I0653876

TOTAL

KAYOS

An
Unfortunate
Lineage

VOLUME
IV

A Novel

Also Available
by **Delaine Christine** through
Kimerah Publishing

AN UNFORTUNATE LINEAGE
Terrible Karisma – I
Kayos Effect – II
Karisma Trouble – III
Total Kayos – IV
Deadly Karisma – V
Kayos Knows – VI

Karisma Kayos: Out of Time
Vol VII (Finale)

TOTAL

KAYOS

An
Unfortunate
Lineage

VOLUME
IV

A Novel

Delaine Christine

Total Kayos
An Unfortunate Lineage Volume II

ISBN-13: 978-1950563166

Copyright © 2020 Delaine Christine

Original Publication 2015 as Angels and Demons: The Blackthorne
Saga, Book Two. Re-published in 2018 with updates under the same
title

This book is a work of fiction. Names, characters, places and incidents
are the product of the author's imagination or are used fictitiously.
Any resemblance to actual events, locales, or persons, living or dead,
is coincidental

All rights reserved. No part of this book may be reproduced, or
transmitted in any form or by any means, electronic or mechanical,
including photocopying, recording or by any information storage and
retrieval system, without written permission from the author, with the
exception of biblical scripture utilized throughout this e-book.

Scripture quotations and scripture references are from the Good News
Translation in Today's English Version- Second Edition Copyright ©
1992 by American Bible Society. Used by Permission.

Book and Cover Design by D. Johnson
Model Pic by Branislav Ostojic, used with permission
Scenic Cover Image by welcomia via 123rf.com
Interior Model Image by Badmanproduction, used with permission

Kimerah Publishing, Elkhart, IN

Printed in the United States of America.

Prophecy

Continues...

For through fiery hair of silver and gold.
and eyes of night filled with silver mists of old.

A seed shall lie within her womb
Three times blessed we can presume.

Not a borrower nor lender she'll be
Her gift to know, her child's to see.

PROLOGUE

I would hope by now
you know not to skip me,
the ever elusive, and
always mysterious…
Vortigern Black.

From one troubling tale, we move on to chaos.

Because why not, right?

Let me put it to you all this way. When I was assisting the author of this here unfortunate story in determining a title I was very adamant with her on my choice. It had to be Total Kayos because, frankly, it fits this story to a T. In the end, I believe Ms. Christine caved for two very good reasons.

One, because as with the second volume in the An Unfortunate Lineage series, I would not get to narrate throughout this story for I wasn't there. She knows full well how antsy I get when I have nothing to do so she's trying to keep me occupied.

That sure didn't last long.

1

And two, because I was right, of course. It's the perfect fit for the title of this story. Although, I don't get why she keeps spelling chaos the way she is. You know? With a K? I noticed she's been doing it with the word Charisma too. I figure it must be one of those artistic license sorts of things.

Who knows?

Now I know some of you are shaking your heads in distress after learning you won't get to hear from me for quite some time. No worries folks. I WILL be back in the next one, and at the very least, regardless of whether Ms. Christine likes it or not, I will be putting my two cents in at the end within the Epilogue.

I would write out this whole story for you if I could, but, here's the thing; a little truth you all should know. I, Vortigern Black, cannot write worth a crap. Though I have lived through the RavenCroft's story, I did not write any of this series. I did, however, meet an author at one point who wrote about the lives of both the Blackthorne's and the RavenCroft's…

-Without any of us being aware of it.

It turned out she had the ability of 'Knowing' a lot like Rafe and his long-lost brother, Bastion RavenCroft. I managed to get my hands on what she wrote and that's how Ms. Christine has come about these stories in order to write them for me...

Or, well … you.

Ms. Christine wanted me to assure you that she is crediting the original author and even has her permission.

Sort of.

(Vortigern coughs nervously.)

The thing is, three of the tales required being pieced together, as they were unfinished works about one of the family's I've been telling you about. Many chapters had been written but they were all over the place and required being pieced together in the correct order – kind of like a puzzle. The last three were finished manuscripts about the other family that required some much-needed editing.

I'll give you one guess as to which families story had to be put in order.

If you guessed the RavenCroft's, you'd be correct, and you probably picked that family because so far their stories have been shorter, right? They're less involved and in need of a bit more explanation, which is one of the reasons why I have been narrating the RavenCroft tales. As you may have noticed in the last volume about the Blackthorne's, my narration skills aren't really necessary, so you'll likely only ever get introductions and re-caps from me.

By the way, what I just told you was your next clue as to my identity. The part about me not being the original author and the fact that I managed to (coughs again) get my hands on it, shall we say? This clue may not make much sense right now but, if you pay close attention in the next volume, you'll find it will.

That said, Ms. Christine has been pretty good about keeping to the original author's story, and more often than not, has copied the dialogue verbatim. Which means...

-Angels and demons are real.

According to the original author anyway, because otherwise, why else would she be writing about them so much in these more faith based Blackthorne tales?

Yeah, still can't get over that one either, but after having read through this story you're about to read, I'm a little more inclined to believe that now.

It still doesn't mean there is a God though. For all we know, the presence of angels and demons is just nature's way of maintaining a balance between good and evil. But don't take my word for it.

Anywho...

3

We are returning once again to Kalispell, Montana in this volume and to the gifted Blackthorne clan that lives there. This particular story is about what I like to call, Kalabernus' RavenCroft's mirror image cousin. Meaning that Drinian Blackthorne is similarly afflicted with the cursed gift to see shadowy demonic creatures. Unlike his cousin in Colorado who wasn't raised with the same ideas, Drinian is a true believer in God and always has been. But he struggles with his faith a little more than the rest of his siblings though, because of what he can see and hear.

Oh, and by now, I think it goes without saying that this is not the first volume in this collection, so if you've happened upon this book first you will definitely want to go back and start from the beginning because otherwise, you will be just plain LOST!

Chapter 1

May 16, 2015
Kalispell, Montana

Veta drove around the Flathead Valley area, taking it all in. The beauty of the mountains and the quaint small-town appearance was obvious even through all the rain pouring down onto her windshield. She had been driving for three days, stopping along the way to give her cat a chance to recuperate from the long days on the road.

Cooped up inside his pet carrier, Drinian was in a right foul mood, even with the sedatives he'd been given earlier in the day to prevent him from crying all the way. The normally gentle, abnormally large black cat did not travel well. Grouchy, he batted at the cage angrily with his one white paw, demanding freedom from his caged existence.

Seeing a vacancy sign off to her left, Veta's attention was drawn to the signage. A drawing of a large black cat with blue eyes and one white paw was pointing towards the hotel. Chuckling at what she deemed irony, she read what it said and gave a short laugh.

"Be at peace, dear; vacancy here. Okay, Lord, I get the picture."

Veta pulled into the parking lot of the Howard's Motel and leaned across the center console to check on her charge. Her long black hair tangled in the head-rest, preventing her from further movement. Eyes flashing with pain, she wrestled the caught tresses from their prison. Achieving her goal after several minutes, she sighed heavily, patted the pet carrier, and reached for the door handle of her car.

"I'll return shortly, Drinian. I just need to get us a room." Stepping from the car, Veta was met by a cool onslaught of rain pounding heavily upon her head, wetting her long tresses in an instant. Instead of running to the office she walked slowly to its door, relishing every drop of rain. Most people thought her insane for she loved the rain but she didn't care what others thought, especially these days.

"Can I help you?" The desk clerk didn't bother to look up from her book when Veta entered the motel lobby.

Irritated by the clerk's lack of professionalism, she waited patiently not saying a word. She took in the pale creamy yellow wallpaper and the intricate floral paintings on the wall. The sparse furniture, more for functionality then comfort, implied that loitering was not encouraged. After several minutes passed, the woman peered over at her from behind her book with a quizzical expression. A strand of her shoulder-length red hair fell across the freckles on her face. She looked questioningly at Veta.

"Ma'am?" The clerk looked up over her spectacles suddenly realizing she was being rude. Gracefully, she swept her tall slender frame from her seat. "My apologies, what can I do for you?"

"Do you accept pets? I have a cat." She noted the woman's name tag said, Lola.

"Yes, cats are fine, just no dogs." Taking in Veta's sodden appearance, Lola's eyes softened. Her clothes had been plastered to her curvaceous medium build by the rain, and her sheer black hair hung limply against her cheeks and shoulders.

"Good. I'd like a room for one please, non-smoking would be preferable." Leaning against the desk she laid her driver's license in front of the woman. Signing the registration she'd been given, she tried hard to keep from dripping on the paper.

"My, you're a long way from home," Lola said, noting that the license listed Maryland as Veta's state of origin.

Accepting her license back, she responded with a sigh. "I don't know that I'd call it home anymore." Attempting to lighten the sad tone in her voice, she smiled back at the woman in front of her, shrugging lightly.

"Are you passing through or thinking to move here?" Lola's insatiable curiosity had gotten the better of her.

Turning around and glancing out the window, Veta viewed the scene in front of her. The thunder clapped and lightning struck close by. Through the flash of light, she could see the jagged line of the great mountains looming up in the distance. They spanned from one edge of her vision to the next, magnifying by mere sight how expansive they must truly be. If it were possible, the rain came down suddenly even harder than it had before. Taking it all in, she turned back to the clerk at the desk who had begun to look at her with concern.

"I have decided to move here."

The finality of the statement washed over Veta with excitement. She didn't know for sure, what it was that she'd seen through the window that made her make this decision so quickly. But she knew, it was the right one to make. When she left Maryland, she'd known she no longer belonged there. Believing strongly that God was calling her elsewhere, she'd prayed fervently then headed west.

It had been a long drive, and she had taken in a few sights along the way. Nothing compared to the view she was witnessing now. There had been no rain until she'd arrived near Kalispell, Montana, and it was as though God cried just for her, letting her know she was where she belonged.

"Okay, Lord, I'm here," she whispered softly as her hand lay against the window pane of her motel room moments later. Fingering the delicate silver cross necklace at the nape of her neck, she rested her head against the window and prayed.

I've lost so much, Lord.

My children.

My husband; a man who claimed to love me, and yet, betrayed me in the worst way, even before we'd married.

I don't know what it is you want of me…

-Need from me.

But as always, Lord, I am your humble servant.

Lead me down the path you wish me to take.

Unseen next to her, the angel Maleeka, rested his hand upon her back caressing her gently, hoping to ease the distress and misery within her. Amazed and in wonder of the woman's never-failing faith in God, even amid such tragedy and loss, he smiled tenderly at her, then gazed out the window along with her as the rain poured down.

"You have suffered much, dear Veta, and yet, your faith has never wavered. For that, you shall be rewarded."

Four glorious wings erupted slowly from Maleeka's back. Soaring up through the motel and out into the rainy night sky, he was met by the angel, Woreash, who had been watching from above.

"Do we stay or go?" Maleeka asked.

Lifting his head to the heavens above, Woreash closed his eyes and hovered where he was, as though waiting for a message from the heavens. After a while he opened his eyes slowly, the grey coloring reflecting the moonlight within its depths. His expression changed to worry as he gazed down upon the motel room, where the woman, Veta, was safely ensconced.

"We stay for now. Her troubles may not be over yet."

Frowning, Maleeka sighed heavily. "Understood."

- - -

Heart pounding, Veta struggled against her sheets.

"No," she cried out, nearly coming up off the bed.

Panting, her eyes searched the room frantically. She fell backwards in distress, her head hitting the pillow.

Veta lay weak upon the foreign bed, the terror of her nightmare running vividly in her head. Staring up at the ceiling she squeezed her eyes shut for a moment, willing her heart to stop pounding so hard in her chest. Tears trickled down her pale cheekbones as she turned on her side, cuddling up close to her pillow, wrapping around it for comfort.

For a while, she lay there crying softly into her pillow. The fear from her dream dissipated slowly from her mind and body. Suddenly, pulling herself up from the bed she pushed off, stumbling slightly as she ran to the bathroom. In her haste, she fell to the floor in front of the toilet and hit her left knee hard against the floor. Slumping over the toilet seat, the sickness overcame her. She vomited into the toilet.

"I c-can't keep d-doing this to myself." She sobbed while wiping her mouth with the washcloth she grabbed from the sink.

Anger surged within her.

Throwing the washcloth across the bathroom, she grabbed her shampoo and conditioner from the counter. Gingerly holding her hand against her belly, she willed the queasiness to subside. She closed her eyes and rested the back of her head against the wall.

Realizing she was still holding the shampoo and conditioner precariously in her hand, she set them down in the shower. Turning on the water, she stepped tentatively into the tub, testing her left knee for support. The hot water ran down her head and back as she pressed her forehead against the smooth plastic shower wall. Wrapping her arms tightly around herself she stood there, shaking for the longest time, crying hard against the overwhelming wave of frustration and desperation building inside her. Veta soon tired of her own tears and hastily began showering, washing her hair with renewed vigor.

Stepping out of the shower, she towel dried her long wavy locks then rubbed herself down with a new towel from the rack on the wall. As she walked out of the bathroom she nearly tripped over her cat, who had taken it upon himself to lie in the middle of the walkway.

"Urgh! Drinian, why must you do that every day?" She spoke vehemently to the massive black cat, who peered at her with his mischievous clear bright blue eyes. Batting at her, with his one and only white paw, he promptly flicked his ears at her and stalked away. Marginally mollified she rolled her eyes and chuckled.

Veta couldn't help but be disgusted with herself for falling for the same trick every time.

Dressing in jeans, a long sleeve white T-shirt, and her favorite tennis shoes, Veta moved gingerly to the mirror to check out the damage. Her face was puffy and swollen from the exhaustive crying. Sighing heavily, as was her response when she looked in the mirror these days, she began correcting the damage she'd done with a heavy dose of concealing makeup.

After blow-drying her bangs, she decided to twist her hair up with a clip on the back of her head. The long, thick black hair was always too much to pile up on her head, so it hung limply, yet fashionable, down the back of her head to her shoulders in big waves. Taking one last look at her poor attempts of tidying herself, she gave up, grabbed her purse with her Bible, and left the motel room in search of a healthy dose of strong coffee.

Nearing the front desk Veta noticed the same woman from the night before. Only this time Lola was scowling at a very tall, semi-attractive man, who happened to be standing behind the counter, arms crossed over his chest.

"Lola, I can't help it. Celia would tan my hide if I hired that girl back and I need the help. Can't you work just one more night?" His plaintive query would have appeared more serious, if it weren't for the comical faces he was making.

"Marshall, stop it!" Lola stifled a laugh. She smacked the desk with her hand. "You know I can't say no when you get this way and I just can't. You know I can't. I have to take care of Raysa today." Turning on her heal, Lola glanced toward the hallway and saw Veta standing in the doorway.

"Don't mind me," Veta said quickly, realizing with embarrassment that she'd been eavesdropping. "I was just looking for some coffee," she finished meekly.

"Morning! I see you're all dried up." Lola glanced over their guest from head to toe. Smiling, she tilted her head toward the door and said in answer, "We're out at the moment. You'll find no better anywhere than at The Coffee Haven. It's just down the road. Walking distance really, so you should see the sign from here."

"Thank you."

Veta quickly walked past the desk towards the exit. She was nearly out the door when she heard the man called, Marshall, asking Lola about her. Leaving before hearing her response, she decided to walk to the coffee shop. The air was cool and smelled strong of pine. Breathing in the fresh mountain air and keeping her eyes on the path from the motel to the shop, she hummed the song 'Amazing Grace' softly to herself, determined to make the best of the day. She chose to ignore its sour beginnings from earlier, as well as the soreness in her injured knee.

"It's a beautiful day, Lord. You've outdone yourself I think," she said aloud. Taking in the quaint small-town view around her, she continued to stroll along.

The walk to the coffee house was short as it was only two blocks away. It was a small shop, newly constructed in the popular modern style of the day, but it had an inviting feel to it. Pushing open the door to the business, she found her way obstructed by an extremely massive man, easily six and a half feet tall. Startled by his sheer height, vast broad chest, and shoulders, Veta's eyes grew wide. She stared up at him. Even more fascinating, were the almost translucent crystal blue eyes that stared back down at her. There was a soft light about them, making them appear as though they were glowing. For some reason, Veta felt instantly at ease, though she imagined some might find them unsettling.

Noting the gigantic thermos mug clasped in the man's beefy hand, she giggled softly and stepped out of his way.

"That's a mighty big mug you've got there." Veta peered up at him, her eyes sparkling with laughter. "Is there any left?" she asked impishly with a smile. He turned to look at her from the door.

"It's only a hundred and twenty-eight ounces; should be a little left," Drinian said with a grin. He eyed the woman before him with appreciation. She was gorgeous. He'd been drawn in by her emerald green eyes and genuine smile. Noting the Bible in her purse and the cross-pendant dangling from her neck, he paused at the door, finding the woman fascinating. He stared at her openly.

Drinian was surprised she'd even spoken to him in the first place. Most women avoided him as a rule. His sheer size, toned physic, and exceptional good looks tended to draw a woman's attention, but his dark countenance and personality often frightened them away.

The man's voice had been surprising. Though very deep it wasn't gravelly or harsh but gentle and soft. "Glad you saved me some. Have a blessed day," she called while moving further into the shop.

Wishing he wasn't already on his way out, Drinian watched her turn away from him. She gazed around the shop as though viewing it for the first time. He suspected she was one of the many tourists, who vacationed in the area but hoped she wasn't just passing through. Closing the door behind him, he stepped out of the shop. Seeing a shadow swirl past him and float inside, he halted abruptly.

Pausing where he was near the shop window, he watched the demon's behavior towards the woman curiously. Then he continued across the street to his sister's Real Estate and Rental Agency. Drinian was not surprised the woman had attracted the attention of one of the demons. She was, after all, very beautiful. Shaking his head as he went, he attempted to push her out of his mind. At the same time, he made a mental note to watch for her when she left the Café. It wouldn't hurt to at least look after all.

Veta peered around the Café while watching the man leave out of the corner of her eye. She had to admit; she'd hoped he was staying awhile. He had been very nice to look at with those amazing crystal eyes of his set against the tanned skin and jet-black hair. And yet she sensed there was something different about him. The man appeared almost lost, like a little boy wishing for something he couldn't have as he stood watching her from outside the window.

Determining God would let him cross her path again in due time if He felt it was warranted, she instead turned her attention to the establishment she'd entered.

She immediately felt at home. There were plushy cushioned chairs around rectangular coffee tables and an L shaped couch was in one corner. Entering further into the shop she noticed small tables, which seated from two to six people, throughout the small cramped space. It had a very homey appearance to it, yet clean and sleek, with its updated furnishings and calm lighting.

Veta made a careful note of the shelves along the walls neatly stocked with various assortments of coffee beans and grounds, eclectic coffee cups and freshly baked bread and sweets. Promising herself she would come back at a later date and investigate the inventory more fully, she gingerly hobbled over to the counter in order to check out their coffee selections.

"What can I get for you, Miss?"

Looking up, Veta was somewhat startled to see a man bearing a striking resemblance to Marshall, the motel clerk from that morning. Though very slightly shorter at five foot eleven, he had light auburn hair and green eyes. Their builds were similar too.

"I'll just have a large dark brewed coffee."

Tapping the glass impatiently, Veta watched him dispense her drink into a mug the size of a soup bowl.

"Do you have brown sugar?" she inquired suddenly, causing the man to turn and look at her with an odd expression.

"Sure do. Want me to add it for you?" he asked politely. Seeing her nod he queried, "How many spoonful's?"

"Two heaping please."

Pausing, his head cocked to one side. He murmured thoughtfully, "That would be the equivalent of...." Making a soft harrumphing sound in his throat, he shook his head slightly. Giving her a curious perusal, he then glanced towards the front of the store.

"Sorry?" Veta inquired at his curious words.

Shaking his head dismissively, the man replied, "Nothing, sorry. Just had a random thought."

Acknowledging his response with a short nod, Veta eyed the breakfast menu, glancing up in time to see a slender woman with a lean medium build walk into the room from the swinging doors at the back of the shop. She had shiny straight black hair that hung to the middle of her back and dark blue eyes set against a tanned skin tone, which was very similar to the man who just left.

"Can I get you anything to eat with your coffee?" she asked lightly, grabbing a pad of paper as she reached the counter.

"I was just eyeing that breakfast croissant you have on your menu. It sounds quite yummy."

"It's one of our best sellers; made fresh every morning."

The waitresses chipper mood perked Veta up even further. Then, glancing at the man making her coffee, she leaned against the counter as she waited. Allowing her weight to press against the counter seemed to help alleviate the pressure on her kneecap, which had begun to throb. Trying to ignore the discomfort, while looking around the shop, she realized there appeared to be artwork displayed on the walls. Noticing the direction of her glance, the man nodded his head towards the paintings.

"Local artists. It gives them a chance to display their works. Sometimes they're even able to sell some. I'm Royce by the way. Royce Howard. You're new to the area?" he asked. He placed Veta's coffee on the counter in front of her and extended his free hand to her.

Hesitating, a moment longer than intended, Veta finally shook his hand, uncomfortable with the familiar contact.

"That obvious, huh?" Self-conscious with his hand in hers, Veta pulled back sooner than expected, managing to knock the freshly made coffee over. Flustered and embarrassed Veta apologized profusely while Royce wiped up the spill and began making another.

"It's no matter. Really. Happens all the time." Chuckling, he finished preparing her new cup as the waitress walked back in with the croissant she ordered.

"This is my wife, Crisalya. We own and run the shop. Most everyone that comes in here about this time of year we usually know, so..."

"New face, new to the place," Veta quipped, trying to forget her earlier spill. She glanced self-consciously over the rim of her mug. Sipping her coffee appreciatively, she settled into one of the nearby tables. Pulling her Bible from her purse, she laid it on the table in front of her with a pad of paper and pen.

"How long have you been in the area?" asked Crisalya. Walking around the counter, she took up a seat at Veta's table when she nodded her approval.

"It's my first day." Veta leafed through her Bible to the passage where she'd left off the morning before.

"You have a place yet?" Crisalya asked while watching the woman before her prepare for her morning devotions. Crisalya viewed her with a curious gaze for the woman was clearly not embarrassed by her faith.

Veta took an immediate liking to the pretty woman seated across from her. Her bright inquisitive expression was truly a delight. Taking comfort in the woman's friendliness, she decided to take a chance and pressed on with her most immediate question.

"I haven't yet. You wouldn't by chance be able to point me in the right direction, would you? I'm looking for a safe neighborhood, small house and all. But I'm not familiar with the area."

"You'll want to see Megorah Ryans at the Ryans Real Estate and Rental Agency." Crisalya wiped her hands on a towel. Getting up, she stepped around the counter and grabbed a card from under the register, passing it over to her.

Handing Veta the card, she pointed through the window. "You see that big green awning across the street?" Nodding, Veta took another bite of the mouthwatering croissant filled with sausage, egg and cheese. She tried to pay attention to what the woman was saying. Distracted by the yummy croissant, she realized too late that she had just asked her a question.

"I'm sorry." Veta spluttered, placing her hand over her mouth in order to keep the croissant from falling out. Face turning red, she looked over at Crisalya. "I didn't catch your question."

Both laughing, Royce and his wife smiled knowingly at her. "It's the croissants. They have that effect on people."

"They are very good. My compliments to the Chef."

Chapter 2

After a brief but pleasant conversation with Crisalya Howard, over her morning devotions and breakfast, Veta left the Coffee Haven. Glancing both ways down the main street, she crossed the road to the agency Crisalya and Royce had pointed out just moments before.

Entering the business, the first thing she noticed was how well organized the office appeared to be. Everything seemed to have its place. Soft jazz music was playing from a speaker in the corner of the room, apparently piped in from another location. Her second observation was that there didn't appear to be anyone there initially. Looking around her, she was unable to locate a bell or buzzer in order to get somebody's attention. Assuming the receptionist had merely gone on a restroom break, Veta decided to take a seat in one of the chairs near the entrance.

Hearing voices getting louder as they approached from a back room, Veta was surprised to realize she recognized one of them.

"I'm sure she'll be ere' any mina. Why don' you jus' wait an ask er' about' it?" A woman with a strong unusual accent walked casually into the room, oblivious to the presence of a customer. Thin and mousy in appearance, she was carrying a food container in one hand and a coffee mug in another. Dropping the items on her desk, she spun around towards the door she'd just come from as the same giant man Veta had seen from The Coffee Haven strolled through it.

"I'm telling you, Freedom. I saw it yesterday and looked it up last night. There's only supposed to be three figures in that painting." Drinian sensed Freedom's reticence at believing him. "Mark my words, there's a demon that has attached itself to the picture over there."

Seeing the direction the man was pointing, Veta flinched. She noticed the painting on the wall next to her. It was a copy of Night Alley by Leonid Afremov. Brows rising curiously she glanced at the painting of which she was quite familiar with, then back over at the man who was now staring at her openly, with his arm still outstretched.

"I'm pretty sure Afremov never painted demons in any of his paintings," Veta said humorously. She tilted her head towards him.

"Thas' jus' a 'opy anyway," Freedom said with a shrug.

Giving in to the inevitability that the beautiful woman before him would soon be fleeing from his sister's place of business, Drinian moved towards the waiting room and gazed at the print hanging on the wall. Next to the two figures standing in the pathway was an unmistakable, thin shadowy figure, staring back at him with an evil grin.

"Yeah, I see you, you filthy demon. Laugh it up now because I will remove you from this place." Scowling darkly, he reached for the painting and yanked it roughly from the wall.

"You realize, of course, you cannot just give it away," Veta said to Drinian, surprising him. She was actually talking to him once again, which was blowing his mind considering what he'd been saying.

"Sorry?"

"The painting." Veta gestured towards the print in his hand. "It's sad to say, but if there is truly a demon that has attached itself to it, then you'll have to burn it. It's the only way to safely get rid of it without it affecting someone else."

"Then burn it I shall." He reluctantly moved to leave. The woman hadn't mocked him but had taken him seriously which startled him. Cocking an eyebrow he gave her a curious look.

"Wha' am I suppose ta tell Mrs. Ryans when she 'ets 'ere?" Freedom asked. "She'll notice it missin' afta' all. It's one 'uf 'er favoris' as ya' well know."

"Right." He felt a little uneasy that the beautiful woman was watching him so closely. "I'll text her. She'll understand."

Pulling his phone out with one hand, he held tightly to the portrait frame. His face flamed with embarrassment as he left the shop.

Veta watched him leave, and then glanced towards the woman called Freedom. "Does he often see demons in paintings?" She wondered at such a troubled soul.

"Firs' time ta mi knowledge. Though c'sa alays been a leatle off, ifn' ya' as' me." Freedom said with a shiver.

Brow furrowing in thought, she glanced at the desk. Veta noticed the gigantic coffee mug she'd seen the man carry from the Coffee Haven.

21

"Oh, no. He left his mug." Grabbing it up from the desk, Veta dropped her purse as she hastily left the rental agency. Glancing both ways, she saw the large man had almost reached the end of the block already. Wishing she knew the man's name, she called loudly, "Wait!"

Startled to hear a woman shouting behind him, Drinian turned to see the black-haired beauty shaking his mug in the air. Feeling as though the wind had almost been knocked out of him at the sight of her smiling radiantly back at him, he inhaled sharply. Catching sight of the demon from earlier messing with the thermos lid, he roared down the street.

"Leave her alone!" His face contorted angrily at the sight of the loathsome creatures attempts to mess with her.

Too little too late. He watched in dismay as hot coffee sloshed out of the mug, down her startled face and white t-shirt. Running down the block, he was within a few feet of her in seconds. Snatching the mug from her small hand, he narrowed his gaze up at the demon that hovered over her, cackling as it slithered about. Unaware that his unexpected action had caused her to lose her balance, he missed seeing her drop to the ground next to him.

"I said, leave her alone." Drinian's deep voice boomed into the air. The demon shrieked in pain. Clasping its long pointy fingered hands near its head it slithered away, howling in its wake.

Staring back up at the tall dark figure from her vantage on the pavement, as he glared toward the sky, Veta's eyes became huge. She could see his massive chest heave anxiously as he peered back down at her. His expression registered concern that he might have been the cause of her fall. The troubled look and sudden ghostly reflection in his eyes at the demons close proximity, made her want to cry for him.

Seeing pity for him in the woman, Drinian scowled down at her. The last thing he wanted from her was pity.

"Are you okay?" he asked gruffly, moving the mug to the hand with the painting. "I didn't … didn't hurt you did I?" He felt clumsy and oafish as he stuttered. The demons, which typically followed him and taunted him, were in full swing, chanting around him that he wasn't a man but a clumsy old bear. Trying to ignore them, Drinian reached down with his free hand, anticipating she'd refuse his help out of fear. It's what most women did anyway.

Surprising him, she extended her hand towards Drinian, without a moment's hesitation. "No, of course not, thank you … oh!"

A tingling sensation, quite similar to getting a shock only stronger, had reverberated through the palm of her hand and up her elbow as their hands clasped together. Feeling somewhat flustered by it, her hand trembled slightly in his as her heart raced.

Unsure of what to make of the sensation himself, Drinian easily lifted her from the ground and set her on her feet as though she were no heavier than a feather. Shaking his hand loosely, he stared down at it, then back at her, swallowing hard. *Lord, what in the world was that*, he thought as he frowned.

Tongue-tied at first, Drinian gestured towards her shirt with the coffee mug, managing to slosh more coffee from within it. "Sorry … for your shirt that is. Not hurt?" She shook her head. "Good. Must away." He said tersely his words clipped and broken. Placing the mug back in his free hand he cleared his throat. Face reddening at how silly he knew he sounded, Drinian turned awkwardly on his heels. He stalked away, wishing desperately he wasn't such an idiot where women were concerned.

Veta watched him walk away, chuckling softly at how sweet he'd seemed then headed back inside the rental agency. The pain in his eyes had been unmistakable and it haunted her. Familiar with such despair herself, she made a conscious decision that she would pray for him to find peace from whatever it was that tormented him.

"Yer' back. 'Ood. Ya' lef'yer' purse," the receptionist said.

"Yes, so I did."

"I'm Freedom, by the way. Freedom Raines."

Thrown by the unusual name, and still recovering from her encounter with the man, it took Veta a moment to respond. "I'm Veta Rohann." She extended her hand in greeting. "I'm looking for a home to rent. Royce and Crisalya Howard, from across the street - they suggested I see…" She glanced down at the card she'd pulled from her purse. "Megorah Ryans."

"I'm sorry. Megorah won' be in till much la'er today. Bu' I can 'elp you." Finally letting go of Veta's hand, Freedom took hold of her cup and sipped it gingerly. "So, tell me. What does yer dream 'ome look like?"

This time, Veta found herself laughing. "I doubt I'll find my dream home for the price I'm looking for. Why don't you just tell me what I can get for $500 a month, including utilities?"

"Naw, really, I can do be'er than tha'." Setting her cup back down after taking a long drink, she watched as Freedom sat far back in her chair, leaned back, closed her eyes and gestured towards Veta with enthusiasm. "Now, describe ta' me your dream 'ome and I shall ge' it fo' you fo' five hundred dollars or less."

"Including utilities?" Her brows rose in disbelief.

"Including … yes, yes." Freedom smiled knowingly, her arms resting upon her chair. "Trust me. I'm really 'ood at this."

"In that case, I'd like a newly renovated log cabin with a mountain view next to a lake or stream. The cabin should have at least two bedrooms and a spacious bath with a hot tub. The kitchen will have plenty of counter space, a gas-powered stove, and a dishwasher. The place will also have central air, a washer and dryer, and…, oh, yes… It must have an attached garage, be completely furnished and accept pets; specifically a cat."

Frowning slightly, Freedom opened one eye and peered over at Veta. "No' osking fo' much are we?"

"See, I told you…"

"Wait!" The woman closed her eyes, squeezing them both shut and scrunched up her face in concentration. "I'm still thinking. Way fo' it."

Confused, Veta couldn't help but ask. "Wait for what exactly?"

She watched the odd woman raise her right index finger to her lips and soundlessly mouth the words, "One momen' please."

Giving the woman a wry smile, she couldn't help but think this was all some theatrical sales ploy but as she watched the woman across from her, she saw Freedoms' expression change from concentration, to a grimace, and then a sad smile. She opened her eyes and looked at her intently.

The woman stared at her for an uncomfortably long moment. Finally, she glanced away and reluctantly stood. Turning towards her desk and taking the remains of her breakfast in hand, she dumped them in the trash. Pivoting on the spot, she walked to a file cabinet, opened a drawer and slid a folder out.

"Twood you like ta see it? I'll drive ya. Le' me jus' get the keys."

- - -

Two hours later, Veta found herself walking out of the Ryans Family Rental Agency with a one-year lease and the keys to her new home in hand. Her heart fluttered in her chest with excitement. She just couldn't believe her luck. Not only did the property she'd rented have everything she'd asked for but it was available right away. Who would have ever imagined being able to rent a beautiful log cabin home like that for only five hundred dollars a month? It looked like it would rent for more like twelve to fourteen hundred.

She had been in such disbelief at her good fortune, that she had asked Freedom on several occasions whether she was absolutely sure about the rental amount. The woman had smiled and shown her the file which listed the rental properties going rate. Walking in a daze along the side-walk, Veta laughed out loud at how much her luck had changed from one state to another.

On the trek back to the motel to check out and get her things, she was remembering with vivid clarity each room of her new home. Spacious and well kept, it was in perfect condition and had a fireplace as well. Something she'd always longed for but had forgotten to mention to Freedom when she'd given the description of her dream home.

Veta couldn't wait to light her first fire and sit by the firelight with a steaming mug of hot chocolate, even if it was the middle of May. The mountain views from her windows were so breathtaking; her hands almost itched to take a pencil to her drawing pad. Some classical music playing with a good book in hand and she'd be in heaven or, at least, as close to heaven as she was going to get for now. Sighing happily, she couldn't help but feel like it was meant to be.

Thank you, God, she prayed as she walked. *You're truly amazing. We both know how rough things have been, but I've always known you were there for me. Maybe this is a sign of good things to come?*

Nearing the motel she began to skip along happily, stumbling slightly because of her knee as she turned in the direction of her vehicle. It wasn't until she was about half-way to her car that she realized something was missing from her view. The U-Haul trailer she'd rented to carry her few belongings, was no longer attached to her car. In its place was an empty space.

Chapter 3

Everything was gone. Veta couldn't believe it. Three hours later, and the shock of it wasn't yet worn off. Turning off the main road onto the tree-lined dirt road that led to her cabin, she banged her hand against the steering wheel in anger.

"We've never had a theft before. Not at this motel. Are you sure you had a U-Haul?" She mimicked Marshall Howard's words in derision. Was she really going to forget that she'd driven through over three different states without a U-Haul attached to her car?

Slowing her speed, she crept along the bumpy road, while letting out an angry howl of despair. The cop had been just as disbelieving. If it hadn't been for Lola having seen her arrive with it the night before, then he probably wouldn't have believed her at all.

Pulling into a clearing, she drove up to the garage of her cabin and attempted to use the garage door for the first time. She watched in disgust as the door promptly refused to open, sitting motionless as if laughing at her useless attempts to reveal its contents by punching the remote button harder and harder. Throwing the remote on the floor of the car, she opened the door, took up the pet carrier, and strode to the front door. Entering her new home, she closed the door and leaned against it, all the while holding the carrier as it banged heavily against her leg. Drinian was obviously restless to get out of his cage. Setting it down and unlatching the cage door, she let him out.

"Go! Investigate. Find mice."

The instant the door opened, Drinian ran from his prison with lightning speed and was off to parts unknown. As she watched him leap across the room, she hollered back at him.

"On second thought, don't find mice."

That was the last thing she needed right now.

After hauling in her luggage and take-out food from the car, Veta went to work setting up Drinian's litter box and setting out fresh water and food. After coaxing her irritating pet out from under the couch with bits of pepperoni, she finally grabbed hold of him. Hefting her thirty-two-pound mega fur ball to his litter box so he'd learn its location, she set him down afterwards in front of his food dish.

Grabbing her take-out from the kitchen counter and curling up on a chair in front of the fireplace, she ate slowly, trying hard not to wallow. She hadn't traveled from Maryland with much as there were few possessions left after she'd sold the house. Veta had been so angry with her late husband Mitch, that she'd sent everything he'd owned to the dump. Everything else she'd given to the Women's Shelter and Rape Clinic that had helped her out after the boys were born. Aside from her laptop and printer, most of the items that had been stolen didn't really have any value other than sentimental.

The items that bothered her the most to lose were her children's memory boxes and the family photos she'd saved. As well as the quilt that her adoptive grandmother had hand quilted for her before she'd passed away sixteen years earlier. Those were priceless items that couldn't be replaced.

"I know we're not supposed to ask why God. So I won't. I am, however, having difficulty understanding what the purpose was for this." She said aloud. *"Was there something I had that someone else needed? If so, then I'd gladly give it to them, you know that. It's theirs, let them have it. But the memory boxes, Lord."* Her voice trembled. *"They were all I had left of my children."*

Sighing heavily, tears threatened to appear in her eyes. She closed the container of her General Tso's chicken with rice and threw it in the wastebasket under the kitchen sink, having lost her appetite. Determining she needed to spend some time with God after a day like today, she pulled her Bible from her purse with trembling hands and set back down on the couch. Leafing through the text to the passage she'd read through hundreds of times since the loss of her children, she rested her hand against the page of the book.

"Come to me, all of you who are tired from carrying your heavy loads and I will give you rest." (Mathew 11:28)

Laughing softly at the passage, she choked back a sob. "My shoulders no longer carry the burden of worldly possessions, that's for sure."

Closing her eyes, she pulled the open Bible towards her, resting it against her chest. Sniffing softly, she felt something fall from between the pages. Glancing down at the cushions of the couch, she noticed one of the many bookmarks she used to mark pages. Picking it up, she read the passage aloud:

"Psalm 30:5, '...Tears may flow in the night, but joy comes in the morning.'"

Veta wept, her face contorting with grief. Crying out in agony, she began shaking her head.

"I'm sorry, Lord. I love you so much. You are my heart. I live for you. But I need a night to weep, to mourn this loss. I pray desperately that there will be joy in the morning, for tonight all I feel is sorrow and pain. I need comfort, Lord. To be held firmly within your arms. To feel someone holding me close, I need..."

Overwhelmed with despair, she dropped her Bible on the couch and stood. She glanced around the cabin feeling lost and forlorn. Realizing she was thirsty after what she'd ate and hadn't bought anything to drink; she ventured into the kitchen and began looking around. Seeing a large unopened bottle of Sangria wine in the fridge, she hesitated, then pulled it out, setting it on the counter. She didn't normally drink, but it had been a rough day and there was nothing else to drink but water. Grabbing her medicine from her purse, she searched for a glass or plastic cup in the cupboards and discovered there were none. Disgusted at the realization she'd have to purchase all new kitchen items, Veta stared at the bottle of wine as tears dripped from her eyes.

Nothing was ever easy, she thought while pulling at the foil wrappings on the bottle top. That didn't really surprise her too much as God did say in the book of Genesis that man would have to work hard for what he had. It was a punishment He had laid down upon mankind with the first sin of Adam and Eve.

Managing to get the foil off, she was grateful, at least, to see there was no cork. It appeared to be a cheap bottle of wine for the top unscrewed easily. Taking her first sip with her pills, she knew full well she shouldn't be mixing them, and yet, at that moment didn't care. The sadness within her was growing and every time that happened she tended to lose her better judgment. Feeling the warmth of the alcohol slide down her throat, she carried the wine and medicine bottle back to the couch, where she sat for a long time in a depressed state, as she drank.

After a while, Veta's head jerked without warning. It occurred to her that she must have dozed off for a bit. Peering at the fireplace sleepily, she wished there was already fire lit within it. Unable to think clearly, her gaze wandered the room to the patio doors. Grasping the bottle by its neck, she struggled up from the couch and headed to the back porch. Veta suspected the hour was very late, but she longed for her first dip in her hot tub and hoped the feel of the water would wash away the sorrow within.

Setting the more than half empty wine bottle down on a patio table, after taking another long drink, she looked out at the landscape. A small lawn that ran into forest met her view. The patio walls were completely glass so she could see the entire expanse of the yard. Blinking in her drowsy state, she picked up the wine bottle and took another long swig while gazing out at the lawn. She found herself suddenly overcome with a wave of emotion, as though she were experiencing the loss of her three children all over again. Weeping in despair, the teardrops fell down her face like rain from a sky, dripping on her shirt and the patio floor.

Above the patio, the angels watched in concern at the scene playing out before them. "Are we too late?" Maleeka asked uneasily. He sensed even from where they hovered the despair that had taken hold of the woman.

"Try to reach her, if you can. I'll attempt to get through to him," Woreash said anxiously. He dove for the woods nearby, startling an owl in flight.

Dropping down through the ceiling of the house, Maleeka watched the woman wince openly while choking down a sob. He could hear her mumbling softly, ticking off on her hand all the things she had lost that day.

"Think not of what you've lost, Veta, but of what you might gain."

Eyes narrowing, she shook her head sadly. Maybe she *had* lost her computer, books and even her small DVD collection of her favorite TV shows. In the end, those things didn't matter. The memory boxes though; they could never be replaced. She knew she had her memories and her dreams with which to recall her children. But sometimes she liked to take out their boxes and pull out their little baby booties or their first baby pictures, so she could touch them and know, having them in her life hadn't just been a dream. Was that such a sin; to want to have something tangible to remember them?

Suspecting the woman had not realized she'd spoken her questions aloud, Maleeka sighed heavily. "There's nothing wrong with wanting something to remember them. Someone else made a poor choice, Veta. I'm so sorry this happened, but please don't let your grief over this loss destroy your better judgment."

Setting the wine bottle down after another dose, she noticed the bottle of medicine on the table. Not thinking straight, her vision blurred through her tears, and she grabbed the bottle, shaking out a couple more pills.

"Wait! Have you taken the medicine already? Think, Veta, please think before you act," the angel begged.

Without meaning to, Veta took her medicine again with another long drink of wine. The angel looked on in distress. She then proceeded to remove the cover from the hot tub. Turning it on, she quickly took off her clothes.

"In the tub, quickly; he shouldn't be seeing you like this." Maleeka implored her as he shot out from the patio door and hovered before her. The angel knew the man would still be able to see her from his vantage in the woods but felt compelled to attempt to cover her, nonetheless.

Feeling a sudden desperate need to be in the water, she picked up the wine bottle. Taking it with her to the hot tub, she stepped in and raised the bottle to her lips again.

"Stop," Maleeka called frantically, wishing the woman could hear him but the alcohol had already dulled her senses. Her despair prevented her from hearing reason. "You're in grave danger." Watching the mass of demons above the patio hot tub, he could see them cackling down at him. Neither being on either side could do anything one way or another at this point. Maleeka's orders were to wait it out and only step in if the demons posed a further threat. The woman's free will to choose took precedence over either sides' position. It was up to her and the man in the woods to decide what happened next.

Relaxing back into the bubbling water, she began another mental tally of all the things she'd lost that day, oblivious to the presence of the otherworldly beings. After a while, she had trouble remembering if she'd added one item or another to her list and thought, who cares? None of it mattered but those boxes. Giving up, as thinking on it was plunging her into an even deeper hole, she shifted around to the other side of the tub. Turning her head abruptly towards the forest, she noticed her head seemed awful light.

Tired, so very tired, she thought on a sigh. She set the empty wine bottle on the edge of the hot tub. Seeing the clock hanging on the back wall of the patio, she was having trouble making out the numbers. She finally managed to decipher that it was past midnight. Not caring how late it was, she rested her head against the tub, vaguely acknowledging the fact that her head was starting to hurt a little and she was feeling awfully hot.

"Get out, Veta, hurry please," Maleeka urged. The angel stood near the patio door next to the living room. "It shouldn't happen this way."

I should get out, she thought. Instead, she lay there, reveling in the sensation of the jets against her back. Her eyelids were getting heavy, and she was having difficulty keeping awake. Her arms were limp, floating up on top of the water. Sensing that staying in the tub much longer might prove dangerous, Veta attempted to move her arms in front of her. Instead, they continued to float in the water. A vague tremor in the left arm was the only sign the arm had acknowledged the instructions sent by her brain. Her last thought as she lost consciousness was.......

- - -

Drinian had been watching from the forest for some time.

At first, because he'd been too stunned that someone was present at the cabin, for he had not known his family had managed to rent it already. But then he realized this very same person was the extremely curvaceous black-haired beauty he'd seen in town. She was now undressing in front of his very eyes.

Grimacing, Drinian looked away, his conscience getting the better of him. He shouldn't be seeing her like that. He wasn't her husband. After a moment, he tentatively turned back, hoping she'd managed to cover herself. Instead, he saw she'd entered the hot tub and was now wading in the middle of it, facing the forest as she took another long drink of her wine bottle. Her eyelids closed over her pretty emerald green eyes as she drank, in what was supposed to be the privacy of her own home.

Seeing the goddess in all her glory, Drinian realized she wasn't just beautiful but gorgeous and definitely all woman. Sweat beaded upon his brow, and he wiped at it feverishly. He had never been with a woman. There had never been one willing to allow him to get that close. Besides, he agreed with his father, such intimacy should be left for the marriage bed as God had intended. Hearing himself groan, he heaved an anxious sigh, longing to know what it would be like to have a woman love him like that. But then most women were afraid of him, so the likelihood of that happening was slim.

When he had first seen her, he'd known he should just move on but Drinian had been alarmed by the many shadows he'd seen floating around inside the cabin patio. Worried the demons had some sadistic ulterior motive in mind he stayed in order to make sure she'd be all right. He didn't want them hurting her.

Grabbing at a nearby tree branch, he broke it off and began whacking it against the tree he'd taken it from, trying to distract himself from the sight of her. Relieved to see her finally settling in the water, he expelled the breath he hadn't realized he'd been holding. When he left his own cabin hours before, it was to find solace in the woods, rather than in the beer bottles strewn across his living room couch and floor. Drinian hadn't anticipated coming upon her, here of all places.

Gazing up at the dark sky, he ran a hand across his tired face, trying to ignore the demons surrounding him on all sides. Their incessant jeering and leering had grown tiresome and he was about to put them in their place; especially since he wasn't too sure he believed them when they'd said he'd need to take his brother Dante's fiancée as his own wife.

Dante had arrived home earlier in the evening for the first time in about five years. He brought with him a woman and her three young children, who were clearly not who they said they were. Apparently having run into trouble, Alaina Jordan, or whatever her true name was, had met his brother by way of his last job with the CIA, as an undercover agent. Dante had decided it was time to bring her home with him when she began having mysterious symptoms. He felt they might require not only medical attention but the capable healing hands of his family as well. He was sure Dante had been right.

Leaning up against a nearby tree as he rested his head against it, Drinian stared up at the dark sky in distress. The notion the woman now lying asleep in his brother's bed might be the one from his mother's prophecy, who could help him gain freedom from his incessant tormentors, was driving him mad. If she was truly in the condition he suspected, then he had no business even going near her. And yet, the demons would have him believe he needed to marry her himself.

Smashing violently with the branch at the tree next to him in frustration, Drinian cried out in despair. His brother would never allow that to happen, and though Alaina was quite pretty, he wasn't sure he wanted to subject her to himself anyway. She had three kids already, after all. What kind of life would it be for a woman with children to be married to a man who could see and hear demons? Always worried that he might hurt her without meaning to because of them. No, it was better to stay single and celibate for the rest of his life, then to subject any woman to that.

Sitting on a stump next to the tree he'd just been abusing, he glanced cautiously down towards the patio once more, thinking it best to move on. The woman in the hot tub could make him want to change his mind, he thought. Imagining what it might be like to have her arms around him, he closed his eyes briefly and smiled bitterly. His torment would never end. He'd die with this, so-called, blessed ability never knowing the love of a woman, and the demons would likely be the last thing he'd see.

The dark chatter of the shadows roused him of his musings, causing him to gaze down towards the patio once more. Moving to turn away and continue down the path, he halted abruptly, when he realized what he'd seen. The shadowy demons floating above the tub had begun swirling around frantically with a feral excitement. Knowing full well this was never a good sign when he saw them act this way, he took a closer look at the woman in the tub.

Her face when she'd entered the patio had been pinched tight, as though she had been very upset by something. Before sitting down in the tub, she'd begun to cry, tears streaming down her face, dripping into the water. He recalled wondering what could have made her so sad to cause her to quickly tilt her head back and take another sip of her wine. She'd apparently emptied the last of it after getting in the hot tub, for she'd shaken it over her mouth, attempting to get one final drop.

Watching her now, though, he saw her set the bottle down, only for it to fall from her grasp into the tub. Her head seemed to spin, as though heavy, then it lolled back against the edge. Drinian's posture became rigid, his senses on alert. Something was wrong. She appeared to be having difficulty keeping her eyes open. His eyes darted past her and the hot tub, settling on the patio furniture. An alarm went off in his head when he saw the medicine bottle sitting on the patio table, where a demon now sat jeering towards her.

"She's not your concern!" A dark spirit howled as he took off for the cabin. His sure-footed steps across the forest floor were swift and quiet. The cool night air, whipping against his face began to clear the fantasies and the shadows that always followed him, from his head. His focus never swayed from her as he ran. With each step, her eyes grew heavier, until finally they lost their battle and closed over those pretty green eyes. Panic seized him. He picked up his pace. Seconds later, the back of her head slid out of sight.

"Let her go." Zalman hissed next to his ear, having taken up its smoky black shape of a man from the torso up. "She's one of ours anyway."

His eyes gleamed with fury, his gaze moving from the demon's evil scowl. Now running at full speed, determined to reach her with haste, he knew full well what Zalman had said was an outright lie. He had seen her with a Bible in her purse and a cross necklace around her neck. For some reason he couldn't quite fathom, the demons wanted her dead. He knew the demons could not physically take a humans life. Drinian was, however, aware that the demons had the ability to torment and influence mankind into making life-ending choices.

Pushing through the brush of the forest, he reached the patio door within seconds and tried to slide it open. The demons pummeled their forms up against the door, pressing against it ferociously, in an attempt to prevent his entrance. As a result, it wouldn't budge.

"What's one more woman?" The dark spirit called Fallon howled angrily. It soared over Drinian's head and around him, attempting to bar his path.

Without pausing for a second, Drinian grasped the sides of one of the patio door panels and lifted it up from its track. He roared at the shadows angrily. Squealing in pain, the monsters wriggled in the air above him, giving him the minute reprieve he needed. Pulling down hard, he ripped the door from its top track and set it precariously against the second door. Rushing onto the patio, Drinian leapt to the top step of the tub and plunged into the water. Lifting her head up by her neck with his right hand, he placed his left arm under her knees and lifted her from the water.

"Fat witch! Only one thing they're good for." Zalman growled angrily then cackled hoarsely. The shadows that had followed him converged onto the patio, floating eerily into the room, swirling around the light fixtures causing them to flicker.

"Enough!" Tired of their incessant presence, Drinian shouted, causing them to shriek in pain once again.

Stepping out of the tub, he glanced down at the woman in his arms. Her face was flushed, and her body was hot and wet to the touch. Nearly losing all sense of reason, he didn't even notice he was wet. What was he doing with this woman in his arms? He had to lay her down, check her pulse, and make sure she was still alive. She might even need CPR.

Laying her upon the patio floor he physically shook his head, attempting to regain his senses. Not seeing a towel anywhere, he pulled off his own shirt and covered her from his view, so he'd be better able to think straight. Kneeling down next to her, he rested his fingers against the point between her jaw and neckline, searching for a pulse.

Feeling she still had a pulse and seeing she was still breathing, he drew a relieved breath. He could see this, as her chest rose and fell gently up and down with every breath.

"Leave her. There are other women more beautiful." This time it was Veranke's oily voice he heard as the demon swirled in front of him and took the shape of a faceless man.

"No one is more beautiful than this woman. I wonder what it is about her that is frightening the troublesome three so," Drinian said to himself. He gazed upon her, ignoring the dark pulsating black form. He wasn't supposed to talk to the demons and often had to make a conscious effort not to.

Suddenly, the shadows began whirling around the room, chattering and squealing incessantly, as though frightened by something they'd seen. Veranke's form became shapeless once again as he exploded onto the lawn and into the night like a blast from a paintball gun. The rest fled across the room, giving the impression they were being chased, stopping in the corners as though having been trapped there. Then, without warning, they fled from the patio, soaring out into the moonlit sky. The shadows behavior didn't faze him. He'd seen them react this way before. He didn't know for sure what caused them to act this way, but he suspected it was God's angels, and he was always grateful to them for abating his tormentors.

Thankful for the reprieve, however short it might be, he found he was now able to give the woman in front of him his full attention. Staring at her longingly the way he was, Drinian knew was shameful, and yet he found his fingers trailing a path down her neck to her collarbone. Inhaling deeply, he marveled at the feel of her skin under his fingertips. His brain kept trying to tell him to pull back but his fingers argued, saying instead, that she just felt too good. His body waged a war with his head and heart. He knew God would want him to leave her alone and his heart was telling him the same, but his body argued for another matter entirely.

The woman's eyes fluttered open and then tried to focus. She reached up towards him with her left hand but it only made it halfway before it fell heavily next to her. By now, he was leaning over her, gazing upon her beautiful face. She spoke then, her voice barely audible.

"Drinian," she whispered softly.

Stunned at hearing his name escape from her lips, he did a double-take. "How did you know my name?" He was sure he had not told it to her at the coffee shop.

She tilted her head up then and pressed her lips against his. Sighing with longing, he found himself kissing her back.

Chapter 4

Leaning all his weight upon his left knee, Drinian took her head in his hand and increased the pressure of their lips together, intensifying the kiss. Realizing what he was doing, his eyes widened, and he abruptly pulled away. Catching his breath, he shook his head in dismay. What was he thinking? He couldn't take advantage of her like that. She appeared dazed, lethargic even, and quite possibly incapable of moving. The woman wasn't in any condition to make any kind of decision, informed or otherwise. Knowing he couldn't just leave her lying on the patio like that, he lifted her carefully from the floor. Carrying her back into the house he headed down the hall to the bedroom where she would be more comfortable.

Grateful to see she was okay, he laid her upon the mattress, realizing there were no sheets or blankets. Frowning, he peered around the room. It occurred to him she must have rented the cabin that day. Heading back to the living room, he grabbed the afghan from the back of the couch and carried it back to the bedroom. Halting just inside the doorway of the small bedroom, he found himself staring into her emerald green eyes. Though clearly foggy from the alcohol and drugs, she appeared to be fully aware of his presence now.

"You really are here?" A slight twinge of fear overcame Veta's senses at his presence. Her tongue felt thick and her voice didn't sound like her own. The room was dark but she could see the hulking form of a man in the doorway of the bedroom. His giant frame obscured much of the soft light trying to creep its way in from the nightlight in the hallway.

"Yes," he said quietly, knowing he had to be honest. Seeing her look down upon the t-shirt he'd covered her with, he went on quickly. "I couldn't find any towels but I have a blanket now." Lifting it so she could see it, he anxiously gestured towards her.

Staring across the short space of the room, her vision blurred a little. Blinking sleepily, she struggled to stay conscious, wanting to see the man in a better light. Recognizing his voice, the fear within her abated; for she knew him to be the same man she'd met earlier in the day.

"I thought I might be dreaming..." She spoke slowly. There was such a sad look in his eye. "What makes you so sad?"

Startled by her question, Drinian didn't know how to respond. He was thoroughly entranced by her.

Not hearing a response, she prompted him. "Is it the demons you see? Do they make you sad?"

"No," Drinian said quickly. In the back of his mind, he remembered the pact he'd made with his siblings never to tell anyone their secret. Then, more slowly, "Yes ... sometimes."

He didn't know what it was about this woman but he felt compelled, for some reason, to tell her the truth.

Admitting his own gift wasn't in any way disclosing his siblings' abilities. Glancing back and forth between the woman and the blanket, it occurred to him he should cover her more. Cautiously moving towards her, not wanting to frighten her, he opened the blanket up in front of him so she could see he had no questionable intentions. Reaching her side, he lay the blanket over her, covering the full length of her from his gaze.

"There. Now you won't … won't get cold," he stuttered, turning to leave.

"You're leaving?" She called to him softly, her eyes glistening. "Why does everyone always leave me?" Her voice was thick as she cried. Her eyes became mere slits as she lay there, feeling desperate. The anguish within her was overpowering. Unsure how she'd managed to get to her bedroom, Veta suspected it had something to do with the man now standing once again in the doorway.

"You want … you want me to stay?" Drinian gaped openly in surprise. No woman had ever wanted him this close before, and he suspected her reticence at his leaving had more to do with the wine talking than anything. Clearly, she was struggling with some internal emotional pain of her own and that troubled him. She seemed so sweet, so genuine. He hated the notion, that she was hurting, and wished he could do something to alleviate her pain.

"Are … are you lonely?" she asked sadly.

Inhaling sharply, Drinian's bright, glowing eyes began to water. "Yes."

Sensing a kindred soul, Veta couldn't help but reach out to him in the quiet darkness of the room. He seemed just as lonely and desperate as she. The urge to hug him was fierce, and she desired nothing more than to ease his suffering so that maybe he could find peace.

"Me too." Feeling melancholic she sighed, choking back a sob. "I don't want to be alone." A tear trickled down her cheek. Shaking her head, she couldn't imagine what it must be like to see the demons that plagued mankind. If only she could make that go away for him.

Drinian saw the pain in her eyes and his heart ached for her. Well aware of how isolating the loneliness could be, he understood her pain and wanted desperately to be able to relieve her of it. Breathing heavily, he watched her eyes sparkle with tears and knew in that instant there wasn't anything he wouldn't do for her.

"You want … you want that I stay?" he asked anxiously, his heart in his throat. The mere suggestion was troubling to him but he knew if she asked it of him, he would stay for her, regardless of the war waging within him.

"Yes, please," she said softly. "Maybe the pain will go away."

"Uh, okay… I'll stay."

- - -

Hovering just above the cabin, swords held aloft, the angels Maleeka and Woreash gazed around, making sure they had chased away the last of the demons. Their mutual silence was born more of the disturbing scene below them then it was of the pesky 'troublesome three.' Keeping their heads averted from the bedroom, they waited patiently as they protected their charges, to see if God would allow the Blackthorne matriarch's prophecy to continue.

"I think they're gone for now," Woreash said quietly.

"Maybe, but they'll be back. They always are," Maleeka said irritably. "You know Zalman won't miss a chance at tormenting him after this."

"Yes, and it's a troubling set of circumstances. Two lonely souls in pain, both seeking solace - comfort."

"It's an understandable outcome I suppose," Maleeka won himself a quelling look from his partner. Shrugging, he went on. "I'm not saying it's right. We both know it's not. I'm just saying that Drinian is feeling desperate. Once Dante marries Saturday, he will be the last of the Blackthorne children who aren't married. He wants what his brother will have; a woman who loves him and children. He believes he'll never have that because of the demons which plague him."

Woreash couldn't help but agree. "Then there is Veta. She is desperate to lose herself for a while and not have to feel the tremendous loss of her children all over again. She worries, that her steadfast belief in our Lord may be preventing her from ever having the happiness during her lifetime, that she sees others having."

Eyeing each other, they watched the bright, white light shoot down from the heavens towards the cabin. The two angels sheathed their swords. They were no longer needed, for now at least.

"And so, for a time, they comfort each other," Maleeka said.

"Yes, understandable, yet still wrong."

"Indeed, which is why, I find this situation so fascinating. They both seek comfort to be free of their pain and yet, their actions are not entirely selfish for their true desire, in this case, is to ease each other's pain. Not necessarily their own." Maleeka spread his great wings, preparing for flight.

"Hhhmm. Maybe so. It still seems a bit self-serving, if you ask me, for them to relieve themselves of some of their own torment, at least for a time. But only for a short while, and then it returns tenfold. That said, mankind's capacity for compassion and love has always fascinated me. As well as their vast misunderstanding of free will, and the power they have over choice."

"Too bad the act outside of marriage comes at such an inevitably high price."

Woreash gazed up toward the heavens then back at his counterpart, flapping his massive wings all the while.

"Agreed."

- - -

Body jerking, Drinian awoke with a start just before dawn, feeling a heavy chill in the air. Staring up at the ceiling, he groaned outwardly at the sight of three dark, shadowy creatures glaring evilly back at him, with their snake-like red, glowing eyes. Scowling back up at them, he heard the soft sound of a woman moaning and was startled to find he was holding a woman in his arms. The initial surprise wore off quickly as the memories of several hours prior came back to him in waves.

Breathing heavily, the magnitude of what they had done hit him full force. Drinian began to panic. His initial response was to get out of there and as quick and quiet as possible. Having disturbed her when he'd jerked awake, he now found himself staring into the depths of a pair of emerald green eyes, which were quickly widening to the size of saucers.

"Please, don't scream," Drinian said frantically, fear evident in his tone and expression.

Breathing heavily, Veta sat up quickly, wishing instantly she hadn't done that. Grabbing at her throbbing head, she stared back in dismay at the giant man now sitting up next to her.

"What … what's happened here?"

"I'm sorry, so sorry!" He stood with haste, forgetting momentarily he was without clothes. Clasping his hands over his head, his ghostly luminous eyes peered frantically around the room. He looked like a caged animal desperate to be set free.

Lip quivering, Veta stared at the man in shock, trying desperately to remember what happened and who he was. She knew she'd seen him before, yesterday at The Coffee Haven, and then again at the Ryans Real Estate and Rental Agency but how had he gotten in her bedroom, in her bed?

"Who are you? What's your name?" she asked while anxiously taking in the sight of him in all his glory.

"You know me. You called me by name."

"No … I don't," she denied. "I didn't…" Confused, she attempted to avert her gaze.

Finding it difficult to keep her eyes off of him she fidgeted nervously where she sat for he was truly amazing to look at. The man's shoulders were vast. His barrel-sized chest was thickly sculpted with muscles, though not in a grotesque way as some muscle builders were. The long muscular arms extending from his shoulders in a hulking fashion, flexed even with the slightest movement.

His strength was clearly born of size, and she suspected, the labor of a hard worker. Catching a glance at his beefy hands, she was amazed by the sheer size of them. Her own small hands would be dwarfed within his. An unsettling sense of disappointment came over her at the realization that she had no memory of them upon her, touching her.

Ashamed by her thoughts, Veta's lashes fluttered softly, almost demurely against her cheeks. She swallowed with difficulty when her gaze forayed further than it should. When she turned her head toward the closet instead, her hand unconsciously clenched at the base of her heart. Her eyes shifted towards him once more. She inhaled suddenly, desperate for the precious oxygen required for consciousness. She was startled to realize she'd stopped breathing. Head jerking at the sound of his voice bringing her back to reality, her chin jutted away from the sight him once again

Nodding his head urgently, he repeated himself, sensing she'd missed what he'd said. "You called me by my name, Drinian."

"Drinian's my cat."

"You named your cat Drinian?" he asked in dismay. The black cat in question walked slowly past his left leg, startling him as it rubbed against him as it moved.

"Are you telling me your name is, Drinian?" She sounded and looked as though she didn't believe him.

"Yes, Drinian Blackthorne." He reached for his pants self-consciously and began putting them on. His awkward movements nearly caused him to trip. Thinking quickly, he realized he still didn't know her last name. "What's yours?"

"You don't know my name?" Her voice rose in horror.

"No, no … wait. I do it's … it's Veta. But you never told me your last name."

"You didn't know my last name and you still… You mean we…? Did we?" She appeared thoroughly distressed as her other hand rested against her belly. Looking back up at him, she saw the guilty look on his face and gasped.

"I'm sorry, so sorry."

"But how?" she wailed. "How did this happen?"

Openly distressed himself, Drinian paced the room. He gazed from her to the demons now floating across the ceiling. They hissed and jeered, cackling at him, for they knew what he'd done and took pleasure in his fear. Sliding their oily looking black substances down toward him, they landed within mere feet of him, brushing against him as they dropped from the ceiling. Flinching away from their cold nauseating presence, Drinian appeared jittery as a result.

"I saw you from the woods."

"You were spying on me?"

"No, it wasn't like that," Drinian said quickly, and then stopped himself, shaking his head. "I mean it's not what you think!" He was disturbed by the conclusions he sensed she was coming to.

"Then tell me, what should I think?" Her voice rose as tears welled in her eyes.

"I saw you, but I was leaving." He tried to explain but was having trouble thinking clearly. "I saw you with wine and pills. You were about to drown."

Hit suddenly with the memory of finding the wine bottle in the fridge, she gasped. Hands covering her mouth, she pinned the afghan covering her to her chest with her elbows.

"Wine and pills, oh no! And I think... Did I take my medicine twice?"

Seeing recognition in her eyes, Drinian latched on to it. "Yes, yes. And you were about to drown. They wanted you to drown so I..."

"Who wanted me to drown?"

"The demons."

"The demons," Veta repeated dully, her face going white.

"Yes, for some reason, they wanted you to drown so I pulled you from the hot tub. I don't know why they did." Drinian hoped the knowledge that he was trying to save her would give her less reason to hate him.

"You're saying demons wanted me dead so you saved me, and then you slept with me?"

The statement even to Drinian's ears sounded ridiculous. Gazing at her face, now stricken with shock and horror, it occurred to him that she didn't remember he could see the demons. Dread overwhelmed him, and his face became slack. He realized instead of helping her, he'd harmed her. Hurt that she couldn't even remember what had happened, he cringed, his face twisting into a wounded expression.

Heart thumping wildly in her chest, Veta's eyes darted about the bedroom then settled back on the man before her. He was huge, he was magnificent, and though clearly all man, his eyes reflected that of a little boy who'd been caught at some mischief and was about to be punished. The hurt and pain she saw in his expression she knew were reflected in her own.

Closing his eyes tightly, Drinian grimaced, choking back a tortured sob. The knowledge, that he had wronged this woman sitting before him was very obvious as he gazed at her cringing form.

"I'm sorry. So, so very sorry," he croaked softly. Opening his eyes, he looked upon her one last time with regret before he fled from the room. The screeching dark shadowy figures swarmed after him.

Crying, she watched him run from the room. Her head throbbed while her heart twisted within her. She didn't understand completely what all had happened yet, but she knew enough. She realized, at that moment, that it wasn't entirely his fault. She drank an entire bottle of wine and accidentally took her medicine twice. In her drunken, drugged haze, she'd been dumb enough to crawl into the hot tub and would have drowned if he hadn't pulled her out.

How he had come to be in her bed she wasn't sure exactly. She suspected she might have encouraged him because of the condition she'd been in. Not in the habit of getting drunk, she wasn't really sure what she was like when she'd had too much, and it was entirely possible she'd asked him to stay with her.

"God, forgive me!" she cried out suddenly. *"Please, forgive me, I'm so sorry. I would never normally…"* Tears welled in her eyes, running down her cheeks in waves as she hiccupped softly. *"God, help me, what have I done?"* Hysteria bubbled up inside her.

Running from the room, Drinian nearly fled the cabin without looking back. Out of the corner of his eye, he saw a purse laying on the counter as he was passing it and stopped abruptly. Taking hold of the purse, he quickly squelched his guilt for snooping by justifying that he needed to know her last name. Pulling out her wallet, he hastily opened it to her ID with shaking hands and saw her picture staring back from her Maryland license, which listed her name as Veta Rohann. Dropping the wallet back in her purse, he heard her cry out to God for forgiveness. He fled in a panicked state from the cabin back through the patio and out into the woods.

Running swiftly, he picked up his pace as he reached the path. Drinian's eyes began to water and burn, and the demons darted about him in a frenzy. Pausing for a moment on the trail, he inhaled the scent of the woods around him, while the shadows circled him. That's when it really hit him, the full magnitude of what he had done. He had been intimate with a woman he didn't really know, during a time when she couldn't make a rational decision for herself.

Did that mean he'd raped her?

Panic seized him. His heart heavy with anguish, tears flooded to his eyes. Tormented by the knowledge he could have hurt Veta in such an egregious manner, he took flight once again and sped through the forest at top speed, feeling the cool mountain air against his skin. What had he been thinking? How could he have lost control of his senses so completely?

Drinian had always prided himself on being more than just gentlemanly with women on the rare occasion when he was in their presence. It's how he had been raised. He had learned to accept the fact, that his ability to see and hear the demons, had made him moody and incapable of feeling. Knowing his personality had suffered for it, he understood the female genders' need to simply enjoy the view of his good looks from a distance.

Noticing his run was taking him along the path towards his father's home, he came to a disturbing notion. He couldn't help but wonder if the demons Veranke, Zalman and Fallen's reticence, at his saving the woman, had been just another of their ploys in order to get him to do their bidding. The fact he had likely just played into, yet another one of the shadows nefarious plans, was becoming quite clear to him.

He stopped suddenly, skidding in the dirt path near a dark patch of the forest. Exclaiming in dismay, he cried out to the Lord.

"What have I done?"

His thoughts turned to his sister, Megorah. He winced outwardly, crying out once again in distress.

Many years back, she had been badly raped by a man that Breydon had known. A man his brother had once called a friend. The issue of respecting women and being sure to listen when they said no or were even remotely unsure about wanting to be intimate in any way was always ingrained into the Blackthorne men even in their early years. But after what happened to her, it was an ultra-sensitive issue in the house. If Megorah were to ever find out what he'd done to this woman, she'd crucify him, forging the cross herself.

Running his hands across his face he felt his heart constrict in his chest. The panic surged within him, causing him to choke back the bile rising in his throat. That's when he realized he was not alone. The troublesome three had followed him from the house along with several of their minions but had curiously disappeared from his side as he'd run. He realized suddenly, they'd simply been waiting; biding their time until he had reached this point in the path, so they could pounce on him at his weakest moment. The shadows flew at him, enveloping him with their nauseating presence. They danced about him, writhing together as their black smoky essence began forming into the shapes of men. Their faceless bodies clung to him, choking at his throat.

"No!" He cried out in anger and frustration for not seeing them coming. It had been a long time since they'd managed to jump him like this. He'd been lost in his thoughts and missed the signs.

"She will destroy you." Veranke taunted him, clinging to Drinian's side.

Shaking his head, he fell to the ground, their deathly cold grip upon him making him even more nauseous.

"She will make you pay for what you've done to her." This time it was Zalman heckling him, as he spoke in Drinian's ear.

Drinian's strangled cry of distress erupted from his throat, forcing them to back away in agony. "No! Get away from me. God, help me, please! I'm so sorry, I wasn't trying to hurt her."

"She'll put you in jail," Veranke spat. "You'll never be free!"

"I'm not free now," he roared at them in indignation, furious with himself for being so stupid and falling into their trap.

"Kill her ... and it goes away," Zalman said with an eerie calm as he spoke. Drinian shook his head violently, bending toward the ground while holding his stomach. He could feel nausea overtaking him. It felt like they were sliding inside him.

"No, I won't do it." Drinian grabbed at his hair. He was in a frantic state. *"Please, God,"* he sobbed. *"Don't leave me. Help me!"*

"We're here, Drinian. We never left you!" The angel Woreash hollered above the clang and clatter of the swords as he and Maleeka battled the troublesome three's many minions. Dozens more erupting from the forest around them, circling the foray, awaiting their turn.

"God would never leave you," Maleeka shouted above the snarling angry roars of the demons at his side. Slashing and smashing into, yet another, he called out to the Lord for aid, the demons numbers too great to handle on their own any longer. In the same instant, a hum could be heard from above the trees as four Guardians dropped down through the branches and leaves.

"No need for the call," Rokon said heartily. His bright silver eyes flashed towards Maleeka. "He knew you'd need help." Whirling his broadsword about, he took out two demons in the same instant.

Seeing the Guardian angels, the demons snarled and gnashed their teeth, shrinking from their foes anxiously.

"Kill her! It's easy, so easy." Fallen wheezed urgently next to Drinian, ignoring the Guardians presence nearby, and yet, ever watchful of them.

"A knife or a rope. Or maybe bare hands. You have big hands. Large strong hands made for CHOKING!"

Zalman screeched at him. Then he laughed at the wild look on Drinian's face as he came up off the ground, hurling himself towards Zalman's smoky black form. He raged at the filthy demon, punching out at him in frustration, knowing full well his fists would just slide through.

"Kill her. Kill the whore!" The three dark spirits attempted to converge upon him, hoping to assault his senses with their evil thoughts. Laughter was ringing in his ears.

Drinian cried out in fear and desperation. His stomach lurched, and he threw up on the forest floor. He attempted to crawl away from the dense path toward the brightly lit portion of the path but before he could reach it everything went black. He passed out amongst the leaves and shadowy patches of trees. Around him, the battle waged on fiercely, as the Guardian angels defended the man now lying upon the forest floor, for God would never leave one of his own, even in their darkest hour.

Chapter 5

There was a phone ringing in the distance. Yet the lethargy Veta was feeling, as she slowly came to a waking state, prevented her from investigating its source. Her eyes felt heavy, her throat dry and pasty. She was conscious of a throbbing sensation in her knee. The phone stopped ringing. She swiftly slipped back into a restless sleep.

What seemed like mere moments later but was actually an hour, Veta woke with a start. The phone was ringing, shattering the quiet of the house again. Only this time, her head didn't feel quite so foggy, though it throbbed with each ring. Slipping out of the bed, the afghan fell with her, tangling around her legs, as she attempted to stumble her way towards the incessant noise. Locating the phone hanging on the wall between the bedroom and the kitchen, she grabbed it up without thinking, merely trying to get the intrusive painful sound to stop. Summoning every ounce of energy she had, she managed a weak and groggy greeting, as she attempted to regain her equilibrium.

"Hello? Hello, Miss Rohann? This is Deputy James Pike of the Breckenridge Sheriff's Department. Have I caught you at a bad time?"

Clearing her throat, she managed to speak, her voice sounding thick, "No, it's fine."

"The Sheriff asked me to have you come in this morning. He wanted to run through what happened with the theft of your U-Haul and get a better listing of the belongings from you." The deputy spoke in a polite but crisp manner.

"Oh, uh, okay." She tried to think. Standing between the bedroom and kitchen, she realized with a shiver, that she was still naked as she leaned against the wall for support. Her head throbbed as she rested her hand against it. It took a moment before she realized Deputy Pike had been speaking to her and she'd missed what he said.

"I'm sorry. What did you say again?" she asked, managing to make her voice sound a little more normal. She realized her eyes were partially swollen from having cried herself to sleep.

"I said, would around ten this morning work for you?" The deputy sounded concerned. "Ms. Rohann, are you all right? Is everything okay there?"

"Ah, yes. Yes, of course, I'm sorry I just woke up to the phone," she explained quickly, not wanting to alarm the deputy unnecessarily.

"Apologies, Ma'am, I didn't mean to wake you." The man sounded flustered.

"No, no you're fine. It's okay I should be getting up anyway." She came back with a halfhearted laugh but she sniffled miserably.

"Can I put you down for ten?" the deputy asked again.

"Um, what time is it?" She knew full well she sounded absolutely stupid.

Chuckling, Deputy Pike responded, "It would be nine in the morning ma'am."

"Can we make that more like ten thirty?" She knew full well she'd never make it back in town and have time to shower if she had to be there earlier.

"Let me check." There was a long pause on the phone. "That should be fine. I'll put you down with the Sheriff then at ten thirty this morning."

"Thank you." Veta hung up the phone and slid down the wall. Blinking her swollen eyes a couple of times, she glanced around.

The last thing she remembered with any clarity was hopping in the hot tub. But she did recall the man called Drinian had been there. The events of what had transpired between them weighed heavily upon her heart. Standing precariously, she stumbled back to the bedroom looking for her bag. It wasn't until she reached the room, that she recalled she'd left the suitcase in the living room. She was about to turn around to head that way when she saw the state of her bed.

There were no sheets because hers had been stolen when the U-Haul was taken. That was not what had caught her attention. Eyes wide she walked towards the bed, staring down at the mattress, as she saw the proof of what had happened between them all over it. For the first time since she awoke the full magnitude of what had happened set in.

Veta whimpered. Tears spilled forth from her burning eyes once again. The cloud that had fogged her brain before was gone. Gasping, she started to recall more of what had happened as though she had dreamt it. But it hadn't been a dream at all for the proof was right there in front of her. Veta ran from the room then and fled to the patio as memories of the events from the night before flooded her mind in waves.

Reaching the patio she stood stock still in horror, looking out onto the patio from the doorway. The hot tub was still on and running from the night before. The empty bottle of wine she'd drunk was floating in the bubbling water, and her pill bottle was still on the table where she left it. What had stopped her in her movement, was the sliding glass door that had been pulled from its tracks and set aside against the other sliding door. A hole gaped through from the patio out onto the lawn of the cabin.

She covered her face in shame and sank to the floor. Sobbing into her hands, she wrapped her other arm around her waist attempting to hold herself as she stared at the floor of the patio. She remembered vaguely now being pulled from the water and placed on the floor by a very big, very beautiful man. The same man who had been in her room, Drinian Blackthorne.

Tears streamed down Veta's face. She lurched forward and threw up on the floor. Pulling her hair out of her face and away from her neck, she cried while crawling back into the living room from the patio. At that moment, she couldn't help but think how stupid she had been. He'd been all over her and she'd let him, welcomed him even, of that she was sure. She now remembered having invited him to stay.

Desperate to get out of there she found a clean pair of jeans and a shirt in her suitcase and threw them on as quickly as possible. She tiptoed back out to the patio for her medicine and clothes from the night before.

Unknown to her, several shadows had crept from the forest onto the patio. Watching her from corners of the room, the demons could see her wadding up her clothes and placing them in a plastic bag from her Chinese takeout. Noticing a puddle on the floor near the doorway one of the shadows gestured towards it with a gleam of mischief in his eye. Exchanging glances with each other they plotted their next accident. As one swooped down to her right and whirled about her, another spread the puddle so it extended further.

"Hurry, sweet Veta," the demon urged at her side. "Drinian's coming back for you, for more." He cackled in a noxious manner.

Shivering as a sudden chill came over her, Veta's head swiveled about in distress. Feeling an uneasy sensation in the pit of her gut as though she were being watched, she gasped when a latent memory from her past washed over her. Overwhelmed with anxiety, she didn't pay attention to where she was stepping as she ran from the patio. Slipping on the water she fell hard, smacking her left knee and arm on the floor. Shaky now and thinking irrationally that Drinian might come back for her again, she hurriedly pulled herself up from the floor and left the patio.

Laughing evilly the demons cheered as they watched her run away. Step one in their plan had succeeded; now on to step two.

Veta was limping badly as she grabbed up her suitcase and purse and carried them to her car. It took a little bit to get her cat Drinian back in his cage but she managed to do it. She half dragged him in her second and last trip out. Backing out of the drive, she turned around and then tore down the driveway squealing her tires in the process.

Speeding down the long driveway, she turned onto Deer Creek Road. As she went, she noticed a black Lexus turning onto the driveway from the opposite direction of where she'd just come from.

"Faster," another demon crowed, having taken a seat next to her in her car. "Better hurry before everyone finds out what you did."

Too afraid to look back, Veta gladly and desperately fled as fast as she could down the road towards town, hoping against hope that her room might still be available back at the motel.

As Veta tore down the road, Megorah Blackthorne pulled into the log cabins driveway. She had to stop suddenly at the assault of emotion she experienced from the other driver. Clearly a woman and most definitely terrified Megorah sat for a moment holding her gut before opening her door. Stepping out of her car, she looked down Deer Creek Road, the direction the woman had gone.

Confused as to what was going on, Megorah could only presume that the woman who'd fled away had been Veta Rohann, the tenant that had mistakenly rented their vacation home. Disappointed at having missed her, and even more distressed by the emotions the woman had been experiencing, she was at a loss for a moment as to what to do.

Getting back into her vehicle, Megorah continued down the long driveway, thinking she would leave a note for the woman on her door. Upon reaching the cabin, she discovered the door had not only been left unlocked but was also left slightly ajar. A little unsettled but not experiencing any bad vibes anywhere from anyone else, she stepped inside the cabin.

Glancing around she didn't see anything amiss initially, other than there were cat dishes in the kitchen. Stepping around the couch, she noticed puddles of water leading from the patio into the living room and down the hall to the bedroom. Checking the patio first, she was alarmed to see the hot tub was still running until she noticed that one of the sliding glass patio doors had been removed from its track from the outside. The patio was left wide open for anyone to enter.

Turning the hot tub off she pulled out her phone and dialed her brother Drinian first to see if he could come out and put the door back on its tracks. Not reaching him, she tried Breydon next, getting him on the first ring.

"This better be good," she heard him growl into the phone.

Smiling, she smirked a little, knowing full well why he was irritable. "Oh, Brey, Brey, did we not sleep well last night?" she teased.

"Ha! You're not funny, Meg. You know exactly why I'm so cranky. Dante really needs to keep better tabs on his fiancée. Maybe then, he'll stop waking us before sunrise."

Her brother was obviously irritable. "Oh, now stop. You know full well you're only cranky because Alaina thinks she communicated with a couple of angels that you cannot see." Meg could hear him making grunting noises over the phone and chuckled. "There *is* actually a purpose to this call."

"Really? You gonna tell me what Dante and Alaina had to speed off to your husbands' clinic for this morning?" he asked.

"Nope. I'm calling about the vacation cabin."

"What about it? I thought you said Freedom rented it." Breydon sounded confused.

"She did. She screwed up too...."

"Now, why doesn't that surprise me? I keep telling you and dad, you need to fire her. She's really kind of useless and too flighty," he said abrasively, interrupting.

Megorah chose to ignore his statement. She'd heard it all before. "Now listen. Something is up here. I was just about to pull into the driveway here at the cabin when this woman comes tearing down the drive and pulls out onto Deer Creek Road at like, breakneck speed. When I get up to the cabin I find the door is unlocked and still partially opened."

"You didn't go in did you?" Breydon asked sharply, alarmed now.

"It's okay, I don't feel a presence here. Anyways, I came inside and I see water all over the floor heading towards the patio. So I go check the patio, right?"

"Megorah…"

"No, now listen to me," she continued. "I check out the patio to find the hot tub is still running and the patio door has been pulled off its track. So I'm wondering…"

"Megorah, you know full well your ability is not always accurate. Get out of that house now!" Breydon shouted into her ear.

Pulling the phone away from her face a little, while she stepped from the patio back into the living room, she turned the corner towards the bedroom.

"Good grief, you don't have to shout in my ear. And thanks by the way for the…." Upon reaching the bedroom she stopped mid-sentence. She had just stepped in when she saw the state of the bed and could smell the pungent odor in the air. It hit her full force upon entering.

"Megorah?" She could hear Breydon over the phone but wasn't able to acknowledge him. She was so stunned by what she saw.

Slithering down from the ceiling, where they had hidden initially, the other two shadowy demons sidled up to her on either side.

"Something happened here," one of them crooned ominously next to her ear.

"Something bad," said the other. His smoky black substance circled her. Only the face of a man could be seen sticking out from the cloud. "As bad as what happened to you fifteen years ago."

Pausing briefly, her eyes darted back and forth before her. She recalled what she'd seen on the patio. Finally piecing the pieces together in her head, the picture that formed frightened her. For a brief moment, she flashed back to an incident she'd had with a man fifteen years prior. Chest heaving with anxiety she made a strangled sound low in her throat.

"Meg!" Breydon shouted again into the phone. Finally, registering his screaming, she took a deep breath and ran from the house.

"Brey, Brey! I think something bad might have happened here in the cabin." She'd run for the front door, fleeing towards her car with the two demons hot on her tail as she exited the house. Grateful to have reached it, she pulled her doors shut and locked them, starting the ignition.

But that didn't keep the demons out. Slithering through a crack in the window, their smoky forms coalesced into the shapes of men and they took up residence in her back seat.

"We're on our way. Get out of there now," her brother ordered.

"I am. I'm pulling down the drive now. I think I..." she paused, taking a deep breath. It occurred to her, Breydon had sounded like he was running when he last spoke. "I have to head back to the clinic. Chase, Dante and Alaina are expecting me back there."

"Good. Go there and stay with them. Please, Meggie," her brother begged.

Megorah could hear the fear in his voice. "I will. I promise." She took another deep breath to steady her voice. "I'm okay. I am, but this, Veta, if that's who she was..." she said as she pulled onto Deer Creek Road towards town. "Then she was really scared, Brey. I mean, terrified scared."

"Don't you worry, Dad and I will take care of it."

Grinning at each other, the shadows watched the woman with excitement. Their task seemed to be coming along nicely. Without warning, the one on the right began howling in pain as a sword sliced through the ceiling of the car. Turning towards each other, their red bulbous eyes widened in dismay. They watched each other explode from the blows the Guardian angel had inflicted from above.

Staring down through the ceiling of the car, the Guardian angel's expression was grim. The troublesome three had set their minions upon Megorah Blackthorne for a purpose. To what end was as yet unknown but it clearly couldn't have been for good.

Chapter 6

Veta sat in her car, staring at the room key, unsure of what to do next. She'd reached the town in what she imagined was record time, only to be told at the motel the room wouldn't be ready for her until almost eleven o'clock. They were apparently short staffed on housekeeping personnel. Looking back down at the room key, she wished mournfully she'd had a chance to take a shower before going to the station to see the Sheriff. Until the meeting at ten thirty, however, she really didn't have a place to go. Veta found herself crying again as she sat there, staring at the key, trying to decide where to go and what she was going to do.

She had nearly an hour until her meeting and she didn't really feel up to sitting in the lobby of the motel. Glancing over at the carrier, she saw that Drinian was sleeping peacefully. She envied him. Staring at its black fur and white paw, Veta couldn't help but think of Drinian, the man, for now, every time she looked at her cat it reminded her of him. Sighing heavily she wiped her eyes and could feel her belly rumble. She wasn't really hungry but she could tell her stomach was upset. She figured it had a lot to do with her medicine and the alcohol she drank the night before. She imagined it had a lot to do with why she had gotten sick on the patio. So stupid, she thought to herself again. Veta knew better than to take her medicine with alcohol, which was why she usually avoided drinking at all.

Her encounter with Drinian, the man with the amazing crystal blue eyes, might have never happened had she been paying attention and not drinking. She had just been so upset over the loss of her memory boxes. Biting at her fist, she decided a cup of coffee, at the very least, was needed and she knew right where she could get that. Starting her engine, Veta pulled back out onto Spokane Avenue and drove down the two short blocks to The Coffee Haven.

Upon entering the coffee house, Veta found she was still limping and a bit jumpy. The man who'd been at the counter the day before wasn't there, nor did she see Crisalya, so she ordered a plain coffee from the teenage girl at the counter. Adding brown sugar, she stirred the overfull cup gently as she took a seat at a small table with her back up against the wall. Her eyes darted back and forth around the room nervously. She blew on her cup and took a sip. It tasted a little bitter compared to what she was used to but she held the cup in her hands anyway as though she needed the warmth.

It occurred to her as she warmed herself with the coffee, that she'd seen Drinian for the first time here at the Coffee Haven. Wondering briefly if he might show up here again this morning, she found her cheeks flushing at the notion. Shaking her head, she tried instead to decide what to do about her living arrangements.

"You can't go back there you know." The demon near her hoped to frighten her further. "Drinian could find you there, and he can find you here. He'll tell everyone too. Soon everyone will know what you did."

Veta didn't think she could go back to that cabin but she'd signed a one-year lease with them. How was she going to explain her need to vacate after only one day?

"Just imagine what the owners will think of you when they find the mess you left there." The shadow continued to taunt with malicious zeal.

Suddenly realizing she'd left the hot tub on, she became even more upset over the knowledge that someone would likely check the cabin and might see the state she'd left it in. Mortified at what they might think, she found herself biting at her hand again, while trying desperately to choke back tears.

"Hi, there!"

Hearing a male voice next to her, Veta was startled out of her reverie. Spilling her coffee for the second time she'd been in the shop, she began mopping it up with her shaking hands as Royce Howard stared at her, his brows furrowing as though something he was seeing bothered him.

His wife came around the counter, with a towel in hand; ready to clean up the mess with a few quick swipes. She had been so lost in her own little pity world she missed seeing Crisalya and Royce enter from the back room.

"I'm so sorry, I guess I'm just a bit jumpy today." Even to Veta, her voice sounded strained and anxious. The demon smiled gleefully at seeing the wretched state he'd managed to place her in, oblivious to the light flashing in behind him.

"Never you mind. It's no big deal," Crisalya said, while cheerfully cleaning up the mess, though she did seem a bit more tired than the day before. Tossing the towel in a bin she stared down at the woman before her. Gradually her expression changed as she gazed at her.

"From the looks of it, you didn't need that coffee anyways."

"Pardon me?"

"You need tea. Not coffee. I have just the right thing for you." She smiled, rubbed her arms, and headed towards the back before Veta could refuse.

"You don't need tea." The demon crooned in an attempt to goad her further. "You need…"

Hearing the sound of a sword sliding from its scabbard, the demon was alerted to the presence of the Guardian angel. Whirling out of its physical form, the creature regained its cloudy mass and attempted to flee towards a nearby window. Halted in its movements, as both Woreash and his broadsword erupted into the shop through the very window, the demon screamed in terror as it was slashed through from both sides.

"What do you suppose they're up to?" The Guardian called Rokon inquired, watching the shadowy demon dissipate as he slid his sword back into his scabbard.

"No good," Woreash said. "They've been ordered to instill fear I would wager."

"I am to stay with her," the Guardian declared. His gaze moved from the heavens back to Woreash's wise face.

"And I have another task." Woreash disappeared, leaving the Guardian to his charge.

"No worries, Veta. We are still with you. God is always with you." Rokon tried to assure the woman. He stood diligently by her side. Placing a hand upon her shoulder he could see her close her eyes and sigh as though an uneasy calm had finally managed to take hold of her.

"That's it. All will be well in time. You'll see."

Minutes later, Crisalya returned with a small tray laden with two cups of tea, a pot of hot water, and scone pastries with butter and honey for two. Placing the tray on the table, she proceeded to serve Veta her tea and placed a scone in front of her as well, after adding butter and honey to it.

Veta glanced over at Crisalya anxiously. "I just don't know if I can eat this today. It looks wonderful; it's just, my belly isn't feeling too well this morning," she said, trying not to sound ungrateful.

"Trust me, you need it more than you think," Crisalya nodded at her encouragingly as the Guardian smiled with reassurance.

"I find," Royce spoke up from the counter. "That it's usually best just to humor her." He glanced over at her briefly then walked away suddenly, disappearing into the back room of the shop.

She couldn't help but wonder if Royce somehow knew what she'd done for the way he'd looked at her.

Nervously, she rubbed her brow with one hand and took up her cup of tea with the other. Taking a sip, she felt the light, warm liquid slide down her throat. It tasted of mint and it had a sweet creamy note to it. Taking another sip, she felt the turmoil inside her ease a bit and her arms and legs stopped trembling quite so much.

"This is very good. What is it?" Veta asked curiously.

"Mint leaf tea. It's often very good, for whatever is ailing a person, though it's most commonly used to ward off nausea." Crisalya's response was a bit distracted. She stirred her own tea and took a sip.

"Is that what you're having?"

"Oh, no, I needed something else today," she said evasively, taking another sip of her tea. They chatted together amicably for a little while about nothing in particular, as they ate their scones. Veta discovered she really was hungry and polished off her pastry to the last bite. Noticing the time was getting close to ten thirty she asked for directions to the Sheriff's office. She attempted to pay her bill, to which Crisalya refused, then headed on out of the shop, missing the exchange between the couple as she left.

"Is she gone?" Royce asked, poking his head around the door of the back room.

"She's leaving now. Why did you disappear like that?" Crisalya asked.

"She's as skittish as a cat this morning," he said in response. "I had the feeling my presence was making her uneasy. I got the sense you noticed it too or you wouldn't have put Lemongrass oil in her tea-cup before bringing it out. You really should not do that, Cris. Not without their knowledge and consent."

Guiltily, Crisalya watched the woman step gingerly along the sidewalk in front of the shop. "I know, Royce, but her anxiety is off the charts right now. I don't have to be Meg to sense that. Something's happened to her. If I can do something to help ease her tension and stress then I feel I should. I just hope what's happened isn't too serious."

Royce grimaced as Veta limped from their view, suspecting his wife's hopes would likely be dashed.

- - -

Standing just inside the cabin doors Breydon and Rafe Blackthorne inspected carefully the kitchen and living space from where they stood. If something had happened in the cabin, that required involving the police, they didn't want to disturb anything. Noticing the cat food dishes and a small puddle of water near the kitchen, Breydon pointed them out to his father.

"Yes, I see them."

"The woman, this Veta, she just moved in yesterday?" Breydon stepped around the couch and headed for the kitchen.

"Yes, but it sure doesn't look like she's planning to stay does it?" Rafe used his well-trained eye to inspect the room. There wasn't really anything in the room, other than the pet dishes, that would imply someone had even been there. Most women he knew would have unloaded their entire belongings within the first day if they could.

Opening a couple of cabinet doors with a tissue, Breydon responded, "No, it sure doesn't."

"Tell me again. What was it that set Megorah off?" Rafe didn't see anything out of the ordinary from where he stood.

"She was just about to pull in the drive when the woman tore out from it and sped towards town. So Meg apparently thought she'd play, Ms. Nancy Drew, and investigates further by coming up to the cabin. When she got here, the door was unlocked and ajar. Being the intelligent individual that she is, she let herself in." Breydon said irritably.

"It's bothersome that this woman left it open and unlocked, but I don't see…"

"She was terrified, Dad," Breydon said, gaining his father's attention. "According to Meg, the woman was scared to death, and she said the patio door is off its track, which was why she thought to call in the first place."

"Let's check it out." Rafe headed towards the patio.

They both stepped out onto the enclosed patio deck and could see where the gaping hole was left where the door had been taken off its track. Walking around the hot tub, Rafe stepped over a small puddle of water and took a good look at the door.

"Whoever did it, I doubt it was a woman." Pausing, he inspected it a little more thoroughly. "It looks like someone knew what they were doing when they took it off. But they did it so forcefully they managed to bend the track."

"They would have to be pretty strong to do that." Breydon moved towards the tub. "The cover is off. Meg said it was still running when she got here. And look," he continued, lifting the wine bottle from the water with a towel. "It's a bottle of red but the water is clear." Glancing around, he didn't see any spilled on the floor either, although there was a wet spot of something between the table and the patio door to the living room.

"What is that smell?" Rafe asked suddenly, glancing around the room. Seeing Breydon looking towards the table, he headed in that direction, then stopped suddenly. "Someone has been sick here." Rafe was starting to get an uneasy feeling about the mental picture he was getting.

"What are you thinking?" Breydon watched his father's quick perusal of the patio deck, knowing full well Rafe's keen mind was working on a theory.

"Front door was left unlocked and ajar with the back-patio door off its track from the outside. The hot tub was left on with an empty bottle of wine and vomit on the floor. We got an extremely frightened young woman speeding away from it all," his brows furrowed. "Frankly, I'm getting kind of a confusing picture. It feels like something is missing from this." Rafe shook his head.

"You know, Meg didn't say anything about the bottle or that." Breydon pointed towards the smelly mess on the floor.

"Your sister's sense of smell has been off since her nose was broken a long time ago," Rafe said with a shrug as he stepped back into the living room. "I'm betting she was more concerned about turning the hot tub off than anything else. So, what ended up spooking you so bad, Meg?" Rafe asked more to himself, as he headed down the hall towards the bedroom. Glancing into the bathroom on the way, he called out to Breydon who was following close behind. "No toiletries in the bathroom. It doesn't even look like it's been used."

Harrumphing out loud, Breydon responded, "This woman is gone."

Seeing Rafe stop abruptly just inside the bedroom doorway, Breydon peered around him to get a good look inside.

"I believe I have a bad feeling I know why," Rafe said with distaste while staring briefly at the mattress on the bed.

Breydon didn't need to see the state of it to know what had happened recently in the room. He could smell the scent of the intimate exchange still lingering there. It was strong too, which meant it had to be recent.

"Are you thinking what I'm thinking?" Breydon asked, looking troubled. Glancing at his father, it was like seeing a mirrored reaction on his face.

Sighing heavily Rafe nodded, "I have a bad feeling Ms. Rohann arrived here yesterday, excited at the prospect of using her new hot tub and wound up getting more than she bargained for." Closing his eyes he breathed in deeply.

Breydon pointed at the bed. "You thinking she might have been forced?"

"I'm thinking someone broke in, by the looks of the back patio, and may well have taken advantage of a woman who was likely drunk at the time. Whether it was consensual or not remains to be seen." Rafe rubbed his hands across his forehead angrily.

"Aren't you getting anything from this Dad? Usually, you have some insight by now." Breydon peered around the room, not seeing any angelic presence whatsoever.

"No, nothing. Truth is, I'm getting a mixed feeling from this room and the patio. It would seem we are meant to decipher this mystery ourselves." Typically by now, the angel at his side would have given him a hint as to what he was dealing with. The absence of his guide had him feeling useless.

"Guess the only way to find out for sure is to find the lady and the best way to find the lady in question would be…"

"Sheriff Blackthorne?" Breydon asked. He left the bedroom and headed towards the front door.

"Yup, time to call Dart." Rafe pulled out his cell phone as he followed.

- - -

From a distance, Drinian leaned against a tree. He could see his father and brother, standing outside the cabin. He knew from where they stood he was thoroughly hidden from their view, so he was not worried about being seen. The foliage here was dense and allowed for shadows to swoop in and out around him, taunting him in their wake.

"They will figure it out. They'll know what you did." Veranke sniveled, swirling around Drinian.

Tearing a branch off the tree in frustration, he whacked it against the ground, becoming irritable at their incessant verbal onslaughts.

A quick glance back down at the cabin, had him growling deep within his throat in frustration. When he awoke after having passed out in the woods, he had initially thought to head to the main house since he was near it at the time. When he'd come upon the hidden trail entrance, that led to the ranch house, he'd seen Alaina sitting outside in the grass, staring up at the northern lights in the sky.

Worried initially, at seeing her alone outside, his concern soon disappeared when he noticed his father watching over her from his bedroom balcony. Then, realizing he wouldn't be able to reach the entrance to the ranch house from any angle without being seen, he'd decided he would have to return to his own cabin. He'd needed a shower badly since he had fallen into his own vomit, and he smelled quite badly.

After showering and changing clothes, he'd taken the trail back down to the main house and witnessed as Dante and his family found Alaina outside. Discovering she had learned of their abilities by angels who had visited her during the night had been intriguing. It had him thinking. His mind was on overdrive and he just couldn't get it to shut down. Suspecting his brother's fiancée might actually be pregnant, after the exchange he'd witnessed between her and Dante, he had become extremely excited.

Over twenty years before his own mother, Lilyandhi Blackthorne had made a prophecy before she died. The full extent with which it affected him and his family were unclear. At its conclusion, it had been hinted by his mother that he might receive relief from his torment. The night before he had suspected that if Alaina *was* pregnant, it might mark the beginning of that very prophecy. After hearing what Alaina had said this morning and seeing that she was experiencing the gifts of 'foresight' and 'knowing,'

Drinian was now sure she was with child. If he was recalling the prophetic numbers in the journal accurately, then it would seem to imply she may well be expecting triplets. He needed to read through his mother's journal again to be sure.

Unusually hungry, Drinian decided to have breakfast at the house since he was already there and figured he'd head back to his cabin afterwards to read. But his sister Megorah had stopped him before he could leave, insisting she needed to see the journal. As he'd watched and listened to her animated argument, as to why she needed to see it, he realized he needed to get back to the family's vacation cabin in order to check on Veta before he could do anything else. With irritation, Meg and Chase had managed to convince him into going back to his home first, in order to pick up the journal and bring it back to them later in the day.

By the time Drinian managed to return to the vacation cabin, it was to find his sister, Megorah, standing on the back patio on her cell phone. He thought she was at the clinic with Dante and Alaina. Apparently, she had decided to swing by the cabin for some reason.

Drinian had watched as she headed back into the house. Then, moments later, witnessed her tear out of the cabin, running for her vehicle as though afraid. Cringing, he'd wondered what had frightened her. Making his way through the woods, he'd come upon the cabin and stepped through the opening of the patio. He'd seen Megorah turn the hot tub off but noticed the wine bottle still floating in the water.

He was about to step through the door to the living room when he paused and turned around. Sniffing at the air, he could smell the acrid scent of vomit. Glancing around the room, he found the spot on the floor where he assumed Veta must have gotten sick. His shoulders slumped and he wanted to kick himself, for he had a feeling that he might be partly the cause. Looking around the living room and into the kitchen he noticed her suitcase was missing. Heading to the bedroom he expected to see it there. He peered quickly into the room. Not seeing the suitcase, he turned around to head out as he could still smell her in the room.

"Disgusting aroma." Zalman chattered in the corner of the room.

"Full of you. Full of her," spat Veranke as he hovered nearby, in the shadowy recesses of the closet.

Stopping suddenly, Drinian turned around and looked back at the bed. Sighing heavily, he realized then, what it was that had set Megorah off, and he worried for her. Rolling his eyes to the heavens, he walked out of the room and nearly tripped on the cat dishes, spilling the water in one of them. Setting them back in place, it occurred to him that it looked like the cat was missing as well. It was then, that he realized she was gone.

Drinian sat for a moment, looking around the cabin, while the dark spirits flitted from one shadowy corner of the room to the next. He could hear them cackling, as though they'd won some sort of victory.

Overcome with remorse and shame, Drinian fell to his knees. Head bent low in submission; he clasped his hands together, as he prayed fervently for God's forgiveness.

I'm so sorry God. I knew better. I know better, and yet, I still took advantage of her, during a time when she was clearly vulnerable. Can you ever forgive me, Lord?

Shoulders shaking, he began to cry softly at first. Imagining what his sisters would say and do if they knew what he had done, as he prayed. Eyes tightly closed, he shook his head in despair, hoping upon hope, that he hadn't physically hurt Veta when he had been with her that night.

Drinian knew he couldn't change what he'd done, nor could he take it back but maybe at the very least, he could quietly attempt to make amends by making things easier for her. Taking a deep breath in order to compose himself, he wiped away the tears from his cheeks, glad that his brothers and father weren't present to see him cry. Resting his hands on his hips, he took a moment to think. She'd need a new place if she was staying in the area, and it occurred to him he might be able to help with that.

A tenant had recently vacated one of the apartments he owned and managed. It needed some superficial cleaning and updates, which he could work on later in the day. He would have to figure out how to let her know it was available somehow, without raising too many red flags. Figuring he could worry about it later, he realized, he had some cleaning up to do of his own here, at this cabin. He needed to get it done quickly before anyone else found out about it.

Drinian was heading to the kitchen to see if there were any paper towels, in order to wipe up the water from the floor, when he heard the dark spirits begin an ominous chant.

"They're coming! They're coming! They're coming! They're coming!"

"Gonna Getcha, you betcha! Gonna Getcha!"

"You're busted! You're busted! You're busted!

Rushing to the kitchen window, he looked out and saw, Breydon, and his father, pulling up the long drive. Eyes growing wide in alarm, he panicked. Whipping around, he sped towards the back patio, leaping over the hot tub, and jumped from the patio out into the yard. His long, strong legs made swift strides through the brush, to his present perch, where he could see them now.

"Close, so close. Could a gotcha. Almost gotcha!" screamed Veranke near his ear.

"Shut it!" Drinian whispered loudly as he continued to thrash the ground angrily with the branch. He watched as they'd headed into the cabin and checked out the patio deck. His presumption was that Megorah had panicked and called Breydon when she'd seen the bedroom. As a result, both his father and brother had come out to investigate. Knowing Rafe as well as he did, he was sure the next call would be to his brother, Dartanian, the Sheriff of Breckenridge County.

"Too late. It's too late!" Zalman cackled, flitting eerily from one tree to the next.

A low growl emitted from Drinian's throat as he turned and stalked away. The shadows were at least right about the cabin. It was too late to clean it before anyone else had seen it. He was going to at least deal with it himself when they'd left. It wasn't his father's responsibility to pay for his mess after all. Tucking the journal further down in his back pocket, so it wouldn't fall out, he headed back towards his cabin.

Chapter 7

Following Crisalya's directions, Veta managed to find her way to the station without too much difficulty. It had taken less time than she thought it would so she was a little earlier than she was expected.

She limped from her car to the front doors of the Sheriff's Department. Taking a deep breath, she pulled open the door and let herself in. Managing a weak smile, she was greeted by Deputy Pike, who was sitting at the front desk.

"Ms. Rohann." He stood quickly, extending his hand to shake hers.

Veta stepped back uneasily at his sudden and unexpected movement. Clearly, she was still a little on edge. Arms outstretched in front, she begged off his handshake with an excuse.

"I'm not feeling too well this morning." She said truthfully as she took a deep breath. The officer looked at her curiously but was kind enough not to take offense or say anything.

"The Sheriff will be with you momentarily. He's just finishing up with something, but I'll let him know you're here," Deputy Pike stated. Stepping away from his desk, he headed towards an office in the far back corner of the building.

The Breckenridge County Sheriff's Department was small but clean and orderly. Noting several of the paintings hanging in the entrance, appeared similar to ones hanging in the Coffee Haven, she wondered briefly, if they were by the same artist. Taking a closer look at the brush strokes, they did, in fact, appear to be from the same hand. Glancing around the room, as she stood waiting, she also noticed several desks had been sectioned off by partitions, though they appeared to be empty. Figuring the other officers were out, either on calls, or patrolling, she didn't think much of it.

Taking a shaky breath, as Veta viewed her surroundings; she couldn't help but feel anxious about being in the Sheriff's office, after what had happened the previous night. A fleeting thought passed through her mind about mentioning the incident but she shook the notion from her head the instant it came to her. Drinian hadn't really done anything wrong, as far as she was concerned. He may have entered her home without permission, but he had clearly done so, in an attempt to save her from drowning in the hot tub and she had invited him to stay, after all.

Resting a hand on her belly, she could feel her stomach doing flip-flops. The tea and scone from The Coffee Haven had aided in helping her nausea subside some, but her stomach was clearly still unsettled.

Rubbing her face in her hands, she ran them through her hair, realizing she hadn't even checked in the mirror to see what she looked like. It occurred to her then, that her appearance might have something to do with the looks she'd been getting from the officer and the Howard's this morning at the coffee shop. Wondering what she did look like, she was about to check her reflection in the signage in the entryway, when she heard a mellow, male voice, coming up behind her.

"Ms. Rohann, I'm Sheriff Dartanian Blackthorne." Veta nearly jumped out of her skin. She turned to face the man in shock. Her eyes went wide and she gasped in horror when she saw the Sheriff and realized who he must be. His name and appearance had gotten her attention. Though, shorter by a couple of inches and a bit smaller all around, the family resemblance was quite clear. The man had to be related to Drinian somehow.

Surprised by Veta's response upon seeing him, Dartanian moved towards her and extended a hand in greeting. "Is something wrong?" he asked when she jerked away as though he had burned her.

Had it just been his build and size, Veta might have been able to compose herself better, but the Sheriff's black hair and crystal-clear blue eyes were a dead giveaway. Realizing the two men must be brothers, she became extremely anxious, at the thought of him learning what had happened between them. Taking three steps back, she tripped as the result of her injured knee. Falling backwards, she hit the floor hard on her bottom. Her sore leg bent unnaturally beneath her. Crying out in pain, she looked up in time to see him coming at her, arms outstretched as if to help her up.

"No, don't touch me." She waived his hands away, tears threatening to spill from her eyes in distress. Her heart was in her throat, and her irises were wide with dismay.

Sheriff Blackthorne backed away, clearly seeing that his presence was distressing the woman, for some reason. Confused by her reaction and why she would feel intimidated by him, he chose, instead, to keep his distance, while waiving at his deputy to see if he could help her up.

"Ma'am, please. Let me help you up," Deputy James Pike offered politely, as he stepped in front of the Sheriff. He extended his hand to her again, but she shook her head.

"No, really." Veta's voice shook and she noticeably trembled on the hard floor. "I'm okay." She winced, the pain in her expression betraying her statement. She attempted to stand. Fumbling, as she tried to get up, Deputy Pike got tired of seeing her struggle and pulled her up the rest of the way. Whimpering, Veta pushed him unceremoniously away.

Flustered, she stared at Sheriff Blackthorne anxiously, waiting to see what he was going to do and worrying that he might already know.

"Ms. Rohann," she heard him say cautiously. "Is there a problem I need to be aware of?" He eyed her curiously giving the woman an assessing look. He was having difficulty getting a good read on her, for the thin energy field surrounding her seemed to be pulsing between black and white, which was a bit unusual. One minute it was bright white and shiny, the next it pulsed black. He didn't get the feel from her, that she was a bad person, but he managed to discern, that something was definitely wrong with her. Or, that maybe something unsettling had happened to her.

Glancing back and forth, between the deputy and the sheriff, Veta shifted her weight to her uninjured leg. "No, no problem at all." A vivid memory from the night before flashed through her mind, causing her to blush. "I just think I need to be going." Face flaming, she turned towards the door.

"Ms. Rohann," Deputy Pike called after her, clearly confused. "You came in to see Sheriff Blackthorne about your U-Haul. Don't you want to see about getting your belongings back?"

Shaking her head, she wiped her arm across her face, and took a shaky breath, thinking quickly. "What are my chances, really, of getting them back?" she asked while balancing on the one leg and clinging to the door.

Sheriff Blackthorne crossed his arms over his chest and stared at her evenly. Glancing at the floor, then back at her, he responded. "I won't deny the chances are slim. We're much more likely to recover the U-Haul than we will the items inside." Dartanian shrugged. "But, by having an itemized list, we'll have a better idea of what belongs to you, should items be recovered."

Veta took a deep breath, taking courage from the knowledge she was close to freedom. She rubbed a shaky hand across her brow. "There are only three items in that U-Haul worth anything to me." Glancing at the door desperate to get away from the man's piercing blue eyes, so reminiscent of Drinian's, she finished by saying, "Find me my children's memory boxes, Deputy Pike and I will be forever in your debt." Pushing on the door, she tried to escape but realized it wasn't budging. Becoming desperate and feeling silly for her behavior, she felt an arm on hers, pulling her back, while another hand reached out to pull the door open.

Looking up into Sheriff Blackthorne's bright eyes, she trembled at his touch. Both seeing and sensing her anxiety, he quickly released his grasp on her arm.

Veta fled, crying in embarrassment as she went. She could feel the hot tears burning down her throat as she half ran, half wobbled to her car. Crumpling into the seat, she got in the car, turned the key in the ignition and sped away, not caring that she was speeding out of the Sheriff's department.

"What do you make of that?" Deputy Pike asked the Sheriff.

Dartanian stood at the door, watching her hobble to the car and speed away.

"I honestly don't know, James. But I get the feeling she's not all that keen on men right now." He turned from the door. "Didn't you say this woman came into town alone?"

"Yes, Sir, just her and her cat. Awful big cat too, but she had papers on him." The deputy said.

"Curious," Sheriff Blackthorne said, pushing away from the door and heading towards the desk.

"What's that, Sir?" James asked in confusion.

"Ms. Rohann said, the only items worth getting back were her children's memory boxes. She indicated three of them." He tapped on the front desk now with a pen.

"Yes, sir, she did. If that's so then," Deputy James Pike scratched at his head, pausing in his confusion. "Well, then where are her kids?"

"That's what I would like to know." Dartanian wrote something down on a piece of paper and placed it in his pocket. "Deputy, I'd like you to run a background check on Ms. Rohann. Let me know what you find out. The file with her social security number should be on my desk."

"Yes, Sir."

"Sheriff Blackthorne," he heard Millie shout from the dispatch room.

"You know, Millie, we do actually have an intercom system," he said dryly.

"But this is so much more fun!" she hollered back, "Rafe's been trying to reach you. Said it was about time you picked up your phone for a taxpayer." Millie poked her curly red head through the door. Seeing Sheriff Blackthorne's stern expression, her face went from smiles to chagrin. "His words, Sir, not mine."

Shaking his head he grinned while he pulled his cell phone from his pocket and turned up the volume. Just then he heard it ring and noticed it was his dad.

He answered the phone. "Yeah, okay, what's up?" Stretching his arms and yawning, he walked towards his office, listening while his father berated him for not picking up his phone.

"I'm assuming you had another reason for trying to reach me, other than to chastise me for my phone etiquette." Yawning as he spoke, Dartanian hoped that Dante and Alaina were figuring out what was wrong with her because he really could use a good night's rest.

"I need you at the cabin, Dart, as soon as possible."

His father's abnormally anxious voice gave him pause. "Why? What's going on? Is this official?" Dartanian asked, stopping as he reached his office door.

"That's going to be up to you, in the end. But either way, I think it's worth taking a look at." Rafe said, without really explaining what was going on.

Sighing with resignation, he yawned once again and turned on his heels, heading for the exit. "All right, I'm on my way."

- - -

Arriving at the cabin, Sheriff Blackthorne stepped out and greeted his dad. After trekking the rest of the distance to the house, he listened as Rafe and Breydon explained how they had come to find the cabin in the state it was in.

"First of all, is Megorah all right?" he asked abruptly, interrupting them as they talked.

"Yeah, she went on to Chase's clinic. She wanted to be there for the results of their testing," Breydon said.

"And what testing would that be exactly?" Dartanian asked, taking a chance they might know something more than him. Stepping into the cabin, he glanced around the room. In the back of his mind, he suspected he already knew what the testing was for, what the results would be, and was agitated because of it.

Shrugging, Breydon peered at the sky in annoyance. "Your guess is as good as anyone else's. It's all very hush, hush, but I'd wager Meg's thinking along the same lines she was last night, just as Chase and Royce had said at breakfast."

Rafe walked in behind them and pointed towards the patio, hoping to get them both back on track. "You'll see what we were talking about on the patio."

Dartanian grunted and headed in that direction. After taking in the scene, he investigated the bent track on the sliding door.

"Royce and Marshall's brother should be able to fix this Brey," he stated, turning back towards the hot tub.

"Way ahead of you," Breydon responded. He'd just finished a text to Cody Howard, who was co-owner of a construction and repair shop. Turning down his phone he asked, "So what do you think?"

Sighing, Dartanian replied, "My problem here is, I can't base a report off of a feeling Megorah got coming here." Seeing the look on Breydon's face, he quickly continued. "That being said, I won't discount the fact, that this woman's behavior, plus the door being off, and the house left open..." he paused then, "It does make me wonder what exactly did happen here." Dartanian's curiosity was mounting.

"We know what happened here," Breydon smirked. Glancing down at his phone again, he then put it away.

Dartanian looked at his dad and his brow rose. Seeing Rafe jerk his head towards the living room, he followed them both and they led him to the bedroom. After glancing in and seeing the state of the room, he stopped suddenly and bent his head, moaning in frustration.

Rolling his eyes to the heavens, he shook his head and mumbled, "Of course, pulsing black, why didn't I see that?" Then he asked, "What did you say this woman's name was?"

"We didn't." Rafe pulled out a small pad of paper and read off a name. "Her name is, Veta..."

"Rohann." Dartanian swore and punched at the wall. Both, Breydon and Rafe, stared at him in bewilderment, their expressions mirroring each other. Groaning, he exhaled and stalked from the room. "Wait to hear from me, Brey, about having Cody repair the door just yet. You know, in case I need to have it dusted for prints."

The sheriff walked with long purposeful strides while trying to determine his best course of action. Rubbing his hands across his face, he thought quickly and headed out of the cabin. He glanced down at his watch.

"Deputy Pike would have called her around nine this morning. She was just waking up, according to her, and couldn't make it until ten thirty but arrived at ten fifteen instead," he said, talking to himself mostly. "What time did Megorah call you, Brey?"

Taking a look at his phone, he didn't respond right away. "Looks like, at nine, twelve. Why?"

Nodding his head in understanding, Dartanian punched in a number on his phone without answering. Hearing Marshall Howard on the other end of the phone, he interrupted him before he could finish his greeting.

"Marshall, this is Sheriff Blackthorne."

"Uh, oh, Sheriff Blackthorne, is it? Must be official," Marshall said wearily.

"It might be. Did you get a Veta Rohann, check back in there by chance? The one who filed the complaint about the stolen U-Haul."

"Let me check, I just got back in." He sounded confused. "Yes, actually, it looks like she did."

"What time was that?"

"Time stamp looks like nine, twenty-three this morning. But she couldn't get in the room yet because it was on the list to be cleaned, so Lola gave her a key and told her to come back at eleven."

"All right, did she say where she was going until then?" he asked, hopefully.

"Let me check with Lola. She checked her in. Hold on." Marshall said, covering the receiver of the phone. A moment later he heard a woman's voice on the other end.

"No, she didn't, Sheriff," Lola said, speaking into the phone now. "But, she was really anxious to get in her room, which didn't make sense, because she'd said yesterday she'd managed to rent a place. She was limping and looking pretty pale and shaken too. I did see her driving south on Spokane, though. Come to think of it, she might have wound up back down at Royce's place again."

"What do you mean, again?" Dartanian asked.

"Why Sheriff, we sent her there yesterday for coffee. Always try to promote the locals, of course," she said cheerily, clearly happy to help out with any gossip she had.

He was about to hang up when he had an afterthought. "Lola, any chance you can tell if she's there now?"

"I can take a look and see if her car is out there. This related to the U-Haul that was stolen?" Lola asked, being nosy.

"You know I can't answer that Lola, just let me know," Dartanian said absentmindedly and hung up.

"What was that about?" Rafe asked as he and Breydon stared at him, looking for answers.

Putting his phone in his pocket, he stood with his hands on his hips, staring back at the cabin.

"Ms. Rohann was at the station this morning," Sheriff Blackthorne said finally.

Stunned, both men glanced at each other than back at Dartanian. "She already reported this?" Rafe asked him.

He shook his head. "No, and that's the bothersome part about this. She was there, at my request, because she'd just come into town the day before and checked in at Marshall Howard's motel. Sometime during the night, her U-Haul was stolen."

"Oh, man," Breydon said as his father winced.

"She didn't discover it until she got back from The Ryans Real Estate Agency yesterday," he went on to explain, "and spent a better part of the afternoon dealing with Deputy Pike on the matter. Problem was, as James is not fully trained yet, he missed getting some information from her, so I had him call her this morning to bring her in to talk to me."

"What happened?" Breydon asked impatiently when his brother stopped.

"That's just it, nothing. She showed up ten minutes early, limping, got one look at me, and bolted." Dartanian ran his hands across his face. "She was there. Right there in my office and she never reported anything because she got spooked by me for some reason." He swore again, kicking at the dirt.

The disturbing information silenced the three men momentarily as they stood outside the cabin, staring off into space. After a while, Breydon spoke up, "Did she say what all was taken?" Breydon asked quietly, unnerved by what had likely happened on his families own property. "Maybe we could at least see to replacing some of it."

Sighing in resignation, while yawning again, Sheriff Blackthorne shook his head. "It's a nice idea, Brey, but she left without giving an itemized list of what was taken. I had the impression anyway, that none of the stuff was worth anything to her, other than the three memory boxes of her kids she wanted back."

This time, Rafe looked at him in confusion. "That doesn't make any sense. She didn't list any children on the lease, just her cat."

"Yeah, I know. I've got Deputy Pike checking into it already." Dartanian shook his head and shrugged, grabbing his keys from his belt buckle. Just then, his phone rang. "Yeah, it's the Sheriff." He listened for a moment and then responded. "Yeah, all right then. Thanks, Lola." Hanging up, he glanced at his dad. "Well, she's back at the motel for now."

"All right. I think this is going to require Meg's genteel touch. I'll get her to contact Ms. Rohann and see if she can find anything out," Rafe said.

"At the very least, should we see to getting her moved into a safer location closer to the station?" Breydon asked. "After all, if there is an attacker, he's still out there, and technically, she still has a lease with you, Dad."

"Sounds like a good plan to start," Dartanian agreed. "That being said, Dad, as I'm sure you've figured out, what we have here is a possible crime scene but without confirmation of that, there isn't a whole lot I can do. Right now your only course of action," he said, pointing to his father, "would be to lodge a complaint against, Ms. Rohann for damages incurred to the property. Of course, if the damages are under five hundred dollars then it becomes a civil case."

Breydon laughed out loud. "The mattress alone was over a thousand bucks." Both Dart and Rafe frowned over at him. Looking back at them, with mischief in his eyes, he chuckled and said, "Hialey and I had to replace it the last time we, uh, borrowed the cabin." He grinned.

Rolling his eyes and groaning in disgust, Dartanian continued. "In which case, we'd file a police report. By doing so, it would allow us to go question her regarding the damages to the door and bed, which may bring to light the incident itself as a result. But there's no guarantee of that."

Grimacing, Rafe pondered on the issue. "I have mixed feelings about having you do that. On the one hand, it would give you a chance to find out about the man who did this. On the other hand, we all know from firsthand experience that by doing so, it could make things worse for her."

"Or better," Dartanian countered, looking his dad square in the face. "It might prompt her to get some help. So far, she hasn't said anything to anyone. She had the perfect opportunity to do so at the station and she didn't. The question is why?"

"She's scared, obviously." Breydon surmised as he sighed heavily, trying to diffuse what he could see to be a potentially volatile debate. Kicking at the dirt on the ground near the drive, he looked up at them. "It's a terrifying thing to go through," he said, awkwardly glancing away, "and embarrassing. If she was drunk, she might not have even realized what happened until she woke up this morning and she may be experiencing guilt because of that." Having dealt with several such cases as a Prosecuting attorney for Breckenridge County, Breydon was very familiar with the trauma the women went through after such an assault.

"This is all assuming, of course, she was actually raped and we don't know that for sure yet. The only evidence we have here is of a possible break-in and that there was a lot of activity in that bedroom last night. The issue with the door could have happened later." Dartanian said, playing devil's advocate.

Rafe and Breydon frowned at him. "Do you really believe that?" Rafe asked. "Based on her behavior alone…"

"Being skittish could just be normal for her," he argued. "Fact of the matter is we don't know anything for sure. Do I think something happened? Yeah, I really do. The energy around her practically screamed it."

"You're seeing black, I take it?" Rafe asked, his attention piqued.

Nodding Dartanian continued. "That said, you know as well as I, that my gift can be deceptive. Discerning good and evil isn't an exact science. Seeing the pulsing black around them could also mean the person is wrestling with a decision that could go either way, or they may just be struggling with personal sins, like drinking or drugs. Either way, my hands are tied for now. I cannot even investigate the possibility unless we start with the damages themselves. Now, do you want to file a report?"

Rafe mulled over his dilemma in his head. Whatever he decided could have equally bad ramifications. Pursuing this could traumatize Veta Rohann if she was a victim of a crime. But not pursuing it could place another young woman in danger of the same fate. In the end, his faith and conscience dictated his decision. Taking a deep breath, he looked at both of his sons. "Lodge the complaint in my name only. I own the property. Meg owns the Agency. This way, Meg can still work with her in order to help relocate her, and Ms. Rohann might feel she still has a friend. If there is a predator out there we need to know who he is."

Nodding in understanding, Sheriff Blackthorne replied, "I already took some pictures of the place but I'll get to work on preserving evidence until my tech guy gets here. I'm gonna need you to stick around a bit longer." Seeing them both nod, he looked to the sky as though to say a prayer, "God, please don't let this turn into a serial rapist situation. That's the last thing we need around here." He headed for his car.

As Dartanian called in for his tech guy, Rafe couldn't help but wonder why Veta had taken such a dislike to him in particular. Narrowing his eyes as he followed his son to the vehicle, Rafe's gut clenched uneasily. He was sure the sensation wasn't going to go away any time soon.

Chapter 8

Arriving back to the motel before the cleaning lady was done with her room Veta promptly tipped the gal ten bucks just to get her to leave and had the foresight, to ask for extra towels as well. She was sure this wouldn't be her last shower for the day. Truth be told it wasn't so much the need to feel clean that drove her to want to feel the water pounding on her body. All her life, even as a child, she welcomed rainstorms and showers pounding down on her. For some reason, it always soothed her, and she didn't know why.

It was nearly noon when Veta was about to step into the shower. She was about to turn on the water when she heard her cell phone ring. Her automatic response was to grab it. It wasn't until she'd answered her phone that she realized she hadn't bothered checking, to see if it was someone she knew first.

"Yes, hello? Am I speaking to, Veta Rohann?" It was the soft voice of a woman that she could hear on the other end.

"That's me. Who's this?" She forced a smile, hoping she didn't sound as suspicious as she felt.

"My name is, Megorah Ryans, of The Ryans Real Estate and Rental Agency." There was a heavy sigh. "I'm so sorry Ms. Rohann, but I'm afraid we might have a bit of a problem this morning."

Dropping her towel to the floor, as she danced in one spot anxiously, Veta winced when she bumped her sore leg against the bed.

"A problem you say, how so?" She hoped she sounded more nonchalant, rather than strained as she suspected she did.

"When you rented the cabin off of Deer Creek Road, you spoke with my receptionist, Freedom Raines, I believe?" Megorah asked, trying to build up to some of the questions she really wanted to ask.

"Yes, I did. She was really helpful in finding me that wonderful place..." She started, and then stopped suddenly, not sure where exactly she was going with it. As she stood, shivering in the middle of the hotel room, cell phone poised at her ear, she couldn't help but wonder how she was going to get out of the lease.

"Ms. Rohann, I'm afraid Freedom made a mistake." Megorah continued, unsure as to why the woman had stopped talking. "It seems she rented the cabin to you, for a sum of only five hundred dollars a month, for an entire year."

"Yes, that's correct," Veta responded, unsure where she was going with this.

"Here's the thing. That cabin actually rents for fifteen hundred dollars a month for only a six-month leasing period," Megorah stated apologetically. "Apparently while she was filing the other day, she dropped a few of the files and some papers got loose. When she tried to put them back she managed to mix up the information of a couple of different rental properties, including the cabin."

Hearing this news, Veta's mind woke up. Seeing a chance to get out of the lease, she jumped on it. "Mrs. Ryans, I do understand. You know, when I spoke with Freedom about the place after seeing it, I asked her if she was sure it only rented for five hundred a month. It's such a beautiful place, it seemed like I was getting it for a steal. And I did, didn't I? She wasn't supposed to rent it for that was she?"

"No, you're quite right. She wasn't," Megorah said softly, concerned she was losing a chance to ask her what she needed.

"My budget is for five hundred a month. I cannot afford fifteen hundred dollars. If you'd like to just refund me the money, I can…"

"Ms. Rohann, am I to understand, you do not want the place anymore?"

Becoming flustered at the question, Veta didn't know how to respond. "Oh, well it's not… I mean to say… I'm sure it's a fine place, I just…" Taking a deep breath, she tried again. "You just said it rents for fifteen hundred, and I don't have that so…"

Frustrated by her ramblings, Megorah decided to gently try another tactic. "Ms. Rohann, are you okay? Did something happen there that you want to talk about?"

"Happen?" Veta choked out, her voice becoming strained. "I don't know what you're talking about. I'm just fine really – P-peachy even." Wincing at her inane choice of words, she placed her hand over her mouth, praying the woman would drop it.

Sighing heavily, Megorah could see she wasn't going to get anywhere with her. "Are you sure, Ms. Rohann?"

"Yes, of course, nothing happened worth mentioning," she said emphatically, completely embarrassed by the conversation, and the woman's possible knowledge of her personal life.

On the other end of the phone, Megorah sat stunned. It was like hearing her own words from fifteen years before thrown right back at her. After taking a second to compose herself, while fighting back tears, she continued.

"May I call you, Veta?" she asked tentatively, hoping they could be more informal. Hearing her assent, she went on, "If you don't mind, what I'd like to do right now is find you an apartment within your price range, that might be more suited to you. Something, a little closer to town that would be ... maybe safer?" She took a chance the woman would get her hint.

Whimpering, Veta choked back a sob. She pulled the phone away from her ear for a moment, hoping on hope, that Mrs. Ryans couldn't hear her.

Safer.

The woman had seen everything in the cabin, and she thought she knew what happened. Too embarrassed by her own behavior, to correct her inaccurate assessment of the situation, she sat heavily on the bed. Mortified, she found herself trembling as she put the phone back to her ear. Realizing only then that the real-estate agent had been trying to get her attention.

"Yes, I think that might be much more agreeable all around." Silent tears sprang from her eyes again. She could hear the woman taking a deep breath on the other end of the phone, and she prayed God would forgive her for allowing the woman to believe what she did.

"Okay, here's what I'm going to do. I'm personally going to handle this one, and I'm going to take a day, or two, and look around if that's okay. I want to make sure this time that you're properly taken care of and set up, does that sound all right?"

"That sounds fine," she said meekly, her voice shaking.

"Do you have a place you feel comfortable staying at until I get you set up?" Megorah asked kindly.

"I'm at the Howard's Motel right now." She inhaled deeply, her voice becoming thick with tears.

"All right. I do have something I have to take care of this afternoon. But, you are a priority on my list, and I will be sure to contact you the moment I find you something."

"I don't want to be a bother." She shook her head guiltily while resting her sore leg on the bed.

"It's not a bother at all. Actually, I think..." Megorah paused. Holding her head in her hand, she winced painfully. "I think under the circumstances, it's the least we can do," she said, tears welling in her own eyes. Clearly, something had happened to her. She could tell by the way Veta spoke and the tenure in her voice, that she was definitely distressed and embarrassed. Megorah didn't have to be standing near the woman to be able to discern she was emotionally in pain.

Saying their goodbyes, Veta hung up the phone and slumped down into her bed, weeping into her pillow.

- - -

Several hours later Veta was startled awake when she heard a loud knock at her door. Sitting up suddenly she was a bit disoriented. Glancing at the clock, she noticed it was nearly four in the afternoon. Realizing she had no clothes on, she grabbed her jeans from the floor and began throwing them on.

"Ms. Rohann? It's, Deputy James Pike," she heard him holler through the door as she tripped and fell to the floor. "Can I have a moment of your time, please?"

"Just a minute!" Veta ran for a shirt. Not finding her undergarments straight-away, she threw on the T-shirt, and then donned her jacket as well, figuring that would help cover up anything inappropriate. Pulling her hair out of her T-shirt, she peered through the curtain of her window to make sure it was really him. Then, opening the door, she forced a bright smile as she leaned her shoulder nonchalantly against the door jam.

Hovering nearby, the Guardian watching her tensed as he felt the sudden chill of a demon's presence. Eyes darting anxiously about, he whirled around and reached for his broadsword. Caught off guard, the angel was surprised to find he was falling through the floor of the motel room. Grabbed by the legs by Fallen and Veranke, the angel cried out in anger and dismay as Zalman shot down from the ceiling unexpectedly. Dragging the Guardian away from his charge to another room they fought brutally.

Knowing, he only had a few seconds to initiate their plan, Zalman awaited his opening anxiously.

"Hi, can I help you with something?" Veta asked nervously.

The deputy looked at her, without saying anything initially. He noted crease lines on her cheek from having lain for a long period of time in one position. She appeared awfully distressed, flustered even. Clearing his throat he peered down at the paper in his hands, then, almost apologetically he handed it over to her. Stepping back from the door a bit, Veta stared at it, then back at him.

"Ma'am, I'm afraid I have a complaint here against you." His tone was formal but he seemed uncomfortable having this conversation with her.

"I'm sorry. You said a complaint against me?" Stunned, she shivered at the sudden chill she was experiencing, as the result of Zalman's presence. She rubbed at her arms.

"Yes, yes." Zalman wheezed anxiously. "Get to the point, Deputy."

"Yes, ma'am, it seems you rented a cabin off Deer Creek Road. The owner is complaining of damage to the property." The deputy pointed to the paper in her hand.

Confused, she gave the deputy an odd look. "I don't understand. I just got off the phone a little bit ago with Mrs. Ryans from the Realtors Agency. She didn't say anything about..."

"She wouldn't, Ma'am. Mrs. Ryans isn't the owner of the property, she just rents it for Mr. Blackthorne," he explained.

Veta's face went white with shock. She shivered again. "Are you t-telling me the Sh-sheriff owns this property?" she stuttered in horror, trying to determine whether it was the brother, or Drinian himself, who owned it.

"That's right, Veta," the demon crooned next to her ear. "The Blackthorne's are everywhere. They're all gonna know of your shameful behavior, you slut."

Surprised by her reaction, the deputy cautiously responded. "No, Ma'am, it's owned by, Rafe Blackthorne, his father."

Stunned by the news, all Veta could see suddenly was black before her eyes as Zalman assaulted her senses with his shadowy essence. Overcome by the overwhelming chill and fear that enveloped her, she passed out. As she fell backwards, Zalman gleefully shoved his way through her, causing her to knock her head on the television stand as she went.

- - -

Glancing at his watch, Drinian realized he'd been working on the apartment for nearly four hours now. It was taking longer than he'd anticipated. There had been broken pipes in the kitchen, and the previous tenant had caused damage to the back of the bedroom door that he hadn't noticed before. Since it was an interior door and he was working on time constraints, instead of replacing it like he normally would, he opted instead, to cover up the damage by putting a full-length mirror over it. The pipes in the kitchen, however, had to be replaced, which had taken the better part of an hour.

Drinian had already put a fresh coat of paint on the walls over the weekend, and he was glad to see that it had brightened the room up quite a bit. The lighter creamy tone, along with the high ceilings, helped make the living room appear larger. He'd also taken the extra time to tile the small floor space in the kitchen, instead of using linoleum. It gave the room a more modern look, while still being functional, and it would last a lot longer.

After repairing the plumbing and the door, he'd finished cleaning up in the kitchen and vacuumed the floors. He'd picked up hardware to put on the cabinets this time and had just finished replacing the old ones when he decided it was time to tackle the bathroom.

Standing in the claw-footed tub, Drinian placed the showerhead on its hook and allowed the hose to fall at will. He had just picked it up the day before and had thought, this particular one would fit in perfectly with this bathroom. Adjusting the head to the pulse setting, his hand rested on the lever for a moment. Then changing his mind, he moved the lever over two more notches to the rain shower setting. He didn't really know this woman, Veta, nor was he sure she'd pick this particular apartment, but for some reason, he figured that setting suited her better.

Stepping out of the tub, he decided to move on to the last item on his list, the toilet handle, when he heard ambulance sirens speeding down Spokane Road. It sounded as though it was heading north towards the train station. Curiosity getting the better of him, he walked out of the bathroom, across the living room, into the bedroom.

Leaning out of the window, he looked towards the station only to realize that the ambulance had stopped at the Howard's Motel. An uneasy feeling rose in the pit of his stomach, and he could hear the shadows laughing and chanting something quietly. Suddenly, there was a flurry of them in the room, swirling and twirling around him. He spun around and confronted them.

"What do you know?" he asked sharply, not caring at that moment that he was breaking his father's cardinal rule where the demons were concerned.

"Die. If the witch dies it all goes away," Fallen hissed slowly as he wheezed. The foray with the Guardian had taken longer than he'd anticipated.

"If who dies?" he asked cautiously. "Do you mean Veta?"

The dark spirits bobbed in front of him, as though dancing in place. Fallen was almost giggling. He watched Drinian sit suddenly on the bed.

"What have you done?" he asked aloud, running his hand across his face. Standing quickly, he ran out of the room and tore out of the apartment, leaving it unlocked behind him. After running down the steps, he slowed his pace once he reached the sidewalk. He had to know if the ambulance was really for her. He needed to know she was all right and that she hadn't been harmed by the shadows.

Walking along the sidewalk, Drinian attempted to move quickly, without receiving any more attention than what he was already getting. Typically, he did not venture into town publicly for all to see, as he tended to unsettle people with his presence. He reached the motel and was peering around the office corner when he was joined by Deputy James Pike.

"Afternoon, Drin. What brings you to town?"

He shrugged, attempting to appear somewhat bored. "I'm working on an apartment down at the old hospital."

"That's right, I forgot. You bought that old place over twenty years ago and turned it into apartments." Deputy Pike hadn't really forgotten. He had tried renting one of them himself shortly after they'd been renovated but Drinian had given it to someone else. Pike had been pretty steamed about it at the time.

"Somebody die?" Drinian asked, pointing towards the ambulance.

The deputy shook his head no, marveling not for the first time, at the man's morbid fascination for death. "I don't think so."

Drinian didn't say anything else and just waited for the deputy to continue. From his experience James liked to talk, so he would eventually tell him everything without being prodded with questions.

"Kind of sad really," the Deputy went on as expected. "There's a really pretty new gal in town. I was serving her complaint papers, for damages incurred on a property she'd rented yesterday, and then vacated suddenly this morning."

Turning his head slowly, he looked at the deputy, trying hard not to show how alarmed he was by the news. "Oh?" he said in response as one eyebrow rose, revealing nothing in his expression and tone. It never occurred to him his dad would ask for damages.

"Yup, the second she found out your dad owned the property, she passed out, hitting her head on the television stand knocking herself out even more, if that were possible. Now, why do you suppose, she got so worked up over that?"

"Couldn't say," He shrugged nonchalantly, suspecting he knew full well why finding out his dad owned the property had upset her. His eyes narrowed, and he stood stock still at the news, brooding. Somehow, he just knew one of the shadows had messed with her, and he had strong suspicions it had been one of the troublesome three. It seemed the decision he'd made where she was concerned had placed her on their radar.

"I heard Crisalya is on in the ER tonight, so Ms. Rohann will receive excellent care," Deputy Pike said, out of the blue.

Turning towards James, Drinian fixed him with a dangerous glare. "Leave her alone James. She's *happily* married now."

Years back, before James Pike had become a deputy, he'd taken quite a shine to his sister, which was not common knowledge by the rest of the Blackthorne family. At the time, she had met and begun dating Royce, which had peeved James something fierce for some reason. Drinian had discovered by pure accident that the man had been keeping tabs on his sister in a rather unethical manner and had put an immediate stop to it.

"That's Deputy Pike now," James said defensively. "And I don't see where it's any of your business," he said bravely, returning the glare.

Drinian stepped forward then and drew himself up to his full six-foot, six-inch height. James Pike was by no means a small man, for he had the build of a football player, but as he was just under six-foot-tall, he towered over him, as a result. Between his vast bulk and hulk-ish build, he knew he made for an intimidating and imposing figure when he needed to. Stepping forward aggressively, he placed his fists on his hips, fixing James with a dark stare.

"Deputy or not, James," he snarled, emphasizing his name. "I'll still put you in the ground if you go near her." He leaned forward and got in his face, poking at his chest in the process. "And being as she's my sister, I'll make it my business." Whirling around on his heels; he made it a point not to look at the ambulance as it was walking away.

Heading back the way he came, Drinian pulled out his phone and dialed Royce. Hearing him come on the line, he said simply, "He's still keeping tabs," then hung up. Drinian wasn't sure which bothered him more right now. The fact that Veta was now on her way to the hospital emergency room, or, that *Deputy* James Pike was still stalking his sister.

Chapter 9

By the time Veta awoke in the hospital emergency room several hours later, she was so rattled by the events of the past twenty-four hours she didn't even want to talk. The fear she'd experienced before she'd blacked out had left her feeling vulnerable and jittery. She listened as the nurse in the room explained to her the doctor would be in shortly, and that the Deputy was hoping to speak with her afterwards. Simply nodding she understood, she didn't say a word, just lay back and began to cry. Moments later, a tall gentleman with brown hair, a swimmer's build, and a kind smile entered and introduced himself as the nurse left.

"Evening, Ms. Rohann, I'm Dr. Chase Ryans. I see you're awake."

She winced slightly and looked away upon seeing another nurse enter the room. Recognizing the woman, as Crisalya Howard from The Coffee Haven, Veta was surprised to see her eyes had appeared to have changed color. They were the same crystal-clear blue as Drinian and Sheriff Blackthorne's eyes.

Seeing her startled expression Crisalya smiled. "It's the eyes that have you thrown, isn't it?" Veta nodded her head but still didn't speak. "You're used to seeing me with my colored contacts. I had one tear earlier and had to replace them with a clear pair."

"Let's check you over Veta. I want to take another look at that cut on your forehead. Then I'll need to ask you some questions, all right?" Dr. Chase Ryans asked, reaching over to remove the bandaging.

Unsettled by the realization that Crisalya might be related to both Drinian and the Sheriff, Veta's eyes shifted anxiously. She'd apparently been renting from their father, too. Lost in her thoughts, she nearly missed seeing the doctor's hand reaching for her. she eyed it wearily but managed to keep from jerking away. She wasn't able to keep her facial expression from appearing pinched as she held her breath, however. Both doctor and nurse exchanged looks at seeing her anxious reaction to them.

Crisalya attempted to calm Veta, by shushing her gently. "It's okay, Honey. He won't hurt you. Doctor Ryans is a really good doctor, and he has gentle hands."

Chase reached for her bandage again, only slower this time, allowing her to adjust to his closeness. Placing his hand on the bandage, he lifted it and took a look at the damage.

"You have a few stitches, that if I might say so myself, were expertly sewn." He smiled down at her. "Since you were unconscious for a couple of hours, I'm concerned you might have a concussion. I think we're going to keep you for the night for observation," he finished as Crisalya absent-mindedly patted her arm.

Veta flinched away, startling her. Narrowing his gaze, Chase noted the woman's response and wondered at it. Seeing his patient's respiration increasing rapidly, he glanced between the women trying to understand the cause of her distress. Her eyes brimmed with tears and for the first time since they entered the room, she spoke.

"I'm s-sorry, Crisalya. I'm so sorry, I just... I can't. I just can't." Veta became increasingly distressed. She'd reached her arms up in a defensive move as if trying to ward her off.

"Nurse Howard, would you mind stepping out for now and asking Amy if she can switch out with you for this one?" Chase glanced over at her meaningfully. He could tell her feelings had been hurt by her crestfallen expression but he couldn't help that. His patient's comfort had to take precedence.

"Of course, I'll send her in."

Dr. Ryans took a seat in one of the rolling chairs at a bit of a distance from Veta. Peering over at her, he could see that she'd been watching him.

"Ms. Rohann, I need to ask you, as your doctor, is there something else I need to know about other than your head and knee injury?" He watched as she glanced quickly down at her left knee, then back at him. "Did someone hurt you?" Waiting patiently for her response, he could see in her eyes that she was struggling with something. After a moment, she spoke quietly.

"I'm not sure." Tears threatened to spill out of her eyes. She looked at him with such a wounded expression that Chase cringed inwardly. He had a bad feeling he knew where this was going.

"Did a woman hurt you? Is that why you're afraid of nurse Howard?"

"No, I'm not afraid of her. Crisalya has been really nice to me since I arrived in town," she said in a small voice, half smiling.

"You seemed awfully distressed by her just now. Can you tell me why?" he asked gently.

Glancing away nervously, she rubbed at her arms in agitation. "We have doctor-patient confidentiality here, right? Whatever I tell you, you can't tell anyone?" she asked anxiously.

Dr. Ryans expelled an uneasy breath and tapped his foot on the floor. "Yeah, that is true," he said cautiously.

"It was her eyes," she said quickly.

Startled, Chase glanced over at her in confusion. "Her eyes. What do you mean?"

Veta took a deep breath, stretching out her arms as she did so, and laid her hands in her lap. "There was a man in my home last night." She spoke softly, swallowing hard. "He wasn't exactly what you'd call invited."

There was an uncomfortable pause before he asked his next question. "Did you know this man?"

"No," she said shaking her head. "Wait, that's not exactly true, I have actually seen him around town, but we've never really been officially introduced. He had..." she took another deep breath. "He had her eyes," she said softly while staring at her hands.

"Wait a minute, you mean to say this man had eyes like Crisalya's?" Too late he realized he used her name informally. Seeing her nod in ascent, Chase looked at her in alarm. "Ms. Rohann, did this man hurt you?" He was unable to masque his alarm and incredulity.

Veta glanced around the room, unsure as to how to answer him. Finally, she spoke as honestly as she could. "I don't think he was trying to hurt me," she said almost defensively. Rubbing a hand across her face, she went on more slowly. "He pulled me out of the hot tub, you see. Oh, this is really embarrassing." She paused, taking another breath.

"Maybe try starting from the beginning. I feel like you've skipped something important here," Chase said softly, treating her with kid gloves.

"It's just, I take medicine for depression, and I took some last night when I got to the new cabin I rented. Only, I was upset when I got there because my U-Haul had been stolen earlier in the day," she explained, wiping her nose with the tissue he produced for her. Proceeding to tell him, how she'd eventually found her way out to the hot tub on her patio, with a bottle of wine, she informed him she had taken her medicine for the second time by accident.

Seeing him nod his head in encouragement she went on. "I got undressed and got in the hot tub, taking the wine with me where I ... well, I finished it off," she said, watching him wince. "I wasn't trying to kill myself, I was just really upset," she said defensively. "You have to understand, everything I owned was in that U-Haul and it wasn't so much the computer and such, it was..." she took a deep breath, "It was losing my children's memory boxes. It's all I have left of them." She choked back a sob in her misery. Her head throbbed from where she'd knocked it on the television stand, and she was feeling a little light headed.

"Why is it all you have left of them?" he asked her gently.

"Because, they..." her face contorted, and her hands flew to her mouth as she finished. "They died in a car accident a year ago."

Doctor Ryans stood then, looking at her with concern.

"So, you took your medicine twice, by accident, and then drank some wine. Are you saying you drank a whole bottle last night?" He reached across her to get a good look at her eyes then ran his hands around her face and neck.

"Yes," she answered quietly, shredding her tissue.

"And then, what happened?" he asked, keeping a close watch on her, suddenly wishing that his brother-in-law, Breydon, was present. The man was exceptionally good at discerning the truth from people.

She looked at him then in earnest. "That's just it, I think I know but I'm not sure. Everything is so fuzzy. It's coming back to me in bits and pieces. I got undressed and got in the hot tub. That's the last thing I really remember well. I remember crying over the boxes and then, I think, I blacked out. But..."

"You blacked out in the water?" Chase asked her in alarm. At Veta's nod, he inquired suspiciously, "Do you remember getting out of the water?" Seeing her shake her head no, he then asked, "Did this man you were talking about pull you out?"

She looked at him and fidgeted. "I think he must have..." Rubbing her chin with the back of her hand, she shook her head. "The next thing I remember clearly is waking up with him next to me in bed. Then I cried myself back to sleep after he fled the cabin." Taking a deep breath her face flushed with embarrassment. "Thing is, it's not entirely his fault cause I'm pretty sure now, that in my depressed and lonely state, I may have asked him to stay and he agreed," she said slowly in mortification, as heat flooded her face and neck.

Chase did a double take, as he realized the implication of what she was saying. From the way she made it sound, one of the Blackthorne men had entered her cabin last night, pulled her from the hot tub to save her from drowning, and then proceeded to take advantage of her, while she was vulnerable. It would have had to have been a Blackthorne for they were the only men in town he knew of with crystal-clear blue eyes.

"When I ran to get my medicine and clothes from the patio this morning, I slipped and fell re-injuring my knee, and that's when I saw the patio door had been taken off its track from the outside," she finished explaining, almost in relief for finally having told someone.

"Ms. Rohann, what exactly are you saying happened last night? Do you believe you were raped?" Chase asked gently, needing her to be very clear about what it was she was saying.

Veta looked up and then closed her eyes. Squeezing them tight she exhaled deeply, while nervously fidgeting with her arm. "I think I might have been ... seduced," she said on a whisper. A tear ran down her face. "But I'm just as guilty." Pausing, she wiped the tear away, struggling to speak. "Because, I think I might have seduced him," she said as she looked imploringly at Dr. Ryans, hoping for understanding. "He just seemed so troubled you see, and I felt compelled, for some reason, to comfort him. But, we were not married. I was drunk and under the influence of medicine. I had no business making a decision like that in that state." She began to hyperventilate.

Dr. Ryans stood there for a moment, simply staring at her. Realizing she was struggling to breathe as Nurse Amy entered the room, he tried to comfort her.

"It's going to be okay. Let's get you calmed down first and we'll deal with the rest."

The nurse stood with Veta while Dr. Ryans stepped outside of the curtain. Leaning against the wall, he put his head back and stared up at the ceiling. One thing was for certain, something had definitely happened to the woman. Frankly, she was lucky to be alive under the circumstances, as the combination of the drugs, alcohol and extreme heat from the hot tub alone could have killed her. Add the fact she'd been sitting in water at the time, and she would have drowned had this man not come along. A naked, disoriented, beautiful woman in a hot tub would have been mighty tempting for most men. But they weren't talking about most men. They were talking about a Blackthorne, of that he was sure and that was what was so bothersome about this. They were all Christian men so he couldn't imagine any of them taking advantage of a woman the way she had been.

Sighing heavily, he glanced down the hall and saw Deputy Pike and Sheriff Blackthorne standing there waiting to talk to her. Seeing him standing outside Veta's room, they moved to walk towards him but he waved them off, shaking his head vigorously. Mouthing the words, not yet, he ducked his head back into the room and spoke quietly to nurse Amy.

"Amy, how's she doing?" From his vantage, he could see the woman had managed to calm down noticeably.

"She's doing much better."

"Good, I'm going to need you to run get a rape kit for me, please," he said quietly. "That is … if you'll agree, Ms. Rohann. We really should at least make sure everything is okay under the circumstances. Don't you think?"

Amy's smile faded and she glanced at Veta sympathetically as she watched the woman nod slowly in embarrassment. "I'll be right back, Dr. Ryans."

Stepping back into the room as the nurse left, Chase took a deep breath before asking his next question. "I know you said you've never been introduced, but do you know the name of the man in question?"

Shifting anxiously, Veta appeared distressed. After a moment she spoke softly, avoiding his gaze. "I'd rather not say."

"All right." Sighing, Chase winced and ran a hand across his face in agitation. "That's your choice, but I should tell you, the Deputy and the Sheriff are waiting to speak to you."

Alarmed by the news, her head shot up and she stared at him wild-eyed. "No, I don't want to talk to Sheriff Blackthorne. Please don't make me."

Deeply troubled by the woman's response, Chase replied uneasily, his expression becoming pinched. "I'll see what I can do."

- - -

Stepping around the curtain of Veta's room, Chase pulled off his gloves and threw them in the bin against the wall. Seeing nurse, Amy exiting the room, he headed down the hall, noting that Rafe Blackthorne had shown up as well.

"All right then, Deputy Pike, she's ready now to answer your questions." The Deputy moved to head down the hall as did Dartanian. Placing a hand on his brothers-in-law chest, he stalled him saying. "No. Not you."

"Chase?" Dartanian questioned, removing his hand. "What do you think you're doing?"

"What I'm doing, is telling you that you cannot go in there," Chase spoke forcefully.

Eyebrows raised, Rafe asked. "What's going on Chase?"

Choosing his words carefully he said, "She does not want to talk to you right now and potentially with good reason." His eyes bore into his brother-in-law, attempting to gauge his reaction. Seeing Dart's confused expression, he tilted his head thoughtfully, his eyes narrowing slightly.

"Why in the world not?" Sheriff Blackthorne asked heatedly. Placing his hands on his hips, he glared at the stubborn man before him.

Shaking his head, Chase explained, "I'm afraid doctor-patient confidentiality prevents me from being able to answer that," he said regretfully. Turning towards Rafe, he went on, "You need to drop this complaint. Do it quick and quiet, and don't ask for damages. Make it go away." Squaring his shoulders, he stared down his father-in-law.

Rafe looked at him curiously. "Why Chase? This is me you're talking to. What's going on? If someone broke in and…"

"Depending on how your lease is worded there technically may not have been a break-in. She's embarrassed and doesn't want what happened to get out and, frankly, I don't think any of you want that either," he said emphatically.

Startled by his words, both men exchanged glances. "What exactly do you mean by 'any of you' Chase?" Dartanian asked, taking exception to his brother-in-law's tone.

Glancing at Rafe meaningfully, Chase responded simply, "Clean up your house." Turning on his heel he walked away and then suddenly he turned back around. "Oh, and Rafe, you might want to consider paying her hospital bill." Turning back around, he walked away.

Rafe silently stood there a moment, stunned by the implication of Chase's last couple statements. "Clean my house? Pay her bill?" Turning on his son, Rafe nearly shouted as he swore uncharacteristically. "What the *devil* is going on here, Dartanian?"

Chapter 10

Just out of a hot shower, early the next morning, Hialey Blackthorne skipped down the steps towards the kitchen, looking forward to getting the first cup of coffee from the pot. When everyone was staying at the Blackthorne Ranch, it was hard to even get a cup of fresh coffee, let alone the first one. This morning, however, Hialey wanted to be in early at the boutique. She was expecting to get a shipment of lingerie that would need to be tagged before the place opened, so it was her first chance at a first cup in weeks.

Hopping the last step as she stretched her arms up high, whispering loudly, "Yes!" she made a beeline for the pot, only to see Drinian sitting in the far corner of the kitchen, sipping at a soup bowl-sized mug of coffee.

Drinian's eyes crinkled at the corners in amusement. He watched her do her little dance at the foot of the steps before making her run to the coffee pot. Chuckling rather uncharacteristically for him, he flashed her a winning smile, raising his cup in greeting.

"Awe, man! What's a girl got to do to get the first cup of coffee around here?" he heard her exclaim. She stood there in frustration, staring at his cup dejectedly and then at the pot. "And that mug should just be illegal in this house. It takes more than half the pot!"

"For starters," Drinian said, peering over his cup at her. "You have to get up before me, and seeing as most nights I'm always up, that'll likely never happen."

Picking up the coffee pot she marched over to him and shoved it in front of his face, saying, "Gee, why don't you just drink it straight from the pot if you're gonna take that much all at once," she vented in disgust.

Drinian laughed quietly as he shook his head. "No, might burn my lip doing that."

"Oh, might burn my lip. Wa, wa, wa, wa." She mimicked the sounds of a baby while turning on her heel and plopping the pot straight on the counter. "Laugh it up, bud." She practically sneered in disgust, as she pivoted with her hands on her small hips. Glaring at him as a smile played upon his lips, she cocked her head to one side almost thoughtfully. "Gee, for some reason you sure seem awful chipper lately."

Drinian tensed slightly at the observation while trying hard to seem casual. Nodding towards the counter, he spoke. "You might want to move that before Meg gets up, or she'll tan your hide for placing it straight on the counter," he warned.

"She can try to tan my hide all she wants. Meg may walk softly, but I…"

"Carry a big stick?" Drinian countered, interrupting her.

Giving him an impish smile she said sheepishly, "I was gonna say, 'carry a mean right hook,' but we'll just go with that. It sounds more feminine."

Drinian laughed out loud, stood, and walked towards her. "Hialey," he said while taking a deep breath, He sighed heavily as his eyes closed. "You are truly amazing. You speak your mind and add laughter in a way everyone can appreciate. It's..." he paused, trying to think of the most appropriate word. "-Refreshing," he said finally. Sipping at his mug, he proceeded to pour the rest of the pot into it, and then added more brown sugar. Once the pot was emptied he took it to the sink, refilling it with water, and began making a new pot.

"You're making a new pot for me?" she asked in surprise.

"I'd say it's about time you got your first cup." He pulled her coffee thermos from the cabinet, setting it next to the pot.

Hialey gave him a funny look. Running her hands through her short, spiky hair, she became suspicious. "Okay, I'm getting compliments and a new pot of coffee." She paused briefly, then asked directly. "What do you want?"

Chuckling again, Drinian emptied the pot of water into the coffee maker and pulled out the coffee grounds. "Truthfully?"

"Truth is always best," Hialey said, internally wishing she lived by that motto more. It was ironic too, considering who she was married to.

"I actually meant what I said." He looked at her meaningfully, as he began adding coffee grounds and turned the coffee maker on. Then, looking somewhat chagrined, he glanced over at her. "But, I actually do have a favor to ask of you, if you're so inclined." Turning towards her, he leaned against the counter and took another sip of his coffee.

"Okay then." Hialey plopped down in one of the bar stool chairs. Gesturing at him she said, "Hit me. What do you want?"

"There's a new lady in town…" he started but Hialey interrupted him.

"You want me to hook you up?" she asked brightly, almost hopefully.

"No." He emphatically shook his head. He saw Hialey slump noticeably and stifled a grin. "That would be a bad idea. Anyways, there's a new lady in town."

"Right, we've established that. Your point?" Hialey asked impatiently.

"She's not from around here."

"I kind of got that when you said, 'there is a new lady in town', Drin." Her tone was sarcastic.

"Hialey…" He was becoming exasperated.

"All right, all right, so there is 'a new lady in town' and…" she prompted while waving her hands in front of her.

"And I've heard she's been having a rough time. She wound up in the hospital last night for something or other," he said nonchalantly as if he really didn't care. But Hialey's senses were on high alert. Somehow this didn't feel like a random thing to her.

"She all right?"

"Yeah, she's fine as far as I know," he said quickly. "They just kept her overnight for observation. She's being released this morning."

"Okay, so what's the favor exactly?" She glanced at the watch on her wrist hoping he'd get to his point soon.

"As I understand it, this gal doesn't know anyone in the area and was taken to the hospital by ambulance. Since you're on your way into town to pick up your shipment, I wondered if you'd pick her up and give her a ride to her motel."

Hialey just looked at him at first. "Let me get this straight. You want me, to pick up some random woman I don't know and give her a lift to her motel room. Have I got that right?"

"Yup." He pushed away from the counter and sauntered back over to his corner.

"How do you know this woman again?" she asked out of the blue.

"I didn't say I did." Drinian's tone was bored, as though he was quickly losing interest in the topic.

"And who would I be saying sent me?" She spun slightly in her seat, nearly falling over.

He shrugged. "Just a friend."

She made a smirking sound, "Right. Just a friend." Then suddenly she said, "Oh, but my shipment's coming directly to the store." Hialey remembered, smacking the counter with her hand. Seeing him shake his head, she started shaking her own.

"Okay, what is with the head shake?"

"It was delivered to the wrong place again," he told her, as he sat holding his cup, waiting for her inevitable response.

Hialey gave him an annoyed look then started banging her head with her hand. "Again?" she practically hollered, slapping the counter this time in frustration. "Who got it this time?"

"Think fish." He sipped at the hot brew and watched her facial expression go from confused to angry.

"You mean to tell me Fishmonger Sam got my bras and panties?" She was horrified. "Oh, I could just die, Drin. I could just die. Man!" She spun around on her stool, in order to face him more directly, and hopped down, her sandaled feet smacking on the kitchen tile. "Why don't they just fire that old coot? He doesn't know Arch Street, from Spokane Road." She moaned in frustration.

"Because that old coot has been delivering the mail since the post office was first opened here in the county," he said matter-of-factly.

Hialey glared at him. "All the more reason to retire him."

"You're speaking to the choir, Honey." Drinian recalled how the shipment of a dozen plungers he'd ordered, for his many apartment bathrooms, had wound up down at the women's shelter. Retrieving the incorrectly delivered and opened box had been not only awkward but embarrassing, to say the least. Upon their curious inquiry, he'd had to explain why he needed so many.

"Well ... then yeah. I could pick this 'new lady in town' up and give her a lift," she said as she tapped her toes on the floor. "What exactly is this to you anyway?" she asked finally.

Drinian just shrugged again. "Nothing really. Heard about it and thought you could help, that's all. It is the Christian thing to do after all."

She pointed at him with a crooked finger. "Well, aren't you being the good Samaritan today? Why don't you go and get her? You could give her a lift," she said, seeing a chance to get him out and with a lady at that. Maybe she could get him a girlfriend, after all. The man had been an absolute grouch for the past five years that she'd known him. Far as she was concerned, he needed a woman in his life.

He looked up at her then, his eyebrows raised. "Are you kidding me? That's an even worse idea, then the first one you had. Besides, I'm not going into town and you are, so it just makes more sense."

"All right then." She sighed in resignation, hating at that moment, that she had to be born with such a kind soul. "What's her name? Does she have to be picked up any certain time?" Hialey asked while pouring coffee into her cup before the pot was finished brewing.

"Nope, anytime, and her name is, Veta Rohann." Drinian tried really hard not to smile as he said the name. Every time he thought of the woman, he couldn't help but picture those beautiful green eyes. The memories from that night flooded back to him, causing him to stare with longing off into space.

Sighing heavily, Hialey cringed noticeably as she took up her coffee thermos, turned, and headed towards the door. "Better get going. I can't even imagine, how long it's going to take me, to get my bras and panties back from that man. He's probably wearing one of them on his head right now," she declared angrily, starting out of the door only to stop suddenly.

"What do you suppose brings people like her here anyway? All it is, is mountains everywhere you go, and as far as I'm concerned it's prettier when the sun is shining."

Drinian glanced out the window thoughtfully. "I would guess, most actually do come for the mountains and the snow, and I'm sure there would be some who'd say there isn't much of a view when it rains. But for me, well, when I see the mountains being drenched by the skies tears, it just feels like I belong somehow."

Hialey watched him staring outside for a moment, as though deep in thought. There really was a whole lot more to that man then most people gave him credit for. Glancing at her watch, she realized what time it was getting and headed out the door.

Chapter 11

Informed by the nurse, that she was being released from the hospital the next morning, Veta realized she had no way of getting back to her motel room. As the nurse aided her into the wheelchair, she mentioned her concern, only to be told her ride was waiting for her at the entrance. Confused as to who it could be, she was anxious when the nurse wheeled her to the front doors, almost half anticipating it might be Drinian. Finding herself uneasy at the notion, she was surprised to find herself almost disappointed when it wasn't him. Glancing at the person standing there waiting, she noted that the woman was a little shorter than her, and very petite, with stylish short auburn hair. She was also wearing, what appeared to be, a sort of uniform.

"Hi! You must be, Veta Rohann," the woman said cheerily.

"Yes, I am. I'm sorry, who are you?"

"I'm Hialey. I was told you'd need a lift back to your motel this morning and to make sure you got there okay." She extended her hand in greeting.

Taking hold of her hand after a short pause Veta shook it, noticing she had a firm handshake for a woman of her size. She also had a friendly face and an infectious smile that made her quite pretty.

Still confused, Veta inquired. "Who told you that?"

Hialey smiled brightly, "A friend. So come on, let's go. You need any help with anything?" she asked, looking around.

Realizing she was looking for bags, Veta chuckled. "No, just me, myself, and I." She smiled back.

"Well, me, myself and I... How about we get you out of here. I can't imagine, you'd want to stick around here any longer than necessary, right?"

Chuckling again softly, she responded, "You would be correct."

Wheeling Veta outside into the fresh air, the nurse helped her up from the wheelchair. Standing, she tested her leg with the brace and limped the last few steps to the navy-blue Dodge Durango in front of her. Inhaling deeply, she paused for a moment before getting into Hialey's vehicle. The breeze felt good against her skin and her long black hair blew around her face. Almost reluctantly, she stepped into the vehicle, noting that it appeared brand new.

"This is nice. I like your vehicle," Veta said as she put her seat belt on.

"Thanks. My husband, Breydon, just bought it for me recently. I kind of totaled out my other one a few weeks ago. I tend to go through cars like crazy." She frowned slightly and made a face.

"And she's not kidding," the angel Maleeka piped in from the back seat, knowing full well neither one would be able to hear him. Smiling ruefully, his blue eyes twinkled. Breydon's wife was forever getting into accidents for no other reason than poor judgment. Watching as Veta glanced at Hialey, Maleeka noticed her eyes widen in alarm.

"Oh, dear. Do I need to be worried?"

"Yes," Maleeka said firmly as he chuckled. The moment they had realized Drinian had enlisted Hialey's aid in transporting Veta from the hospital, the Lord had sent him to watch over her during the transfer.

Grinning back at her, Hialey laughed. "I won't lie, I did kind of wonder why they asked me, of all people. I mean it's my third vehicle this year," she said conspiratorially.

"Not true, Hialey. You know full well it's the fifth. You're just not counting the two you totaled of Breydon's." Maleeka chastised as he scoffed. It was times like these when he wished the humans could hear him.

If it were possible, Veta's eye grew wider. "But it's only May," Veta said in alarm, marveling at how a person could go through so many vehicles so quickly.

Seeing her expression, Hialey continued. "In my defense, it was not my fault, two out of the three times. But, no worries, I'll get you where you're going."

"Again, not counting the two you totaled of Breydon's," the angel countered, groaning.

"Who was it that asked you again?" Veta asked, thinking she might be able to trip the woman up.

Hialey glanced over at her as she put the car in motion. She just grinned again, flashing her pearly whites. "A friend," was all she would say.

"Well, tell this friend thanks, because I figured I'd be hobbling my way back to the motel." Veta winced as she touched the bandage on her head gently.

"Wait until you arrive safely at the motel first. Then you can have her tell Drinian thanks," the angel suggested dryly.

Seeing the gesture, Hialey's curiosity was piqued and she couldn't help but ask, "Looks like you got a nasty knock on the head there. So, I take it you're gonna live?"

"Yes, so it would seem. I'm afraid the story isn't so glamorous though. I kind of knocked myself out really," she admitted while blushing.

"No, you didn't. That was the demons fault." Maleeka scowled, peering around them. His senses were on high alert to any possible further attempts by the troublesome three. Fortunately, the guardian who'd been watching out for her had survived, but he had required healing by the Lord's hand.

Hialey laughed. "How'd you manage that?"

Veta smiled ruefully. "I passed out first, then knocked myself out even further, by hitting my head on the television stand in the motel room."

Harrumphing softly, at the inaccuracy of her statement, Maleeka stayed quiet for the moment as he worried over the woman in front of him. She had always had such strong faith. He hoped recent events wouldn't change her. Now, more than ever, she was going to need her faith for things would soon become very difficult for her.

"Oh, my!" Hialey's eyes widened. "What on earth did you do that for? Seems a bit overkill really," she said, trying to turn it into a joke.

Veta laughed out loud. It was the first time she had since she'd arrived in Montana and it felt good. Glancing over at the woman next to her, she was awful grateful to whoever sent her.

Smiling ruefully, the angel watched Veta's face light up. He understood why Drinian had asked Hialey to give her a lift. Her fun and infectious personality were exactly what Veta needed right now in order to help build up her spirits.

"So, I heard you weren't local, how long have you been in town?"

"Two days."

"Wait, did you say two days?" Hialey laughed again in astonishment.

Reaching forward suddenly, Maleeka touched her urgently on the shoulder, in order to gain her attention. "There's a stop light, Hialey," he said forcefully in her ear.

"Wow, what a way to start a vacation." She skidded to a stop at a red light. Grimacing, she apologized. "Sorry almost missed that."

Recovering from her near heart attack, she responded, "I'm not on vacation. I was planning on moving here."

"Hhmmm. Was – past tense. I take it you're thinking to move on instead? I wouldn't blame you, I guess. What made you think to stay in the first place?"

Having caught the past tense in her wording as well, the angel Maleeka turned abruptly towards Veta with concern. "Please, do not make a hasty decision you will likely regret."

Veta sighed, pondering her last question for a moment before replying, "I don't know. When I got here it was raining so some would say, I suppose, there wasn't much of a view. But ... then I looked out the window and I saw the mountains were being drenched by the skies tears, and it just felt like I belonged somehow." Realizing how maudlin that sounded, she glanced over at her temporary chauffer apologetically. "Sorry, that probably sounded depressing." Noticing the surprised expression on her face, she asked her curiously. "What's the look for?"

"It's funny, it's just … someone else I know made a similar statement recently." Shrugging it off, Hialey went on. "So, even after that, you're still thinking of moving on?"

"Honestly, I don't know. I have to stick around for at least a little while. My U-Haul was stolen when I first arrived in town, so I'm sort of waiting to see how that all turns out."

"Wait, wait, wait! Did you just say your U-Haul was stolen when you got here?" Hialey's eyes sparkled with laughter. Seeing Veta nod in response, she exclaimed, "Dang girl! You're having some awful lousy luck aren't you?"'

"It's not bad luck," Maleeka insisted, as Woreash popped in next to him. "It's called humans making poor choices and demons being a nuisance."

Eyeing the two women in front of him, the angel Woreash turned to Maleeka as he spoke. "You know they cannot hear you unless He deems otherwise, so why do you even bother with the monologue?"

Sitting back in her seat, Veta sighed and closed her eyes. "Yes, so it would seem," she said aloud, although she was thinking to herself 'you have no idea.'

Maleeka grinned. "Because I know full well He's up there listening. I might as well give him something to laugh about. He's still pretty angry over the trick Zalman pulled after all. What are *you* doing here *anyway*? I thought you'd been given another charge to tend to for today."

"Five accidents since the beginning of the year; the Lord feels a second presence may be warranted in this case."

"Why? Because he thinks demons may be involved in her accidents?" Maleeka inquired, gesturing towards the woman in the driver's seat. Shaking his head, Maleeka continued. "No, this woman, Hialey, is merely accident prone."

"Indeed, and she's transferring a woman linked to a prophecy, who's recently been attacked by demons."

Glancing at Woreash uneasily, Maleeka saw the anxiety in his grey eyes. Staying silent, he merely nodded his understanding, for there really wasn't anything more to say. Turning his attention back to the women in front of him, he listened as they chatted amicably.

"Personally, I hope you stay because you seem like the type of person I could become good friends with." Hialey pulled into the motel parking lot. Both the angels sighed in relief. "So, that being said, I'm gonna give you my number, and if you decide to stick around for more than a couple days then call me. We can get coffee sometime," she said brightly, turning to look at her.

Smiling back at her, Veta responded genuinely, "I think I'd like that." Exchanging numbers, she thanked Hialey for the ride, asking her to be sure to thank the "friend" as well. Gingerly stepping out of the vehicle, she waved her goodbye as Hialey squealed her tires and nearly hit a car while attempting to pull out. Laughing out loud, Veta said to no one in particular, "That girl is gonna need a fourth new car real soon if she's not careful."

"Sixth." Woreash corrected, smiling after the Dodge Durango, then down at the beautiful woman at his side. Poor Maleeka had been instructed to stick with Hialey for a while until she reached her shop and was clearly annoyed by the task. Chuckling softly, he stayed with Veta as she hobbled toward the motel entrance.

After stopping at the front desk for a new room key, Veta went straight to her room. Though still out of sorts, her spirits had lifted a bit after her ride from the hospital with Hialey. Upon entering her room, she closed the door and locked it, applying the deadbolt as well. She didn't really feel afraid anymore. She was, however, unsettled by the events of the past two days.

"That's right. Put your mind at ease, sweet Veta," Woreash soothed, touching the woman's arm gently.

Tossing the room key on the table, she sat down on the bed in order to allow her left leg to rest. Having been awakened periodically during the night, she hadn't really slept too well at the hospital, so she was pretty tired still. Deciding to lie back for a while and get some rest, she curled up on her side and promptly fell asleep, as the angel watched over her; protectively enclosing her in his wings.

- - -

Rafe Blackthorne stared at his phone. He had made and received several phone calls that morning that had left him feeling more than a little disturbed. Concerned for Ms. Veta Rohann's safety, he'd contacted a taxi service to arrange her transportation from the hospital to her motel, asking to remain nameless. Completing that call he moved on to the next by contacting Cody Howard to have him go out to the cabin and repair the patio door. It wasn't until he attempted to make the third call, that things started getting a little peculiar. The uneasy feeling he'd had since stepping foot into the cabin yesterday began to increase exponentially.

The cleaning service he usually used phoned him, asking what he wanted to be done with the old mattress, as a delivery truck had arrived at the cabin with the new one. When he asked the cleaning lady what she was doing there, she stated she'd been contacted the previous day by an anonymous party, wanting to have it cleaned. Rafe sat back in his chair, crossing the service off his list of calls to make. Someone else, it seemed, had already dealt with it. Glancing down at his list, he crossed off the Mattress Factory as well, for it would appear that the mattress had already been replaced also.

His next call was to the hospital in order to take care of Ms. Rohann's medical bills. Rafe was still unsure why Dr. Ryans felt it was necessary for him to do this, but Chase had always impressed him as being a man of good character. If he felt that someone in the Blackthorne family had wronged this woman somehow, he trusted his judgment.

After getting off that call, however, he became increasingly agitated for an unidentified party had apparently already paid her medical bill in full. Not only that but when he had the billing department transfer him to customer service, he was informed that Veta Rohann had already checked out and had been picked up. When he asked the receptionist if she knew who the person was that had picked her up, she replied it had been his own daughter-in-law, Hialey.

Reclining in his chair, he turned and looked up at the oil painting of his late wife behind him. As he gazed at her beautiful tanned face, he began to have a sick feeling in the pit of his stomach.

"Lilyandhi, is it possible? Did one of our sons take advantage of this woman?" he asked her aloud. He often found himself talking to her when he was distressed or in the middle of a dilemma and he most definitely was in a quandary. Clearly, someone was attempting to either, cover their tracks, or make amends, or possibly even a little of both. The question now was, which son.

Rafe pondered that notion, having a hard time believing that any of them would do that. Veta's reaction to Dartanian at the Sheriff's office made him the logical suspect initially, but Rafe quickly squelched that notion. Dart was about as in love with his wife, Lylia, as he himself had been with his own wife, Lilyandhi. The next logical candidate would be Dante as he was his identical twin. Shaking his head though, he quickly put a kibosh to that notion. Dante had just arrived home with a fiancée he was clearly in love with, whether he realized it yet or not. They were about to be married on Saturday.

Rolling his eyes and sighing heavily, he considered Breydon. He seemed the more likely candidate out of the four sons. He hadn't seemed too surprised yesterday when they'd found the mattress in the soiled condition. He even admitted to having it replaced once before without Rafe being aware of it. Additionally, he had been awful quick to call Cody out to repair the damages to the door. Rafe knew he was hiding something from the family as well. Something embarrassing, he didn't want them to know about and that he'd sworn Hialey to secrecy. Could this be it, Rafe wondered? Was it possible his son, Breydon, had been suffering from some kind of sinful side effect, from a gift he wasn't supposed to have?

Breydon's mind was constantly drawn to women, and he did have a rather long and unfortunate history of girlfriends. He'd even gone so far as to frequent exotic dance clubs which was where he'd met Hialey until she quit and opened her shop. They often fought, most frequently, over an embarrassing problem with porn he'd developed within the past year. Rafe had discovered the unfortunate habit by accident. Linking his fingers behind his head, he sighed and crossed his legs, allowing his boots to bump the desk.

If his theory was correct that could explain a lot. It did not, however, explain why Breydon would involve his wife, Hialey, by asking her to give a woman he'd been intimate with, a ride back to her motel room.

Troubled by his thoughts he nearly missed hearing the phone ring. Tensing, he somehow knew full well he was likely not going to like what he was about to hear. Staring at it briefly, he allowed it to ring for a moment, and then finally picked up the receiver.

"Rafe Blackthorne speaking."

"This is Cody Howard. About the door you wanted to be repaired... Can you tell me which one it is you're wanting to be fixed?"

The man sounded confused.

"That would be the back-patio door that is currently setting off of its track." Rafe grabbed a pen, preparing to write a reminder note. There was a pause at the other end of the phone which halted his movements.

"Cody?" Rafe asked, curious as to the silence, his pen stilled in his hand.

"I don't know who fixed it, but it would seem it has already been repaired. There are no doors off anymore." He sounded almost disappointed.

"Is the cleaning lady still there, by chance?" Rafe asked, hoping she might have seen something.

"She's loading up as we speak, why?"

"Do me a favor. Ask her if the door was already repaired when she got there." Rafe tried to sound casual about the request. There was silence on the other end for a moment, and then he heard voices talking in the background.

"She says it was already fixed when she got here. She didn't see anyone but the delivery guy for the bed." Chuckling, Cody continued. "Did Breydon have another incident here and forget to tell you he took care of it again?"

Stunned, Rafe managed to regain his composure quickly and responded by saying, "No, just got mixed signals, I guess. Thanks anyways, Cody. Sorry for the trouble, I'll pay you for your time."

"Don't worry about it. As much business as you guys give me, there's no need. We'll catch you next time," Cody finished and ended the call.

Dropping the phone on the desk Rafe stood suddenly, tossing his pen across the room as he struggled to keep from swearing. Another incident? Exactly how many women had Breydon taken to the cabin? Was that why he insisted it only be rented six months of the year?

Making a sour face at the distasteful behavior his son was committing, Rafe could only presume that past indiscretions had been willing participants. But, this latest foray was unacceptable, because the woman in question had clearly been wronged. Disappointed by his son's obvious lack of respect for his wife, he grimaced. Rafe had thought he'd taught his children better than to cheat on their spouses. Grabbing his cowboy hat he decided to head down to the stables to let off some steam. One thing was for sure. The next time he talked to that boy, he'd be putting him in his place.

Chapter 12

Thursday evening, Drinian sat at the kitchen table in his father's home pretending to look over the papers he'd pulled out of the file for the apartment he'd completed. Having grabbed a beer from the stash he'd placed in the fridge when he'd first arrived, he was almost done with it already. His contact at the hospital had told him that Veta had come in with the head injury and been kept overnight for observation. They'd also told him about the rape kit Chase had performed on her, and the reaction she'd had to Crisalya upon seeing her there without her colored contacts.

Rubbing his eyes wearily, he got up and headed toward the fridge, tossing his bottle in the recycling in the process. Standing in front of the open door of the fridge, he stared at the bottles for a while, debating how many he wanted to limit himself to tonight. He typically tried keeping his quota under four, but when the demons were bad, a drunken haze made handling them so much easier. Sighing heavily, he grabbed three more beers and headed back to the table, allowing his worn-out body to fall heavily into his chair.

It bothered Drinian a great deal that he'd caused Veta so much trouble, and his conscious was starting to get the better of him. He was also hurt by the fact that Veta had apparently claimed she'd been raped. He knew he wasn't experienced with women like his brothers but had thought he'd been able to please her that night. Troubled by the notion that they both might not have agreed, he tried to think back to that night to see if he could recall a moment when she'd been hesitant. She'd never said no that he could recall and had actually encouraged him. Maybe he was remembering things wrong. Either way, she had surprisingly not reported it to Dartanian. If she had, he imagined he would have heard from his brother by now.

Distressed by his thoughts, he ran a hand across his face and rubbed his eyes again. The disturbing news wasn't the only reason he was so tired. It seemed as though, since the night he'd been intimate with Veta, the shadows wouldn't leave him alone. He hadn't had a moment's peace for whatever used to keep them at bay wasn't doing its job. So he hadn't really slept well since and was considering staying at the main house tonight because of it. His father had been saying a prayer for protection upon the ranch house ever since he'd been born. Though they could still get in, they seemed much less inclined to disturb him in this house for that reason. Thinking it might be wise to start doing that with his own home and wondering why he had never thought of it before, Drinian lifted his shoulders to stretch them.

Glancing around the kitchen, he wondered what was taking Megorah so long. He knew she was in the house as he'd seen her arrive when he was in the yard. Drinian had assumed she would be coming straight to the kitchen since it was her and Chase's turn on kitchen duty. He wanted to already be at the table when they came in.

The night before, he had overheard Megorah talking about, how she was looking for a place for the Rohann woman for five hundred or less, including utilities. Typically, he'd rent this one for seven hundred, and the utilities would not be included. However, considering the circumstances, he thought he could make an exception this time. He felt he owed her even more. He was a little uncomfortable with the idea of taking money from her period but figured he'd simply not bother cashing her checks if Veta wound up renting it from him.

He figured, by laying everything on the apartment out on the table, she'd see him perusing it and ask him about it. Hearing a noise from the stairwell, he leaned back casually in his chair, watching as Megorah and Chase came into the kitchen.

"Starting early tonight, I see," Megorah said with disapproval, nodding towards the beer in his hand. There was concern in her eyes, and she looked at him curiously.

Shrugging nonchalantly, he didn't really respond but glanced back down at the papers before him. He knew his family didn't like that he drank but it wasn't really their decision, and they weren't the ones being tortured by demons.

"What's for dinner?" he asked without lifting his head.

"We figured we'd go easy and have spaghetti. You know, kid-friendly and all." Chase said while pulling spaghetti sauce and pasta from the pantry.

"You might want to rethink that unless you're planning to go meatless." Drinian glanced up towards them finally. Seeing them both stop suddenly and turn to stare at him, he cocked his head.

"Why?" They said in unison, making him chuckle inwardly.

"Dad used the unfrozen hamburger for burgers earlier today and there isn't enough of the leftover Italian sausage from breakfast for that."

"Are you kidding me?" Megorah practically hollered. Slamming the pot on the stove, she glared at him angrily. Her temper wasn't so irate though to miss the fact that Drinian seemed more talkative than usual. He was even using full sentences.

"Nope, they were really good too," he said, continuing to make notes. "Just the way I like them, medium-rare and nice and thick."

Chase and Megorah both stared at each other without saying a word.

"Now what are we gonna do?" Chase asked in exasperation.

"French bread pizzas." Drinian offered as a suggestion. "You could make them out of the garlic bread."

"Do we have everything to do that?" Megorah asked as she leaned into the fridge, looking for cheese. Pulling out a package of mozzarella, she tossed it on the counter along with the two packages of pepperoni, eyeing the cheese in irritation.

"Is that all the mozzarella?" Chase eyed the bag of cheese skeptically. Seeing his wife, he sighed in exasperation. "That's not going to be enough."

"So, mix it with the bag of cheddar that's in there," Drinian said while continuing to peruse his apartment information, getting frustrated.

Megorah leaned back into the fridge and grabbed the bag of cheddar, throwing it on the counter as well. Staring at the two, thirty-two-ounce bags of cheese they both eyed it anxiously. Taking that moment to look over at them, Drinian rolled his eyes in exasperation. Getting up, he carried his papers with him and set them on the counter. Reaching around them, he grabbed a large bowl and grater from the cabinet and then proceeded to dump both packages of cheese into the bowl.

Peering into the fridge, he took the sixteen-ounce block of Monterey Jack out and shredded it into the bowl. After completing that, while they stood there and stared at him, he turned back to the fridge. Grabbing the Italian sausage leftover from breakfast that morning, along with onions, green and red peppers, and a jar of mushrooms he tossed all the ingredients onto the counter. He then pulled the parmesan cheese from the cupboard and set it along with the rest of the ingredients.

"Now, you guys get all those French bread garlic loaves from the pantry that you were going to use for the spaghetti, and you've got enough stuff to make French bread pizzas for everyone. As long as you use the cheese sparingly, that is."

"But there's no pizza sauce. What do we use for pizza sauce?" Chase called from the pantry as he came walking out with half a dozen loaves of French bread.

Drinian shrugged. "Use the spaghetti sauce, instead."

"Well, aren't you just a culinary wiz … and a life saver." Megorah smiled back at him brightly. "Anything I can do for you in return?" she asked suddenly.

Drinian had been about to head back to the table when he stopped and turned to look at her. Tilting his head, as if pondering her query for a moment, he finally responded.

"Actually, do you know of anyone looking for an apartment? I have one that just came available," he said, trying to sound nonchalant.

"Is that the info on it?" She pointed to the papers on the counter.

He could see her interest had been piqued. He nodded as he smiled inwardly.

Megorah glanced over the details of the apartment in question, her excitement mounting. She'd found a couple for Veta to look at, but she was nervous about whether they'd actually work for her. Seeing the listing price, she glanced up at him in surprise.

"You're only listing it for five hundred?"

"Yeah, I'm kind of anxious to get it rented and not have to bother with it anymore. I might even be willing to cover most utilities just to be done with it. The building has been paid off for several years now so the rent would still cover my expenses and then some." Striding back towards the table he sat down and grabbed up his beer. Taking a swig, he eyed her over the bottle, his eyes twinkling as he could see her noticeably getting excited.

"Are you thinking for this, Veta?" Chase asked her suddenly.

Not expecting to hear her name, Drinian nearly choked on his beer, spluttering as he sat up suddenly and began coughing uncontrollably.

Ignoring her brother's predicament, Megorah set the papers down and got to work on making the French bread pizzas. Splitting the loaves open she laid them on the pans her husband had gotten out and began spooning sauce onto the bread.

"Drin, I might actually have someone for you. I'm supposed to be showing some tomorrow to a gal looking for a place. Mind if I borrow that folder and show it to her?"

"Not at all." Drinian grinned. "I'm betting she'll like the shower and tub the best," he said, without thinking. That had been easier than he'd thought.

- - -

The next morning Megorah contacted Veta to let her know there were three apartments she had for her to look at and choose from. Agreeing to meet that afternoon, she confirmed she'd be at the rental agency at one-thirty in order to go check them out.

Stepping in the shower for the second time that morning, Veta simply stood under the water, allowing it to trickle down over her head and shoulders. She'd already washed first thing that morning, but it seemed as though she felt the need to be under the lukewarm water, for reasons she couldn't explain. The day before, she'd decided it wasn't because she felt dirty, but instead because she wanted to remember as much as she could.

Each time she stepped under the showerhead, she found herself thinking back over the events of that night at the cabin. Allowing the water to pour down over her, she discovered she would remember more of what had happened. She could even practically feel his hands running up and down her body, as though investigating a woman for the first time.

Whether it was real or imagined, it seemed as though the more she stood there, allowing the water to soothe her, the more she would recall and it was important to her to remember. She wanted to be able to clearly see Drinian's face. So far the picture was still a bit hazy to her. All she was able to recollect was his gentle pale blue eyes, black hair and his deep tan skin color.

Sighing, as the water loosened her muscles around her neck, she rested her head against the shower wall. Her problem was, she was finding that the more pieces she managed to put together, the more she realized how much she had shamefully enjoyed the experience.

Drinian had been very gentle with her. The way he had held her after they had been together the first time had been so affectionate, so loving. It had been such a tender moment that it almost made her heartache for the wanting of it. Blinking back tears, as she rested her hand against her chest, she allowed the water to wash them away and decided it was time to get out of the shower. She didn't want to be late meeting Megorah at the rental agency, and she still needed to get a bite to eat.

By the time she'd dried off and dressed, Veta had managed to push the thoughts of that night out of her mind, at least for the time being. After towel drying her hair, she blew it with a curling brush and hairdryer, allowing it to fall in waves around her face. Deciding to skip the makeup regimen, she simply dabbed a bit of blush on her cheeks and chap-stick on her lips. Glancing briefly in the mirror, she was grateful she'd been blessed with thick black lashes that framed her green eyes in a flattering fashion, for it meant never really having to use mascara, except on special occasions. Sliding her feet into her tennis shoes and grabbing her purse, she was out the door.

Megorah had already agreed to drive to the apartments for her, so she could concentrate on the roads and be able to familiarize herself with the area better. So instead of taking her car, she opted to test out her leg and walked the two short blocks down to The Coffee Haven for lunch. Veta hadn't been there since the incident at the hospital. She figured it was high time she made her apologies to Crisalya, regardless of her own unease.

By the time she'd reached The Coffee Haven, she was seriously rethinking having walked there. The leg brace on her knee did not allow for her to bend very well, which meant utilizing her hip more. She appeared a bit tired and winded as a result when she'd entered the coffee house and to her disappointment, the person she had been expecting and almost hoping to see wasn't there. The question she had to ask herself though, was whether she was really hoping to see Crisalya or someone else instead?

After deciding on a chicken salad croissant sandwich and a raspberry iced tea, she sat and ate quietly, staring at the Bible on her table. It had been a couple of days since she'd done her devotions. She'd felt so much guilt over the choice she'd made. Taking a deep breath she decided her faith could use a good dose of the Lord's word. What had happened wasn't his fault. As much as she would like to place the blame elsewhere, in the end, it had been her choice, regardless of Drinian's actions. She even worried a little, at what he might be going through right now. She wondered if the demons would torture him even worse than they already did.

Putting the thoughts on hold, Veta delved into her devotions for the day, finding it ironic that they covered forgiveness and penance. Saying a prayer, in the end, requesting that God might give them both peace and forgive them of their actions, she set her Bible and devotions book aside in order to eat.

She was halfway through her lunch, when a beautiful blonde woman, with striking dark blue eyes, entered the coffee house. She had a medium build, with a perfect hourglass shape and stood shorter than her, at about five foot, six inches with heels. Smiling brightly, she greeted the young woman at the register by name, making it obvious to Veta, that she was a regular. After ordering a couple of mocha and caramel Frappuccino's each, she stood waiting for them to be made.

Realizing she hadn't taken her pain medicine yet, Veta reached down to grab it from her purse. In doing so, she managed to knock over the remainder of her iced tea. Not noticing what she'd done at first she went to pull the medicine bottle out only to feel an icy cold substance drizzling across her neck and down her hair. Startled, she banged her head on the table and managed to slip off her chair.

"Oh, for the love," she cried out in frustration. If she wasn't spilling drinks, she was injuring herself. She just couldn't win. As she sat there on the floor, the pretty blonde bent down with a hand towel she must have grabbed from the cashier and handed it to Veta.

"Would this help?" she asked kindly. Her eyes held a hint of humor.

"Thank you. Lord, help me, it's the third time I've spilled something in here, and I've only been in here three times," Veta exclaimed, as she dabbed at her head first with the towel.

"Come tomorrow you can make it four," the woman said cheerily, starting to chuckle.

Groaning, she adjusted her position on the floor so she could mop up what she spilled. "Something tells me Crisalya and Royce might not appreciate that so much," she mumbled while managing to finish cleaning up her mess.

Surprised, the woman asked, "You know the Howard's?" seeing Veta nod in ascent she went on. "And here, I thought, I knew everyone in town. Where are my manners? I'm Lylia, and you are?" she asked, extending her hand to her.

"Veta…Veta Rohann. I just moved here. Or, at least, I think I may be moving here." She sighed heavily as she shook her hand.

"Not sure yet, are you?" Lylia's face piqued with curiosity. Noting Veta had a brace on her leg, she proceeded to help her up from the floor.

"Thank you," Veta said, having returned to her chair. "It's still, as yet, undecided. I am looking for a place right now but if my luck keeps going the way it's been, I may move on soon." Seeing the remnants of ice and tea on the table, she continued to wipe it up while they talked. "You're welcome to sit while you wait," she offered, waving her hand to the extra chair.

Lylia glanced over at the barista who was making her drinks and decided to sit down. "Don't mind if I do. Chastity isn't quite as quick making them yet as Royce and Crisalya are. She's still fairly new." She rolled her eyes. "You're having some bad luck you say?"

Shrugging, she couldn't really think of a really good response without having to go into detail, so she replied, "I've had better weeks. Nothing, a few prayers wouldn't cure."

Lylia's eyes grew wide then. She smiled, noting the Bible and devotions book on the table. "Do you attend church?" she asked cautiously.

"I used to back in Maryland. I've only been in town here since Sunday evening, so obviously, I haven't had time to check any out in the area yet."

"I'm not sure what faith you practice, but the United Methodist Church my family attends in Whitefish is pretty good. The Pastor there has been around awhile, but she keeps the services surprisingly up to date for all generations really. Kind of a happy medium, you could say."

"I grew up in a Methodist church," she responded, expressing interest. "Where's that located?"

"It's off Wisconsin Avenue. Here, let me write down the address for you. Are you familiar with the area yet?" Lylia pulled out a notepad and wrote the information down.

"No, but there's a public computer at the motel, I can MapQuest it," she said, becoming excited.

"There is an adult Sunday school class at nine, but the service itself is at ten-fifteen," Lylia explained as she finished writing and handed Veta the paper she'd torn from her notebook. "I often help out in the nursery because of my daughter Kayla, but we may not make it this weekend due to a family gathering."

"I'm sorry to hear that. I might just take you up on checking that out though." Veta smiled. Glancing down at the paper, she folded it and tucked it into her wallet for safe keeping.

"Lylia, I've got your drinks for you," Chastity called from the counter as she set the Frappuccino's into a carrier. "I'm sorry it took so long but I had a blender go down. So I was working with just the one today."

"Do you want me to mention it to Royce when I see him?" Lylia asked with concern.

"Would you? I'll make a note and leave it for him but he may not see it until tomorrow. He forgot to give me his new cell number," the barista said

Lylia looked at her in surprise. "I didn't know he'd gotten a new one, but I'll do that." Grabbing her drinks, she turned towards Veta. "I hope you do. Maybe I'll see you there next week." Giving her an encouraging bright smile, Lylia proceeded on out the door.

Chapter 13

Veta watched Lylia go, then glanced down at the remains of her meal. Unexpectedly full after only a sandwich, she found she was also very thirsty for some reason. She finished cleaning up her mess and ordered another raspberry tea to go. Twenty minutes later, she left the coffee house and was crossing the street to the Ryans Family Rental Agency. She was becoming increasingly optimistic and excited over the prospect of looking at apartments. Meeting Lylia had made any reservations about wanting to stay go away. There really were some nice people living in the area. Not wanting to let her last experience ruin her outlook, she decided to be positive.

Preparing to open the agency's doors, Veta saw a Black Lexus pull up in front of the building. Recognizing the woman in the vehicle as the same one who had pulled into the drive at the cabin four days ago, she paused. As the woman stepped out of her vehicle, she called out to Veta.

"Are you, Ms. Rohann?" she asked as she walked around her vehicle, extending her hand. "I'm, Megorah Ryans. We talked on the phone?"

The woman was about the same size and build as Hialey, only she seemed a bit shorter maybe. Her black hair was extremely long, hanging down past her waist, and she was wearing a long flowing skirt with a stylish but blousy, royal blue shirt. Sporting sunglasses and carrying a very large purse, that almost looked like a bag, she stood there with her small slender hand outstretched.

Her face flushing a little Veta stretched her hand in greeting and shook hers. "Yes, hi. It's nice to finally meet you." Without warning, she found herself feeling a bit uncomfortable near her so she directed her gaze at her feet.

"I have everything we need in my suitcase here." Megorah gestured to her giant purse with a quirky smile. "So, if you want to get started I can show you some of the stats on our way." It was clear she was trying to keep things light, while still being professional.

Grateful to her for her efforts, Veta inhaled deeply, remembering her conversation moments ago with Lylia. "That sounds great." She smiled back at her, deciding she was looking forward to the afternoon. She was a little anxious about being around the woman, knowing that she knew what she did, but wasn't going to let it bring her down. Following her back to her car, she opened the door of the Lexus and carefully slid in.

"As I told you over the phone, there are three apartments we're looking at today. Two I found, and one other rather interesting one, that I was made aware of last night. We'll probably hit that one last, but the other two are close together. I figure we could check those out first." Megorah pulled files out of her bag and selected a sheet from each one, handing them over to Veta. Glancing down at the papers, she realized they had pictures of the exterior of the buildings, as well as layout diagrams, room sizes, and a detailed account of what utilities were covered and the cost of deposits and rental fees.

"All of these rent for a full year?" She perused the sheets while trying to pay attention to where they were going.

"Yes. You'll notice they all allow pets as well, though, this one here requires proof your pets have been both spayed and de-clawed." Maintaining her grip on the steering wheel with her left hand, she used the right to point out the unit in question.

"That's all right, he's already had both done, and I have papers on him."

"Perfect. One of them is a house that has an apartment both above and below. Separate entrances, but it's the upper one that's available right now, which might be problematic with your leg," she explained, gesturing towards Veta's brace. "But then again, I guess all three of them are on the second floor, so either way you'll have stairs." Megorah frowned and looked both ways before turning.

"It's okay, I'll manage. This won't be on forever." She patted the brace and smile ruefully. "What about these other two?"

"The other one I picked is above a business, just a few blocks away from the first. It's nice and clean, and longer than it is wide." She peered over at her. It appeared as though she had a disturbing thought just then, although Veta was having trouble telling for sure with her sunglass barrier.

"And the third one?" she asked curiously, seeing it was listed with a compact sized kitchen stove and was unfurnished.

"That one has an interesting history to it. The building it's in used to house the old hospital before the new one was built. It was turned into apartments thirty-five years ago and remodeled again about twenty years later by the newest owner." Megorah paused suddenly, as though she had just remembered something. Her mouth pinched tight, and she clenched at the wheel.

"Is something wrong, Mrs. Ryans?" she asked in concern.

Shaking her head, she plastered a smile on her face and said, "No, of course not. Everything is fine," she said quietly. "You'll notice, the living room is unfurnished, and there is no table in the kitchen because it's more of a kitchenette than a full-sized one. But, I was told, that there is a twin sized bed, with a bookshelf style headboard in the bedroom, and it has a large double closet with a built-in set of drawers in one of them."

Veta tilted her head at Megorah, thoughtfully. She appeared to be struggling with something but was determined not to let it affect her. "It has a full bath, not just a shower?" she asked, trying to keep the conversation flowing.

Megorah nodded. "The owner seemed to think you'd like the bathtub and shower setup in particular, for some reason."

Thinking that was an odd statement, she chose to ignore it in the interest of keeping things genial. "That sounds promising, although I must admit I was hoping for a fully furnished apartment. Are the other two furnished?"

Hesitating slightly, Megorah glanced over at her uncomfortably, as she pulled in front of a two-story house with wide wood siding. It had narrow stairs leading up the side.

Taking a deep breath, she spoke, "I'll be honest with you. I *have* been having difficulty finding a place for you that is fully furnished in your price range. I understand these two I've found have some furnishings that have been left behind by previous tenants but none are fully furnished. I've been told that some of the items aren't in the best of condition." Seeing the disappointment in Veta's expression, she turned towards her as she parked. She contemplated for a moment before speaking. "I had actually thought to have one of them furnished for you, but not knowing which one you'd prefer, I was leery about doing that. Especially not knowing what you'd like."

"Why would you feel you'd need to do that?" Veta asked cautiously, knowing full well what her answer was likely to be.

"I feel somewhat responsible for what happened to you at the cabin," she said softly, looking directly at her. Veta turned her head away and peered out at her surroundings as her face flamed. The conversation was starting to touch on a subject she wasn't sure she was inclined to discuss.

Deciding there really was no avoiding it in the end, she turned back with a heavy sigh. "Why would you feel responsible for that? You weren't there, shoving my medicine down my throat, twice, and forcing an entire bottle of wine down my throat."

Megorah looked at her in horror, "Is that what happened? Someone forced you to…"

"Oh, no, you misunderstand. Look, Mrs. Ryans…"

"Please, call me Megorah, or Meg. Most friends and family call me, Meg." She smiled warmly.

"Meg," Veta continued with a weak smile of her own. "The only person responsible for that night is me. I was upset, took too much of my medicine, drank too much wine, and got in a hot tub. It was stupid and dangerous. The man who came along actually saved my life because I passed out in the hot tub."

Alarmed, Megorah exclaimed, "You could have drowned!"

Nodding her head in agreement she stared down at her feet trying to avoid her startled gaze. Finally peering over at Meg, she saw her rub her hand across her face. Then she leaned back with her arms across her chest.

Shaking her head, Meg went on, "But I don't understand. Did you know this man? I mean you let him in?"

"I'd seen him around town a couple of times but, no, I didn't really know him. He must have come in through the patio door when I passed out," she admitted.

"But then, why would you..." Megorah started to ask, but then, suddenly stopped. Her eyes widened behind her sunglasses

Veta sat with her hands in her lap. Her face flushed with heat and her eyes began to water. Tilting her head back she forced them down. Attempting a rather weak half smile once again, she looked at Meg anxiously.

"I am embarrassed to admit, I don't really remember everything yet, you see, because of the medicine and alcohol. I mean, I know what happened, obviously, but I don't exactly recall everything, just yet." Shrugging, she fidgeted and said, "Bits and pieces are still coming back to me." She laughed nervously, glancing away, unable to handle Meg staring at her anymore.

"Oh, Veta, this man took advantage of you, didn't he? You couldn't say, no, but you couldn't really say, yes." Megorah cringed inwardly, imagining the situation in her head. "You were weak, disoriented and unable to defend yourself against someone who broke into your home," she finished choking back a sob.

Alarmed at Meg's conclusion, Veta turned in her seat. "Please Meg, don't be upset. Look, it wasn't like you might think. He didn't hurt me." Seeing her doubtful expression, as Megorah peered down at her leg, she added. "He didn't hit me, tie me up, or abuse me," Veta explained as her mind flashed back to fifteen years prior. "It wasn't like the last time. And this knee injury; it actually happened the first morning after I arrived. I re-injured it when I slipped and fell at the cabin in my haste to leave." Realizing she said too much, she quickly moved on, noting Megorah's startled glance her way.

"From what I can recall, we both appeared to be hurting that night, and I am ashamed to admit, I may well have invited him to stay. So it's just as much my fault, as his." Veta paused a moment, embarrassed at her own admission, and blushed. "What I do remember, is that he was actually very gentle, really, it's just..." she sighed then, and her hands trembled, as she reached up to push her hair out of the way in order to stare out the window, unable to finish.

"You woke up, realized what had happened after seeing the state of your bedroom and the patio door off. Then, you got scared, because you couldn't remember anything and didn't really know who the man was." Megorah finished her thought for her as she looked away lost in her own memories.

Grimacing, Veta sat back in her seat. They both stared out the window together. "Something like that I suppose." She knew who the man was but wasn't inclined towards saying who. "You're very intuitive."

Meg laughed derisively for Veta was very close to the truth, "It's supposed to be a blessing, but at times, it feels like a curse." Leaning her head back against the headrest, she peered over at the attractive woman next to her. Her beauty had marked her as a desirable target for many a man she was sure. "This time, I'm making sure you're located somewhere you'll be safer." Reaching over and patting her on her injured leg, she exclaimed suddenly. "Let's go see if we can't find you a new place."

Smiling brightly Veta agreed, glad for the change of topic. They got out and headed up to the apartment on the second floor. It was very small, and though, it was a full kitchen, it turned out to be a one-room flat. Veta had been hoping for something a little bigger. The bathroom was very small, and the garden tub had been converted quite oddly into a shower. Plus, the pull-out couch was nothing more than a futon mattress on crates.

"Okay, I think this is a no." Her response to the place was emphatic.

Megorah grinned mischievously. "What, you don't want to sleep on crates? It's all the rage!" They both giggled and promptly left.

Hoping the next apartment would be better, they headed over to Fishmonger Sam's building since it was located above the store there. The stairway was narrow and steep, making it difficult for Veta to get up the steps with her leg in the brace. By the time she managed to hobble herself to the top of the stairs, she was disappointed to see that this apartment wasn't a whole lot better. Though both had been clean and well kept, they didn't have the space she was wanting. The one above the store, at least, had a separate bedroom, but it was small, had no bed, and an extremely narrow closet. The bathroom was bigger but only had a shower, and the fridge didn't have a freezer. Becoming discouraged, they made their way down the steps and back out to the car.

"I'm sure the next one will be better."

"I'm sure it will." Veta tried to masque her disappointment so far.

Clearly a lousy actress, Megorah took her arm and gently shook it. "No worries. I'll find you something it just might take a little longer than I thought. Besides, worst case scenario, I'll set you up on the ranch."

"The ranch, what's that?"

"My Dad owns a horse ranch and it has tons of rooms. I mean, the place is huge. I'm sure my dad wouldn't mind if I set you up there for a while." She turned down Spokane Avenue and parked near a large, older style building.

"Oh, no, Meg! I couldn't possibly impose." She couldn't imagine any elderly gentleman wanting a widowed female traipsing around his home. "I'm sure this next one will be just fine." She glanced up at the building nervously. It appeared to have three floors, and hers was supposed to be on the second. "Huh, it's kind of an oddly shaped building, isn't it?" she said absent-mindedly. They got out and headed up the stairs. These were much easier to manage. They were wider and nowhere near as steep, having been smartly rebuilt as though to accommodate a person who might be handicapped.

Upon entering the apartment both Megorah and Veta stood in the entrance and looked around the room in surprise. The almost triangular shaped living room and kitchen area were set up in an open floor plan style, giving it a more spacious look. The space wasn't large, by any means, but allowed for much more room than the other two had. The kitchen was more of a kitchenette in style, as there was a compact sized stove, which Veta had never seen before, and a refrigerator that had a freezer but was perfect for one person. Everything appeared to have been recently cleaned and freshly painted. There was even room to put a small table for two or an island with bar stools.

After fully inspecting the living and kitchen space, which didn't take long, they checked out the bedroom. It was small, narrow even, but it fit a twin sized bed perfectly. She noticed it already had, what appeared to be, a brand-new pillow top mattress on it.

"Look, Meg! There are drawers built in underneath this bed. I can store things here and won't have to buy a dresser," she said in delight, her eyes lighting up. This would definitely save her some money.

"It almost looks like someone took an old, tall bookshelf to use as a headboard, along with a shorter one for the footboard," Megorah said as she inspected it.

"Then, they added three smaller drawers here, and two larger ones down here," she pointed out as she closed the smaller ones and opened the others.

"That is really quite clever. It's an excellent use of space." Meg opened the closet doors. She was garnering a greater amount of respect for her brother's woodworking skills the more she saw. Gasping, she whirled around and pointed inside the closet. "If you like that then get a load of this!" She giggled in delight, gaining her attention.

Turning, Veta's eyes grew wide. Not only did the closets have lights she could turn on, but they had organizers as well. The double sized closet sported both long and short spaces for hanging clothes, in addition to more drawer space, as well as, shoe racks.

"Someone really knew what they were doing here, I've never seen space so well utilized." She gazed into the closets in wonder, noting it even sported a mirror she could use for applying makeup if she wanted.

They looked at each other, and Veta could tell they were both thinking the same thing. "Okay, the deal breaker will be the bathroom," Megorah sang out as she practically ran from the room.

Laughing, she limped after her, nearly missing the full-length mirror behind the bedroom door. The bathroom was across from the living room and behind the kitchen, which seemed an odd placement to her until she realized it was probably more practical for the purpose of plumbing to have it there. Coming up behind Meg, she nearly bumped into her as she stood stock still in the doorway.

"Are you seeing this?"

"No, not really," Veta said with amusement. Laughing, Megorah moved so she could get through.

The moment she stepped in the bathroom, the first words out of her mouth were, "I'll take it."

It wasn't a large bathroom, by any means, for it was mostly built for functionality, but someone had taken it upon themselves to add a free-standing, old fashioned, claw style tub, and it was huge. The shower curtain hung all the way around the tub, and the shower head hung from an extension on the wall.

"Look," Megorah cried, stepping into the shower to investigate. "The shower head is even detachable."

"It appears to also have various settings as well," she noted with excitement. The one she was most anxious to try out appeared to be a rain shower setting.

Smiling, Meg glanced over at Veta. "I think we just found your new home."

Chapter 14

They promptly left the apartment and quickly headed back to the office to fill out a new lease form for her new home. As they sat at Meg's desk, Veta couldn't help but imagine how she would decorate the place. Granted, she was going to have to furnish the living room and get a table for the kitchen, but she figured she could do that pretty cheap if she could find a second-hand shop somewhere. Thinking she'd ask Megorah if she knew of a good place, she waited patiently while she made copies of her new lease.

Megorah walked out of the back room with keys and her lease in hand. Laying them on the desk, she sat and reclined back in her chair, while sipping the last of her Frappuccino she'd brought from the car.

"I love these things but whenever my sister-in-law gets them for me she gets large. Honestly, I'm better off with a small. They take me forever to drink." Setting the cup next to her computer, she turned her attention back to Veta. "How do you feel about this one? Is it okay?"

Chuckling, Veta took hold of her keys. "Not a dream home, per se, but definitely much better than the other two. You know, you really don't have to do this. The rent I mean. I'm more than willing to cover first and last month's rent and deposits."

"Absolutely not." Shaking her head, Megorah looked at her sternly. "Your money will transfer over to this lease. I'll make sure of it. There's no need to strap yourself, and you can't tell me it wouldn't. Otherwise, you wouldn't be looking for a rental for only five hundred a month. Besides, you needed something fully furnished and you're not getting it."

"I was hoping for furnished, I won't deny it. Especially now that I'll have to replace everything that was stolen."

"That's why I was hoping one of the other apartments would have worked out."

Cocking her head to one side, Veta peered over at the woman in confusion. "I don't understand, what do you mean?"

"The one you chose isn't in a bad area or anything. It's just, the other two would have been closer to the Sheriff's Department." Megorah turned towards her computer and took off her sunglasses. Hearing Veta gasp, she turned back to see she'd closed her eyes and was leaning back in her chair with her hands over her face. "What's wrong?" Concern was etched in her voice. She could feel the sudden wave of anxiety emanating from her, as she sat with her hands over her face, shaking her head.

"I'm okay," she said weakly, trying to hide her shaking hands and avoid the realtor's gaze. "If I'd known that, I probably wouldn't have wasted your time looking at them." A wave of relief washed over her. She was glad to know the place she'd chosen wasn't any closer to Sheriff

Blackthorne than necessary. The last thing she wanted was for Drinian's brother to find out what had happened, especially since he was the Sheriff.

Surprised by her statement and the sudden distress she could sense from her, Megorah couldn't help but ask, "Why on earth for? After everything that's happened, what with your U-Haul being stolen and … everything. I would have thought you would rather be closer?" She watched the woman's face closely, trying to determine the root of her anxiety.

Chuckling nervously as she rubbed her neck, Veta looked everywhere but at the woman before her, trying to avoid her direct gaze initially. "The last thing I want is to be closer to Sheriff Blackthorne. The farther away the better." The words came more forcefully then she'd intended. Realizing her mistake, she anxiously looked the woman before her in the eye for the first time.

Startled by the mention of her brother, and the woman's obvious dislike for him, Megorah stared back at her in silence. Veta's eyes grew huge as she swallowed hard and shrank into her chair. Megorah could feel the new unexpected wave of anxiety from the woman.

Veta locked gazes once again with a pair of crystal-clear blue eyes. It was as though she were seeing the woman across from her for the first time. Then her eyes darted fearfully to the keys in her hand. "Do you mind if I ask? Your eye coloring… Are they common in this area?"

The change of subject was abrupt, throwing Megorah off guard. "No. They're a family trait. I know the pale blue color is more commonly found on albinos so with our tan skin and black hair, it tends to unsettle people sometimes when they see us. My sister is more self-conscious about it than the rest of us which is why she usually wears colored contacts."

"A family trait." Veta's voice shook. She took a deep breath. "So, Sheriff Blackthorne?" Her voice sounding strained.

"He's my older brother."

"I see." Her face turned beet red and she continued to stare down at her keys. "The owner of the cabin, are they the same owners of this property?" She lifted the copy of her lease with shaking fingers.

Becoming more and more alarmed by Veta's line of questioning, and the obvious anxiety she was experiencing, Megorah replied, "The owner of the cabin was my father, Rafe Blackthorne. This property is owned by another party. Why?"

Veta closed her eyes tight, exhaling deeply with relief. Opening her eyes, she looked back at her new friend but was having trouble seeing her clearly. Her vision seemed to be blurry, and the room had a feeling of unreality to it. A wave of panic seized her, from out of nowhere, and she was finding it suddenly very hard to breathe.

Glaring with malicious intent upon the woman below him, the demon, unseen by the human's eyes, pressed his smoky hands further into her chest as he knelt on her lap. Watching briefly, the panic he was instilling within her, he cackled with glee at her distress. Peering around him anxiously, at the battle being waged around him, Zalman noted his minions were holding their own against the angels, Woreash and Maleeka, for the moment. They'd come quite suddenly, but the angels had been ready for them, nonetheless, so they wouldn't have much time to complete their task. Everything had to fall into place within a specific timeframe, or they would fail in their orders, which had been laid out for them by the master himself. Unconcerned for the moment, of the Ryans woman, sitting at her desk staring at Veta in stunned silence, Zalman leaned in and crooned into Veta's ear.

"They're all gonna know. Everyone will know of the sin you committed," he crooned. His red eyes glowed, burning into hers. The way her green eyes stared back at him, if he didn't know better, he'd say she could see him, but the demon knew that wasn't possible, yet. The woman below him started breathing heavily, the hysteria within overpowering her senses.

Megorah watched as Veta seemed to be having a panic attack right there in her office. What was even more startling was the implication as to why she was experiencing the attack, for the fear now appeared to be linked to her family somehow. Swallowing hard, her voice trembled as she spoke quietly to Veta. An extremely disturbing possibility began weighing upon her. "Why don't you like Dartanian? You act like you're afraid of him for some reason." Her eyes bore into Veta's, suspiciously.

"No, no. I'm not afraid of him. Really." Veta's voice rose with the sudden hysteria and fear she was experiencing. She couldn't understand why she was becoming so worked up, but the notion of Drinian's family finding out about them frightened her for some reason.

Megorah gasped, her hands flying to her face. Veta didn't have to say a thing, it was written all over her face. She knew who her rescuer had been, the man who had taken advantage of her, and it was the reason why she disliked Dartanian. Shaking her head, Meg couldn't believe it was true. But the overwhelming anxiety coming from the woman sitting across from her was unmistakable when she'd spoke her brother's name.

"You know who it was, don't you? The man who broke into the cabin," Megorah questioned her, needing to actually hear her say it. "You said you'd even seen him around town … you're just not saying because…"

Clearing her throat Veta chose her words carefully as she shook her head no. Her voice trembled. She smiled nervously, her chest heaving in distress. "I know, yes. I figure the man had probably just been out for a walk, you know, and was watching from the woods maybe when he saw me in trouble," she said evasively, avoiding Megorah's gaze.

"Stupid woman," Zalman laughed, snarling near Veta's face. "Still haven't figured out who Mrs. Megorah Ryans is, have you?"

"Get off of her, you foul, loathsome creature!" Maleeka slashed through a demon that had been hindering his progress. Ignoring its cry as it fizzled to the floor, Maleeka's glowing blue eyes narrowed upon Zalman as he lunged for him. Ensnaring the demon around his shoulders, the angel managed to yank him from his perch. Erupting into the air, swords suddenly appeared in Zalman's hands and he hovered above her. Whirling his double-bladed swords toward Maleeka he growled angrily. The angel deflected his blows.

"I don't know what your game is Zalman, but you won't win this."

"Less talking, more fighting," Woreash called out irritably, managing to finally push Fallen and Veranke into a corner.

In that same moment, Veta made a sudden connection in her head of which she hadn't picked up on before. Megorah Ryans was a Mrs.

"Ryans," Veta said suddenly. "You wouldn't happen to be related somehow to Dr. Chase Ryans, would you?"

Confused by the question Meg answered, "He's my husband."

Veta giggled hysterically. She was leasing a property from the sister of the man she had been intimate with. The sister, who was married to the doctor whom she had told what happened, and had, in fact, performed a rape kit on her. To top it off, the man who originally owned the cabin in question, who had a complaint for damages against her was both of their father's. It occurred to Veta then that she also happened to frequent the coffee house owned and run by one of his other daughters as well, and the county Sheriff was Drinian's brother, by extension Megorah's as well. Seriously, what were the odds, she thought to herself in a panic.

"Listen, Meg, thanks so much for your help today." She stood up too fast, causing her to feel lightheaded. Wobbling slightly, she maneuvered around the chair as her whole body seemed to tremble noticeably. Tears were threatening at the corner of her eyes as she spoke. "I really do appreciate it, as I couldn't have done it without you."

"Veta, wait!" Meg said in alarm. Sensing her overwhelming distress she stood suddenly.

"Stop!" the angel Woreash called to the woman from the corner of the room where he'd been pinned down by Veranke and Fallen. "Maleeka, can you follow?"

The urge to flee was great. Veta couldn't find her way out of there fast enough. Though trying to spare Megorah's feelings, she awkwardly picked up her copy of the lease, while avoiding her gaze. "I really do need to go. I figure, I have just enough time to check out and can move right in tonight if I hurry." She spoke with a false sense of excitement while trying to mask the overwhelming desire to hurl and then run. Turning towards the door, she called out to Meg as she left, "I only have suitcases after all." she waved, plastering a false smile on her face. "Thanks again!"

Attempting to fend off Zalman and two of his minions the Guardian leaped after Veta in order to secure her safety across the street. He was halted by several more vaporous black demons, slithering past her through the open doorway.

Megorah grabbed her cell phone as fast as she could and waited impatiently for the other end to pick up. She watched in horror as Veta buckled over just outside the Agency doors. She then attempted to limp across the street. Unseen by her eyes, two demons in their truest form urged her forward. Hissing and snapping at her with their snake-like tongues, they escorted her as she went.

"Pick up, pick up, pick up…" Megorah urged, waiting impatiently for him to answer. Then suddenly he was there.

"Royce speaking…."

"Please tell me you're at The Haven," Megorah said frantically, cutting him off.

Startled by her abruptness Royce responded, "Yeah, I'm…"

"Royce, listen. Veta just left here. She's crossing the street and I think she might … no, she is, she's in the throes of a panic attack. Can you…"

Royce didn't give her the time to finish as he hastily hung up.

"I'll be back for my order," he shouted to Chastity as he ran for the front door of the shop. He watched the scene before him in dismay as he yanked the door open and leaped through it. Veta was limping from the rental agency to the middle of the road unaware that a car was speeding down the road towards her.

All around the car, half a dozen demons flew about, urging the vehicle forward. Their ugly grey scaly faces twisted with rage, as their bat-like wings flapped urgently,

169

in an attempt to speed the car along faster. Howling angrily as the Howard man ran into the middle of the street after the woman, they snarled and gnashed their teeth. Seeing the human take her by the arms, they roared with fury as several Guardian angels streaked down from the heavens. Braking ranks, two sped towards the demons and the vehicle, while the other two dove for the woman and man in the street.

Screeching loudly, the demon with Veta found its attention divided between the Guardian now assaulting him, and the woman being urged across the street by the other Guardian and the Howard man. The demons inside the rental agency spilled out, chased by Woreash and Maleeka. Holy light exploded about them and their wings sprung from their backs. The battle waged even as the car sped by, barely missing Royce's leg as he lifted Veta, with the Guardian's assistance, away from danger.

Helping Veta up, as they'd fallen to the ground upon reaching the sidewalk, Royce could see how pale and shaken she was. Breathing heavily himself from the exertion, he watched her gasp and hold her stomach, as though she were about to be sick.

"Thank you," Veta stuttered out finally, attempting to crawl back up into a standing position, with the man's help, not realizing who it was next to her yet. "I'm so sorry. That was really stupid of me, I never even looked before crossing," she gasped out, the fear from the moment slowly starting to dissipate. Overwhelmed by her roiling emotions, her eyes brimmed with tears and her face showed clear distress.

Veta bent over again where she stood, trying to catch her breath. The world seemed to be spinning around her, and she couldn't seem to stay standing.

"Veta, are you okay?" she heard the male voice say next to her, as he laid a hand upon her shoulder. Startled, she stood erect too fast and found herself losing her balance. Arms reached out and caught her, holding her up where she stood. Glancing up at the man next to her, Veta finally realized it was Royce Howard from the coffee shop.

"I'm not feeling s-so good," she stuttered, blinking her glistening eyes. Bright lights seemed to swirl and flash before her as she gazed up into the sky.

Concerned, Royce held her up but was prepared to carry her if it were necessary. "Can you walk?" he asked.

"I'm not sure," she said weakly, attempting to take a few steps.

Crouching down a little, Royce wrapped one of her arms around his shoulder and placed his hand at her waist, being sure to tell her what he was doing as he did it, so she wouldn't be startled. She nodded in understanding and attempted to get her breathing under control. He half walked; half carried her the two blocks to the motel.

Deferring his head in the direction of the motel he asked, "Which room?"

"Six. Room s-six, first f-floor." Anxiety surged within her.

Royce guided her the rest of the way. Leaning her up against the door, he took her things from her as well as her key and promptly let her into her room. He stepped in briefly, in order to help her to her bed, and then left her things on the table.

"Are you going to be okay? That was an awfully close call. Is there anyone I can call for you?" Royce noticed how ashen her face appeared to be. Tears were starting to stream from her eyes as she sat on the bed, trembling while holding herself.

"No." Veta shook her head. "There's no one," she said quietly, looking away from him. Her face contorted in distress. "Th-thank you. I'll be okay now." She wiped at her wet face.

"Are you sure?" He was leery about leaving her alone like this. Seeing her nod in the affirmative, he wished her a good night and closed her door for her.

Royce couldn't help but feel a bit anxious about leaving her alone in her condition. Deciding to stop down at the front desk, he asked the clerk to check in on her within the half hour, explaining briefly why he wanted her to do so.

"You mean the gal that got sent to the hospital the other day?" Jenny asked curiously.

"Yes. Veta Rohann, in room six. I'm a little concerned about the state she's in after nearly being run down. I just want to make sure she's going to be okay," Royce said.

"No problem. I'll give her a call in fifteen minutes, and then stop by in an hour if I need to," she said sweetly.

Thinking he'd probably done all he could at that point, Royce left, with an unsettled feeling in his gut. The woman had nearly gotten killed, trying to cross the street, and the cold that had engulfed him as he'd reached her led him to believe she might not have actually been alone. The thought occurred to him, that he might want to talk to Drinian to see if he could come into town in the next day or two, to check the situation out. If there were demons plaguing her, as Royce suspected, then maybe Drinian could cause them some pain and convince them to leave her alone.

Wishing he'd had more time to stick around and maybe help Veta, he rushed back to his shop instead, in order to pick up the food and drinks he needed for the rehearsal dinner that night. Before he left, he placed an order for chicken soup and a fruit smoothie to be sent down to room six of the Howard's Motel around five-thirty. He suspected Veta might not be up for going out tonight and got the feeling from the look of her, that she required the sustenance for some reason.

Chapter 15

The angels watched Royce leave her room, glancing back towards her door upon exiting. After a moment they saw him head down towards the main office and go inside. If the angel Phillipe hadn't gotten to him when he had, then he wouldn't have been there for Veta when she needed him. And, he wouldn't have gotten the peace of the puzzle, he needed. The timing was everything after all. It helped, that Royce had a helpful spirit and kind heart.

"He's a good man, Royce. I've always liked him." Through the window Maleeka watched him speak to the woman at the desk. Gazing off into the near distance, two blocks down the street, he could see the Guardians were tying up loose ends with the last of the minions. The troublesome three had, of course, fled the scene, the moment Royce had gotten Veta to safety.

"He treats Crisalya very well," the angel called Woreash replied.

Gliding through the motel room door they stood together, watching Veta as she wept and struggled to breathe. Clearly in distress, her face contorted in discomfort as she bent over and held her waist.

"I'll stay with her for now," Woreash said suddenly, eyeing the woman with concern. "Go back to the house. The Blackthorne home is in disarray, and there is a wedding that must be held."

Nodding in agreement he sighed heavily. "I wish things could have been different. That they could have come together in another way," Maleeka continued sadly. He could see their presence seemed to be helping to calm Veta already.

"It has caused much trouble indeed but in the end, I believe it may well have been the only way, Maleeka. We almost didn't find her in time. The demons have been most troublesome where this one is concerned."

Maleeka stayed for a moment, deep in thought and agitated by his statement. He floated around to the other side of the bed, startling the cat, causing him to speed off towards the bathroom to hide. Leaning towards Veta, as he sat on the bed, he whispered near her ear.

"Don't be afraid. All will come to pass as it should." Lifting up from the bed, he soared up and out through the afternoon sky, the blousy white fabric of his pants, flapping against his legs as he went. He thought of the Blackthorne Ranch and was instantly there.

Maleeka fretted over whom to start with first as he hovered over the expansive house. The late matriarch's wedding dress hadn't fit and Alaina still had the journal. Then suddenly he knew who needed him most. Gliding down toward the house, he fell through the roof to her destination.

- - -

175

After Megorah got off the phone with Royce she headed straight home, finding her husband standing in the bathroom, getting ready for the rehearsal dinner. After confronting him about her conversation with Veta she became even more alarmed when she saw how closed lipped he was being about her hospital visit.

"Need I remind you that I am bound by doctor-patient confidentiality? Even if I wanted to tell you what was discussed, I couldn't. You know that." Chase tried hard to contain his emotions but to no avail.

Seeing him struggle, Megorah's eyes grew wide and filled with tears. "He did it, didn't he? Dartanian raped her."

"Now, wait just a minute," he said, trying to get his wife to calm down. She was quickly becoming hysterical. Choosing his words wisely while trying to keep to his oath, he spoke softly. "Even if there is something to this. Why are you assuming she was raped and that it was Dart? Did she say something to you?" he asked, wanting to determine what exactly Veta had said to her.

"No, she didn't have to." She stomped angrily away from her husband and threw her purse on the bed. "I mentioned I was trying to get an apartment for her closer to the Sheriff's Department and she became very upset, anxious even. She said she wouldn't want a place anywhere near Sheriff Blackthorne." Megorah whirled around suddenly as a thoughtful expression played upon her face. "And you know, she had no idea I was related until I took off my sunglasses and she saw my eyes. That's when she started getting really scared and asked me about them."

Nodding his head, he encouraged her to continue. "What did you tell her?"

"That it was a family trait. The only people I knew of in the area that had them were my family."

"Meggie, does she know you have three other brothers, or just you, Dart, and Crisalya?"

She looked at him then, as though shell shocked. Dropping to the bed, she peered up at Chase as he walked over to her and stood before her.

"Oh, no!" Megorah cried out suddenly. "Of course, it wasn't Dart at all."

She sat there for a moment, thinking it through, realizing that the much more likely candidate was Dante. Shaking her head back and forth, Megorah started to cry.

"I just knew. I knew it couldn't be Dart, but I guess it never occurred to me that it might be Dante either. Dart loves Lylia so much so I was having such a hard time imagining him ever doing that to her."

Chase shook his head in agreement. "No, you're right. I don't think Dart would ever cheat on Lylia, let alone take advantage of a woman like that," he said quietly.

Sniffling as tears fell from her eyes, she rested her head against her husband's chest, allowing him to soothe her, by running his hands through her hair.

"But Dante didn't get to grow up with us, so he was raised differently. It's much more likely, that he…." Megorah couldn't finish the statement. Burying her face deeper into her husband's body, she began to sob uncontrollably.

"Dante was out of the house that night too. Poor, Alaina," she said between sobs. "Pregnant with triplets, and she's about to marry a man who would do that."

"Meggie…" Chase lifted her face to his so he could see her. "We don't know anything for sure," he said softly, watching her face contort with pain.

177

"Maybe not, but who else *could* it be?" She leaned back into him, her heart breaking for Alaina.

- - -

At the same time, Chase and Megorah were in the middle of their discussion, Breydon was closing the door behind him as he stepped into his father's study. For some odd reason, he couldn't help but feel like a high school teenager, who'd been called in for a tongue lashing. Glancing at his dad, he moved further into the room and stood near the bookcase.

"Have a seat, Breydon." Rafe pulled out the chair to his desk and sat down. His tone was serious, and he was looking at him with, what appeared to be disappointment.

Eyeing his dad suspiciously, Breydon asked tentatively, "What's going on dad? Why such formality?" he asked, choosing instead to stay standing where he was. Thirty-six years old and his father could still intimidate him.

Inhaling deeply, Rafe leaned back in his chair. "Something has been brought to my attention, that I feel warrants a discussion."

"Oh? And what would that be exactly?" He stared at his father warily.

Instead of answering right away Rafe asked, "What is it you're not telling me?" He looked at his son then, with an expression that said he knew something that Breydon knew he wasn't going to like.

Confused, Breydon stood there for a moment without saying anything and silence filled the room. For a second, he became anxious that Hialey might have finally broken down and said something to his family about his secret. He quickly dismissed the notion, as in the end, he knew he could thoroughly trust her with that, and his life, if ever need be.

Taking a deep breath himself, he finally responded. "Honestly, I don't know what you're talking about."

Rafe came up out of his chair, throwing the calculator he'd just picked up across the room and glared at him. "Enough," he hollered, his patience nonexistent where this issue was concerned. "You best start talking, boy or I'm going to have your brother march you straight down to that jail cell in handcuffs for all the world to see!"

Startled by the sudden outburst and alarmed at such a quick turn it had taken, he stared at his dad with a look of utter bewilderment. "What in the world?" he said after a moment but was cut off before he could say any more.

"If you think, you can continue this sort of behavior, and that there aren't going to be ramifications from it, then you're sadly mistaken."

Taken aback by his dad's words and self-righteous tone, he narrowed his gaze at him and responded in kind. "First of all, you know full well Dart couldn't arrest me without charging me with something first. Second, a man's got a right to know what he's being accused of, before being arrested, and third, to what behavior specifically are you referring?" he finished heatedly as the lawyer in him began kicking in.

Rafe stood with his knuckles on his hips and picked up a paper from his desk. "Our recent tenant vacated the premises rather suddenly, as you well know. When she left there was damage to the property. When I called to have it repaired, Cody informed me it had already been repaired by someone else. At the same time, the cleaning lady was already there, and wanting to know what to do with the old mattress, as someone had been kind enough to have a new one delivered."

Breydon did a double take as he stared at his dad. Rafe continued, not missing his reaction, "When I called the hospital to try and pay her bill, I was informed it had already been covered in full by an anonymous party." He narrowed his gaze upon his son and shook the paper in front of him. "Would you care to explain this?"

"Explain what, exactly? What is it that you think I did in the first place?" Feeling more than a little affronted by the conversation, he wondered why his father felt he needed to cover her medical bill in the first place.

"I want to know, why you felt the need to take care of these things behind my back, for starters. And, as for the incident with, Ms. Rohann…"

"Wait a minute." Breydon shook his hand in the air. "I didn't have anything to do with any of that. As for Ms. Rohann, I had absolutely *nothing* to do with her. Furthermore, I resent the implication." He stared at his father angrily while shouting him down. Without realizing it he'd moved towards his dad's desk and found himself leaning over it, glaring at him in indignation.

"Nice try." Rafe pointed at the phone without taking his gaze off of his son. "I have Cody Howard himself, quoted as saying, 'Did Breydon have another incident here and forget to tell you he took care of it again?'"

Breydon paled noticeably and stepped back from the desk. He had the appearance of a man quickly sinking in quicksand. "That … that has nothing to do with this."

Rafe's eyes slanted at his son, confused by his response. Exasperated, he sighed and spoke in a plaintive manner. "Why won't you talk to me? Tell me what happened? Is this about this side effect you're having, from being able to see the angels?"

Recoiling, he wondered if his dad realized how close he'd managed to touch upon that issue.

Reeling back he gave his father a dejected look and pointed at the paper his father still held. "I may be sick, but I'm not that sick. I cannot believe you'd think I'd do that. I'd never cheat on my wife, none of us ever would. Regardless of whether we're Christian men or not, that's what *you* taught us!"

Staring blankly back at his son, Rafe became thoughtful. His son's response to his accusations had been most illuminating. Gazing off toward the balcony doors, he pondered the situation as his son continued to glare at him.

"Dad," Breydon said finally, gaining his attention. "I'm the Prosecuting Attorney of Breckenridge County," he hollered angrily. "And I found my own twin sister, brutally raped out in that barn, nearly fifteen years ago. What could possibly make you think that I, of all people, could ever take advantage of a woman like that?"

Chapter 16

A half an hour later, Dante Blackthorne was heading down the stairs to the kitchen when he ran into Hialey. Seeing her shrink back, placing her hands in front of her as if trying to ward him off, he chuckled humorously.

"To what, do I owe this greeting?" He bent down enough to chuck her playfully on the nose.

Fixing him with a feisty glare, Hialey retorted back, "I figure I better warn you off of any attempt to pull me into a heated discussion."

"Heated discussion about what, exactly?" Dante gave her a perplexed look and smiled affectionately. The tiny woman was a true delight to be around sometimes.

"Oh, I don't know," Hialey quipped. Dropping her arms and shrugging she smiled. Her eyes filled with mischief. "I figured it was the right thing to say, considering."

"Considering what?" He laughed, bewildered by what she'd said.

"I'm telling you, it's the atmosphere in this house, man. It's like, ripe for a fight, you know?" She walked down the stairs beside him, her voice full of excitement. "A little while ago, I hear Meg come running in the house, shouting for Chase. I walked by their room a bit later, and I hear them in a heated discussion," she said conspiratorially.

"Really? Meg and Chase fighting, that's pretty rare, isn't it?" Dante watched curiously as her head bobbed up and down.

"Yeah, and at the same time, Rafe comes looking for Breydon, and pulls him into the study." She said as her eyes went wide.

Dante cringed inwardly, thinking to himself how that didn't sound good.

"Now, mind you, I wasn't eavesdropping or anything." Hialey paused a moment on the stairs, leaning back as though to make a point.

"Oh, of course not." His eyes twinkled with.

"But, whatever Rafe said to my husband, did not make him happy. That man was shouting!" She sounded awestruck. Dante could see why, because frankly, he was in awe too as no one ever dared raise their voice to Rafe Blackthorne.

"No one yells at dad." He shook his head in disbelief.

"I'm telling you, he did. You know," she paused again, peering up at him thoughtfully, her eyes lighting with excitement. "This could make for a very interesting evening." She raised her eyebrows playfully.

"By interesting, do you mean, uncomfortable and awkward?" He wiggled his eyebrows right back at her as they stepped down into the kitchen at the same time, laughing. As they both glanced into the kitchen, they saw Royce and Crisalya hard at work, preparing the nights meal. Megorah sat at the bar stool, adding what appeared to be a whipped potato filling to several trays of potato skins.

"What do you want?" Megorah spat at Dante. She glared at him angrily, and then turned back to the potatoes, as though not caring what he had to say.

Both Hialey and Dante turned and looked at each other, eyes wide. "I'm going with uncomfortable and awkward," Hialey said. They both nodded their heads in unison and rolled their eyes.

Coming around the counter, Dante moved to take up a seat at the bar stool. As soon as he sat down, Megorah shot daggers at him with her eyes, lifted her tray, and moved everything over to the table to work instead. Dante glanced over at Royce and Crisalya, mouthing the words, "What did I do?"

Seeing Royce peer over at Meg, he shrugged, while continuing to fashion crescent rolls on a tray. Crisalya, on the other hand, glanced back and forth between Meg and Dante several times before fixing him with a rather curious stare.

Having witnessed the entire by-play, Hialey finally stamped her feet and loudly said, "Okay. What have I missed here?" she asked, drawing everyone's attention.

Sighing, in what could only be construed as exasperation, Megorah asked, as she finished the last two potatoes. "What do you mean?"

"Clearly, the women are mad at Dante for some reason." She said in an imperious tone as she pointed towards him. "So, can I know why I should be mad at him too?"

"Gee, thanks Hialey. I'm feeling the love over here," Dante said in aggravation.

"Love!" Megorah scoffed loudly, dropping her utensils with a bang. "And what, could a man like you, possibly know about love?"

"Excuse me? What is that supposed to mean?" Dante could feel everyone staring at him. Something had clearly gotten under her skin today.

Pushing away from her chair angrily, Megorah stood facing him. "How could you, Dante? I just don't understand. You know what I went through, you were there..." she paused then, as her lips trembled and tears threatened at her eyes. "And you're getting married, Dante. What would Alaina think, if she knew?"

Staring at her, utterly confounded, Dante stood and confronted his sister. "First of all, I think I'd really like to know what kind of man you think I am, exactly, and secondly..."

"You know full well," Megorah declared, interrupting him as she shouted. "What were you thinking? How could you?" Wheeling around, she fled out the patio door into the yard.

Spinning around, Dante looked at each of them and asked, "Can someone please tell me what is going on here?"

Dante watched Crisalya peer over at him with a hurt expression on her face. Throwing down her towel, she followed Meg without saying a word.

Hialey glanced from Dante to Royce, then back again. Plastering an angry expression on her face she stuck her hand in the air and hollered, as though somewhat apprehensive, "Yeah!" Then she stomped out of the kitchen after the other two women.

Royce stared down at all the unprepared trays, then back out onto the patio wearily. Resting his hands on the counter, he didn't look up right away. When he did, Dante was staring at him expectantly.

"I couldn't say for sure, that I know exactly what's going on, but I've managed to piece a few things together over the last few days," Royce said finally while glancing out the patio door. "I gather, they think they have the rest of the story, though I'm willing to bet each one of them is wrong."

"Okay, well, give me what you've got because so far I'm completely out of the loop here." Dante was anxious to finally have some answers.

"You really are ... out of the loop that is? You have no idea what's going on?" Royce asked cautiously. Seeing Dante shake his head Royce raised his eyebrows. Lifting a piece of dough, he began rolling another crescent. "Wash your hands and help me out here." He nodded toward the empty trays.

"Are you kidding? This rehearsal dinner wasn't even my idea," he exclaimed in frustration.

Noting Dante's mulish expression Royce asked, "Do you want answers? If so, then wash."

Groaning as he scowled in resignation, Dante did as he was told and began helping Royce prepare his own rehearsal dinner.

Royce didn't start right away. He was trying to formulate how best to explain what he did know. "Here's what I know for sure. There's a new woman in town, about our age; very beautiful, with ebony black hair and green eyes. She arrived in town, apparently, the same night you and Alaina did."

Dante turned towards him in alarm.

"Now, just hold on. She's from Maryland. It seems she's the one who rented Rafe's cabin."

Nodding in recollection, Dante rolled two crescents at once as he talked. "Dad mentioned something about that the afternoon we came back from the doctor's office. He'd said she'd had some bad luck or something, and Meg was trying to find her another place."

"I think she did just that today actually, because Meg called me in distress, needing help with her." Royce finished rolling the rest of his crescents and placed them in the oven.

"Why? What kind of help?"

"Veta was trying to get across the street and back to the motel, while in the middle of a panic attack, and hobbling with an injured knee."

"How did that happen?" Dante asked, continuing to work on his tray of crescents.

"What, the leg?" Royce shook his head. "I don't know, but I think it was already an issue. She was limping the first morning she came into the shop. Anyway, I barely managed to get her out of the street, before a car nearly hit us."

"You're kidding?"

"Wish I was. She was so close to getting hit, Dante. I nearly got clipped myself, just trying to help." Resting his hands on the counter momentarily, Royce hesitated then made a decision. "I think demons are messing with her."

"What makes you think that?" Dante's attention was on high alert at this piece of news.

"Because, when I reached her in the street, I felt a frigid cold engulf me," Royce said pointedly, knowing full well Dante would know what that meant. "And because she's had way too much bad luck since she's been in town."

"We need to get Drinian involved then. He might be able to help her out." Dante's concern was evident in his tone.

Nodding agreement, Royce continued. "I got her back to the motel all right, but she was still pretty well in full panic attack mode. I had to leave her because I had to get back here for this," he said guiltily, indicating the trays laden with food.

"What does all this have to do with me?" Dante finished his tray and placed it in the oven.

Royce took a deep breath and went on. "Crisalya tells me, this same gal arrived at the hospital emergency room by ambulance Tuesday evening. Cris was on call that night and so was Chase. She'd torn a contact earlier in the day, so Cris had to switch out her colored ones she usually wears, for her clear ones."

Dante nodded again, remembering that his sister had often been self-conscious about the looks she'd get from patients over her eyes.

"Anyway, she goes into the ER room with Chase to attend to this, Veta, and the woman freaks out when she sees Crisalya's eyes. So much so, Chase has to ask her to leave because she appeared almost frightened of her."

"Of Crisalya? She's about as gentle a soul, as anyone I've ever met."

Royce shrugged and continued. "The rest of the night, she said it was like Chase was trying to avoid her." He stopped for a moment in his work then and turned towards his brother-in-law. "Now, she's not really allowed to tell me personal stuff about patients, but what she did say, was that she found out later on from the nurse that switched with her, that it turned out something pretty bad had happened to her, the night before at the cabin."

"Something bad. As in what?" Dante asked in alarm, trying to keep up.

"I couldn't say for sure. But what I can tell you, is I overheard Rafe telling the cleaning lady over the phone to have the delivery men toss the mattress from the cabin in the dumpster and burn it." Royce paused for effect, exchanging a meaningful look with Dante.

Stretching his neck uncomfortably, Dante heaved a heavy sigh.

"Not long after that," Royce continued, "I'm walking by his study again, and he's asking my brother, Cody if the cleaning lady knew who fixed the patio door on the cabin he'd called him out to fix."

"Wait, what?" Both Dante's voice and expression were incredulous. He stared at Royce, holding the crescent dough as it dangled limply from his hand. "Wait a minute, this Veta, she never met Megorah before today, isn't that right? Because Freedom had rented it to her?" He was starting to put things together in his head. Seeing Royce nod, he stared at him for a moment. Suddenly his eyes grew wide in alarm.

"Yup, that's right, you're getting there," Royce said, all the while continuing to prepare food trays. "Keep following those clues and you come to a fairly disturbing conclusion."

"The conclusion being that this woman, Veta, was likely assaulted at the cabin the first night she was there, by someone who was strong enough to come in through the patio door. That same someone having to be a Blackthorne because…" his shoulders slumped then, and he glanced at Royce. "…because she's afraid of our eyes." Pausing, he watched Royce nod in agreement. "And Megorah thinks it was me, why?" Dante was both hurt and disturbed by her assumption.

"Honestly, I couldn't really say for sure, but you have to understand…" Royce placed more pans in the ovens, then moved on to building a giant bowl of salad. "Dartanian has been married a lot longer, and she grew up with your brothers. I think she'll have a harder time believing the other three to be capable of it than she would you. Your relationship with Alaina is new, and well, clearly complicated. Plus, we haven't seen you much over the years." Seeing Dante's wounded expression, Royce turned to him and said, "If it's any consolation, I really don't think it was you. The fact is though, someone clearly messed with this woman, or she wouldn't be acting the way she was today. She was running scared. No doubt about that."

Dante was uneasy and no longer inclined towards finishing the crescent rolls. "You think it's still one of us though, don't you?"

Sighing heavily, Royce wiped his hands on a towel and leaned against the counter, staring at the floor in contemplation. "Man, I hate to think it'd be any of you, but yes, I would say, it had to have been a Blackthorne. According to Cody, both Breydon and Rafe said the door was completely wrenched from the track. An inordinate amount of strength would be necessary in order to do that and no one else in the county has eyes like the Blackthorne children."

"You said you don't think it's me. You're closer to them Royce, so who do you think it was?" Dante asked directly, knowing he needed to get to the bottom of this quickly. Royce merely stood there for a moment, staring out the patio door. Then finally he turned towards Dante.

Dante fixed Royce with a stare, but his angelic guide wasn't giving him anything.

Continuing to dry his hands in the towel he was using, Royce answered in a roundabout way. "Rafe taught you all some extremely good morals and values as you were growing up; especially where women are concerned. Never hit or hurt a woman, always ask first, never push them if they're unsure, and most importantly, never cheat on your wife or girlfriend."

"Yes, that's true. God knows, I'd never cheat on my future wife. I love her too much, even if she doesn't know it yet," Dante said in full agreement. He remembered the look on Alaina's face as she'd run back into the bathroom and recalled the thought she'd hoped to keep from him, as it ran through his head. Smiling stupidly at the memory, he just looked back at Royce, knowing full well how much she loved him too.

"I'm really glad to hear that. It's nice to know you've finally found your place. That being said, here's my question to you, who else isn't married?"

Staring back at his brother-in-law, their eyes locked. Wincing openly, Dante groaned softly. "Drin."

Chapter 17

Drinian stood just outside the kitchen doors, listening in on Royce and Dante's conversation. Having heard everything, he turned suddenly in a panic, only to find his path barred by Alaina. He didn't know how long she'd been standing there for sure, but by the expression on her face, he'd guess she'd heard everything as well.

"Quite a lot going on in this house tonight, wouldn't you say?" she asked quietly, not wanting to attract the attention of the men in the other room.

"So it would seem." Drinian's response was cautious and he stood straighter than normal.

4r5Merely nodding in agreement along with him, she stood staring at him for a moment, as if trying to gauge what to say next.

"You know, Crisalya doesn't know what to believe. She can't imagine any of her brothers behaving that way. But Rafe and Dartanian, well, they think it's Breydon and as you know, Meg and Chase think its Dante." Alaina paused. "And Hialey was unaware until now, just as he was." She indicated the kitchen doorway. "Lylia, it seems, has her own worries right now and rightfully so." She stopped suddenly which left Drinian to wonder what was occupying Lylia's thoughts. "Royce was the only one who thought it was you, until now." She tilted her head to one side and glanced at him as though attempting to size him up. "I wonder why?"

"I'm sure I don't know…"

"It's not me, you know," Alaina said softly, cutting him off. Her eyes filled with sadness, as she stared back into his. It was as though she could see through him, and it scared Drinian. What secrets could she unravel, that were better off left hidden?

"I don't know what you mean." He shook his head slowly, eyeing her with unease.

"I think you do." She showed him the red rose she'd found on her pillow that morning. Alaina watched him stare down at the rose then back up at her.

Shifting nervously, he could feel the anxiety building in his chest. Taking a deep breath he took a step toward her as she continued to hold in her hand the black baccara rose he'd laid upon her pillow that morning.

"Alaina, I could…"

She cut him off again.

"No, Drin," she said apologetically, giving him a slow, mournful smiled. "I believe, I am merely the beginning." She took his hand in hers and placed the black baccara rose in it. "Not the end."

Puzzled by her words, Drinian looked at her in distress as he glanced towards the kitchen and back again. She shook her head at him, smiling brightly. He marveled at how just a few days in Crisalya and Royce's care could make such a difference in her. She seemed so much healthier now, compared to when she'd first arrived.

"It's okay, no one needs to know." She stepped back from him, placing distance between them for good measure.

Inhaling and exhaling deeply, Drinian nodded his head in understanding. They both knew he had enough to worry about right now, without adding to the mix the clearly ridiculous proposal he'd made to her that morning. Recalling the story in his mother's journals from two hundred years ago, he'd thought and acted irrationally. The demons had insisted that in order for the prophecy to continue on, he would need to marry Alaina, rather than his brother, Dante. But they had been messing with him, trying to confuse him. Berating himself for not listening to his father, once again, Drinian became agitated. He knew better than to listen to anything the demons said. It was why he was always to ignore them as best he could.

Upon further reflection of his own, at that moment, he realized it simply didn't make sense that he'd need to take his brother's fiancée for his wife. Squeezing his tired eyes shut tightly, he placed a hand to his brow in distress and confusion. Obviously, the demons were messing with him. He was angry with himself for falling for their tricks once again and weary of trying to decipher their true intentions. Standing straighter, he moved to leave but felt the palm of her hand stay him from his course.

"I have one question for you, however," Alaina spoke quickly, determined not to let him get away yet. "Be honest, did you…" she paused then, carefully choosing her words. "Were you intimate with this woman, this Veta Rohann?" She searched his eyes.

The look of anguish in his face was unmistakable. His face colored significantly, and he turned his head away from her in shame.

"Oh, Drin…"

"I didn't mean to. I knew… I knew I shouldn't." He shook his head, trying desperately to tamp down his emotions. He refused to break down in front of her, as the fresh humiliation of his proposal being rebuffed still stung. He had the look of a man haunted by more than just shadows.

"Then why?"

Drinian managed to change his facial expression, in order to replicate indifference. "I honestly don't know. It's been ingrained in us to respect women since I can first remember. I knew it was wrong," he admitted finally, "But it's not what everyone thinks. You have to believe me."

"What do you mean?" She was trying to give him the benefit of the doubt. There were always two sides to every story, after all.

"We were both troubled and in pain; lonely. She asked me to stay. So I did, but I was only trying to comfort her. And once I got started I just…"

"Couldn't stop?" She finished for him as he sighed heavily.

Face flaming Drinian bowed his head, needing to take his eyes off her. "I've never been…" he started, and then huffed out his massive chest anxiously. Clearing his throat he tried to continue, as his eyes misted. "I've never been with…"

"Oh… I see," Alaina said in surprise. Gazing upon him tenderly, she could see the raw emotion in his face, and her heart hurt for him. The situation he found himself in was clearly troubling him, and he seemed wounded by it.

Inhaling sharply, Drinian spoke quietly. "It was like something was egging me on."

"Is it possible?"

Unsure exactly what she was referring to he gave her an inquisitive look. "What do you mean? Is what possible?"

"That something was egging you on."

"You mean, like the shadows?" He shook his head. "No, the demons had left me by then." Drinian paused in thought and found he was repeating himself. "They left me." Glancing back at Alaina in astonishment, he came to a revelation.

"What is it, Drin?"

"They do that sometimes, the demons. They'll leave me suddenly and without warning as though they're being chased away by something. I don't know what or who does it for sure, but it happens usually when I am most tired and in need of rest. They don't allow me to sleep much you see; the shadows that is. At one point, I thought it might be the messengers, you know? The angels Breydon sees. But I'm not sure."

Alaina pondered thoughtfully. "Is it possible, whatever chased them away might have encouraged you? Drinian, the shadows, they can influence you can't they? To do things you might not otherwise do?"

"Oh, yes. Especially when I am at my weakest."

"Were you tired that night?"

"Exhausted." He rolled his eyes and gave a long-suffering sigh. "You and Dante arrived home that night. I hadn't slept for a couple of days. Actually," he mused. "I hadn't slept well for the past month. It seemed like, whatever it was that normally kept them at bay in the evenings wasn't doing its job well. They would show up one night and chase the dark spirits away, but then disappear for two to three nights, before they'd return to withhold them again."

Alaina contemplated what significance there might be in that. "Angels and demons. Whether one or the other might have influenced you, remains to be seen. I cannot imagine it would have been the angels. In the end, though, God has given us free will. We make choices, Drinian. Sometimes they are not always good ones, but sometimes God has a way of making a lot of good come from the bad. This may turn out all right in the end."

There was silence between them. After a while, Drinian found his voice again. "Listen, Alaina, about what happened with Veta…" he said, but again she let him off the hook.

"It's not my place to say anything. When it's time for it to come out, it will."

Her statement startled him. "I don't see that there's a need…"

"Oh, but there is…it will come out. It's inevitable. The question is, will you and Veta be ready when that happens?"

Floating nearby, Maleeka smiled warmly, gazing upon the two of them, as they dispersed. "Good girl, Alaina. That's just what he needed to hear."

- - -

Hialey stared at the two women before her as Megorah informed them of what had happened at her office that day. Listening to them discussing openly, back and forth, what they knew, she was amazed they weren't being more considerate of her own position. After all, her husband was one of the Blackthorne brothers who was presently being considered as suspects. Though somewhat relieved to see neither one believed Breydon was the culprit in question, Hialey began to form her own conclusions.

Knowing what she did about men and their ways, from her previous work experience as an exotic dancer, she thought she had a pretty good idea of what had happened. Listening intently, as Megorah went on to tell them what Veta had said to her in her car, she wondered how Veta would be feeling to have her private conversation and experience discussed with someone else.

After hearing Meg explain the condition Veta had been in when she'd entered the hot tub, Hialey winced inwardly. The poor woman had been ripe to be taken advantage of. She could almost sympathize with how she must have felt when she woke up the morning after.

Hialey recalled her conversation with Veta when she'd picked her up from the hospital that Wednesday morning. She'd seemed like such a nice woman. Hialey had high hopes of a possible friendship developing from that. However, the more she listened, the more she realized that a friendship might be impossible.

Presently, Meg and Crisalya did not know that Hialey had given Veta a ride home at Drinian's request. She intended to keep it that way for now, as it seemed she had a dilemma of her own. One thing she knew for certain, neither Dante or Dart was guilty of taking advantage of Veta. As much as Hialey hated to admit it, her husband seemed a much more likely candidate, which disturbed her a great deal. She knew he would never intentionally cheat on her, but his problem tended to inhibit his common sense at times. And she knew Breydon had been out in the woods that night, trying to walk off some of his aggression.

What bothered her was that Breydon had never said anything to her about what had been going on. He told her the cabin had been rented, but he never told her about what he and Rafe found at the cabin, and what their suspicions were. Standing there next to her sisters-in-law, Hialey closed her eyes, imagining what had transpired. She pictured the view someone walking by the cabin might have gotten, as Veta had entered the water, naked with a wine bottle in hand.

Grimacing, she realized that Breydon would have had an extremely tempting view. Knowing Breydon's tendency towards heroism where women were concerned, she could imagine him tearing off the patio door and pulling her from the water. The end result might have been inevitable considering the state he'd been in that night.

The fact that Drinian had requested she give the woman a ride back to her motel, however, was what was giving her a moment's pause. She couldn't imagine Breydon being okay with that if he had been the one. She was glad she hadn't gotten around to mentioning it yet.

Her mind wandered back to her conversation with Drinian that morning. Hialey recalled he'd been trying really hard to act as though, it didn't matter to him either way, whether she helped Veta out that morning. Eyes narrowing, Hialey shook her head unable to discount the possibility that it might have just as easily been Drinian. He didn't sleep much and tended to wander the woods as well. This commonality, she realized, played well into Alaina's theory, that Breydon was being tormented by an ability he wasn't meant to have.

"What is it Hialey." Megorah's question drew her attention back to the conversation at hand.

Hialey realized that Meg and Crisalya had been watching her, shaking her head in silence.

She shrugged it off. "I had no idea the extent of this. That poor woman," she said with real feeling. "Imagine what she must be going through right now. It sounds to me like she's absolutely mortified over the situation and wanting to keep this to herself, you know?" She hoped they'd get the hint.

Feeling properly chastised, both Megorah and Crisalya glanced guiltily at each other.

"I'm so sorry, Hialey," Crisalya exclaimed without warning. "I really don't think Breydon would ever do something like that."

"I know. As much as I hate to say it, your theory *is* entirely possible though. But again it's just a theory. In the end, it could be either one. Really it could be any of them." She shrugged, trying to appear unfettered by the news. Both women looked at her with doubtful expressions. "Come on guys. They're men! Yeah, they may have been raised and taught never to take advantage of a woman, but even the best of men can fall unintentionally. God gave us all free will after all. Anyone can be tempted, even a married man who loves his wife. I saw it happen over and over again when I used to dance."

"You did?" Megorah was intrigued. Hialey rarely spoke of when she used to get paid to pole dance for men.

"It wasn't just single men that came into the bar. We'd get guys who had girlfriends, wives and boyfriend's, for that matter." Chuckling inwardly, she watched both women make faces at her last statement. "All we really know from what you've said is that it had to have been one of them. To make blatant accusations and suppositions is unfair to all of them, without having all the facts."

"Now you just sound like Breydon." Crisalya was annoyed.

"What can I say? It comes from being married to a lawyer." She smiled as she wrapped her arms around both women's shoulders. "Now, I have the feeling Royce could use some help getting this dinner around. How about we drop this for a while, head in, and help him out? What do you say?" Silently agreeing, they all walked slowly together back to the patio.

Unknown to the women as they walked away, the angel Woreash, having left Veta in Phillipe's capable care, was close by. Gazing at them, as they disappeared through the patio doors into the kitchen, he then lifted his head toward the heavens.

"All right Lord. Is that everyone?" Holding steady where he was, he soon began to chuckle. "Which hidden room is he in?" Receiving his answer, he promptly disappeared.

In the blink of an eye, Woreash found himself standing over Rafe Blackthorne in the secret room between his bedroom and the library. Gazing down upon the man, sitting reclined in his desk chair; he could see him staring at the flat screen above him on the wall.

"Did you catch all that?" Woreash asked of him. "What did you miss that you need to see?" Peering at the screen himself, he noted Rafe was watching the women as they settled in to assist Royce with the rest of dinner.

"Hhhmm. So you saw the discussion in the kitchen between Dante and Royce," he said quietly next to the man.

"Is it possible," Rafe spoke aloud, drawing a troubled breath. "Lord, have I misjudged my sons? Do I owe Breydon an apology?"

"Rafe, who was in the living room just now?" The angel prodded, gently attempting to guide him.

Making a clicking noise with his tongue, Rafe sat up momentarily. Grabbing a remote from his desk, he pointed it toward the screen. As the picture expanded out and readjusted, the next view was of a full detailed diagram of the main level. Watching, as the heat signature of two figures quickly moved away from the kitchen doors in the living room, he frowned.

"Who has been eavesdropping in the living room?" he asked thoughtfully, quickly clicking with the arrow on the screen, so that he might catch who they were. Seeing Alaina take the front stairs to her bedroom, he also caught Drinian moving around the steps and heading down the hall towards the main floor library.

Debating what to do next, Rafe sat pondering his dilemma.

"What do you say, Lord? Would you say this instance requires a rewind?" Expelling air through his mouth, he sat back again in his chair, kicking his feet up against the wall adjoining the library. Running his hands through his hair, he grimaced.

Sidling up closer to him, Woreash bent down next to Rafe's ear. "You are the head of this house. What do you need to know, in order to protect the people within it?"

Rafe turned towards the angel as though he could see him, his crystal-clear blue eyes appearing troubled. He gazed through him at the family picture he had hanging on the opposite wall.

"Ah, Lord. I hate eavesdropping and spying on my own children." He stood suddenly Directing his gaze towards the ceiling of his hidden room, he continued. "It makes me feel like some kind of a perverted voyeur, rather than a normal father."

Still holding the remote, he pointed it again towards the screen. Clicking on the menu on the right side, he arrowed down to the recording section. When he'd installed the cameras around his house many years back, it had been for protection and security alone. Rafe had never imagined he'd have to utilize them in this way, but he'd found there had been a few times over the years, where circumstances had warranted this kind of use.

Locating the footage from the front living room, he rewound it till he saw Alaina coming upon Drinian, as he eavesdropped outside the door. Taking a deep breath, he watched and listened. He could hear Royce and Dante speaking briefly from the kitchen. After hearing what was said between Alaina and Drinian when he'd attempted to leave, Rafe groaned.

"Son, what were you thinking?" Rafe exploded in disgust. "Did you completely miss the lesson on respecting women?"

"He is a man after all, and an extremely lonely, as well as, tormented one, at that," Woreash chided, trying to get the Blackthorne patriarch to calm down and see reason. "The circumstances are troubling, yes, but you still do not have the full story."

Dropping the remote on the small narrow desk behind him, Rafe turned, running his hands through his hair once again in agitation. "What am I supposed to do with this knowledge, Lord? Do I confront him?"

Gazing upon Rafe curiously, Woreash looked toward the ceiling for guidance. "Lord, what say you?" After a moment he nodded his understanding. "Wait, for now, Rafe. They both need a little time. Now, find out who else knows. What was the discussion between the women in the yard?"

Expelling another uneasy breath, Rafe stared at the floor, clearly disturbed by the situation. Glancing at his watch, he noted the time. Returning the view on the screen to the kitchen, briefly, he saw his two daughters and Hialey, assisting Royce and Dante with the rest of dinner prep.

"All right, Lord. Looks like there might be enough time to determine what was said in the yard. Returning to the menu, he found the footage he needed. Sitting back in his chair, he kicked back once again and listened to what had been said. Though, a bit difficult at times to make out, what was said being at such a distance, he managed to decipher what he missed by reading their lips.

Chuckling finally in irritation, he leaned further back in his chair and groaned. "My girls think it was, Dante. Royce, Dante and now Hialey suspect it might be, Drin, and Alaina knows it was him but doesn't intend on saying anything. Dart still thinks it was Breydon, and Chase suspects its Dante, but Breydon is now thinking, it might have been, Dart. Good grief what a mess!" He threw his arms and head back in frustration. "I feel like I'm in the middle of a soap opera."

Switching the view on the screen back to the kitchen, he sighed in exasperation upon hearing Megorah ask if anyone had seen where their father had disappeared to.

"Shoot, the rehearsal and dinner." He scowled, having nearly forgotten. "Better get down there."

Looking around him on the floor, he realized his slippers were missing, and then glanced in annoyance at the screen. He noted Megorah was now on her way up the kitchen stairs. Rafe opted to head through the passage door of his closet, which led into his bedroom, rather than going through the one into the library. Tossing a towel around his shoulders, he opened his bedroom door, managing to catch her as she was about to enter his study.

"Yes, yes, Meg," he called down the hallway to her. "Go back down, I'm on my way."

"Dad, everything is running so late tonight. The children are getting hungry."

"I know, now go."

Watching her disappear, he strolled slowly down the hall after her and peered around the corner. Hearing someone possibly coming from the front stairwell, he peered around the wall to see Alaina walking from her room and heading down the stairs towards the front entrance.

She grinned at him. "Hi, Rafe; beat you down there."

He smiled back at her. "I'm sure you will. I'll be down shortly." Leaning back, he glanced around him before tiptoeing along the hallway past the back stairwell that led to the kitchen. Quickly entering his secret room just past the stairs, he closed and latched the door, then grabbed the slippers he'd left there earlier in the day. After peering at the main floor diagram of his house, he opted instead to drop through the passage in the floor to the bathroom below him, rather than to waste time taking the stairs.

Landing softly on the tiled bathroom floor, as a panther would, he propped one foot on the toilet and leaned his other knee against the wall for support. Reaching up, he returned the paneling to the ceiling so no one could see the passage. Hopping quietly down from the toilet, he was placing his slippers back on his feet when he stood suddenly, staring at the mirror in front of him as the darkness surrounded him.

"Wait a minute," he said aloud suddenly, frowning in confusion. "Am I to gather Drinian proposed to Alaina this morning? Lord, why in the world would he do that, he doesn't even know her?"

Perplexed and not paying attention, he opened the bathroom door without thinking. Exiting the bathroom, he was standing in the hallway near the kitchen, when he heard Alaina call to him as she stepped down from the last of the stairs.

"How did you get down here before me?"

Thinking quickly, he replied. "There *is* another set of stairs."

"I didn't see you just now on the back stairs," Chase could be heard to say from behind him, causing Rafe to turn.

Not skipping a beat, Rafe grinned at them both while extending both hands above him and shaking them. "It's magic," he exclaimed good-naturedly, using a mysterious voice as he said it. "It is, after all, in the air. Besides," he continued, his eyes twinkling with mystery at their quizzical stares. "This old man is a lot faster than he looks. Now come, I suspect we'll be having the rehearsal dinner before the rehearsal."

Chapter 18

On Sunday Veta woke early and decided to take Lylia up on her suggestion to try out her church. Pleased by the service and welcomed warmly by many of the regular attendees, she stayed for fellowship afterwards. While munching on a cookie and gingerly sipping at a hot tea, she met a few more of the church members, one of whom recommended several local resale shops. For the rest of the week, she found herself wandering through the various shops in order to locate the items she needed.

Managing to find a couch with sections that reclined, a small table with four chairs, and a coffee table, in addition to, a couple of tall lamps, Veta realized she'd need a way to get them to her apartment. Fortunately, the owner of one of the shops was aware of a delivery service that could deliver the items for her the next day, for a small fee. By the end of the week, she'd managed to replace most of the essential items needed that she'd lost in order to furnish her apartment.

Tired of take-out food, she headed to the grocery store to fill her fridge and to get some Alka-Seltzer for her stomach. She'd noticed it had been upset the last few mornings and was hoping it might help ease her discomfort. Having spent much of her time otherwise cooped up in her new home, she found she was starting to get a little stir crazy by Friday, especially since she had not replaced her television yet. Deciding to go out for lunch, she headed to the Coffee Haven, where she ran into Lylia again as she was placing her lunch order.

"Why don't you join me?" Lylia asked as she paid for her meal from Chastity. "My husband couldn't make it today because of work." She was clearly disappointed.

"It's his loss then." Veta took her raspberry tea to the table and sat down across from Lylia.

Lylia gave a rueful smile before sitting nervously, noting that her hands shook a bit. It had been a rough week back at the Blackthorne Ranch. She constantly found herself running into either Alaina or Dante around the house and grounds. Their ability to be able to discern what she was thinking all the time was starting to grate on her nerves. As a result, Lylia was getting anxious to move back to their own house, rather than staying at the ranch house with everyone. She'd hoped to head back this weekend with Kayla, but then Megorah got the bright idea to have a Memorial Day cook-out on Sunday since they'd missed being able to do that due to the wedding.

Eyeing Lylia, as she took a bite of her sandwich, Veta couldn't help but notice she appeared cross for some reason. After asking if everything was okay, Lylia proceeded to explain about the Sunday cook-out.

"I thought the family gathering you mentioned was for Memorial Day weekend." Veta appeared a little surprised.

"Oh, no, my brother-in-law returned home with a fiancée quite suddenly this past Monday. They needed to get married kind of quick, so they had the ceremony Saturday night at the house. It was a small gathering for just family, you know, very private." Lylia noted her curious expression and realized she nearly said too much. "It's a long story," she answered nervously, having discovered the near blunder.

Lylia couldn't really explain why they had to marry so quickly. To do so, would either risk sharing the secret about Alaina's origins with a stranger or find herself sharing about the couples unplanned pregnancy and Lylia abhorred gossip. Annoyed by this additional complication with Dante and his wife's situation, she chose to change the subject.

"We're having a big gathering at the house for the whole family on Sunday after church. You're welcome to come and meet my family," Lylia offered almost jokingly, thinking it might be nice to have someone there who was normal.

"You know what? That sounds like it could be fun," Veta said between bites. Thus far, she had yet to order anything from the Coffee Haven that she didn't like. She commented as such as well. The roast beef and Swiss sandwich with au jus sauce that she'd ordered today were delicious.

"Really?" Lylia said hopefully, pausing in eating.

"Yeah, it's fantastic! Do you want to try it?"

Laughing at the misunderstanding, she waved her off.

"No silly, I mean, do you really want to come Sunday?" Lylia asked more seriously.

Veta could tell Lylia really seemed excited about having her there for some reason. Shrugging, she gave her a grin.

"Why not, it might be nice to get out and meet some new people." Veta wiped her mouth. Relieved to finally have something in her belly, she noted it was starting to feel much better. When she'd awakened that morning, her stomach had been so upset she'd nearly gotten sick, so she hadn't bothered to eat any breakfast. Taking a long sip of her tea, she also noticed she just couldn't seem to get enough to drink lately, either.

Smiling brightly Lylia sat back in her chair, for the first time actually looking forward to the cook-out on Sunday. It'd be awfully nice having a fresh face out at the ranch to talk to.

"What are you doing with the rest of your day?" Lylia asked.

"Not sure. I figured I'd probably try and replace my television so I have something to watch this weekend." Putting her sandwich down, she sighed wearily.

Lylia looked at her new friend with sympathy. Having mentioned in their earlier conversations that her things had been stolen, she could only imagine how difficult it must be to have to furnish a new place on little to no funds.

"Getting expensive is it?"

"Yes. I wasn't planning on these expenses when I decided to move. I'll probably have to start looking for work, sooner than expected." Out of the corner of her eye, Veta thought she saw a shadowy form standing near the front of the shop outside. She did a double take, as the black figure had looked like a man, but without a face. Glancing in that direction again, she looked closer, no longer able to see anything as a chill rolled down her back. Tilting her head, while peering in that direction, she must have had an odd expression on her face because suddenly Lylia touched her shoulder.

"Are you okay?" There was concern in her voice as she spoke.

"What? Oh, sorry, it's just ... I thought I saw..." Veta's voice trailed off as she stared toward the windows. She could have sworn someone was standing there a moment ago, but now they were gone. Thinking that was odd, she tried to shake it off when she heard Lylia trying to get her attention.

"What is it? I can tell something is bothering you."

Veta stilled in her chair and peered at Lylia, coming back around to their original conversation. Not wanting her to think she was going crazy she contemplated how much she was willing to divulge. Wanting to keep things on a lighter note, she opted not to go into a lot of detail.

"I lost something that was of great value to me but wasn't really worth anything to anyone else; a memory sake, if you will. Of all the items that were taken, I just wish I had a way of getting them back somehow."

It was obvious to Lylia that there was more to it than that, but she could tell Veta wasn't quite ready to open up yet. Not wanting to pry, she pondered on the dilemma thoughtfully. After a moment an idea occurred to her as if it had been whispered in her ear.

"If it means that much to you, one thing you could try would be to put out an ad in the paper." Seeing Veta's confused expression, she elaborated. "You know, appeal to the thief's conscious somehow. Maybe they'd see it."

Sipping on her tea, Veta really thought hard about what she was suggesting. She stared at Lylia, transfixed. It seemed her eyes were playing tricks on her again because she could have sworn she'd just seen a bright light flash next to Lylia and wasn't sure quite what to make of it. Turning her thoughts back to Lylia's suggestion, she recalled the pastor had just covered in the sermon on

Sunday about how everyone has a conscious. Whether or not they listened to it made the difference. If she worded it just right she might be able to convince the thief to return, at least, the memory boxes if they knew they wouldn't get in trouble.

"You know what? That is an excellent idea," Veta said with excitement as she stood. "Can you point me toward the local paper?" she asked, clearing her things quickly from the table.

"You haven't even finished your sandwich." Lylia glanced up at Veta in surprise. Pulling out a pen and a pad of paper from her purse she began to write.

"That's okay. I'm getting full anyway so I'll finish it later. You gave me a really good idea and I want to move on it quickly." She smiled brightly.

Lylia ripped a piece of paper from her pad and handed it to Veta.

"The first address is to the ranch. I'm assuming you can still map quest?"

"Yes, I found the library. They have computer access, and it's not too far from where I live."

"Good. The second there is directions to the local newspaper office. It's just downtown here, not far."

"Thanks so much, Lylia. You've been a real help." Veta said genuinely. Turning towards the door she spun around suddenly glancing over at Lylia. "I almost forgot. Should I bring something?"

"If you want, but you don't have to. My father-in-law always supplies everything. Maybe I'll see you at church," Lylia called.

"I'll be there." She happily turned back and moved to open the door of the coffee house.

Veta knew she shouldn't get her hopes up, but she just had a feeling if she gave them a bit of a story, she might be able to get her memory boxes returned to her. That was all she really wanted. Everything else could be replaced.

Halting abruptly, as Drinian's hulking frame appeared in the doorway, blocking her path; she stared up at him in surprise. Her face colored noticeably.

"You're ... you're leaving," Drinian stuttered. Both a look of surprise and disappointment crossed his handsome features.

Having made it a point to be somewhat allusive around the ranch since the wedding, Royce hadn't been able to catch up with him until that morning. Informing him of what had happened last Friday, Drinian had agreed to watch Veta from a distance, in order to see if she was having any further demon problems. So far there hadn't been too much activity but he'd caught one a moment before, attempting to wriggle its way into the Coffee Haven. He had taken pleasure at causing it pain.

"Yes, I was. I am, that is," she corrected herself, having trouble focusing as her chest heaved anxiously. Fumbling with her purse she dropped her drink, spilling it on him, managing to make a mess once again.

Grabbing for her purse, she reached for the cup as well, connecting with his fingers as he attempted to help her clean the mess up.

"I'm so sorry," Veta exclaimed, her face flaming brighter when she saw her tea staining the legs of his jeans. Her hands trembled nervously at his touch as he took her hand in his and helped her from the floor, noticing the brace was no longer on her leg.

Fixing her with his gorgeous eyes, he stared intently at her. "No, *I'm* sorry," he whispered quietly. He pulled her slightly towards him, trying not to be too obvious.

Eyes darting towards Lylia who was walking towards her with a towel in her hand, Veta smiled anxiously up at him. "It's okay. Really it is," she replied, feeling flustered in his presence, knowing full well he was apologizing for something else entirely. He was just as big as she remembered, and she was having difficulty thinking straight with him so close.

"Don't let this guy scare you." Lylia handed Drinian the towel, rather than Veta. "Look what you did, Drin. You must have scared the poor woman half to death," she chastised

Staring down at the towel in his hand, Drinian frowned back at Lylia in irritation. He then looked at Veta with a wounded expression, wondering if that was really the case.

"Oh, no! That's not ... I'm not afraid," Veta said quickly, hoping to erase the hurt expression from his brow.

"It's okay. Most women are," Drinian said, sounding forlorn. He bent down to soak up the tea with the towel and pick up the ice from the floor. "You want ... you want to take her to the counter and get her a new tea? Tell them I'll cover it." He directed his words toward Lylia.

"It's okay, really. I was on my way out anyway." Veta peered at her watch, wishing she could stick around. He looked so lost and hurt. She hadn't seen him until today and had hoped to talk with him about what had happened between them.

"No, he's right. The least he can do is buy you a new drink." Lylia shook her head in disapproval at Drinian. Guiding her towards the counter she asked Chastity for a new drink, telling her to put it on Drinian's tab.

Chastity giggled, glancing over at Drinian as he stood, holding the towel full of ice, looking dejected. "It's not the first time he's had to do this." She handed Veta her new drink. "Of Course, most women usually run away before he can replace their drink or food," she continued as she laughed. "I can't blame them really. He's nice to look at and all, but he gives even me the willies."

Seeing Lylia smiling as well, Veta became cross. "That's not funny," she said sharply, coming to Drinian's defense. "You shouldn't make fun of people. It's cruel and hurtful." Walking away without looking back, she didn't really care if everyone was staring or not. Casting a glance Drinian's way, she smiled at him sweetly as she passed.

"Thank you, for the drink. You didn't have to," she said shyly.

"You're welcome," he said softly. Peering down at her, he held the door open for her.

Walking slowly out the door, Veta briefly glanced back at him as she left, wishing once again that she didn't have this errand to run right now.

Closing the door behind her, Drinian watched her walk away along the sidewalk. The look on his face must have registered longing for Lylia sidled up to him and touched him gently on the arm.

"Are you okay?" she asked softly, disturbed a little by the tortured look on his face.

"She's so beautiful Lylia." His voice was filled with barely restrained emotion.

Staring after her, she glanced up at Drinian and could see the despair there. "Yes, she is. I'm sure someday you'll find someone, but a woman like that deserves a man…"

"That's just it, I'm no man." He abruptly cut her off. The contempt in his voice was unmistakable. "I'm just a monster."

Yanking the door open, he stalked from the shop, disappearing in the opposite direction, forgetting he needed to pay for Veta's drink.

Chapter 19

Sunday morning after church, Dante Blackthorne sat at the kitchen table, leafing through the newspaper while he listened to all the children playing in the yard. Chuckling at their antics, he overheard Storman exclaiming over the water balloons Breydon was tossing at his twin brother from his dad's upstairs study. Paying more attention to Dartanian's outraged cries, as Breydon finally hit his mark; Dante nearly missed the article on the bottom of the front page.

It might not have caught his attention if it weren't for the name of the woman who'd authored it. As he began reading he sat forward, his attention on full alert as Veta spoke of the items she hoped to have returned. Standing suddenly, he carried the paper with him as he walked out onto the patio; only to get nailed by one of the water balloons himself.

"Dang it, Brey, knock it off for a minute, will you?" He hollered up at him only to hear his brother laughing uproariously at him. Shaking the paper and his hands at the same time, in order to try and keep them dry, he looked up in time to see his dad and Hialey grinning from ear to ear.

"Might have known the two of you were up there," he called dryly.

Looking down, Rafe could tell his son was more than a little cross, and that he had something on his mind. "What's up, Dante?"

"You have to come down and hear this." He waved them down. Shaking the newspaper in the air, he hadn't intended on getting everyone's attention, but he realized now that he had it.

"Find something interesting?" Dartanian put the grill lid down, having just flipped the burgers. Walking towards them along with the rest of the family he wrung out his shirt in the process.

"You could say that." He was a little anxious now about whether or not he should read it in front of everyone. Eyeing his dad, as he came through the patio doors, he glanced down at the paper. Deciding the article itself wouldn't throw up any flags to the ladies; he went ahead and began reading it aloud.

All I have left. Special addition by Veta Rohann.

He started reading, noting varying reactions to Veta's name.

We all have things we cherish. Things that help us remember better times past. Items, that when touched, help us remember what we have lost. Or, like in my case, loved ones we've loved and lost. And when those things are lost or stolen, it can be as though you're losing your loved ones all over again.

Dante paused. Rafe cocked his eyebrow in inquiry. "Just wait," he said then continued.

Upon arriving in Whitefish, I personally found myself in such a position. I came from Maryland, with only a U-Haul. It housed all of my worldly belongings. Upon arriving on Saturday, May 17th, I checked into a local motel, where the U-Haul was stolen.

"That was nice of her not to mention Marshall's motel," Royce murmured quietly, as they listened.

Though I know all those things are replaceable, there are three items inside which can never be replaced. They hold no value to anyone else but me for they are memory boxes for each of my children. Each box holds such items as their first lost baby tooth, a lock from their first haircut, baby booties, baby pictures, and baby clothes they wore home from the hospital when they were born.

"Of course, I have the same sort of items in our kid's boxes." Megorah glanced over at Chase, exchanging looks with him.

Chase stood quietly as he listened, gazing at his wife with unease. He'd never told Megorah what Veta had said at the hospital, figuring Veta had her reasons for keeping what happened to her children to herself.

My twin boys, Casey and Aaron, each had a baby spoon engraved with their names, dates, and times they were born. And my daughter, Sarah, had a tiny hairbrush, also engraved with the same information. All had hand

and footprints done in ceramic casts when they were one year old as well as other sentimental memorabilia.

Pausing for a breath, Dante went on.

I hold no ill will towards the party, who took the U-Haul and have no expectation of receiving any of the items back, that might be worth anything to that person. That being said, I can't help but wonder if I might appeal to the individual who took the U-Haul for the memory boxes alone. If you are a thief with a conscience or one who is merely trying to get by, might you be willing to return these items to me, with my assurance of no reprisal?

"Wow. She's willing to give up everything, just for those boxes." Hialey's eyes grew wide.

"It's not really giving them up when she'll likely never see those things again anyway. She seems to understand that pretty, well from the sounds of it." With a heavy sigh, Dartanian kicked at the ground.

More often than not, stolen property was never recovered. But having done a background check, he knew a lot more about the woman than anyone else and was already aware of why she was so desperate to see the items returned.

Sensing Dartanian already knew Dante turned towards Hialey instead, saying. "This next part explains why."

Were my children still with me, I might not make such a bold request. But as it happens, they were killed in an auto accident one year ago, last Sunday. Aaron and Casey were only thirteen years old when it happened and my daughter Sarah was only nine.

Lylia gasped unexpectedly, winning her a couple startled stares. "Oh no... Poor thing! She never said anything about that."

"Honey, you know Veta?" Dartanian asked cautiously. He glanced towards Rafe then Breydon.

"I just met her last Friday at The Coffee Haven. How horrible for her. I couldn't even imagine," Lylia finished on a whisper, overcome with emotion.

Dante and Dartanian exchanged looks then glanced around the gathering. Looking back down at the paper, Dante lifted it towards him and read the last of what was there.

These memory boxes are all I have left of them. For obvious reasons, I can only hope you're a thief with a heart. Should you choose to return them to me, you may contact the newspaper anonymously.

Snatching the paper from Dante, Breydon flipped the page up, noting the article had been placed at the bottom of the page. Taking a closer look, he then turned towards Rafe and glared.

"If I'd been them, I would have led with that article at the top of the page." His acrimonious tone was evident. Turning away from him, he handed the paper back to Dante roughly, still feeling stung by his father's false assumptions.

"I didn't see her at church this morning; I sure hope she's okay." Lylia leaned against Dartanian. "She was acting kind of funny when I invited her here on Friday. I'd hoped she'd come here after church, but maybe with the article, she didn't want extra attention?"

Rafe inhaled sharply. "Lylia, are you saying that she now attends our church and that you invited her here today for lunch?"

"Yes. She's new in town, and I thought it might be nice if she met some more people," she said, becoming somewhat anxious when Rafe just stared at her.

"Does she know you're a Blackthorne?" Chase spoke sharper than he'd intended.

"Well, I … I don't know. Why? Does it matter?" She was both surprised and confused at hearing what sounded like alarm in his voice. At that very moment, the doorbell reverberated throughout the house.

"She must have decided to come. Come on everyone!" Lylia raced into the house to get the door.

Uneasy looks were exchanged amongst family members, as they all headed into the living room with trepidation. It was clear to everyone that Lylia was unaware of the mystery plaguing the household with regard to her new friend.

Opting to stand in the background, for the moment, Rafe headed towards the furthest kitchen door and just stood there, peering out into the living room. As Lylia answered the door, he could hear Veta's soft voice when they greeted each other.

"I'm so glad you came! Did you find the house okay?"

"Yes, thank you, I didn't have any trouble. Although, the signage for the ranch must have fallen down at some point because I might not have found it if it weren't for the number on the mailbox."

Rafe made a mental note to have one of the ranch hands go out on Monday and put it back up. Wincing inwardly, he realized that because it had been down, Ms. Rohann likely had no warning as to whose home she'd just entered.

"Are you all right?" Lylia could be heard to inquire suddenly, noting her friend's drawn face and tired eyes. "Are you upset because of the article this morning? Did something happen?"

"No, no," Veta reassured her while pressing her free hand against her forehead. She had been feeling ill all morning long, which had kept her from attending church. Having awakened from some of the worst nightmares she'd ever had, she was still feeling a little shaken up by them. Smiling weakly at Lylia, she continued. "You saw that I take it?"

"My brother-in-law was reading it to us, a little bit ago. I'm so sorry. I had no idea." Realizing her friend was still standing awkwardly in the entryway, she waved her on in.

"Is that why you weren't at church?" She looked at Veta with concern, as she closed the door behind her. She could tell the woman in front of her didn't seem quite right for some reason. It almost reminded her of how Drinian would get after having a bad bout with his shadows.

"No, actually I must admit I wasn't feeling well this morning." She still trembled a little. "Let's just say it was kind of an odd night and leave it at that." Peering around the entryway, Veta was a bit surprised by its interior. Though a grand house in size, it had been highly deceptive in appearance from the outside. She had anticipated it would be lavishly decorated. Yet she was pleased to see it had been very tastefully furnished with comfort in mind.

In the kitchen, Rafe cringed inwardly as he listened. He was about to step forward into the living room to head off the inevitable when he saw Drinian come in from the porch. Drinian nodded towards him, then grabbed a root beer from the fridge and turned towards his dad.

"I only see kids outside. Where is everybody?" Knocking the cap off the bottle, he took a swig.

Rafe's eyebrow's rose. Eyes narrowing upon his son, he glanced towards the other room and up into the entryway.

"They're in the front living room, greeting our guest," he said nonchalantly. He could see that Lylia had not yet moved into the living room, where Dante, Dartanian, and Breydon were standing together, trying to see into the entryway. Eyeing his daughters, Alaina, and Hialey, with some misgivings for what he was about to allow, Rafe watched, as Drinian strode towards the other kitchen door. He wanted to gauge Ms. Rohann's reaction to seeing his son.

"We have a guest?" Drinian inquired, pushing through the door into the living room.

Lylia was bringing Ms. Rohann down into the same room and appeared to be getting ready to introduce her to the family. Veta didn't seem to have noticed his sons quite yet but Drinian, on the other hand, stopped cold at first sight of her, his mouth dropping, the root beer precariously dangling from his hand.

"I'd like you to meet my family."

Oblivious to his reaction, Lylia spoke casually as she steered her friend over to the two steps leading down into the living room.

Veta stopped suddenly upon seeing Megorah and Crisalya's, anxious eyes staring back at her, while they stood next to their husband's. Dr. Chase Ryans looked upon Veta with sympathy, as he reached an arm around his wife and held her close.

"It's nice to see you," Chase said cordially in greeting. He could see her respiration become choppy and she paled noticeably. He watched her glance warily around the room.

"Lylia, whose house is this?" Her voice shook and her hands trembled, causing her Tupperware bowl of Jell-O salad to shake. Eyes widening in alarm, Veta took in the three men with crystal-clear blue eyes near the fireplace. For a moment, she thought she was seeing double. Two identical men, both looking like the Sheriff were standing next to each other. She blinked trying to clear her vision but the double didn't go away. Then, there was another who looked very similar, though a bit leaner, who was standing right next to them. It wasn't until her eyes fell upon the very large man who'd just come in through the kitchen doorway, that she dropped her bowl and gasped. Jell-O, peaches, and whipped cream splattered everywhere.

All eyes turned towards, Drinian, as Veta's face turned white with stark terror. Veta wavered where she stood. Instantly feeling queasy, her head seemed to spin at the sight before her. Grabbing at her stomach, she watched in horror as wispy black smoke seemed to shoot out from behind the man and envelope her, curling around her, as she stood precariously near the steps. She let out a strangled cry of shock and fear, as the slithering forms seemed to surround her, attempting to ensnare her as though with tentacles. She tensed noticeably, her body shook, and the lamp flickered near her.

"Veta!" Unaware of her friend's full distress Lylia gasped, stepping back away from the container as it had fallen. When she turned back to look at her, she realized the woman looked like she was about to pass out.

Rafe watched in dismay as Drinian roared angrily then leaped across the furniture to catch Veta as she fainted.

"Leave her alone," he bellowed, glaring towards where she would have fallen. Turning suddenly, he held her protectively and he growled dangerously. "I told you to stop messing with her." Hearing the dark spirits screech in agony all around them, as they finally shrank away, and fled through the front windows of the house, he held her close. He carried her as though accustomed to having her in his arms.

Feeling anxious, and angry with the demons Drinian laid her gently on the couch. Grabbing the afghan from the chair where it had been left, he tossed it over her tucking it carefully around her. Looking down at her, his face reddened noticeably, when he realized how familiar he'd just been acting towards her. Glancing towards his dad, the look Drinian gave him was full of shame and remorse.

"I'm sorry," Drinian said quietly, his voice cracking in the silence as everyone but Alaina stared at him in varying stages of surprise.

"Not as sorry as *you* will be." Hialey's voice was deadly. She glared angrily at him and stalked off towards the kitchen, fuming outwardly. Drinian winced, catching Breydon's attention.

"Now, why..." Breydon stared his brother down. "Why is my wife presently plotting revenge? I know why *she* has a right to be mad at you," he said, pointing towards Veta's unconscious form on the couch. "And why I should very shortly be getting an apology from dad, but why..."

"I asked Hialey to pick Veta up from the hospital Tuesday morning." Drinian interrupted. "She asked me why and wanted to know what she was to me. I told her..."

"You told her what exactly?" There was steel in Megorah's voice. Her eyes began filling with tears. She moved towards her brother, unable to believe she'd been so wrong. She'd been so sure it had been Dante, but it was very clear from both Veta and Drinian's response to each other, that he was responsible for what had happened to her at the cabin.

Glancing towards Alaina, Drinian winced at the sight of her looking back at him with sympathy. Chuckling nervously, he gave her with a half-smile and rubbed at his face.

"I told Hialey, she wasn't anything to me."

He knew it was coming before he felt it, the fierce whack from Megorah's hand as she slapped him hard across the face, leaving behind a resounding silence. His cheek stung where she'd hit him. He stared down at his sister, inhaling sharply as tears stung the back of his eyes. Staring back up at him, the wounded expression on her face mirroring his own, she then stalked off after Hialey only to stop suddenly in front of Dante.

"I'm so sorry. I thought it was you. That was so unfair of me." Running from the room, she tore after Hialey as Dante watched her go, hurt plainly reflected in his eyes as well.

"Would someone please tell me what's going on!" Lylia stamped her feet in frustration. She lifted her arms and gestured towards her husband, waiting for a response. He exchanged looks with his younger brother.

"Care to explain, Drin?" Dartanian asked evenly, his posture indicating he might pummel him if he didn't.

Drinian took a deep breath. "I was out walking Monday night when I saw Veta at the old vacation cabin, skinny dipping in the hot tub." Sighing heavily, he looked away from Lylia's raised brow and continued. "I saw a medicine jar on the table and an empty bottle of wine in her hand. She looked ... like she was in trouble. So I ran down to the patio, yanked the door off when I saw her head go under the water, and pulled her from the hot tub."

"Apart from you seeing her naked that's not so bad," Lylia said in confusion. "What's Megorah getting all riled up about? It sounds to me like you saved her life."

Rafe strode into the living room and confronted his son.

"You saved her life, which is highly commendable but then you took advantage of her. Am I right?" Rafe asked in a quiet tone. The disappointment in his voice was evident.

Drinian didn't look at him at first. Hearing Lylia gasp suddenly in understanding, he looked over at her. Guilt was written all over his face.

"Drinian did you … did you rape her?" She was horrified at the thought.

"No. I swear it wasn't like that." Distressed and a little angry by her assumption, he tried to explain. "I was only trying to help her. But she was … she *is so beautiful*." Drinian let out a tortured sigh, more than a little embarrassed. Rolling his eyes, he grimaced uncomfortably and looked down at Veta's still form on the couch. "And she seemed so lonely and in need of comfort when she asked me to stay. I wasn't trying to hurt her," he said imploringly, trying to get them to understand. He turned on the spot, glancing around at everyone in turn. Becoming choked up, his shoulders fell helplessly as if in defeat, looking much like a little boy, having been caught playing somewhere he shouldn't.

Kneeling down next to her, he tenderly ran his shaking hand along Veta's cheek. "The demons are messing with you because of me, Veta. I keep telling them to leave you alone, but I have no real control over them. I'm so sorry," he whispered aloud, kissing her absent-

227

mindedly on the forehead. Getting up, he was about to walk away toward the kitchen when Dante reached out and handed him the article.

"You might want to read this."

Taking the article from him, Drinian read it through. Though his expression was devoid of emotion, internally his gut clenched. Only now was he beginning to understand the depths to which she'd been wronged since she'd arrived in town. Dropping the article wordlessly, he paused at the door and stopped without turning around.

"Burgers are burning, Dart," he said in a hoarse voice, and then disappeared through the kitchen door. *Lord*, he thought, *will this torment ever end?*

Chapter 20

Restlessly, Veta turned in her sleep. Her eyelashes flickered and her face contorted as though in anguish or fear. She reached out as she slept as she always had for the book to throw in his face. Thrashing, one arm flailed about, trying to push him away, as the other lay limp at her side.

"No, no, James no!" She screamed, coming awake suddenly. Perspiration spilled from her brow. She sat upright, her heart lurching roughly against the wall of her chest. Eyes wide with fright, she found herself staring into her daughters face, just as she had last night, waking from one nightmare to the next. Only this time, she was not in her apartment.

Sobbing uncontrollably, she reached out for her daughter, wanting to hold her, to touch her once more. Tears streamed down her face as her hand slid through Sarah's arm. She let out a strangled cry of fear, confused by what was happening. Had she awoke to another nightmare or was this real?

"Sarah!"

Alarmed that her hand had gone right through her daughter, Veta frantically tried to wrap her arms around her. Disappearing before her eyes in a puff of smoke, Veta cried out once more not wanting her to go.

"No! Sarah, don't go!" The inky black smoke seemed to split, each cloud exploding as a bright light flashed before her eyes. A figure of a very tall man with shoulder length blonde hair and pale blue eyes, garbed in loose-fitting white clothing hovered before her. Holding a sword in hand as he gazed upon her, his eyes were gentle yet fierce.

"Who are you?" she asked quietly. Though trembling she was no longer afraid. An unexpected calm overcame her.

"You can see me." The man's voice was as soft as a caress. "Good, Maleeka will be pleased with this news."

"Who's Maleeka?"

"Ms. Rohann, who are you talking to?" Rafe asked, gaining her attention. He stood in the doorway of the kitchen, staring at Veta curiously. He looked past her but could see nothing.

"Don't you know?" She stared back at him, her eyes wide and glistening. Turning towards the fireplace, she reached out to the figure, wanting desperately to be closer to him but unsure why. Stopping suddenly she frowned. "He's gone. Where did he go?" Distressed, she glanced around the room. Untangling herself from the afghan, she stood on wobbly legs.

The light from the kitchen spilled into the room. It illuminated the space in front of the fireplace, allowing Rafe a clear view of Veta's disheveled appearance. He could see how his son might have struggled to control himself. Even in this state, she was extremely beautiful. Her face was pale, and she seemed to tremble while turning on the spot, as though desperate to find whoever she'd been speaking to.

"I'm sorry; you must have been waking from a dream," he said gently, watching her response with concern.

"But, I could have sworn..." Confused, she glanced around her once again, sniffling while wiping at her eyes and face with her hands.

"You've been out for some time, Ms. Rohann. I sat with you for quite a while, but it became apparent around dinner time that you might need the rest," Rafe said, hearing the partition opening between the kitchen and living room. "We heard you from the kitchen. You were having a nightmare. I came in hoping only to wake you from it."

Breydon peered through the partition - having overheard what was being said. "Do you often talk in your sleep?" He could have sworn he'd heard another voice in the living room, just before his dad had entered but clearly, there was no one there now.

"Let her be," Rafe insisted

"It's okay." More than a little embarrassed Veta gave a shaky laugh. "I do sometimes, yes, for I'm prone to nightmares. I'm sorry I didn't mean to disturb you." Glancing through the partition at Lylia, she noticed her sitting next to the Sheriff. She was staring back at her, wide-eyed. "Sometimes nightmares can just be so real."

"No need to apologize," Drinian said, coming into view. "I'm quite familiar with that terrifying feeling when waking myself."

He had been sitting at the table near the patio doors where she could not initially see him but had overheard everything. Including her reaction as she awoke, crying out the name James in fear, not his. Beer in hand, he took a sip while watching her closely.

Drinian had thought for much of the day about how Veta had responded when she'd seen him and fainted. He could have sworn she had acted as though she was actually seeing the demons that had chased him through the door and assaulted her, as she'd entered the living room. When he'd seen her at The Ryans Rental Agency, he'd thought it rather odd she'd been so accepting of the fact he was seeing demons.

Straightening suddenly, she stared back at him and took a deep breath, trying to regain her composure. "Of course, I can't even imagine what it must be like for you, what with being able to see demons."

The noise in the kitchen halted abruptly as Drinian winced.

"Drin, what *exactly* have you told her?" Rafe asked cautiously.

"In my defense, I didn't really tell *her* anything." Seeing the warning look, he became defensive. "She was at the rental agency when I was talking to Freedom about that painting with the demon in it. She sort of overheard me."

"Are you telling me she knows?" Dante's expression was incredulous and angry when he came into view.

Seeing the man, now standing near the Sheriff who was still seated, Veta did a double take. "Identical twins, of course," she mumbled softly. She'd thought she'd been seeing double earlier.

"She knows I can see the demons if that's what you're asking." Drinian was showing clear signs of agitation. He gave his brother a hard look.

"I didn't realize it was a family secret. I promise I won't say anything." Veta tried to assure the man with the scar on his brow, who was now watching her very closely with an intense expression. "Besides, even if I were to say something most people wouldn't believe me anyway. They tend to think you're crazy when you say you can see such things as angels and demons."

"Of course," Drinian responded. "Because you would *have* to be crazy to be able to see *angels*, right Breydon?" Grinning at his younger brother, he took another swig of beer.

"You're not funny," Breydon said irritably, casting a warning glare his way.

"No, I imagine my behavior lately has been anything but funny to everyone." Drinian sighed in resignation, putting his beer down on the table. Placing his hands on his hips, he faced Veta head-on, appearing more than a little uncomfortable.

"It would seem I owe you several apologies. The first of which, would be for earlier today. I truly am sorry that I terrified you so…"

"That wasn't you," Veta said urgently, interrupting him. "I could never be afraid of you, Drinian." Her voice compelled him to believe her.

Pleasantly surprised by her response, he queried her further. "Then what were you so afraid of, Veta?" he asked with disbelief. He looked back at her, searching her face. "Because it was fear I saw in those beautiful emerald green eyes of yours."

The man before her looked angry. If she were to leave him to believe what he did then he was rightfully so. Veta stared at him, her face flushing as she watched him look her over. Glancing away in embarrassment, she realized she'd been eyeing him as well.

Unable to elicit a response from her, he sighed heavily and moved on. Taking his beer bottle back up in his hand, as though it were a safety net, he took another drink for courage. Swallowing hard, he proceeded.

"I did something unconscionable."

"Oh?"

"Yes, it would seem I took advantage of you when you were somewhat incapacitated." Taking a deep breath, his face reddened as he continued. "An apology, I'm sure, doesn't quite..."

"Wait, Drinian, please." Veta interrupted him again. She leaned forward, raising her hand in the air awkwardly, uncomfortable with discussing things so publicly. "Could we just talk about this alone? Maybe somewhere more private?"

Taken aback, Drinian's face registered surprise. He peered over at his father, standing near the kitchen doorway in the living room. Seeing Rafe's brows raise in fascination, a small kernel of hope lit within him.

"You want ... you feel safe being alone with me?"

She giggled, tickled by what she was hearing. "Why wouldn't I?"

"Most women are afraid of me. They're afraid I might hurt them," he said sheepishly as his family looked on while listening in. "My presence makes them uncomfortable and edgy – afraid."

"You didn't hurt me the last time we were alone together. Why would you now?" She blushed, gazing upon him with a shy gentle smile.

"Yes, why would you, Drin?" Rafe asked, his eyes alighting with hope. Was it possible his son had finally met a woman who wouldn't run away from him? Inhaling deeply, he tucked one hand in his pocket as he ran the other across his face and down his mouth.

"Tell you what," Rafe started. "Ms. Rohann is it?"

"Please, call me Veta," she insisted, her mouth feeling suddenly dry. Her bashful gaze shifted to the gentleman who was still standing just inside the living room. He appeared to be a slightly older version of the Sheriff with lighter skin. She wondered if he was another brother. "You are?"

"My apologies, I am Rafe Blackthorne, Drinian's father."

Stunned, Veta gawked at him openly. "You're Rafe Blackthorne?" Seeing him nod she turned towards Drinian. "How old are you exactly?"

Chuckling in response, his eyes lit up. "Forty."

"But you can't possibly be more than fifty," she exclaimed, staring back over at the Blackthorne patriarch.

Rafe smiled and winked at his son who was shaking his head. "I turned sixty in March, actually."

"I don't believe you," Veta said, winning herself a hearty laugh from Rafe. His children guffawed from the kitchen.

"Regardless, it is true."

"I can attest to that," Breydon called from the kitchen. "He *is* telling the truth." His eyes twinkled with unrestrained mirth.

Glaring at his son, Rafe shushed him and assessed the woman before him discreetly. "Veta then. May I invite you to sit and converse here in the living room with both Drinian and me? We can close the partition. Breydon?" He gestured towards his youngest son to close the partition walls. "Why don't you do that? And, Drinian, come on out here."

There was a flurry of activity and noise as the walls were closed. Veta was a little confused as to why the Blackthorne patriarch felt he needed to be present. "I don't want to be rude but I can't help but wonder why this is any of your business."

Rafe chuckled softly, respecting her directness.

"She has a fair point." Drinian sauntered into the living room, beer still in hand.

Rafe gave his son a stern look. "I am the head of this house, Veta. You are a single woman in my home who may or may not have been wronged by my son. I do realize you both are adults but it would be negligent of me to leave you alone in his presence until I know for sure no legal action needs to be taken against him."

Drinian's eyes gleamed with resentment. His mouth curved up on one side in a wry smile as he sat back in a plushy chair near the fireplace.

Veta didn't say anything right away. She opted to lean against the back of the chair near the partition wall. Instead, she stared down at her feet, both surprised and a little embarrassed, by the man's protective nature. Seeing Rafe gesture towards the couch in front of the fireplace, she watched as he sat in the chair across from Drinian.

Cringing inwardly at how awkward she could only imagine the conversation was about to become, she walked around the chair and tentatively took a seat on the couch he had indicated. Placing her hands in her lap, she glanced first at Drinian then Rafe.

"No legal action is necessary, Mr. Blackthorne."

"Rafe, please. No need to be so formal." He leaned forward, clasping his hands together in front of him. "It's important to me that you feel you can be honest about this. I don't want you to feel afraid of accusing him of wrongdoing in front of me. If there was misconduct on my son's part, I have no qualms about having Sheriff Blackthorne arrest him and haul him to jail."

"You would have your son arrest your other son?"

"Yes," Rafe insisted adamantly while gesturing towards Drinian to keep quiet. "You have to understand, Veta, I take both God's law, as well as man's law very seriously. Regardless of whether or not he is my son, if he hurt you in any way or forced himself on you, he will be arrested." Noting she was about to interrupt, he halted her with his hand. "By the same token, Dartanian, being the Sheriff of this county, won't hesitate to arrest him for the same reason."

"I see."

Setting his beer bottle down on the end table next to him, Drinian fidgeted in his seat, appearing agitated. "I'm awful glad everyone's so willing to throw me in jail." He mumbled darkly as he brooded.

"Hush," Rafe ordered. "You'll have your chance in a minute. Now, Veta..." He turned towards her, his expression softening. "Did my son hurt you in any way?" he asked calmly, his concerned tone genuine.

Veta's eyes made quick work of Rafe Blackthorne's features, clearly able to see where Drinian had gotten his exceptional looks and his eyes for they were the same. She found herself relaxing in his presence in spite of the circumstances.

"No." She smiled shyly. "He never hurt me."

"I know this must be very awkward for you, and I do not wish to make you uncomfortable, but I must ask. Did my son force himself on you?"

Abashed, he looked away from him and began fiddling with her fingers. "There was no force."

"Did he take advantage of you?" Rafe pressed.

Biting her lip, Veta sheepishly peered over at Rafe through her lashes. "I think that's between me, Drinian, and God. Don't you think?"

237

Sitting back in his chair, Rafe sighed. He peered at her thoughtfully, his expression blank. Exchanging glances with Drinian, she fidgeted on the couch, her face turning red.

Taking a deep breath, Rafe finally looked over at his son. "I won't lie to you, Drin. I'm not happy about what's transpired."

Leaning forward, Drinian's jaw clenched. "Did you have a talk like this with Dante before he got married?"

Startled and confused by the question, Veta glanced between the two men, sensing she'd missed something.

"The circumstances were slightly different and you know that. You and I will talk later."

"No, we really won't," he said adamantly.

"Yes, we will," Rafe ground out. He stood and stared momentarily down at his son then walked away toward the kitchen.

"Wow, he's pretty intense," Veta said once he'd disappeared through the kitchen doors.

"He takes his role as father and head of this house very serious." A bland smile was plastered across Drinian's lips. "Some would say he's a bit old fashioned, but I must admit, I have an inordinate amount of respect for that man; even more so now, as an adult. For that reason, he and I will likely talk later, and I shall sit through the tongue lashing, I expect I probably deserve."

"You didn't really do anything wrong."

"Didn't I?" He leaned forward in his seat, taking up a similar pose his father had had only moments before. "I think we both know you weren't quite yourself that night. Now I understand better why, having seen the article in the morning paper."

"Maybe that's true," Veta conceded with a frown. "But regardless of my state of mind, I did ask you to stay.

I tempted you, just as Eve tempted Adam in the Garden of Eden."

"Maybe so." He slowly stood and walked towards her, gauging her reaction as he moved closer. Seeing no reticence at his close proximity, he took up a seat next to her and tentatively took her hands into his. "But you were vulnerable and I had just pulled you from the hot tub, where you'd nearly drowned. I am a Christian man, Veta. I have been since a very young age."

"Really? How old were you?"

"Eight years old."

"I was five."

"You're serious?" Drinian spluttered, staring back at her in surprise. Seeing her nod he blinked. "Wow, that's amazing. But I'm getting off subject here. My point is, especially since I am a Christian, I had no business messing with you regardless of whether you'd tempted me, for I knew better."

"Even the best of men; Christian or not, can make bad choices now and again." Veta reached up and brushed her fingers against his furrowed brow. The simple gesture made Drinian sigh. "Even as a Christian woman, I faltered myself that night. I allowed myself to give in to despair, which led me to the state I was in. As far as I'm concerned you saved my life that night so we're equal in our burden."

"It would seem we both agree that we sinned." He smiled sheepishly at her.

Grinning back at him, Veta chuckled. "So it would seem."

"I'll tell you what. I get the feeling we could go back and forth on this all night. What do you say we just agree that we both made bad choices?"

"Agreed. I have already asked for God's forgiveness, have you Drinian?" She asked softly.

"Yes." He harrumphed softly. "More than once."

"What would you say, if I suggested we just move on from here?"

His interest definitely piqued, Drinian tried not to appear too eager. "Move on. Meaning, what exactly?"

Before she could respond, the partition wall opened abruptly and Dante peered out into the living room. Not far behind him stood his brother Dartanian as he grabbed a pie plate from the counter.

"Just checking. Dad seemed to think it was getting awful quiet out there," he said on a grin. The scar on his brow was more noticeable as he bent his head to take a bite of his pie.

"Identical twins," Veta murmured, peering back up at Drinian. "Wow, I'm going to have difficulty getting used to that."

Dante watched nonchalantly as Drinian scowled back at him. "You have awful lousy timing."

"And don't think it wasn't intentional." He continued to smirk mischievously.

Glancing around the living room and out the windows, she could see it had become dark out and it was raining heavily. It occurred to her how late it must be getting. She smiled anxiously.

"I don't want to impose on you all any more than I already have, and Drinian is waiting at home to be fed. I think it best if I just go."

"Did you just say Drinian was waiting at home to be fed?" Rafe asked in confusion. He'd propped the kitchen door open with his foot so he could see.

"Yes. Drinian is my cat."

"You named your cat Drinian?" Breydon barked, laughing aloud.

"Yes." Veta blushed, becoming flustered by the coincidence.

"Why don't those of us who haven't officially met introduce ourselves?" Rafe said quickly. He strode toward her and guided Veta into the kitchen. His hope was to distract her from leaving just yet for he sensed that his son really liked her. "I believe you've met Hialey but not her husband Breydon."

Breydon nodded towards her in greeting. "Nice to meet you," he said, giving her a once over as he did so, winning himself a swift kick from Hialey. He yelped in pain.

"As you probably heard, this here is my son Dante and his new wife Alaina," Rafe continued, indicating the man standing near the partition with pie plate in hand, and the woman who had come up next to him.

"Lylia mentioned to me that you were married last weekend. Congratulations," Veta acknowledged, a little confounded by the sudden introductions when she had been intending to leave.

"And though you've met Dartanian and Lylia, you may not be aware that they're married," Rafe continued, gesturing in their direction.

"Oh." Startled by the news, she glanced between the two of them. "But of course you are." She giggled hysterically. Though Dart greeted her by glancing in her direction for some reason Lylia couldn't seem to look her in the eye.

"From what I gather, I believe you've met pretty much everyone else," he said kindly as he nodded toward Drinian, who sat staring at her from one of the bar stools, having strolled into the kitchen as his father spoke.

Drinian's eyes twinkled. He saw the befuddled look on her face. "You understand my families surprise at the name of your cat, of course. After all, I have a rather uncommon name so you can imagine it's not often when we come by it elsewhere."

Seeing Veta glance at the counter towards the various pies that were set out, he picked one up and held it out towards her.

"Would you like some pie? We could ... call it a peace offering." The corners of his mouth twitched with humor. He gazed over at her hopefully. "You know, forgive each other but not necessarily forget?" His voice was deep and sensual as he spoke, and he gave her a look that she could tell held a great deal of meaning. Shivering slightly she raised her hand to her chest. Noticing his gaze dropping in that direction, she drew her hand away self-consciously.

Veta could swear her heart skipped a beat. She stared at the extremely handsome man before her. He gave her a knowing look and she blushed like a schoolgirl. A sensation akin to acceptance washed over her at that moment. It was as though a wave of understanding and peace over their first encounter together had overcome her. Any unease she might have had promptly melted away upon seeing the bright smile light up his face. If it were possible, he was even more attractive when he showed off his pearly whites.

"I haven't eaten anything today," she admitted slowly. She peered over at him shyly. "I suppose, I could be cajoled into having a piece of the pie." That exact moment, her stomach growled loudly for everyone to hear. Laughing in embarrassment, she glanced at the pie plate hungrily and her face flushed. "Or maybe two?" she said, taking it from him.

"As it would happen, there are two pieces left there. Royce, we need a fork." Drinian hollered, grinning again happily, slapping at his thigh with the palm of his hand.

Royce reached into the silverware drawer in front of him and handed it across the counter, staring at Drinian thoughtfully.

"Would you like some coffee with that, Veta?" Royce asked suddenly.

"That would be great," she said, not sure where to sit. Drinian motioned her towards the bar stool next to him. Unsure at first, she walked over slowly and crawled onto the stool, allowing him to help her up. Her leg brushed against his accidentally. She adjusted herself and she caught his eye when he handed her the fork.

"The sugar and creamer are over here if you want sweetener." Hialey got up from her seat and brought it over to the counter.

"Oh, no. Veta likes her coffee black with brown sugar," Royce said, intentionally being a bit louder than usual. Grabbing the bag from the counter, he added two teaspoonfuls. Stirring it, he handed it to Drinian and watched in amusement as his brother-in-law stared down at the mug in surprise.

"You named your cat Drinian and you like brown sugar in your coffee." He looked somewhat bemused.

"Yeah, I know. I also like long walks in the rain, potato chips dipped in applesauce, and would waste an entire day watching, 'Monk', marathons," she said between mouthfuls. She couldn't believe how hungry she was, and the apple pie was really good. "I guess you could say I'm a little weird." Without realizing it, she'd garnered the attention of everyone in the room. They noted the extraordinary similarities between her and Drinian's tastes. Sipping at her coffee appreciatively, she polished off the two pieces of pie faster than she had intended.

"You seem to be enjoying that pie," Drinian noted. She pushed the empty tin away. "I take it you're an apple pie fan?"

She bobbed her head in response. "But my first love will always be cheesecake." She closed her eyes on a wave of relief for finally having something in her stomach. Pressing her hand to her belly, she opened her eyes. "Now, if you were to give me an entire New York style cheesecake with cherry topping, I'd love you forever."

Breydon nearly choked on his coffee upon hearing her pronouncement. Standing suddenly, he wiped at the coffee he managed to spill on the table.

Drinian, however, merely peered at her over his beer then finished it off quickly. Eyes sparkling, he deferred his head towards Royce, who was still standing near the coffee pot.

"I'll have to remember that," he said quietly in answer. "Royce, you want to hand me the coffee pot?"

"You want coffee?" Royce's mouth dropped open in surprise. He'd never known Drinian to drink coffee so late after having begun his regimen of beer.

"Yup, I figure I better stay sober if I'm gonna take her for a walk in the rain," he said with a wink toward Veta.

Chapter 21

Megorah watched the couple sitting at the counter with a cautious eye. It had been a surprising turn of events seeing Drinian and Veta sitting together so amicably. After her fainting spell earlier in the day, she had been certain that Dartanian would be handcuffing her brother and hauling him downtown to jail. As far as she was concerned he still deserved it. But then, she wasn't Veta, nor had she been there that night. Clearly, the experience hadn't been anything like what she'd been through fifteen years before.

They were definitely hitting it off it seemed. They appeared to have a lot in common, and Megorah could tell that her brother was very interested in Veta. At present, they were sitting together companionably sharing coffee and pie. Sensing Veta's comfort and ease in Drinian's presence, she smiled softly, gladdened for once to see a woman unafraid of her brother. Megorah couldn't help but wonder if this was a good sign, and she could tell her dad was thinking the same thing, even without having the ability to discern thoughts.

Lylia, on the other hand, was clearly irritated and even flummoxed by the turn of events. For whatever the reason, she appeared to be extremely disappointed that they were hitting it off so well. Finding her behavior curious, she opted to ignore it, for the time being, wanting instead to concentrate her thoughts on the way Veta had been acting earlier.

Megorah was troubled by her response toward Drinian when she first saw him. She could tell he had picked up on something odd as well. Veta had said she hadn't been afraid of him, but clearly, she'd been scared of something else, which she'd never clarified.

Having heard Veta's reaction when she woke, Megorah could sense that something truly horrible had happened to her at some point in her life. Her fear had been immediate and strong at that moment. But from all appearances, Veta didn't seem afraid of Drinian at all. For the first time, in quite a long time, she could see a genuine smile cross her brother's face as he sat next to this woman. She hoped desperately it wouldn't be the last time she saw that smile.

She tensed when she heard Drinian invite Veta for a walk. Anxious to hear what her response would be, she nearly missed seeing Lylia's head snap up suddenly. The look on her face led Megorah to believe she'd just had an epiphany of sorts. Wishing she could discern thoughts, at that moment, she watched as Lylia excused herself, feigning exhaustion, and headed up to her bedroom. Just the opposite, Megorah had felt the excitement, even a surge of adrenaline coming from her. Making a mental note to check on Lylia in the morning, she dismissed her peculiar behavior and watched Drinian lead Veta out onto the patio.

"Crazy," Hialey cried out suddenly as they strolled out into the rain. "They're a couple of crazies they are." She watched them in dismay.

Megorah chuckled while sipping her coffee, then took a bite of her pie. "Now, Hialey," she began to say, as though pandering to a child.

"No," Hialey said loudly, shaking a finger at Meg. "He's crazy for doing what he did, she's crazy for letting him get away with it, and they're both crazy for walking out in that rain. I mean really." She scowled as she vented.

"You're just mad…"

"Darn right I am. Oh, he's gonna get it. When he least expects it he will." Hialey fumed.

"They'd make a really good-looking couple though, wouldn't they?" Crisalya glanced hopefully out the patio doors, ignoring Hialey's comical tirade. Nighttime had descended, so it was hard to see anything now, especially with the rain.

"Girls, no matchmaking. Let's not get our hopes up yet. We don't know where this is going, and we don't know enough about her." Rafe tried to rein his daughters in. They were forever trying to match make for Drinian, and it usually never ended well.

"What do you want to know about her?" Dartanian asked cautiously. He peered over at his dad while leaning back in his chair. Concerned by Lylia's hasty departure he was somewhat distracted.

"What do you know that I don't?" Rafe eyed his son suspiciously.

"Nothing you can't find for yourself I'm sure," Dartanian said evasively, gaining both Dante and Royce's attention. Chuckling internally he noted, not for the first time, that they were usually the ones to pick up on this sort of talk.

247

"I see. So there's something else to find?" Rafe sounded disappointed.

Sighing, Dartanian grimaced noticeably. "Unfortunately, yes."

Rafe stared down at his empty coffee mug, deep in thought. Recalling, how Veta had responded when she awoke, he had a sneaky suspicion he knew what that something was going to be. Leaning forward in his chair, he stared down at the floor, and then glanced cautiously over at the women near the patio.

"What are we talking about here, Dart?"

Pausing, the Sheriff in him cast a furtive glance towards the women as well. Seeing Hialey speaking with animation, while she shared for the third time how she managed to get her order of lingerie back from fishmonger Sam, he stood and stretched uncomfortably. Striding toward the counter, he grabbed the coffee pot and poured Rafe another full cup, suspecting he was likely going to need it. Leaving the pot on the table in front of him, Dartanian lowered his voice.

"Think Meg, only worse."

Startled, Rafe looked up at him in alarm. He heard Alaina laughing at Hialey, from the other table. "How could it possibly be worse?" He tried to keep his floored voice in an undertone.

Dartanian raked his hand across his face, ignoring the questioning expressions he was getting from Dante and Royce. Turning on his heels, he headed towards the stairs, calling back at them as he went.

"Trust me. It just is."

Watching him disappear from view, the three men stared back at each other. Royce watched, as Rafe got up, taking his coffee cup with him, and headed upstairs to his study. At the same time, Dante grabbed a root beer from the fridge, and then headed towards the front of the house, presumably to his own study.

Royce sat with his half-empty juice bottle, stewing inwardly as he contemplated. "It's times like these, I wish I had government contacts too."

- - -

They walked together in silence at first, as they crossed the lawn, both unsure about what to say. Drinian guided her, toward the path he normally took, to his cabin in the woods, but Veta stopped, eying it wearily.

"It's okay, you're safe with me." He coaxed her to join him along the path.

Veta raised an eyebrow at him humorously. "Am I now?"

"For the most part, anyway." He grinned back at her; the depth of his meaning clear in his tone. Drinian didn't know why, but he couldn't seem to keep from smiling in her presence. Anxious about being so near her, he tentatively reached out and took her hand in his.

"Walk with me," he said simply as he turned toward the path, very gently tugging at her arm. Veta quietly walked alongside him, peering up at him every so often, as the rain pelted down over her face and shoulders. She'd been a little surprised at his invitation at first; not realizing he'd been serious when he'd commented about staying sober for their walk. Never before had she known anyone who liked to walk in this kind of weather as she did.

The warm summer rain came down in a steady stream, drenching them as they went for neither of them was wearing coats. Periodically, Drinian would pause as they strode along the path, pointing out various landmarks which appeared to be extremely important to him.

"You walk along this path often," she said, more as a statement than a question.

Nodding, he replied, "Yes, it leads to my cabin. So I walk it nearly every day."

"No wonder you're in such good shape," she mumbled thoughtfully. Feeling unusually relaxed in his presence she sighed, closed her eyes, and lifted her face towards the sky. The rain had turned to a light mist, and it fell upon her skin. Reveling in the sensation, she didn't realize he was staring at her.

Marveling at her beauty Drinian watched her closely. Her jet-black hair clung to her face and neck, drawing his gaze towards the soft pale skin near her collar bone. Her clothes clung to her body, allowing him to see every curve. As far as he was concerned, for a woman who had birthed three children, a set of twins at that, she had a rather remarkable figure.

Veta opened her eyes, noting that he'd been watching her. The desire for him to bend down and kiss her was so strong she found she had to look away. Deciding the silence might be dangerous for them, she continued along the path with him, trying to think of something to say.

"Drinian?" she said finally, stopping suddenly in her tracks.

Not expecting her to stop, he bumped into her accidentally. Taking hold of her shoulders, to keep from ploughing her over, he steadied himself as he looked down at her.

"What exactly would you like to see happen? Between us, that is."

During the short time they sat together and talked, she had picked up on numerous similarities and common interests between them. Starting to wonder if the Lord had brought her to Montana with a distinct purpose in mind, she peered up at the dark sky thoughtfully, waiting for his response as the mist fell upon her. Regardless of how they'd come together, she couldn't help but get the feeling God had guided her for a reason to the man next to her. If the Lord wanted her at his side, then she felt compelled to take that possibility seriously.

Swallowing hard, Drinian gave her an awkward look. Wiping his hands anxiously across his wet chest, he took a deep breath. "I suppose, I'd like to see you from time to time." His voice was deep and sensual, causing her to shiver lightly. "You know – date. That is if you're so inclined. I find myself liking you a lot," he admitted slowly, the words feeling awkward coming from his mouth.

Looking worried Veta peered down the trail still deep in thought. Startled briefly by an unexpected bright light flashing next to her, she blinked then felt a tickling sensation against her right ear. Brushing it away she turned toward Drinian.

Seeing her troubled expression, Drinian hoped he hadn't scared her off already. "There's no rush of course. I don't want to pressure you or be pushy. Or if your just not interested, I suppose I can understand," he said on a sorrowful note.

Smiling at how sweet and considerate he was trying to be, she leaned up towards him, touching her fingertips to his cheek. "No, it's not that at all. I like you too if it helps."

Beaming at the news, Drinian considered her words carefully. "Then, what is it? I can tell there is some resistance to the notion. Is it because I can see the demons?"

"No, that has nothing to do with it," she said dismissively, then sighed in resignation. "This is probably more like a third or fourth date discussion when a couple is considering becoming more serious but…" Pausing, she took a deep breath and went on. "Considering our situation is … a bit different, I figure you should probably know. I need to be honest, Drinian, losing my children in the car accident, though tragic, it was not the only bad thing that has happened to me."

"What is it? You can tell me anything."

She didn't say anything at first, but moved further along the path, walking ahead of him as though needing a bit of distance. Lightening flashed across the sky, thunder rumbling in its wake, but it didn't seem to faze her.

After a while she began to speak, telling him about an incident she'd had while in college. Explaining to him what happened to her, when the football players assaulted her, Drinian inhaled sharply, stunned at what she was saying.

"*They* forced themselves on you?" he asked, placing emphasis on the word they.

"Yes. James hit me pretty hard, a couple of times actually. He messed me up pretty good. So I lost consciousness and wasn't aware of what all was happening to me." She was nervous and flustered at having to put the incident to words. She'd only ever had to tell one other before. That had been her late husband Mitch. In the end, it had turned out he had already known. Taking a deep breath, she bravely went on, telling him about how she'd been found.

"No one came looking for you?" he asked incredulously upon hearing no one had noticed her missing until the next day.

"It was May and end of the session. Finals were over. Most people had, or were already, heading home. My roommate was distracted with her end of year party. She didn't notice me missing until late Sunday night when she finally woke up from her drunken stupor."

Watching his reaction closely, Veta reached out and took hold of a nearby tree trunk. She swung back and forth as she spoke, trying to gauge his response to what she was saying. She was nervous about telling him something so personal.

Sensing he was about to speak she stopped him. "There's more, just wait." She grimaced at the look he gave her. With a heavy heart, she began telling him about the fourth man she'd been unaware of until the police had questioned her at the hospital. Staring back at Drinian anxiously, her eyes began to water, though one wouldn't have been able to tell with the rain washing down over her.

"I never knew who he was … until last year."

Eyeing her with concern Drinian stepped closer to her. Reaching out, he touched her cheek gently. His expression softened.

"Your article said your sons were thirteen when they died the year before."

"Yes." She understood where he was going with his inquiry. "I never knew for sure who their father was until last year either," she said softly, almost sadly.

"I take it the police finally caught him, and that's how you found out?"

Veta searched his face, unsure why she was telling him all of this. She never spoke of it. Now, all of a sudden, she found herself baring her soul to him. It was as though something was nagging her to share with him about her past. In the end, she supposed she knew that if they were to consider seeing each other, he needed and deserved to know.

Laughing bitterly, she leaned up against the tree for support. The mist continued to fall all around them. Her face contorted with pain as the betrayal sliced at her heart, still so prevalent after a year.

"In May of last year, I'd picked up my children from school then picked up my husband, Professor Mitchell Gaylord from the hospital." Veta willed herself not to close her eyes for fear of reliving the moment once again. "He'd had a surgical procedure which required anesthesia and he was really loopy, acting almost like he was drunk. At first, I didn't think he knew what he was saying." She started to cry as she choked back a tortured laugh. "But then he started talking about how we'd been together before I had the boys, which wasn't possible."

"What do you mean?" Drinian's brows furrowed in confusion, trying hard to follow what she was saying. He was getting an uneasy sensation in his stomach and didn't like it.

"People used to say, that my boys looked like Mitch, and we'd all laugh because we knew they weren't his. Mitch and I didn't start dating until nearly a year after they were born. I'd always been honest with Aaron and Cody. But that day in the car, in front of my sons and our daughter, my husband tells me about how he remembers our first time together in the library and he acted as if it was a fond memory for him."

Stunned, Drinian stared back at her. "Are you saying your own husband was the fourth man?"

Veta slumped to the ground, her knees digging into the soft earth and then stared up at him miserably. Tears welled in her eyes and anger surged within her. "I was married to that rat for eleven years! The whole time, having to apologize for the nightmares and disturbing his sleep. Right there in my very house was one of the very predators who'd violated me. And what was even worse? He knew! He knew he was their father!" The hurt and pain were still raw in her voice.

Kneeling down next to her Drinian listened with rapt attention, distressed by the suffering she had experienced. It hurt him to see her in so much pain but he knew to stay quiet, for as painful as it was, he also knew she needed to let it out.

"Twins run in his family. Mitch used to joke about it when I was pregnant with Sarah. It pleased him when others would notice and he'd laugh. Then he would say that's right, those are my boys all right, and he'd give me this look." She sobbed then as thunder reverberated around them. The sky seemed to open up with a new flood of water. "I just thought he was taking ownership of them as an adoptive father would. I didn't realize he was really mocking me when he said it." Not bothering to wipe the rain from her face, her expression contorted painfully.

"That was the day they all died," she said finally as she began shaking her head from side to side. "I was in such shock as to what he'd told me. I wasn't paying attention and people were honking behind me. I barely glanced at the light and just sped through the intersection. I didn't even see it coming, and I was looking in that direction. The tanker came barreling through the light and crashed into our car, killing everyone. Everyone but me."

She cried in anguish as the memory played out in her head.

"They said a man by the name of Bastion pulled me out because I was the only one he could get to. The car was just so mangled."

Gentle, strong hands took hold of her shoulders. Moments later she found herself wrapped in a warm and strong embrace, as her back pressed into his massive chest. She reveled in the feel of him next to her. No words were spoken; no move was made for what seemed an endless amount of time as the rain poured down over them. It was as though the sky was trying to help wash away the past. The hurt. All Veta wanted at that moment was for the pain to go away. So she just knelt there, being held like a child as she wept.

After a time, Veta realized she'd stopped crying. Spent from the sheer exhaustion of emotion she attempted to disengage herself from Drinian's embrace. Instead of relinquishing her, he surprised her, by picking her up in his arms. The sound of his feet squishing into the soft, waterlogged grass, met her ears as he reached the lawn leading up to the house. Easily carrying her along the path and across the lawn, he eventually reached the patio. Seeing that the doors had been left open for him, he realized his father must have seen him coming. Grateful to Rafe for his discretion, he entered the empty kitchen and headed into the living room. Chuckling internally upon seeing the fire going in the fireplace he moved to set her down on the couch.

"Oh, wait, please. I'm sopping wet." She snuffled anxiously as Drinian placed her on the blankets he saw spread across the couch.

"I know." He sat down next to her and pulled her against his chest. "You look really good wet, too." Pulling the blanket, that had been thrown over the back of the couch, over them, Drinian simply held her there as they both gazed into the fire.

"I truly am so sorry. That's more than any one woman should ever have to endure in a lifetime." Bending down, he gently kissed her forehead then snuggled her closer. Grabbing one of the towels his father had laid nearby, he wrapped it around her hair in order to help dry it some.

"I know God wouldn't want me to think this way but sometimes I wish this man Bastion who saved me, had just left me there to die in the explosion. Because at times, I feel like I killed my babies and deserved to die along with them." Whimpering softly, she buried her head into his chest.

"No, don't say that," he said quickly. "The devil wants you to think that but you cannot blame yourself for their deaths. Besides, from the way it sounds it was an accident; a terrible horrible accident. One that wasn't even caused by you." Drinian's own memories of loss from fifteen years before came back to haunt him as they flooded into his mind. Recalling in vivid detail, his horse, Rohn, falling away from him, as her footing had slipped on the wet narrow trail, he inhaled sharply.

Finally connecting the dots, Drinian's eyes grew wide; his horse Rohn, Veta Rohann. Was it really just a coincidence? And she'd named her cat, Drinian.

"Veta, when did you say the assault happened?"

"Fifteen years ago. May the eighteenth," she answered on a shrug, causing Drinian to tense slightly at the news. Not noticing his discomfort she continued. "I thought I was over the anger and the hurt. I've prayed about it and asked God to help me find peace. But clearly, I'm still struggling with the loss and I'm just so mad at Mitch. I don't know how else to be." New tears trickled down her face and she turned towards him.

Dismissing his musings for the moment, he turned his attention back to the woman before him, for her needs were more important. "You're still grieving," he said softly, remembering it had taken over a year before he got

257

on the back of another horse. Unable to imagine attempting to recover from the loss of a child, let alone three of them, he said a silent prayer that he'd find the right words to comfort her.

"You take the time you need to grieve. Then you move on." He tenderly stroked her cheek with his fingers. "Even Jesus mourned the loss of those He loved, Lazarus, being one of them."

"Yes, it's in the New Testament as I recall. John 11:35 says, 'Jesus wept.' I only remember it so well because it happens to be the shortest verse in The Bible." A half-smiled played at her lips as she curled her fingers into his shirt.

"He also tells us in Ecclesiastes, chapter three, verse four that 'He sets the time for sorrow and the time for joy, the time…'"

"…For mourning and the time for dancing," Veta finished for him. Drinian could feel her head nod gently against his chest as she sighed forlornly next to him. "Yes, I'm quite familiar with that one as well. I think I won't ever fully get over the loss of them. I know God is saying there will come a time when I'll want and even need to celebrate their life rather than mourn them. I thought I was getting there but I guess losing the memory boxes was kind of like losing them all over again."

Impressed at her knowledge of the Bible, and her perspective on it, he peered down at her intently as though confused. "How is it you've been able to maintain your belief in God after everything you've been through? Most in your position, would curse God, and become bitter."

Sitting forward, Veta turned and faced him. Her lashes fluttered momentarily against her cheeks, and she placed the palm of one hand against his chest near his heart. A twitch at the corner of her mouth gave away her humor at the inquiry.

"After everything I've been through, how can I not believe?" Seeing twin crinkles in his brow at the question, she proceeded to explain why she felt so strongly on the matter. "God was there with me that day in the library. I know it in my heart. I admit I may not have felt His presence at that moment. There was too much else happening to me at the time and it was my first experience with a man. But He was there, Drinian. Or at the very least an angel was protecting me. Of that I am sure."

Angered to hear that the men had stolen her virtue, he was equally appalled at the notion of an angel being present when it happened and scoffed. "How can you say that? You're telling me, you believe an angel of God was there, just watching four men abuse you?"

"I'm saying, I believe one of God's angels was protecting me from being killed that night. The doctors told me it was a miracle I hadn't suffered brain damage. They hit me in the head so many times, I required plastic surgery afterwards. I could have been blinded but I wasn't. I lived and I can see."

A sound of disgust erupted from Drinian's throat and his free hand thumped against the couch. He knew full well there was such a thing as angels for his brother Breydon could see them, and at times even talk to them. But the notion that one would have been present at such a deplorable act, and not waged war to prevent it, angered him. The mere thought that any man had harmed her in that manner, was making the darkness within him grow stronger, more feral. The desire to kill the men who hurt her increased in the same token.

"You see the demons that plague us, and yet, do not believe there are angels who protect us?" Veta asked, thoroughly perplexed by his response.

"If an angel was there, then he should have prevented it from happening in the first place."

"You're presuming the angel in question would have had a choice in the matter."

"Everyone has a choice…"

"*Mankind* has a choice," she interrupted hastily. "Angels, on the other hand, are not human, but God's holy warriors and messengers. They perform God's will at His behest and oftentimes after man has made *his* choice, regardless of the consequences to himself and others around him," she finished harshly.

Staring at her in confusion at first, Drinian was at a loss initially as to where she was going with what she was saying. Leaning back, he peered thoughtfully into the fire. After a moment a look of understanding softened his features. His head swayed up and down.

"You're speaking of mankind's free will."

"Yes. Bad things happen to good people every day because people make bad choices, not because God says it will happen. Can He prevent it? Of course. He is all powerful, after all. But sometimes…"

"Sometimes there is a lesson that needs to be learned."

"Exactly."

"And not necessarily by the person experiencing the suffering in question, but by those inflicting the harm." Drinian was somewhat annoyed to have his father's words being reiterated to him from such a beautiful mouth. Rafe had taught him this in his youth, and it was more than a little unsettling to be reminded of it by the extraordinary woman sitting next to him.

"And sometimes, it's meant to serve as a warning to others. I, a single woman, incapable of defending myself for I'd had no training, had no business being alone in that library that night and so late."

"A woman should be able to feel safe in familiar surroundings."

"That is a valid point, but a woman should also be mindful of her surroundings and not place herself in a dangerous position. Make no mistake, I don't blame myself for what *they* did to *me*, Drinian, for that was *their* choice. But I do blame myself for making the choice to be in the library in the first place when I shouldn't have been, and so late at that. After what happened to me, a new awareness group called the SMART program was created in order to educate college students – freshman in particular – on how to make safer choices." Rubbing at her face Veta's eyes began to droop, showing clear signs of exhaustion. Reaching out to her, he pulled her towards him, encouraging her to snuggle up next to him for warmth.

"It was a horrible thing to happen." She yawned. "No one should ever have to experience it but a lot of good did come from it. God blessed me with two children that day, and the SMART program was implemented the next semester."

"Some would not have viewed becoming pregnant from such an experience as a blessing. Especially with twins. They would have chosen to rid themselves of such a burden."

"Yes, and that would be *their* choice. Personally, I have never viewed my sons as burdens, but as gifts from God. I chose to have them. They lived for thirteen years until God called them home."

Sensing the sadness was starting to sink into her once again, Drinian shifted her into a more comfortable position. "Rest now, Veta."

She rested her head against his shoulder wearily. "But my cat," she said weakly not really wanting to leave anymore.

"I think he'll survive the night. We'll check on him together in the morning."

It felt so good holding her near. Drinian had never had any contact like this with a woman before, and it was only now that he realized how desperately he'd wanted it.

Before long they had both fallen into a peaceful sleep.

Chapter 22

Maleeka floated from room to room, as though checking up on those within to ensure their safety. After leaving the last room, he stopped at the landing and peered down. He watched Rafe stoking the fire and was pleased by his gesture for his son. In the past, he had always been so strict where his unwed children's partners were concerned, which was as it should be, but in this case, it was different. For Drinian and his situation were very different from the rest.

Seeing Rafe turn abruptly towards the kitchen he laughed aloud at seeing him become flustered and run from the room. In the man's haste, he attempted to leap across the chair and would have made it if he hadn't caught his large cowboy boot on the cushion. Hearing him swear and limp swiftly out of the room and up the stairs, the angel chuckled with humor.

"You're a good man with a tender heart," Maleeka said as Rafe walked past him on the landing. Stopping suddenly the man turned back, slanting his head thoughtfully. He raised his hand to his chest and patted at the place where his heart lay.

Rafe spoke quietly. "My love, though I wish it were you, I know it is not." Glancing about the stairwell and the entryway, he could still feel the sensation as though he were being watched but chose to move on, not wanting to disturb Drinian and Veta's time together. Turning once again, he headed down the hall taking the back way to his wing of the house. He figured he'd check in on them from the hidden room in his closet in a little while, just to make sure things were staying PG.

Feeling another presence join him, Maleeka turned to see Woreash by his side. As always, his wise eyes scanned his surroundings for the presence of the demons before greeting him accordingly.

"There are times when it seems that man might know you're there." The older messenger said. His age-worn eyes peered over at him then at the figure disappearing down the hall.

Turning their attention back to their charge, they floated down from the landing to the entryway below. They watched as Drinian carried Veta into the front living room and placed her gently on the couch.

"How did it go? Did you convince her to tell him?"

"Listen and you'll see." The messenger pointed his steady hand towards them. His expression was blank but Maleeka thought he saw a twinkle in his eye.

Listening, as Veta spoke of her anger at her children's death, Maleeka's hand flew to his chest. He could hear Drinian talk of her need to grieve and to eventually move on. The angel was pleased by his response. The man had handled himself well.

"She was so distressed earlier when Phillipe had to rip away the demon who'd taken her daughter's form. It's too much all at once."

"We cannot keep the dark ones from her forever. She will have to learn to deal with it. The quicker the better." The elder angel spoke forcefully, his brow furrowing in agitation.

"I suppose so. This one has just been through so much. I hate the thought of her having to endure any more than necessary."

"She is strong and can overcome. That's why she was handpicked for him." Eying his partner, Woreash inquired, "Can you manage the shadows and the troublesome three alone tonight? Or will you need assistance?"

"I take it you're going to work on Lylia?"

Smiling halfheartedly, the older messenger began floating toward the landing.

"She is quite bright that one. I only hope I can get through to her."

His counterpart disappeared.

He couldn't help but feel somewhat anxious about Lylia. Maleeka knew the woman was the obvious choice for she was, after all, Dartanian's wife. But her response to the Blackthorne children's abilities was starting to unsettle him. He couldn't help but wonder if she would be able to handle what was coming. She'd never really experienced a hardship like the others. That did seem to be a pre-requisite of sorts for some reason.

Pushing the uneasy thought out of the way, Maleeka watched Drinian as he slept, holding the woman in his arms. It pleased him to see them together. They were quite a good-looking couple as Crisalya had said and it was good to see things might be finally coming along. If this relationship stayed its course then it would give him and Woreash more time away to work on the other situation they had. They couldn't afford any more setbacks from the troublesome three and their minions.

Soon things would start to become more obvious, too. Lylia was already starting to figure things out in her head. Out of all of the Blackthorne's it had not occurred to him that she would be the one to start piecing it all together. He had presumed it would be Megorah since she was more familiar with Lilyandhi's journals.

Sighing heavily he glanced around, making sure the demons were staying at bay. It was important tonight that they keep their distance, so the couple could sleep peacefully. The gifts would finally present themselves fully soon. It was imperative they were all together to witness it and help her through it.

- - -

The next morning Drinian and Veta were found asleep on the couch. Having come down towards the front of the house, thinking he'd left his briefcase near the door, Breydon discovered them curled up together. In pure mischief mode, he crept up behind the couch and was about to whack Drinian across the back of the head for fun, when Rafe peered through the partition.

"Don't even think about it." Rafe glared, scowling with disapproval. "Thirty-eight years old and still acting like a ten-year-old."

Disappointed he'd been caught; Breydon gave a mischievous grin as he carried his briefcase with him into the kitchen. Setting it down near the table he strode over towards the coffee pot. Grabbing a mug from the cupboard, he poured himself a cup.

"One should never allow their age to prevent them from having a little fun." Breydon's response won him another scowl from his father. He chuckled. "Have they been there all night?" He watched his dad pull eggs and sausage from the fridge. Seeing him nod Breydon continued to eye his dad wearily. He was also grabbing onions, tomatoes and peppers, and began chopping them for what appeared to be omelets.

"*You're* making breakfast this morning?" Breydon asked in amazement.

Rafe worked in silence while frying the sausage, breaking it up in the pan.

Setting his mug down loudly, Breydon cleared his throat in disgust. He glared at his dad in frustration as Meg and Chase along with Hialey and Dartanian wander into the kitchen from the stairs.

"Let me get this straight. Not only did you let Drin have a woman in the house overnight, but you're taking his turn making breakfast this morning?"

"Veta's still here?" Hialey grinned mischievously. She ran around the counter and looked out through the partition. Seeing them cuddled up on the couch one hand flew to her chest and the other flew to her mouth. "You weren't kidding."

Having just come downstairs, Crisalya gawked at them. "How sweet."

"You all let them awaken at their own pace. Don't be like Breydon who tried to smack Drin awake." Rafe placed four pans on the stove. Tossing butter in each pan, he began adding ingredients to each of the pans, starting with whipped eggs.

Staring at the mess Rafe was making his children, now all present but Drinian, eyed him in dismay.

"Is he really trying to make omelets again?" Dartanian sounded perturbed.

"Yup. Trying, being the operative word." Breydon took a big gulp of his coffee.

Megorah became increasingly concerned at her dad's hurried movements. "Oh, dear."

"*This* is going to be her first breakfast in this house?" Dante was horrified at the notion.

"Not if I can help it. Cris?" Royce called, waving towards his wife for help.

"I'm on it." Crisalya took the spatula from her dad's hand and not so gently pushed him out of the way. "Dad, really. After forty years, you'd think you'd know better than to try and make an omelet. They never turn out right." She grinned at the wounded look he gave her.

Rafe's shoulders fell in defeat. Peering into the living room, he conceded, handing off the hot pad as well.

"Don't worry, Rafe. I'll take care of the omelets." Royce took over at the stove. Having all the ingredients, already handy, was going to make his job easier. After removing the mess Rafe had already started into one fry pan, he cooked up the egg mixture with a little more sausage, peppers, and onions, then threw it all in a casserole dish. Layering it with cheese from the fridge and a sauce from the cabinet, he put it in the oven to bake. Adding more butter to the now empty pans he began creating omelets.

Grumpy over being kicked from his own stove, Rafe disappeared into the pantry. When he came back he was carrying several boxes of donuts in his arms. He set them on the counter as Royce handed him a platter.

Everyone pitched in when the kids started coming down. The adults pulled out the cereal boxes, milk, juice and bananas and settled the children at the table near the patio. Picking their respective favorites, the kids began chowing down while laughing as Saruman – Astraia's son – made faces at his brother Storman.

The general noise and hubbub of the early morning ritual in the kitchen gradually awoke the sleeping couple in the other room. Drinian woke first, realizing that he hadn't actually been dreaming when he felt Veta still curled up in his arms. He stared down at her sleeping form as she slowly came awake. Somehow during the night she had adjusted and was now lying with her head in his lap. Content sitting as they were together, he smiled down at her.

Veta woke from one of the more peaceful night's sleep she'd had in a long time. She stared up at Drinian, gazing into his amazing eyes without saying a word. Comfortable, lying as she was, Veta was reluctant to move, and she had the sneaky suspicion he was feeling the same way. She felt his fingers gently grazing her cheek, as he stared into her bright green eyes. His voice was soft and deep as he spoke to her in a hushed tone.

"I believe my family is making breakfast if you're interested. It was … supposed to be my day to cook, but it seems they've taken matters into their own hands."

Leaning up reluctantly, Veta peered over toward the kitchen. She could see Royce cooking at the stove, while Crisalya was handing around plates of food to everyone at the table. Chase was grabbing a donut from the counter as was Dante, and they were fighting over who was going to get the last apple fritter.

"Wow. Is it always like that around here?" She was amazed at the noise and general camaraderie. "I mean, so many people all working together and enjoying each other's company. Like a real family." Her voice softened as she looked upon the familial setting with longing.

Drinian watched the play of emotions cross her face. The way Veta spoke, she sounded almost envious of what he had. Glancing into the kitchen, he really looked at the scene from an outsider's perspective for the first time. He'd never realized until that moment, how something as simple as having a family could be so appealing to others.

"Do you not have any family of your own left?"

"None that I'm aware of anymore." She shrugged sadly and sat up. "I was adopted, and my adoptive parents were killed in an accident when I was seventeen. What little family they did have was distant, so I never really knew any of them.

"Come. I'll share mine with you." He realized he still felt a bit damp in places as he stood. Reaching for her hand, he helped her up.

The instant she stood; a wave of nausea overcame her. Veta grabbed at her stomach. Dizziness soon followed though she managed to maintain her balance.

Observing the trouble she was having he helped steady her with an arm about her waist. Stepping into her, he allowed her to rest against him momentarily.

"You okay there?" he asked gently, against her hair.

Feeling the dizziness subside, Veta nodded her head. Though her stomach was still upset, she no longer felt as though she were going to be sick.

"Sorry. I guess I need more than two pieces of pie in a day." She chuckled, trying to play it off as being nothing. She was starting to become concerned by the incessant stomach discomfort and was beginning to think she might want to have it checked out. Hoping that getting some food in her belly would help it go away, she allowed Drinian to pull her along to the kitchen.

"Mihapmak, Drin," Crisalya called as they entered. Turning towards them she stopped suddenly and eyed

Veta thoughtfully. Leaving the kitchen she headed towards the pantry.

"Nice to finally see you join the living, Drin. Veta." Breydon greeted them between mouthfuls.

Veta could see the adults were having omelets, and they looked delicious. Following Drinian to the table, he pulled out a chair for her at the very end of it. Taking a seat she peered shyly around at everyone. It seemed as though her presence wasn't being viewed as anything other than normal.

"What do you like in your omelets, Veta?" Royce called across the kitchen, briefly glancing in her direction. Turning back, he poured more egg mix in a pan and began adding ingredients before she could reply. The sounds and smells of butter and eggs sizzling, over the general morning conversation filled her with a warm sensation as she sat there. She almost felt like she belonged there with them. Hearing children giggling at the table near the patio, she watched as several of them grabbed their dishes, carried them to the sink, and ran from the kitchen.

"Everything sounds good this morning." She eyed the donut tray on the counter. Turning unexpectedly, Dante leaned across to the counter and grabbed the platter of donuts. Handing it off to Drinian, he motioned for him to pass it to Veta.

"I take it this sounds good to you?" Drinian proffered the platter.

"I'm not sure actually," she said in surprise while eyeing what appeared to be a glazed blueberry donut thoughtfully. She was unsure if her stomach could handle it. Before she could choose, Rafe had come around and set two large mugs of coffee in front of her and Drinian.

"Black coffee with brown sugar, right?" Rafe asked.

Two more children left the table near the patio and headed out of the kitchen, leaving their cereal bowls behind.

"Why … yes. Thank you." Veta was more than a little stunned that the Blackthorne patriarch had remembered her preference.

"Oh, no. That's the last thing *she* wants this morning." Crisalya chastised her dad. She took the offending mug away from Veta and replaced it with a different one. "Royce, why don't you keep the onions out of that last one?"

"I'm already on it." He flipped two omelets out onto two different plates. Adding strawberries to both plates and hash brown potatoes to only one, he handed them across the counter to Crisalya as the last couple children left the kitchen on a dead run for the playroom.

"Here you go, Honey. That should help. Maybe even with a little toast." Crisalya grabbed the platter of toast and added a slice to both their plates.

Overwhelmed by the hospitality and a little unnerved by Crisalya's uncanny ability to sense what she needed, Veta wasn't sure where to start.

"What did you give her?" Lylia asked as Veta took a bite of her omelet. It was filled with sausage, cheese, peppers and tomatoes. It tasted amazing only it seemed to need some black pepper.

"Lemon Balm Tea," Crisalya said off-handedly in answer as she walked away. Coming to an unexpected halt, she spun around and eyed Veta with a look of astonishment on her face. At the same time, Lylia's head spun towards Veta. She stared at her wide-eyed.

Several other heads swiveled Veta's direction, including Drinian's, as she took another bite of her omelet.

Oblivious to the attention she was getting, Veta continued to eat ravenously.

"I thought you had that on hand for Alaina? You know, for her nausea." Megorah's brows furrowed suspiciously. Her gaze moved between Drinian and Veta.

"I don't mind," Alaina said, turning towards Veta as she smiled. "If Crisalya thinks she needs it, then I suppose she needs it."

Dante put his fork down on the table and eyed his wife. A curious expression crossed his chiseled tan features.

"This is very good but it needs pepper." Glancing down the table Veta saw salt and pepper shakers at the other end, near Dartanian and Rafe.

"Could you pass the pepper please?" She called, raising her right hand without thinking. Looking down at her plate she took her tea up with her left hand for a sip.

In that same instant, the living room door swung open. Drinian watched as a thirteen-year-old boy with hazel eyes and black hair sped to the table. Grabbing up the pepper shaker the boy crawled onto the table. He then carried it down the length of the table to Veta, placing it into her hand.

"Here you go Mama," the boy said, turning to Drinian with an evil grin.

"No." Drinian exhaled, his heart dropping to the floor at his feet.

There were several startled gasps and many stunned looks among everyone present, as the pepper shaker had found its way on its own volition down the table. They were unable to see the boy as Drinian could.

"Thank you, Cody," Veta said automatically then proceeded to shake the pepper over her omelet. Peering up

273

into her sons face Veta almost giggled as she smiled. "Cody, Honey, what are you doing on the table?"

Gaping at her openly, Drinian pushed his chair back with a start. Pointing at the figure on the table, he glanced frantically back and forth between Veta and the boy as it twisted its head unnaturally towards him, a gleam in its red eyes. Drinian looked at Veta, his eyes widening in dismay. He stammered, while his family looked on in confusion and alarm.

"You … you can see it?"

Peering over at Drinian curiously, Veta replied, "If by 'it' you mean my son Cody, then yes I… I…" Faltering in her speech, her head swiveled from Drinian to the figure of the boy now sitting hunched on the table in the butter. Only now she realized he was hovering there and his head was twisted grotesquely toward Drinian. Face gaping in horror, she watched the boy who looked so much like her son Cody, turn towards her and smile with a dark evil glimmer in his eye.

"Hi, Mommy. You miss me?" The unnatural sound of the boy's voice elicited an alarmed gasp from her lips.

Shoving forcefully back away from the table, she cried out in anguish and dismay as a bright flash of light exploded just to her left behind Hialey. What was happening? How could she possibly be seeing her son's spirit? She didn't think it was possible.

"Oh, jeez!" Breydon exclaimed, having been startled by the unexpected sight of a Guardian angel near the table between Veta and his wife. Its thick muscled arms slashed through the air, with a giant broadsword.

Screaming, Veta stretched her arms toward the table where her son once had been. She watched as the figure of the boy vanished without warning and was replaced by an inky greenish-back cloud of smoke. It expanded suddenly, billowing up and out across the table. The demons scaly face and giant hide erupted from within it and attempted to take flight. Halted in its progression by the force of the broadsword slashing through its hide, the demon squealed in pain, exploded without warning, then fizzled to the floor.

A keening wail emitted from Veta's throat at witnessing what had just happened. Her face contorted in agony and she stared upon the angel, now sheathing its sword at its side.

"That, that was my son!" She stared at the man before her who now looked upon her with pity. "How could you do that to my son?" She wailed in confusion over what had just happened.

"My sincerest apologies. We knew they would attempt something this morning but this... This was beyond cruel even for them." The angel Phillipe spoke calmly, his voice barely above a whisper as he spoke.

"Bring him back! Please bring my son's spirit back!" Tears rolled down her cheeks.

"That was not your son." The angel shook his head. "Spirits and ghosts do not exist. The Lord designates where souls shall rest upon a person's death. You should know that for it is written."

"My... my son is dead." Veta stammered, chest heaving with hysteria. Her eyes darted wildly about. Drinian stared upon her, in shock at the realization she had seen the demon, and it had taken her sons form to torment her.

"That's right, your son is with God." The angel spoke in a gentle soothing manner as he gazed upon her with sympathy.

"Then, what was that just now? A demon?" She was in shock.

"Yes."

"And you're … an angel," she said evenly suddenly knowing somehow that was the truth. Her arms stretched wide as she stood there before the angel. Veta sensed his answer even before he gave it, and the tension and fear within her suddenly abated.

"Yes."

"Wait a minute, you can see him?" Breydon gaped, pointing toward the angel standing next to her. Phillipe turned towards Breydon, deferring his head almost regally towards him as if to say what he was thinking was true. At that moment, Breydon knew as he gazed across the table towards his brother Drinian that Veta was, in fact, seeing both angels and demons.

"You're seeing them. Both of them. Angels and demons." Breydon's voice held within it the steely truth he was so adept at gaining from those around him.

Silence fell over the table as everyone shoved back in their chairs and stood. They stared down the table towards Veta as she trembled next to Drinian.

Stunned by what he'd just seen and heard, Drinian gazed wearily upon the dark-haired beauty next to him.

Clearing her throat self-consciously, Veta peered over at Drinian.

"How?" She whispered on a whimper. Her eyes searched his for answers then darted back towards Breydon. It occurred to her what Breydon's words meant, for though he could see the angels and Drinian could see the demons, it seemed neither could see them both as she just had.

"Veta, do you know what just happened?" Drinian asked her cautiously. His chest heaved with a mixture of excitement and anxiety at the realization of what this must mean.

"The boy looked like my son but he wasn't my son," she said in reply. The Blackthorne family members exchanged uneasy glances. "He couldn't be. There's no such thing as ghosts and spirits."

Clearing his throat Rafe dropped the newspaper he'd been holding and strode toward Veta, his expression appearing just as cautious as his son's. Having witnessed the pepper shaker carry itself down toward the end of the table, he'd known instantly what was happening and had been unable to prevent it from occurring.

"Veta, you say you saw someone who looked like your son?" Rafe asked. "Just now."

"Yes, but ... but he wasn't my son." She glanced towards the angel towering over her at her side then back at Rafe, trying to understand how it was possible she was seeing what she was and wondering if she was starting to go crazy.

"You're not crazy, sweet Veta." The angel spoke, knowing full well what she was thinking. "But you have been blessed," Phillipe said, gaining Breydon's attention.

"How? Why? I don't understand." Shaking her head in confusion, Veta clasped her hands together anxiously as they trembled slightly. Overwhelmed by the notion she was seeing a messenger from God, she moved one hand to her chest as the other pressed against her belly.

Lylia watched the scene play out before her as anger surged within her. Staring upon Veta, her expression changed suddenly from indifference to resentment. Her eyes seemed to flare and she flung her napkin on the table. Glaring across the table at her husband Dartanian, she swore at him angrily not caring at that moment that an angel might be present. The green-eyed monster known as jealousy festered within her, growing too great to squelch any longer.

"Now how much you want to bet she's pregnant?" Lylia asked in a snappish manner, her face coloring angrily. Slamming the chair into the table she stalked off out of the kitchen and back up the staircase to her room.

Chapter 23

Alarmed by what had just happened Veta didn't know what to think. It took her a moment to register what Lylia had said. She stared at Drinian, her alarm turning to shock.

"Why on earth would Lylia think I was pregnant, based off of what just happened?" Veta asked of Drinian then the room at large, presuming wrongly that everyone present had seen what she had.

"Messenger," Breydon spoke tentatively, gaining Veta's attention. "Can you tell me if there is any truth to…"

"Here now, I say to all of you. I am the Lord's messenger, Phillipe, and I am here to tell you, that Lylia is not wrong." Phillipe said softly, his gentle gaze swiveling from Breydon to Veta, then to Drinian. Watching Drinian's eyes become saucers the angel beamed openly at him. Other voices around the room could be heard exclaiming in surprise upon seeing the angel hovering next to Veta.

Drinian's chest heaved with emotion. He stumbled backwards, leaning up against the island counter for support. Gasping for air as his face streamed with tears, he

279

stared upon the bright glowing figure hovering before him. For the first time in his life, he was seeing one of God's holy angels. All of his life they had eluded him.

"I see… I see you." Drinian stammered as his family looked on in varying stages of shock, dismay and awe.

"Yes, Drinian, for though you have never been able to see our kind before this day, God has deemed this message is not for you and Veta alone but for all present to hear it. Though I daresay, sometime in the future you will be able to see us more frequently." Phillipe said with a smile as his eyes danced.

"But how can I be pregnant?" Veta asked suddenly in confusion. She gazed in wonder upon Phillipe's glowing countenance. "I can't have children anymore. The doctor told me after Sarah…"

"Anything is possible through God's grace." The angel Phillipe bent his head towards her. "Congratulations, Drinian, you shall soon become a father. It is the Lord's desire that the two of you shall become one in marriage." With that final statement, he promptly disappeared.

"Whoa!" Breydon exclaimed in shock while gaping at Drinian.

"Breydon, are they always so big and bright and, well, big?" Hialey stammered next to her husband in awe, having recovered quicker than most.

Stunned at what had just happened and what she'd heard, Veta's eyes wandered the room in a daze, eventually latching onto Drinian's. They stood silently staring upon each other, unable to speak.

Sensing everyone's eyes upon her Veta ran her hand across her face in agitation. Self-consciously she began backing further away from the table. Though she felt no fear, she did sense an inordinate amount of anxiety surging within her.

"What's going on here Drinian?" Her gaze shifted to his again as though searching for answers. The knowledge she was pregnant was overwhelming her. She suddenly had the distinct impression there was so much more going on. "You can see demons but not angels," she said finally, pointing at Drinian. Then gesturing towards Breydon she continued, "And you can see angels but not demons?"

Gazing surreptitiously towards his father Breydon observed Rafe gave a brief nod towards him, as though to say it was okay to answer. Inhaling deeply he placed his mug on the table.

"You are correct."

"How am I seeing both?" She pressed her hand further into her belly. "What the angel Phillipe said, about me being pregnant. Does that have something to do with it?" She stared up at Drinian, imploring him for answers. "What aren't you telling me? Did I really just see that?" Gesturing wildly towards the table where the demon had taken her son's form but moments ago, Veta couldn't help but think she was starting to go crazy. Angels and demons, how was this even possible? She knew such things happened during the time of the Bible but this was the year 2015. What she had experienced seemed almost surreal somehow.

"To answer your second question first..." Rafe paused, then glanced around at each one of his children, in turn, settling last on Drinian. Making a hasty decision for them all he continued. "What he's not telling you happens to be a family secret. One that would affect all of them if it would happen to get out."

"A family secret," she repeated anxiously. She stared back at Rafe still trying to recover from having been in the presence of an angel. Seeing him nod, she glanced over at Drinian, noticing he was watching her intently.

"Yes. My children are unlike most for they have been gifted with … special abilities."

"Special abilities," she repeated automatically, having difficulty processing what was being said. "But how," she began in astonishment. Rafe interrupted her by raising his hand to silence her.

"These gifts were bestowed by God along both lines of our family and have culminated into what they have now. Being pregnant with Drinian's child is how you were able to see the angels and demons." He spoke quietly, hoping he hadn't just scared her away.

Not saying anything at first, she looked around at everyone, wondering if they'd all gone crazy, too. Her other hand flew to her belly as she glanced Drinian's way out of the corner of her eye. She had been irritatingly nauseous for the past week. Veta hadn't thought she could have children anymore but according to the angel she was now pregnant.

"You know, I didn't think I could have any more kids either," Alaina said suddenly, interrupting Veta's train of thought. "I'd had a tubal ligation after my boys were born. And yet, two weeks ago I found out I was pregnant. A messenger told me as well. I do understand a little how you're feeling right now."

"We're not crazy," Dante said, trying to reassure her. "I can sense your instinct right now is to run but I would strongly encourage you to at least hear us out."

Veta's first instinct was, in fact, to flee. Unsure what exactly was going on she glanced around at them wearily. When the angel had been present she had felt no fear but now anxiety surged within her. Her breathing became heavy. Glancing down at the tea on the table a nagging thought occurred to her. Crisalya had switched out her coffee with herbal tea. Was it possible she was imagining this? Had Crisalya slipped her something for some reason?

"Crisalya would never do that," Dante said promptly as if he were reading her mind. "Lemon Balm Tea is for nausea. She was just trying to help you."

"How did she know I was nauseous?" Veta's eyes narrowed suspiciously upon Crisalya then Dante. The air next to him was vague and hazy, holding a soft light. Blinking twice she tried to clear her vision, thinking her eyes were playing tricks on her. But the view didn't change. "And how do you keep doing that? It's as though you can read my..."

"Mind," Dante finished for her, staring around at each of his siblings in turn. "Are we all in agreement?" He asked them quietly, peering down toward Drinian. Dante could see the hopeful expression on his face. He looked at Veta with such wanting that it nearly hurt to see him so desperate.

"I don't think we have a choice," Dartanian said aloud irritably. He wiped at his mouth with a napkin, threw it on the table then sidled up next to his brother. Staring back at the woman at the end of the table, he could tell her anxiety was building, even without having his sister's ability. He was concerned about how she was going to take the news especially upon learning she was with child. "Meg?"

"This is too important," Megorah responded with an affirming nod. She turned towards Veta. "Yesterday, when you first saw Drinian and fainted, you were seeing the demons then weren't you?" Seeing Veta swallow hard and bob her head in ascent, she continued. "And the pepper shaker this morning..." she went on, her brows furrowing thoughtfully in agitation. "The demons are messing with you, as they did with the Indian woman from mom's story two hundred years ago. If this were to happen in our time and in public at that…" Her speech faltered as a sudden chill could be felt in the air around them. The chair Veta had been sitting in shot across the room.

Letting out a startled cry, Veta jumped as the chair skittered across the floor, having been shoved there by three black shapeless cloudy substances now hovering before her. Hands outstretched and shoulders hunched she cringed inwardly, the cold emanating from them enveloping her. Backing up towards the nearest cabinet, away from the three black vaporous faceless figures, she put her trembling hands up as though to ward them off.

"Who are you? What do you want from me?" Veta cried out, frightened by what was happening. She suddenly felt like she'd stepped into a fantasy fiction movie.

Drinian's arms flexed, his hands balling into fists. He growled at the troublesome three, his angry visage becoming dark and ominous. "Get out of my father's house," he roared. "You have no place here. Those within these walls serve the Lord."

Shrieking and clawing at their heads the demons snarled, baring their teeth. Their red eyes glowed with menace, writhing in place as Drinian continued to yell. Desperate to be free of the pain, the inky black vaporous creatures took on a cloud-like form and soared from the kitchen out through the patio. Wisps of black tentacles trailed behind them.

Shrinking away from the scene, Veta watched in horror as they disappeared. Her irises were wide with fright and her pupils began to dilate in shock.

"It's really important, Veta. Never speak to them directly." Rafe urged, gaining her attention. At her questioning look, he explained. "They must be treated with indifference and ignored at all cost. If you encourage discussion by responding to the demons, then you give them an opening..."

"An opening? To what exactly?" She wailed as she slumped to the floor, tears threatening at her eyes. Suddenly, somehow knowing what he meant she replied. "They want to turn me away from God. So they can use this gift against Him. Tell me the truth Breydon, I know you cannot lie. Truth is your gift."

"Whoa." Both Hialey and Crisalya exclaimed in surprise, watching as Veta had slumped on the floor.

"And you Megorah, you sense my fear and you, Dante, you're not reading my mind you're ... being given my thoughts by the angel at your side." She gestured toward the hazy light next to him. The knowledge was coming to her in waves. It was almost dizzying at its intensity.

Megorah came around the table and knelt down next to Veta on the floor. Her skirts billowed around her legs and feet. Eyeing her thoughtfully, a soft sad smile played at the corners of her lips. Taking Veta's trembling hands in hers, she looked her in the eye with a knowing expression.

"I understand your fear," Megorah said, feeling Dante's presence as he quietly stepped around her in order to kneel down next to his sister's side for support. "This is all very new, alarming even. I'd wager that the demons are trying to instill fear within you in order to separate you from my brother. I'm concerned about your state of mind right now. Any chance I can get you to calm down a bit? I can sense how anxious you are, but there's no need to be afraid. We'd never hurt you, nor would Drinian."

"Oh, I know he wouldn't," she said quickly, winning herself a bright smile from Crisalya. "I just don't know ... what to think right now," she said quietly. Confused and anxious, she looked imploringly at Drinian then glanced once again towards the table where her son had been moments before.

She'd thought briefly it might have been her son's spirit, but then had known it couldn't be since ghosts and spirits don't exist. Demons, however, were real and would take on the form of a lost loved one in order to torment or trick a person into believing they were real. Overwhelmed by what she was learning, and what had happened, she leaned up against the cabinets behind her.

Kneeling down on the floor next to her, Drinian took Veta's hands from Megorah. Consumed by the knowledge that she was pregnant with his child, he struggled momentarily with how to begin. Glancing at Megorah as though seeking permission she nodded in assent.

"It's going to infuriate Lylia to no end but go ahead. I think under the circumstances she has the right to know."

Drinian turned back towards Veta. "My mother was a full-blooded Indian, and the last in the line in her tribe which had been gifted with ... certain abilities," he explained. He paused, searching for the right words. "When she met my father, she learned that these gifts or abilities had been blessed to them by God and not mother earth as they had originally been taught by their elders. That's when she became a Christian." Drinian said cautiously, trying to gauge her reaction. Taking a deep breath he went on.

"Now, we don't know why God has bestowed them along our line as He has, and for that matter, we might never know. Most people can actually have discerning tendencies. Ours are just much more prevalent than in most, for we were all born with a specific ability as my father said moments ago. As you deduced, Megorah can sense people's emotional state. Breydon can discern the truth as well as see angels. Dartanian can discern good and evil within a person by way of a dark or white light which seems to surround most people. Dante can discern thoughts. Crisalya is a…."

"A healer. Of course, that makes sense now." Veta began to understand Crisalya's behavior that morning and at the shop. Seeing Drinian nod Veta became embarrassed at the realization that Dante might have known what she'd been thinking all morning.

"And I have the ability to see demons," Drinian said finally. "As you now well know, they appear as a shadowy form, or essence, which is why I grew up calling them shadows. Sometimes, they will take on a corporeal form if they are really strong. But they typically don't have clear facial features when they do unless they are attempting to look like someone specific. Like this morning when the demon took on your son's appearance." His voice filled with raw emotion as he watched Veta's face contort in agony at the memory. "I'm so sorry. That was beyond cruel of them. I wish I could stop them from tormenting you but I have no real power over them; only God does. It would seem I'm only able to cause them pain with the sound of my voice when I become angry or belligerent. Only then will they stay at a distance and that's only to keep from experiencing the pain."

"Have you always been able to see them?" She asked, wiping tears from her eyes with shaky hands. She wasn't so much afraid anymore as she was disturbed by what she'd seen.

"They have plagued me my entire life," he said quietly in response, sitting down next to her on the floor. He looked tired, and his handsome features had become drawn.

Taking it all in, Veta just sat there deep in thought over what she'd learned, and what the angel Phillipe had said. Thinking back over Crisalya and Megorah's behavior, she realized she could pinpoint when they had been utilizing their gifts with her.

"I won't try and discount what you're telling me." Drinian instantly dropped her hands and pushed back away from her, disappointed. "Because based off of what I've experienced and seen just this morning, I tend to believe you," she said, trying to reassure him that she didn't think he was nuts. "But to clarify, you're saying…"

"That you can see angels and demons because you're pregnant with my child who will, in turn, be born with this gift," he finished for her, his voice filling once again with raw emotion as he spoke. The distress in his eyes was evident, as was the faint inkling of hope there as well. The wounded little boy was back once again in his demeanor. His shoulders hunched uneasily, and his lips twitched anxiously. Appearing lost and vulnerable, she sensed sadness within him.

"Gee, are you sure you don't discern thoughts?" She asked tremulously, hoping to alleviate some of the tension of the moment.

Chuckling softly, Drinian chucked her chin playfully. Inching toward Veta, he watched her closely, waiting to see if she'd bolt on him. Reaching for her hands again he was amazed to see that after everything she'd learned, she hadn't flinched from his touch. Sighing heavily he leaned his head back briefly then eyed her carefully. He proceeded to massage her hands gently with his fingers.

"I'm afraid I'm going to be spending a lot of time apologizing to you. See, the thing is, none of us Blackthorne men are supposed to be able to have children. Though, it would seem that has changed recently for some reason," he said, as though an afterthought. "The same thing happened recently with Dante and Alaina. She'd been experiencing some unusual symptoms and he thought she was sick. He brought her here to the ranch two weeks ago. That's when they discovered she was actually pregnant. What she was experiencing were the abilities that her children will one day be born with."

"I see. You mean Alaina can also discern thoughts, like Dante?"

"Yes, she can also have prophetic dreams." Taking a deep breath he went on. "And she also frequently seems to know things, without knowing why. My grandmother Saphire called it, the gift of 'Knowing'."

"You mean her child will have three gifts?" Veta peered over at Alaina across the room, noting she was shaking her head.

"No, she's pregnant with triplets. Each child will have its own gift."

"Wait. What does that mean for me? I'm seeing both Angels and demons."

"And you would appear to be presenting with the ability to know things without knowing why as well," Rafe interjected, "which could imply you're expecting twins."

Frowning in consternation Veta was confused. "But seeing angels and demons; aren't those two separate abilities?"

"It should be a conjoined gift," Megorah said, gaining Veta's attention.

"But then, why…"

"Why are they separated between Breydon and Drinian?" Dante finished for her. He bowed his head in frustration.

Veta gazed around at them all in confusion. Dartanian finally replied after a moment, eliminating the silence. "It seems our mother may have made a mistake when we were born."

"It's a bit of a long story." Drinian rested his head against the wall again. In the back of his mind, he realized he desperately needed to find the journal of his mother's that had disappeared. He needed to read through it, and refresh his memory, on what Lilyandhi's prophecy said. The numbers seemed extremely important all of a sudden.

Sitting next to Drinian, Veta leaned back against the wall for support. Having been stunned into silence for a while, she simply rested there, trying to take in everything she'd just learned as a measure of calm overcame her.

What he was saying would seem to make sense. She'd never been able to see angels and demons before now. Standing unexpectedly, Veta adjusted her shirt awkwardly. Turning towards the door to leave, she could hear Drinian inhaling sharply as he came up from the floor.

"Veta, wait please." The distress in Drinian's voice was obvious. She couldn't help but feel a little guilty for the worried expression on his face. He'd looked so hopeful at her moments ago when he'd spoke.

"Drin, I just..." Veta raised her hands up in the air and anxiously backed away. She could feel herself trembling at his close proximity. No one she'd ever known had ever been able to affect her the way he did. "Please. It's a lot to take in all at once. I just … please, Drin." Her eyes were tearing up and she choked back a sob. "I understand, I do," she said almost pleadingly. "I won't say anything to anyone. I won't," she promised as she continued backing away. Her eyes darted frantically around the room, imploring them to understand. "I just… I need some time … and I have to go." Turning hastily she ran from the kitchen and out the front door.

- - -

Watching her flee from the room, Woreash flung himself across the room in front of Drinian. He could sense the man's first instinct and knew he had to temper it for now.

"Maleeka, go! She cannot be alone right now. I'll follow shortly."

Sensing the woman's distress as she ran through the living room Maleeka floated in step with her. Eyeing her closely, he could tell something was wrong and it had nothing to do with what had just happened.

Chapter 24

An uneasy quiet settled over the kitchen.

Drinian stared after Veta through the partially opened kitchen door. His first instinct was to go after her. To chase her down, drag her over his shoulder and hall her back to his cabin. But he knew, that would merely frighten her even more. She was clearly scared enough as it was. Instead, for the longest time, he didn't move or speak. Sighing heavily he finally turned around only to see that his family had been watching him carefully.

"What are you looking at?" He growled angrily and stalked over to the table. Sitting heavily in his chair, dwarfing it, he reached for his coffee mug. Scowling over at Veta's partially eaten breakfast plate, he worried that she hadn't gotten enough to eat. Being pregnant she would need all the nourishment she could get.

"Drin," Megorah spoke up finally. "It will all work out in the end. You'll see."

He turned on her viciously. "Really? You think so do you? Because every woman wants to be taken advantage of and seduced by a man, then find out they're pregnant with a freak of nature," he said bitterly.

Rafe lashed out at his son. "Drinian Tolin Blackthorne, your child will not be a freak of nature."

Standing abruptly, knocking over his chair, Drinian glared at his father. "Oh, I know that. I'm just saying exactly what I can only imagine is running through her head right now. Ten to one she'll have herself in an abortion clinic by this afternoon."

"We can't let that happen," Crisalya declared urgently.

"Are you, of all people, going to advocate for a woman to carry a child she doesn't want to have?" Royce said surprising everyone. He stared down his wife.

Crisalya's face turned bright red. Eyes brimming with tears she threw down the platter she'd been holding in her hand, stalked out of the patio door and out onto the lawn.

Though the exchange was suspicious, Rafe and Megorah were too distracted by the current situation to think much of it. Making a beeline for her brother, Megorah reached up and took his face in her hands. She could see the defeated expression on his face and feel the sadness in his heart as he stood with shoulders slumped. His lips quivered. He was trying desperately to reign in his emotions in an attempt to hide them from her.

"Drin, you don't know that for sure. Not every woman who finds herself unexpectedly pregnant will have it aborted."

Drinian tried to pull away from her but she held him fast.

"She is not Elizabeth," she said firmly, maintaining her grip on his face. "The men in this family make presumptions of that nature about a woman because of what happened between Dante and his first wife. I know.

293

I get that." Megorah finally let go of him. "But that was one situation, and you and Veta are two entirely different individuals."

Hialey spoke up suddenly. "She just needs time, Drin, as she said. All of this is new to her and I imagine a little scary."

"But not too much time," Dartanian interjected, winning himself a scowl from Hialey. "Because she's a ticking time bomb right now." Seeing Megorah staring back at him crossly, he shrugged his shoulders and glanced down at his watch. "All I'm saying is up until now all of the abilities that we've had experience with haven't been that obvious. The demons are openly messing with her though and moving objects in her presence in order to accomplish it. If they do that in public someone could see. You can't leave her alone for too long, Drin," Dartanian finished, becoming anxious at the late hour.

"I hate to say it but he's right," Rafe agreed. "Go, Dart. I know you need to get to the station. We've all still got our lives to live here. Breydon, you too. I remember you said last night you had an early morning appointment."

Grabbing up his suitcase Breydon reached out and gave Drinian a brotherly tap on the shoulder. Drinian acknowledged the gesture as Breydon leaned toward Hialey and kissed her goodbye.

"I need to motor as well. My shop should be opening real soon," Hialey quipped, pulling Breydon back down for another kiss. Glancing apologetically toward her brother-in-law she headed toward the door.

"I hate to say it but I need to get out of here too." Royce came around the counter while glancing out the patio door. "I was supposed to open the Haven this morning." Turning towards Drinian, he paused a moment, thinking twice about whether or not to say something.

"Drin, if it's any consolation, I suspect that her twin sons might have been the product of a rape." Royce began tentatively. Drinian eyed Royce with something akin to admiration. It wasn't the first time he'd noticed how perceptive the man could be.

"You would actually be correct on that." Seeing both his dad's and Dartanian's expressions, Drinian rolled his eyes in exasperation. "She told me all about it last night. Let me guess. You all did background checks?" Nodding somewhat sheepishly, Dartanian and Rafe exchanged looks.

"All I'm saying is, a woman who would carry to term, give birth to, and keep children from such an experience, is not going to give up a child that easily." Royce continued. Having said his mind, he headed on out, anxious now to get to the coffee house. He was already late opening his own business.

Dartanian followed not far behind him, after hastily thumping his brother on the back on his way.

"Wow, Chase really does miss everything doesn't he?" Megorah said suddenly, glancing over at her brother.

"Where is Chase? The clinic?" Rafe asked, realizing for the first time he hadn't seen him since he'd been fighting with Dante over the apple fritters. "I didn't even notice him leave."

Megorah replied, "He had to go in early, so he took a donut and coffee with him." Walking around the counter, she reached for the dishwasher, pulling a Tupperware container out and setting it on the counter.

"Drin, you have a good excuse for going and seeing her this afternoon. She left this behind." She pointed at the container.

"She's going to see that coming from a mile away." Rolling his eyes Drinian scoffed and kicked at the chair in front of him moodily.

"Oh, I'm sure." Megorah acknowledged, "especially now with her gift of 'Knowing.' But it may just get your foot in the door. And that's all that matters right now."

- - -

Veta spent the morning holed up at home, literally on pins and needles. Her agitation was almost palpable. Sitting curled up on her couch, she eyed the bag on her kitchen table anxiously. When she'd arrived home she'd taken a long shower, and then stood in her house robe staring at her open fridge, trying to determine what she wanted to try eating. Eventually, she'd opted for a bagel with egg and cheese along with orange juice. It hadn't tasted near as good as the omelet Royce had made and it sat heavy in her stomach.

Since she hadn't gotten around to buying a television yet she sat down on the couch with her book as she drank a glass of water. But she couldn't seem to get into the story. The bag on the table kept drawing her attention. Deciding that continuing to read was pointless, she got up and wandered over to the table. Taking a deep breath, she pulled the box from the bag with shaking fingers as a wave of excitement, as well as, trepidation hit her. Seeing a soft light flicker nearby she sensed there might be an angelic presence at her side and was grateful for it. The shadows didn't seem inclined to leave her alone. She could see their black cloudy formless shapes peering eerily out at her, as they cowered in the corners of her apartment; their mannerism that of a predator waiting to pounce. Knowing the angel was near put her at ease. Veta couldn't even imagine what Drinian went through only seeing the demons.

"Please God. Please let this be real, don't let this be a cruel joke," she said quietly, trying to get her emotions under control. Sniffling softly her hands trembled as she tore open the box of the early pregnancy test and headed towards the bathroom. It wasn't so much that she didn't believe what the angel had said, that prompted her to take the test. It was more a desire to confirm everything was real and she wasn't going crazy. The further she'd driven away from the Blackthorne ranch house, the more she sensed the demons were attempting to plague her with doubtful thoughts. Mumbling miserably, she sneezed for the third time that morning, stepped towards the sink and stared at her drawn appearance in the mirror.

"This is obviously just a formality." she couldn't help but say aloud. After all, how else could she explain how she could see the demons and angels? Not to mention how she'd known of the Blackthorne's abilities even before being told.

Veta sneezed again as she read the instructions then proceeded to take the test. Setting it on the sink counter, she dropped her house robe and hopped into the shower. Turning on the water, she stood for a long time under the shower head, reveling in the feel of the water as it poured down over her. Holding herself, she remembered how Drinian had embraced her the night before after she'd told him about her past.

It had felt so good being carried back to the house in his big strong arms as the rain had washed down over them. Veta had felt so safe with him. And when she woke up that morning he was gazing down at her with those beautiful eyes of his. Veta had been lost. Which was insane, of course, because it became very clear at breakfast that she didn't really know anything about him.

After a long time, Veta stepped out of the shower and dried herself off. Putting her robe back on, she sneezed again and grabbed a tissue to blow her nose. Just great, she thought to herself. Her throat was scratchy and she could feel pressure on her sinuses. Now, after everything, she was also coming down with a cold. Staring at the test on the sink she finally worked up the nerve and reached for it. Glancing down she saw the plus sign on the stick and sighed. A weak smile played at the corner of her lips.

"Those nasty demons are trying to make me believe otherwise; shame on them." Still holding on to the test, she wandered out into the living room in a daze and lay down on the couch.

Staring at the test in her hand, Veta began to come to terms with the knowledge, that she was, in fact, pregnant. Laying her hand on her stomach she smiled wistfully, daydreaming of holding a tiny baby in her arms again. Her eyes welled with tears when she thought of the children she'd lost, wishing they could meet their new brothers or sisters.

Turning on her side, she noticed her head felt heavy and her body ached. Unusually tired, she allowed herself to fall asleep, hoping her dreams would allow her some peace for a while.

When Veta woke a long time later her eyes were blurry and she felt feverish. Shaking uncontrollably from chills, she suddenly realized someone was kneeling over her. Blinking several times Veta could feel a cool damp washcloth being held to her forehead. She could see Drinian's worried face hovering above her. Tilting her head to the side she could see through the window that the sun appeared to be setting.

"Drinian?" she asked groggily. Her throat felt nearly swollen shut but she coughed painfully anyway, nearly gagging on phlegm.

Turning her on her side so she could cough into a tissue he'd brought up next to her, Drinian stared down at her in concern. When he had arrived at her apartment an hour ago, he had become agitated, when he'd banged on her door and no one answered. Her car was parked near the building. He was sure she was home, so he'd peered through the window.

Stunned and angry to see her being lifted four feet above the couch by a demon, he'd frantically searched his key ring for his master key. Afraid the demons intent was to drop her in an attempt to harm her, he'd used it to let himself in.

Upon entering, Drinian had hastily placed the flowers, casserole dish and Tupperware bowl on the coffee table, then cautiously strode around it towards her. The demon had glowered at him as if daring him to yell. He'd stared at the demon as though in a stand-off, willing it not to drop her.

"If you let her fall, I warn you Veranke, I will cause you more pain then you could possibly ever imagine," Drinian warned in a dangerously ominous tone. He'd watched as the demon sniggered through a wheezing cough then nudged at her robe, causing it to fall open and bare her shapely leg.

Sensing the presence of numerous other demons within the room Drinian had quickly assessed the situation. A flurry of inky greenish-black demonic figures had been whirling about the room as though in the midst of a fight. Long black swords could be seen slashing and bashing at what he could only presume were angels attempting to defend the woman hovering above the couch. Not wanting to alarm her more than necessary, Drinian snarled at the demon as he spanned the distance between them in three long strides. He lunged for her just as Veranke dropped her forcefully towards the floor next to the couch.

Feeling as though he were being lifted up off the floor and flung across the room in order to catch her, he had a moment's sensation of unreality. His arms ensnared her mere seconds before she'd hit the floor. Carefully wrapping his arm around her, Drinian gently laid her back on the couch. He bellowed towards the demons, forcing them from the room with the sound of his voice, and he imagined, the assistance of the angels present. Grateful for their help in protecting Veta, he'd taken a moment to say a brief prayer of gratitude over her still sleeping form on the couch. Laying a hand on her shoulder it was then he'd felt how hot she was and realized she was in real trouble.

Drinian attempted to cool her off by using ice water and wet washcloths on her forehead. It had taken quite some time to finally even get a response from her.

"Veta, honey. How long have you been like this?" he asked, bending over her.

"Don't know," she said quietly. Her face was flushed and he could see bags under her eyes. "I lay down sometime before lunch." She felt chilled to the bone and couldn't seem to stop shaking.

"Veta, you're on fire, Honey. I can't get your fever down," Drinian said quietly near her. He smelled really good like he'd just come from a shower. She noticed he was wearing a dress shirt and slacks. Seeing the flowers and casserole pan on the coffee table she realized he'd been attempting to romance her and was touched by his thoughtfulness.

"Drinian, how did you get in?" she asked as he laid another cool washcloth on her forehead. Hazy glowing lights seemed to float across the ceiling playfully. She watched in wonder, the mere sight of them putting her at ease.

Shrugging, he replied, "I own the building. I have a master key. Megorah didn't tell you?" Seeing her shake her head no, Drinian grimaced. "I knocked several times then peered through your window. When I saw one of the demons making you float above your couch I became worried it was trying to hurt you."

Veta raised her hand to her cheek and could feel how hot and sweaty she was, even with the cool washcloth. Shaking noticeably, she pulled her hand away and it fell limply to her side. It was then that she realized the stick for the pregnancy test was no longer in her hand.

"Drinian?" she could hear herself speaking weakly as her eyes flew open. "Drinian, I'm pregnant!" she cried out in alarm. It occurred to her a fever could be very dangerous to the babies.

"I know, the angel told us." Grinning from ear to ear, he turned toward the test on the table and smiled down at it. "And I saw the test." Looking back at her he realized she was starting to cry.

"Veta, it's okay, Honey. I promise I'll be here. I'll help you through this."

"You don't understand," Veta said urgently. "A fever right now could be dangerous. I could miscarry. I need to go to the hospital, now, please. Please, help me." she cried as she tried to lift up from the couch but became dizzy. Looking past him she could have sworn she saw a dark figure poised near the fridge with a sword in hand as though awaiting an assault. Seeing it charge towards them she flinched. Out of the corner of her eye, one of the golden lights above the ceiling took on the form of a man with fierce green eyes and golden hair. Shooting down from the ceiling he halted the demon's movements with his own gleaming broadsword. The angel, who had called itself Phillipe at the Blackthorne house, forced the demon back towards the kitchen.

"Then let's go. I'll take you myself." Drinian said, reaching down to lift her from the couch. Fear enveloped him at her words. Concerned for both Veta and his children, he stared at her anxiously. Ignoring the sniping dark shadows who had rushed up behind him in an attempt to hinder him, he hastily tried pulling her into him as an unseen entity seemed to force the demons back.

Suddenly, she pushed his hands away and stared up at him. The movement caused her to nearly fall on the floor. Something he'd just said finally registered to her.

"No. No, Drinian, wait! Did you say I was floating when you came in?" Seeing him nod she stared at him briefly, realizing even in her foggy haze what that meant. Shaking her head, she looked up at him as he lifted her into his arms.

"You can't take me to the hospital, Drin, or the clinic. What if the demons make me float, or they move things in my presence again? It will look like I am doing it. How will we explain that?" Dizzy, she glanced about the room. Even with the lights, it seemed to be growing darker for some reason. She couldn't understand why.

"I don't care. You need help." He carried her out the door. She coughed violently next to him, and he headed quickly down the steps to his SUV. The pesky shadows who had taken positions outside her apartment, swooped low about his feet, attempting to trip him but he deftly stepped past them, accustomed to their wily ways.

Holding her close, he opened the passenger door with his free hand and placed her in the seat.

Brushing her hair out of her face, he buckled her seat belt and kissed her gently on the forehead. A shadow swooped past him through the vehicle, startling Veta, causing her to gasp, but it dissipated quickly. Drinian was close by. She knew, for certain now, that God's angels were attempting to protect her. She did not need to be afraid.

Running around the vehicle Drinian jumped in and started the engine. Her hand reached out and covered his as he attempted to put the vehicle in motion. Glancing over at her, they locked eyes and he could see her pleading with him.

"Drin, no, I won't be the cause of your family's secret getting out," she said imploringly while swatting at a pesky shadowy substance near her cheek.

Drinian stared straight ahead of him, deep in thought.

"What do you expect me to do, Veta, nothing? Because I won't do that; I can't put your life or the lives of our babies at risk just to keep our secret from becoming public knowledge. No one in my family would ever ask that." He sat back heavily in the driver's seat and put the vehicle in motion. Turning towards her, he asked impatiently, "Do you want these babies, Veta?"

Tears filled her eyes. Sobbing, she placed her hand across her stomach hugging herself as though afraid to let go. "Drinian, I want them so bad. I can almost feel them in my arms. I can't lose another one." she cried as she began coughing heavily. Her face contorted in pain and discomfort. Squeezing her eyes shut she tried to ignore the dark substances flitting before her eyes, along with the bright golden lights which attempted to chase them away through the closed windows of the vehicle.

Sighing with relief Drinian drove south on Spokane Avenue at an accelerated speed. Reaching over, he patted her leg and smiled at her, worry lines etched in his face.

"Then we most definitely need to get you some help."

Drinian could hear Veranke cackling near his ear, and he sensed Veta shiver next to him. Gritting his teeth he stared straight ahead, ignoring the dark spirits incessant chanting that his babies would soon die.

"Drinian, what about Dr. Ryans?" Veta said urgently, becoming angry at the demons words and foul language. Turning her head towards the demon who had positioned himself between herself and Drinian, she glared defiantly. "These filthy demons cannot win; will not win. God has always and will always take care of me." she insisted firmly, determined to thwart whatever evil plans they might have for her and her children.

Snarling at her, Veranke began to speak only to be interrupted by the presence of an unexpected glowing light coming up through the floor of the vehicle still in motion. Grasping hold of the demon's neck, the angel smiled broadly at Veta and thrust them both up through the ceiling of the vehicle removing the foul creature from their presence.

Smiling as Drinian realized the suggestion she was making, he turned towards her abruptly, as he drove.

"Chase is at the ranch right now."

Drinian could see Fallen hovering just outside the vehicle next to Veta through the passenger window. The shadow turned suddenly toward him with an angry visage. The idea seemed to be upsetting him, leading Drinian to believe it was their best and safest option.

"Then take me there. Take me home," she said wearily. She leaned back in the seat and rested her head against it, closing her eyes to the images all around her.

Already at peace and unafraid in Drinian's presence, she found the notion of going back to the Blackthorne Horse Ranch just as comforting for some reason.

Drinian's heart skipped a beat at her words. She wanted their babies just as much as he did, and she'd called the ranch home. It was more than he could have ever hoped for when he'd left the ranch earlier in the day. Swatting at Veranke and Fallen with his wiper blades as they attempted to obscure his vision of the road, he swerved but managed to stay on course. Unseen by his eyes, the angel Phillipe was met by Maleeka and Woreash. They proceeded to chase the demons away from the vehicle. Outside the vehicle, a swarm of demons ascended from the ground creeping and clawing up from their dominion, instilling a chill in the air, only to be met by additional Guardians from the heavens above. The sun had set, but there was still enough light in the sky, to prevent the shadows from stopping him.

He took the roads at high rates of speed, making it back to the Blackthorne Ranch in record time, just as the dark of nighttime was setting in. Coming around the vehicle, he pulled her from her seat, kicking the door shut as he turned towards the house. The demons attempted to converge upon him in an attempt to force him to drop her, but he would not be deterred from getting her the help she needed. Drinian had just reached the patio steps when the front doors were flung open before him. Standing in the doorway was his father and his sister Megorah.

"Drin, what is it? What's wrong?" Rafe asked anxiously, seeing Veta lying limply in his son's arms. Suddenly, Drinian heard eerie cries from the demons. They seemed to be assaulted on all sides, by an unseen force. Within seconds they had been driven away.

"Felt me coming did you?" Drinian replied, looking intently at Meg while stepping through the door and into the entryway. Relief over the absence of the shadow overwhelmed him. "She's sick. Where's Chase?" he asked urgently. Sensing his distress Megorah lifted her hand to Veta's forehead.

"Dad, she's on fire!" she cried anxiously. Calling out to Chase, she sped toward the kitchen.

"She's feverish. I can't get it to go down."

Rafe watched his son pace back and forth as he carried her. Drinian looked as though, he was afraid to put her down.

"Why did you bring her here instead of the hospital then?" Chase called out crossly as he came running from the kitchen, having heard the commotion.

"Because, when I got there she was floating," Drinian replied, smiling briefly. "She was afraid to go to the hospital and didn't want to risk…"

"Our secret getting out," Dante finished for him as he came strolling out from the other kitchen door. "That's awfully noble of her. But can you help her here Chase, or should we take her to the ER instead anyway?"

Chase was quiet. Frowning with concern he felt Veta's forehead, then checked her pulse.

"Do we know how long she's been like this?" Chase asked.

"She said she lay down before noon, so I'm not really sure. But she was already feverish when I got there, and that was around six thirty." Drinian answered, watching the play of emotions on his brother-in-law's face. Even with his exceptional bedside manner, Drinian could tell the time frame concerned him.

"I should be able to help her here. Since finding out about Alaina, I've been keeping items on hand here at the house and our residence that we might need for such occasions as this." Chase finally replied a little sheepishly. Dante stared at Chase in surprise, for the first time appreciating the lengths with which his brother-in-law would go in order to protect their family.

"Take her upstairs then, Drin. To your old room." Rafe said, guiding him towards the stairs.

"I can check her temperature from there," Chase explained, as he followed quickly behind Drinian. "We can determine from there, whether she'll need an ice bath, though from the feel of her she's gonna need it. Meg can you grab my bag from our room?" he called down to her. "And someone, get Crisalya. I may need her help, too.

- - -

Sheathing their swords, for the time being, Woreash and Maleeka watched with trepidation as Drinian carried Veta up the stairs. Upon entering Drinian's old room, they followed close behind and stood just inside the bedroom where Chase directed him to lay her on the bed. Moments later Megorah came running into the room with Dr. Ryans medical bag, and Crisalya followed close behind.

"Did we get him to her too late?" Maleeka asked in concern, worry lines creasing his youthful face. His long dark hair fell in a wild mess around his shoulders and down his back. Their recent battle with the demons had ruffled him a little more than usual. They had been more aggressive than normal.

"It's too soon to tell." Woreash shook his head and watched Chase take Veta's temperature.

"But, Woreash if she loses the babies now, then..."

"Right now, we must wait and see how this transpires. There's little more we can do for her. It's now in Dr. Ryans hands and God's."

Nodding in understanding his face fell slightly. He turned toward the bed and watched Chase move toward the bathroom. Megorah was attempting to push Drinian out of the bedroom and Crisalya had begun trying to wrestle Veta from her robe. It appeared Megorah was having difficulty getting Drinian to leave so they could get her ready for the bath.

Chuckling softly, Woreash reached out and laid his hand upon Drinian's shoulder, stilling him.

"Let them work, Drinian. They must get her fever down." Woreash spoke quietly but firmly next to him. The man stood, clearly struggling with an inner turmoil. His protective desire to be close by her side was strong. Seeing his shoulders fall in defeat, his head drooped and he turned toward the door in order to allow some privacy for her. Yet he still refused to leave the room.

"Humans," Maleeka said almost disapprovingly, "can be so stubborn."

Turning their heads away as Crisalya pulled the robe from Veta and began helping her from the bed; they stood with their hands resting on Drinian's shoulder. Seeing Chase enter the bedroom out of the corner of his eye, Woreash spanned the distance between them in order to chastise him accordingly.

Noting Chase was already turning away, he stood by his side as they waited for the women to pass by. Sensing the doctor's anxiety and concern over Veta's high fever, he rested his hand upon his shoulder.

"Think doctor. Is there anything else you can do for her?" Woreash asked, prodding him gently, yet knowing that the decision to do anything else must be his. He could see the indecision upon the man's face as he debated back and forth, whether using the drug as well was warranted, and whether it would be safe.

"Stay put, Drin," Chase said without warning. He strode past him and out of the room. Running quickly down to his own bedroom, he searched frantically in their bathroom cabinet under the sink. Staring down at the package of paracetamol in his hand, he clasped his fingers around it tightly.

"Only use it, if you feel it will not harm the babies," Woreash said, impressing upon Chase, the importance of precaution, where they were concerned.

"They should be okay," Chase spoke aloud. "And if I use a small amount along with the ice bath..." Hastily leaving his bathroom, he headed back down the hall.

Chase noted that Rafe had arrived and was arguing with Drinian as he entered the bedroom, he ignored them. Walking towards the bathroom he called out to Crisalya. She stuck her head out in order to talk with him.

"I believe they have it in order now," Woreash said with amusement as he watched Rafe and Drinian arguing.

"They are very protective of their women." Maleeka nodded in the direction of Drinian and Rafe.

"It would seem to be especially strong in Blackthorne men." Woreash agreed. "Though, propriety and reason often seem to go out the window when one is in danger."

"Agreed, it is good they still have their patriarch."

"Yes," Woreash said. "But his time in this world is not infinite. Hopefully, he will have impressed upon them the Lord's values before that time is up."

Seeing shadows attempting to wriggle their way in through the cracked patio door, they both pulled their swords from their scabbards. Glancing towards each other, they moved in tandem toward the door, preparing for the battle to come.

Chapter 25

After checking Veta over thoroughly and taking her temperature, Chase determined an ice bath was definitely warranted. The women had assisted in getting Veta in the tub, after struggling to get Drinian to leave long enough to do so. Much to Rafe's annoyance, Drinian kept trying to go into the bathroom in order to be by her side. A shouting match had ensued when Rafe tried to have Drinian dragged from the bedroom, but after a while Rafe finally gave up, seeing that his son wasn't going to be budged.

Wanting to nip the fever in the bud quickly, Chase had also given a small dose of a drug called Paracetamol. Dissolving the tablet in water first they managed to get her to drink it using a dropper since she was barely lucid. Confused as to why Chase was having the girls give it to her that way, Drinian argued with him. After reminding him that he was a doctor, after all, Chase continued to appease him, stating it would help bring down the fever faster that way.

The news got around quickly that the demon Veranke had been floating Veta above her couch when Drinian had seen her through the window. Having told Chase he'd found the positive pregnancy test on her at her apartment, excitement grew. There would be a set of twins joining the family within the next year, along with Dante and Alaina's triplets. Finally, after Chase managed to get the temperature down for at least the time being, Drinian had insisted on helping to pull her from the tub to place her in his old bed.

"If Crisalya and Megorah can manage to get her in then I'm sure they can get her out just fine as well." Rafe could be heard hollering through the bedroom as Megorah drained the bath. Shaking her head, she eyed Veta then grinned.

"Have they really been going at it, all this time?" Veta asked in awe while watching the water starting to recede through the ice. She was freezing now, and her body shook violently from the chill.

Crisalya giggled. "Oh yeah, you were out of it for a while, but it got pretty heated when dad tried to yank him out of the bedroom earlier."

"Oh, my," Veta said quietly, listening to Drinian shouting down his dad.

"No doubt they're more than capable, but I'm not willing to take the risk of her being dropped coming out." Veta could hear him yell back at his father.

"Drinian, it's not right and you know it. We have children in this house…"

"I don't really care."

"Now you just listen here, boy, this is still my house…."

"No worries. I got one of my own. I'll take her there."

"Drinian," Veta called out suddenly, startling Crisalya and Megorah.

"Yeah, baby, you okay?" she could hear him holler back through the door.

Tickled, at his endearing usage of the word, baby, in regard to her, Veta's eyes twinkled in amusement. "Tell him I'll marry you. See if that helps." she hollered back. Tired of hearing them argue and figuring it just made sense to have both parents of their children in the same house, she waited in the stunned silence that followed. Seconds later, Drinian's shocked face peered around the door frame at her, causing Megorah to hastily toss a towel over Veta as she still lay in the tub.

"Did you just say, what I think you just said?" he asked quietly, wide-eyed with wonder.

"Yes. I figure our kids will need both of us, right?" she replied simply. "And besides, the angel Phillipe did say God desires us to be wed after all."

Taking a deep breath, he spun on his heel toward the bedroom. Immediately turning back, he grabbed onto the door frame and swung back in playfully.

"Veta Rohann, will you marry me?" he asked, grinning rather stupidly, from ear to ear.

"Yes. I think I just said that." She grinned right back at him.

Drinian whooped loudly and swung backwards, nearly busting down the closet door falling into it. Laughing happily, he pulled himself up and disappeared back into the bedroom.

"Ha." They heard Drinian say as he confronted his dad once more. "No disrespect intended, but I'm forty years old and we're getting married."

After a moment of silence, she could here Rafe reply. "Maybe so but you aren't married yet." If Veta wasn't mistaken, she could swear she could actually hear Rafe smiling.

"Oh, for the love of might!" Drinian shouted back, in exasperation, growling at the same time.

"This is why I love staying at the house," Crisalya said, next to her as she rested her chin in her arm against the tub. Glancing over at her Veta could see her smiling as her eyes sparkled with laughter. "It's forever much more fun around here."

"Will you really marry him?" Megorah asked anxiously, helping Veta from the tub. Sitting precariously on the side, they wrapped the robe she'd worn earlier back around her as she shook from the cold.

Veta bowed her head as she spoke. "Yes, are you okay with that?" she asked nervously, her teeth chattering as she watched for their response intently.

Glancing back and forth the Blackthorne sisters squealed excitedly, both of them hugging her at the same time. Veta couldn't help but giggle. Pushing them both away she laughed out loud at seeing their expressions, causing her to cough.

"You guys need to get away from me, or you'll get what I have," she said finally, coughing some more, proving her point.

"Drinian, your fiancée is waiting for you." Megorah promptly called out. They watched him barrel through the door, slumping only slightly when he saw she was already in her robe.

He stared at her with an almost disbelieving look in his eye as he came closer. Bending down he picked her up as if she were a fragile China doll and proudly walked into his bedroom with her.

"I'd like you to officially meet my fiancée," Drinian said, holding her tightly, not wanting to let her go.

Megorah and Crisalya followed out of the bathroom behind them, all the while, trying really hard not to laugh. Running past them out the bedroom door, they could be heard pounding down the stairs towards the kitchen. If Veta didn't know better, she'd swear she was surrounded by a bunch of teenagers.

Watching his daughters run from the room, Rafe acknowledged the introduction with a nod. He stood with his arms across his chest, staring back at Drinian, struggling just as much as his daughters had been, to keep from laughing. His eyes twinkled merrily at the bullheaded look his son had on his face. Never before had Rafe ever seen Drinian so happy. He couldn't help but hope it would stay that way.

"You sure you want to put up with this bull-headed bear for the rest of your life?" Rafe asked, looking at Veta rather seriously.

Glancing up at Drinian as he held her, Veta looked back at Rafe. "Well, I suppose you've put up with him for the last forty, right? Only fair I take him off your hands for the next forty." Veta replied quietly. She could feel Drinian exhale deeply, as though he'd been holding his breath.

"In all seriousness, Veta. There is still a lot you don't know about this family and my son." he continued, pointing at Drinian. "Whether you're married to him or not, you're already privy to secrets, which have been kept from outsiders for hundreds of years. Not even our ranch hands are aware of what my children can do. And some of them have been with us for over twenty-five years." He paused for effect. "That being said, your actions today lead me to believe, that we can trust you to protect what you do know. I wonder though if our views on other issues, such as marriage, for example, would be met with as much gravitas."

Rafe was clearly concerned about whether or not she was truly sincere about her intentions. Laughing internally, Veta couldn't help but think the rolls should be reversed on that score, but in the interest of peace, she kept that notion to herself.

"Mr. Blackthorne, I do take marriage very seriously. Though I must admit that if Mitch had lived, I might not still be married today. I daresay the circumstances, in that case, were exceptional." Veta looked back at him.

"I would agree wholeheartedly. And you can call me, Rafe," he said quietly, staring back at her with compassion. She could tell by his response he had somehow learned about what had happened to her. Face flushing angrily, she looked up at Drinian.

"Veta," Drinian said cautiously, seeing the hurt in her eyes. Peering down at her, he shook his head at her earnestly. "You can be assured I did not say anything to him."

"He didn't have to. I used to work for the CIA, Veta. I have…connections." Rafe replied, surprising his son. His time in service was normally not something he spoke of. "I'm very protective where my sons and daughters are concerned, for reasons I think would be obvious; more so even than most parents as a result."

"Rafe, I don't want to have to try and raise my children without their father. I can't, I just won't, especially under these circumstances. I remember how hard it was to be a single parent of twin boys. I have done it before; I could do it again if I had to. But this, this is different. I don't know how to raise twins, with gifts like these. This is beyond anything…." Pausing she took a deep breath and found herself in the midst of another coughing fit.

Drinian inhaled sharply and stood, still holding her close. Closing his eyes he cringed inwardly at the thought the only reason she might be marrying him was out of fear. Though, the thought was somewhat ironic to him as most women avoided him out of fear. When her coughing subsided he voiced his concern.

"Are you agreeing to this only because you're afraid?" he asked softly. He set down with her on the bed, leaving her in his lap. Face drawn with hurt, he looked back at her, his excitement from a moment before diminishing.

Veta really looked at him, raising her hand to his cheek. Touching him softly with her small fingers she stared at him, mesmerized by his luminous blue eyes. She sensed in him, a kindred spirit, a damaged soul, of sorts, like her own. And understood the kind of pain he must feel, as a result.

"Drinian, if I didn't really want to marry you, I wouldn't. But I won't sit here and lie to you either. I am a little scared. This is all knew to me." She gestured around her. "It would be foolish of me not to be at least a little bit apprehensive. And yes, there is practicality in my decision." Avoiding his gaze she looked down, playing with the buttons on his shirt. "I know I don't know you well, Drinian. What I do know is that for some reason, within only a few hours of being with you I felt safe. Do you understand?" she asked urgently. "I became comfortable enough with you to tell you about everything that had happened to me. And I've never spoken of this to anyone before, other than Mitch. It was painful to tell him, but it wasn't with you. I'm not ready yet to say for sure I know what that means. But it clearly means something. Don't you think?"

Feeling her leaning into him as though needing comfort, Drinian stared up at his father in wonder. He'd longed for someone to share his life with for such a long time. He had come to believe it could never happen for him. Reaching around her back, he lay a hand upon her brow and simply stared at her.

"I would have to agree. For it means something to me."

"Rafe, whatever I don't know yet I'm confident in time Drinian or you will tell me when I need to know." she finished almost wearily. Tired and becoming a little chilly, Veta shivered noticeably, wanting desperately to curl up in bed and sleep for a while.

"All right then. When you kids want to get married?" Rafe asked suddenly.

"Sorry?" she asked, looking at him blankly. The fever was down but she was clearly still not able to think straight.

"For the wedding ceremony. You know, seeing as Drinian's so unwilling to let you out of his sight I figure we should probably get you two married pretty quickly or the children will be asking questions. After all, it won't take long for you to start showing."

Drinian simply stared at Veta with a blank expression. Clearly, they had not thought that far yet.

"What day is today again?" Veta asked suddenly.

"Monday."

"Okay, Friday then. I'd think I should be mostly over this by then." She yawned against his shoulder.

Startled, Rafe stared back at Veta and Drinian in surprise. Drinian laughed out loud and Rafe watched him wrap both his arms around her as he chuckled. "Friday it is then. You heard her dad. Spread the word," he said loudly.

And with that, Drinian turned away from his dad picked Veta up and laid her on the bed. Taking his cue, Rafe walked out of his son's room, closing the door behind him. Shaking his head as he grinned, delighted by her response, Rafe started for the stairs at a dead run. Halfway down, he slowed his pace. Squaring his shoulders, he coughed to clear his throat and had managed a straight face by the time he'd entered the kitchen.

Rafe could hear the gossip flowing before his foot even hit the bottom stair. Glancing into the kitchen at his eldest daughter he called out her name.

"Megorah!" he shouted sternly. All conversation ceased as he strode towards the table. Hands on hips, he glared around at everyone. "Do you suppose you all can pull together a wedding by Friday?" he asked, struggling to keep his face straight.

Rafe watched with enjoyment as Breydon's eyes bulged in his head.

"You mean to tell me that fine looking woman, really did consent to marry him?" he said aloud, earning himself a resounding whack across the head from his wife Hialey.

"Fine looking woman, eh?" Hialey vented angrily. Her scowl quickly turned to a bright smile as a thought came to her. "And I know exactly what I'm gonna do for him for his wedding." she declared with an evil grin. Clearly, she had not forgotten her promise of vengeance.

Dante and Alaina swiveled around suddenly, both staring at her in horror.

"No Hialey, don't!" they both cried out in unison.

Not sure he really wanted to know what that was all about; Rafe chose to ignore them all.

"So?" His brow rose in question at Meg. "Can you do it?"

"Well, we managed to do it for Alaina and Dante. I don't see why we couldn't do it for them too," she exclaimed with excitement.

- - -

At the same time, Drinian was attempting to tuck his new fiancée in. Setting her on the bed he reached down to pull the ties of her robe away when he stilled suddenly. Realizing he was being awfully presumptuous, he stated as such, telling her he would give her a chance to disrobe of her own accord more privately. Knowing how sick she was and how much she needed rest, he went in search of something for her to wear to bed.

"I'm sure I have a T-shirt in here, you can borrow for tonight." Pulling out several drawers of his dresser, he found a white one folded neatly in one corner. Shaking it out, he carried it over to the bed and stood before her, holding it out for her to take. Reaching out, she took the shirt from him gratefully, her green eyes sparkling back at him as though knowing full well what his first instinct had been.

Pointing at him with one finger she ran it in a circular motion in front of her. Getting her meaning, his face jerked in a comical fashion as though startled, and he spun around facing the wall as he spoke.

"Right, of course. No looking yet."

Giggling, she coughed and pulled the robe down off her shoulders so she could put on the t-shirt. Fumbling with the fabric at first, she managed to get it on so she was covered from his view.

"You can turn around, Drinian."

Inhaling deeply, Drinian spun back around and stared at her. Entranced by her beauty even in her ill state, he was reluctant to cover her with the blankets. The over-sized t-shirt hung on her provocatively. Kneeling down on the bed he wrapped one arm around her, reveling in the feel of the soft pale skin of her arms against his fingers. Grazing the nape of her neck with his lips, he kissed her there, noticing her breathing becoming rapid. Afraid she might begin coughing he pulled away.

Giggling again, as he turned her and tucked her legs under the blankets, she watched Drinian's slow movements to cover her and began to cough once more. By the time he'd finally managed to pull the blankets up over her chest, he was still gazing down at her longingly.

"I take it you were enjoying the view?" she asked playfully and was rewarded with a sheepish grin.

"Very much."

Hearing a knock on the door and Chase's voice calling through to him Drinian expelled an exasperated sigh.

"Drinian, I'd like to check her temperature again. Can I come in?" Chase called again, as he waited.

"Yeah, come on in." Drinian hollered back almost irritably.

Striding in with a thermometer and a glass of ice water in hand, Chase set the glass on the table next to the bed. Hands on hips, he stared down at Veta almost sternly.

"Now that you're out of the bath I expect you to get some sleep. Hear me Drin?" he asked, turning towards the giant brute sitting on the bed next to her.

"I hear you."

"Don't you think you should get some rest while you can as well?" Chase asked while placing the thermometer in her mouth. "I know you haven't been getting much sleep lately. And the way Rafe talks, the shadows aren't bothering you right now." Chase stood, waiting for the temp to register. He glanced again towards Drinian.

"I will when I know she's out of danger," Drinian replied calmly.

Hearing the thermometer beep, Chase pulled it from Veta's mouth, checking the reading. Shaking it gently, he slid the cap back on and tucked it in his pocket.

"She's out of the woods for now." sounding pleased at seeing his patient beginning to recover, Chase peered down at Veta. "Try and get some sleep and drink as much water as possible," he said, as she acknowledged his instructions. Eyeing Drinian, Chase sighed heavily. "Rafe said the couch in the living room would suit you just fine," he said meaningfully with a stern look in his eye.

Veta and Drinian exchanged looks. Veta could see Drinian poking uncomfortably at the blankets on the bed as he grimaced. She could tell he didn't like the idea of having to leave her alone. Chuckling at his protective nature, she chose to enjoy his presence for as long as she could.

"I'm okay with him staying with me till I fall asleep." she responded at first, but then a thought occurred to her. "But maybe you shouldn't get too close Drin. I wouldn't want you getting sick."

Touched by her concern, Drinian reached out and took her hand. Chase glanced between the two of them and laughed.

"This scoundrel, are you kidding? He never gets sick," Chase declared, moving towards the bedroom door. "But let's not tempt fate. No kissing her right now, Drin. Keep your distance, Doctors orders." Seeing the impudent look on Drinian's face, Chase stopped abruptly and glared at him sternly. "You know how dangerous it is for you when you do get sick. It's been fifteen years, Drin. I don't want to go through that again. And remember, only till she falls asleep. Then Rafe wants you downstairs, and you know he will know."

Rolling his eyes at him, Drinian exhaled in exasperation. Saluting him, as if he were his commander in chief, he finally replied, "Yes sir."

"Besides," Chase continued, pausing near the door. "I hear you're getting married Friday. We wouldn't want you to miss that. Someone else might have to take your place." Grinning mischievously, Chase ducked as the remote from the television barely missed his head. Chuckling, he closed the door behind him as he went.

"What did he mean by that?" Veta asked as Drinian lay down next to her above the blankets. Resting his head on one hand, he peered down at her, tugging at her blanket with the other.

"By what?"

"The part about it being dangerous for you; when you do get sick."

Shrugging, Drinian was thoughtful for a moment. Finally, he responded, "Thing is, he's right. I rarely, if ever, become ill. The few rare times I have it nearly killed me."

Anxious at his words, she looked at him with concern. "Then you really do need to stay away from me, because this stuff is messing with my head."

Leaning over Drinian kissed her gently on the forehead. Standing suddenly he crossed the room and turned out the lights.

Remembering what Chase had said about drinking lots of water, Veta reached out and took a long drink of the ice-cold water next to her, swallowing it painfully. Settling back on the bed she watched his movements. Moments later he was back, lying on top of the blankets next to her. She supposed she should be shocked by the familiarity with which they were behaving with each other, having only known each other for such a short time. But for some reason, being with him and near him like this, just felt right.

Pulling her close he held her with her back to him. Sighing contentedly he rested there with her not saying a word. After a moment he spoke quietly in the enshrouded room of shadows along the walls and ceilings. At least this time they were the shadows resulting from the absence of light and not of demons.

"I feel so undeserving of you, Veta. Thank you for agreeing to marry me. You have my word; I'll spend the rest of my life trying to make you happy." And in the absence of the shadows, they both promptly fell asleep.

In the quiet of his hidden room, on the opposite side of the house, Rafe leaned back in his chair, watching the monitor on the wall. Having turned it on just moments before, he caught the sight of Veta as she struggled to drink from the glass of water Chase had brought her. Sipping at the hot toddy, a secret vice of his which tended to settle his nerves, Rafe sent a quick text to Royce, thanking him for being kind enough to make it for him. Tossing his cell phone onto his desk he took another drink. Setting it down abruptly on the desk next to him, he watched Drinian crawl into bed next to Veta.

"Awe, Drin. Don't do it son. You're gonna fall asleep there." Rafe exclaimed on a scowl. Deep in thought, he tapped his foot on the wall in front of him. After a while, he could hear the steady rhythm of his sons snoring signifying that he'd fallen asleep. Pursing his lips in irritation, Rafe frowned.

"Dagnabit. Saw that coming a mile away." Rafe said aloud. Shoulders drooping in defeat he turned off the monitor screen but left the sound on. Swiveling around towards his desk he clasped his hands together before him and bowed his head in prayer.

"Well, Lord, at least if they're sleeping they aren't messing around, I guess. Please send an angel to watch over and protect them as they sleep, Lord. And please help my son refrain from anything more inappropriate.

I must admit though, however wrong it might be, I sure couldn't blame the boy if he did. You sure broke the mold with that one I'd say. Veta is quite beautiful and she seems most genuine. Thank you, God. Out of all my children, I'd say Drinian is the most deserving right now of a little happiness. I pray that whatever plan you might have for the two of them, that it stays its course."

Chapter 26

For the next two days, Veta was confined to her bed. She had orders to stay there and rest. Periodically, she was visited by Hialey, Alaina and the Blackthorne sisters who proceeded to congratulate her on her impending nuptials. Insisting she had no real preferences on specifics of the wedding, other than to have Irises if they could find them, she'd given Crisalya and Megorah free reign over the planning phase of their wedding, much to Alaina's alarm.

"You won't be lacking for decorations," Alaina said dryly, as Megorah and Crisalya ran from the room excitedly. "When they planned mine they had streamers everywhere. If I didn't know better I'd say they lived for planning weddings."

"Or, at the very least, mine," Drinian said mildly, watching them disappear. Chuckling, he got up from his chair, stretched and yawned. He'd made only one request of them in private and as long as they saw to that, he didn't care.

Absentmindedly, he scratched at the stubble at his jaw. Veta's cat had been purring loudly at his feet for some time now. Apparently bored of that, it jumped up on the bed and nestled between her legs. When they'd realized she would be staying at the house for a while, Dartanian had gone by her place and picked up her cat. It had caused a bit of a problem initially, as every time someone called for the cat, Drinian would respond as well. When he ignored his dad calling for him, upon seeing the cat in question running past him with a pen in its mouth, they realized a change was necessary. After much laughter at hearing Rafe expound on the matter, she had finally agreed to call her cat, Little Drin, in the interest of keeping the peace.

Enjoying the sight of the handsome man next to her, it occurred to Veta that he'd barely left her presence in the past two days for more than a few minutes at a time, much to his father's annoyance. Though she'd enjoyed their 'Dexter' marathon they'd been having, she was concerned he was going stir crazy. So she suggested they try taking a walk. After getting permission from Chase and borrowing some clothes from Crisalya, they left the house by way of the kitchen patio. Wanting to see where he lived, she strolled with him through the forest toward his cabin.

"Is that where you'd like to live after the wedding Friday?" she asked as she attempted to keep pace next to him.

"If it's all right with you. I hope you like it."

"Will there be enough room? You know, with the twins coming?" She was a little concerned that a small cabin wouldn't have sufficient space.

"I'd say so." Drinian grinned at her. He could tell she was thinking that his cabin in the woods was a small one. She had no idea what was in store for her, and he was anxious to see her reaction. Glancing around him, Drinian could sense the demons amongst the shadows as they neared his home. They'd been suspiciously docile in the past day, showing themselves for only brief moments at a time. By no means was he complaining, though it left him wondering what they might be up to. Normally they were never this complacent.

The path widened as they came out into a clearing. Veta's eyes grew as she looked out over a very large log style cabin nestled next to an expansive pond. She could see a boat docked near the house and a playground on the lawn on the opposite side of the garage. There was a huge deck with a tasteful selection of patio furniture, and the rose bushes all around the house had been well tended.

"Drinian!" Running towards the house to get a better look at the flowers she cried out in delight. They weren't just any rose bushes for they held the purest black flower she'd ever seen.

"They're Black Baccara roses. I planted one bush the year Rohn died in his honor. That one bush became many over time."

She touched one reverently in fascination.

"Clearly they have flourished here." She admired them for a bit before she asked in confusion, "Who was Rohn?"

"My best and oldest friend," he said wistfully. "She was an extraordinarily beautiful black stallion. I'd had her since I was ten. The shadows caused an accident that led to her death. She was split down the chest, so I had to put her down."

Veta could see that the memory was still painful to him. Reaching out she took his hand in hers.

"I'm so sorry, Drin. That must have been so hard." She glanced down at the bushes which had clearly been well taken care of. "I didn't realize they could affect things in that way."

"You'd be surprised. Sometimes they can convince you to do things that go against your very nature when you're at your weakest." He gave her a meaningful look.

Realizing what she thought he meant by that she faced him, stepping back a few steps so she could look up at him.

"You mean that night at the cabin, don't you?"

"My father instilled some pretty strict guidelines in us at an early age, where women were concerned. Never hit, never abuse and most importantly, never take advantage of a woman, unable to say, yes, or, no. Course, he tried to instill the whole waiting to get married thing as well, but he knew the likelihood of that was small for some of us, Breydon in particular." Seeing the humor in her expression he gave an awkward lopsided smile, deciding he had better elaborate.

"We Blackthorne men have a rather strong drive where intimacy is concerned. Once we hit puberty it can become almost overpowering."

Veta laughed. "Really? Are you sure it's not just a man's way of explaining away why it's okay for a man to be sexually active and not a woman?"

"Uh, yeah, see for any other man I'd say you were right but with us it is different."

"How so?" Sensing he was being serious her interest had been piqued. "Does it have something to do with your abilities?"

"I couldn't say for sure on that but it *would* appear to run along the Blackthorne family line. Once we become active it's like an insatiable need for it. I never understood it completely myself, until more recently of course, but it's almost … primal in nature. When we don't get it regularly it makes us extremely…"

"Aggressive and irritable?" She was beginning to understand his most recent behavior. He usually had such a gentle way about him. It had been one of the first things she had noticed. But in the last several days since they had been spending time together, she'd noticed he had become a lot more difficult around his family. In particular his father.

"You could say moody even."

"Hhhmm. I've noticed." She grinned.

He rolled his eyes at her uneasily. "It can sometimes, even make us dangerous."

"Drin?" Seeing he was lost in thought, as though disturbed, she touched his arm gently in order to get his attention. "I'm confused. If that's true then how…?"

"I know what you're going to ask. How could I have gone without until a few weeks ago if that were true?" Seeing her nod, he continued, "Look, you have to understand, Veta, you're not like most women. No woman has ever wanted to get barely even within an arms-reach of me, let alone to be intimate. So it was never really a huge issue with me until now. Besides, dad put us through some rigorous training where this is concerned." Hearing her hearty laughter at his last words, he grimaced and ran his hands through his hair in frustration. "Oh, now don't laugh. It's embarrassing enough as it is."

"Sorry. I'm sorry." Batting at him with one hand she held the other over her mouth in an attempt to squelch her giggling. Veta struggled to keep from laughing further for the notion of such 'training,' as he put it, was making her giggle. "I take it that's why you didn't fall asleep in your old bedroom with me last night?"

"Yes," Drinian admitted shyly, his face turning red. "I don't want to hurt you, and I was afraid that I might. Besides, every woman deserves a man who's willing to wait for them until they're wedding night. My mother once told me that having a sense of security with a man is extremely important for a woman and she can't possibly have that feeling unless the man she's with is willing to wait for her."

"It's true. It's an issue of trust and we tend to question a person's motives more when we don't have that." She agreed with a sigh. "It can really mess with our heads. I saw it happen all the time with my friends in college and later on in the workforce. And it doesn't seem to matter what our faith is. Your mother, she sounds like she was a very smart woman."

"She was. She would have liked you a lot." He said seriously, surprising her. "Anyway, Dad taught us effective ways to 'get through dry spells,' as he called them. And no, I'm not going to tell you what they are," he said quickly, noticing she was about to speak. "It relieves the immediate need during that time but doesn't rid us of the aggressive tendencies or irritability. It's one of the reasons why in the last twenty years or so, I've made myself a bit of a recluse out here. Unfortunately, I believe it left me vulnerable to the demons exploitation of me when I saw you that night from the woods."

"You think they influenced you?" She reached out to him, trying to get him to look at her.

"I know they did. They had to. Veta, you're so beautiful." His voice filled with emotion and he stepped away from her self-consciously. "Any man in his right mind would enjoy looking upon you and being with you. But … that night, my only intention when I saw you was to get you out of that water before you drowned. I'd thought they'd left me, once I'd pulled you out. They were acting awfully weird and they really didn't want me to help you."

Recalling what he'd told her when she'd woke up next to him that night, Veta realized what he was saying. "They wanted you to let me die, didn't they?" Seeing him nod, her hand flew to her chest, and she wondered, not for the first time, why the demons were so against her.

"At times they fly about, as though being chased away, and then they'll disappear for a time. That's when I'm finally able to sleep, usually. But I wonder if maybe one stayed behind that night and was whispering in my ear. I was very tired and hadn't slept in some time." Embarrassed, he turned to her, hoping she'd understand. "I think they were angry with me for saving you, so they convinced me to hurt you."

"But you didn't hurt me, Drin."

"Didn't I?" He turned on her angrily.

"No, you really didn't. And besides, God gave us free will. You made a choice that night just as…"

Interrupting her, Drinian spun towards her. "That's just it, you didn't ask for this life. You weren't given a choice because I made it for you." Roughly taking her small fragile hand in his, he half guided, half dragged her up the stairs to the patio door. Flinging it open he pulled her inside.

"Look around you. See? I can give a woman everything they could possibly want." Veta gazed around the living room and into the kitchen, nearly awestruck at the sheer size and grandeur of his gorgeous log home. "It's beautiful isn't it?" He watched her reaction closely.

"It's amazing. I've never…"

"I built it," he interrupted again. She stared back at him in surprise. "And yet, no woman would ever willingly have me, or it, knowing the darkness within." He thumped at his chest miserably. "Not without lack of choice." Taking a deep breath he went on. "You've agreed to marry me. I can only presume that you wouldn't do so if you truly didn't want to, though I imagine its more because of the children you carry." Drinian pointed toward her belly and Veta covered it with her hand shyly, flushing slightly.

"It's important to me that you understand what you're getting in me when we take our vows Friday night, which is why I'm telling you all of this. After everything you've already been through, you deserve so much better. I don't want there to be any more surprises for you." Turning away from her again, he leaned up against the glass windowpane, staring out at the pond and surrounding forest.

"What is it you're trying to say exactly?" She was starting to understand what he was afraid of.

"I am not like my brothers or father. I cannot make you the promise that I will never hurt you because I just might. I don't mean to, and I don't want to." His eyes brimmed with tears, and he fought to hold them back. "But I … I might not be able to keep from doing so because of the shadows." The pain in his eyes was real and for the first time, she began to truly understand how tortured he truly was. She stood silently next to him for a time as she peered out over the pond.

"Veta," he said finally, turning towards her. Taking her hands in his he looked down at her and took a deep breath. "I would not hold it against you if you decided not to go through with this. You don't know me very well, and I can imagine after learning this now you're probably afraid…"

"I am not afraid of you," Veta said sharply, surprising them both. "I have never been afraid of you… But I won't lie these demons you told me about, the 'troublesome three', they do frighten me, yes. Frankly, I think, I'd be stupid not to be afraid of them after hearing what happened to your horse, but I'm not afraid of you," she declared adamantly.

"Maybe this isn't such a good idea." Worry lines creased Drinian's handsome features. Releasing her hands he turned on the spot as he spoke while walking away. "Maybe it would be better if I just supported you from a distance."

"Is that what you really want? To be a part-time father?" She asked in disgust. He continued to stroll on out of the house onto the patio. Resting his hands on the railing, he peered out over the calm waters of his pond, his gaze falling upon the ducks splashing in its waters.

"I never get what I want," he said quietly. He brooded there for a time as the bright yellow sun beat down upon his shoulders.

Veta stood in the patio doorway staring at him, her eyes filling with tears as panic overcame her. She found she was crying and her heart began to ache. Afraid she was once again finding herself at the crux of becoming a single mother of twins all over again, she sniffled loudly and sobbed.

Hearing her crying Drinian looked back at her in surprise. He didn't understand her. Any other woman would be running from him without a glance back. Instead, she stood in his doorway as though desperate to plant herself there forever.

"Veta?"

The wind had picked up, and her long black tresses blew around her face as her body trembled. As she sobbed the sun reflected upon the tears streaming down her cheeks. They sparkled, flashing in the light like diamonds. Desperately trying to get her emotions under control, Veta took several deep breaths in quick succession.

"Please, Drinian," she found herself begging shamelessly. The tears continued to stream down her face staining her cheeks. "I've raised twins alone before, for almost two years, and it's the hardest thing I've ever done in my life. I can't do it again." Stretching her arms out wide, she walked briskly towards him. "I know God was with me through it all, and I've no doubt He would be there for me again, but I don't want to do this alone this time. Please don't make me do this alone. It's too much. You heard what the angel said God wants us together. Would you really go against God's plan for you, for us? Knowing, that it's what He wants to happen?"

Drinian stared back at her. He was in awe of the power of her faith shining in her brilliant emerald eyes. Setting his own fears aside he reached out and took hold of her. Pulling her toward him and into his arms he kissed her hungrily. Holding her gently as she hiccupped next to him, he soothed her by running his hands against her back.

"And so I shall heed His word and you won't do it alone," he said fervently, holding her close. "Only death could keep me from marrying you Friday evening."

Sighing in relief, Veta clung to him. She could feel the attraction between them growing. Though their shirts were between them, she could feel her skin flushing with heat beneath the fabric. Sensing his breathing becoming erratic, she leaned into him and tilted her head back, wanting to look him in his amazing luminous blue eyes.

Drinian could see the flicker of desire in her eyes and could feel the softness of her body molding into his, as though she were made for him. Moaning slightly, he kissed her again, his large hands tentatively resting against her back. Then suddenly he pulled away, refusing to allow his sanity to be taken from him once again.

"I want to be with you again, Veta, more than anything right now. But not until we're properly married. I would have waited for you had we met in a different manner,. I know it's not much and it may be too little, too late but…"

Shushing his ramblings with her fingertips, Veta was both touched and grateful for his thoughtfulness. Resting her head against his chest she sighed contentedly into him.

"Where were you fifteen years ago?" she asked quietly.

"Right here, Honey. Right here."

After a time, they slowly headed back to the ranch house, walking hand in hand. As they neared the lawn near the kitchen, Drinian sneezed loudly, causing a pair of nearby blue jays to fly away in fright.

"God Bless you." Veta giggled, then stopped suddenly. Turning towards him, she eyed him closely. "Are you feeling all right?"

Shrugging it off he beamed down at her. "I'm on top of the world. How could I feel any better?" He backed towards the patio near the kitchen, with his eyes full of mischief. Without warning, he ducked into the kitchen while calling back at her. "I'll grab you something cold to drink."

Standing on the patio looking out on the lawn, an uneasy feeling began in the pit of her belly. She noticed what appeared to be a thin woman in a long flowing white skirt, with a wide belt and blousy long sleeve shirt, standing near the playground. Her long black hair blew around her, obstructing Veta's view of her face. At first, she thought it was Megorah because of the hair, but then she realized the woman's hair color was shinier and not quite as long as Meg's was. Plus, the woman's height and build seemed larger even from the distance she was viewing her.

The woman looked back at her, appearing concerned. Her deep blue eyes were intent upon Veta's face.

"You can see me?" the figure called out suddenly, across the yard. The voice sounded deeper than what Veta had anticipated. "Oh, dear, that's not good."

Tilting her head at the odd question and statement, Veta was about to reply when she heard Drinian come up behind her. Turning, she took the tall glass of iced tea he offered and sipped at it.

"Drinian, who's the woman in the yard?"

Glancing around, his eyes narrowed in confusion. "What woman?"

"The one near the..." Her voice trailed off. She glanced toward the playground, noting the woman was gone. "Oh, she disappeared. I wonder why?"

"Probably one of the gals that dad has clean the house. I think they come on Wednesdays and they're usually pretty shy. Though, normally they're not here this late," he said dismissively. "Come, let's go inside. We can watch Dartanian and Lylia attempt to cook together."

He was clearly in a jovial mood. She smiled at him as he guided her toward the patio doors, encouraging her inside. Watching her as she walked, he enjoyed the view and then sneezed quietly into his sleeve once more.

Veta stopped abruptly in the patio doorway, staring at the couple at the stove. Already in a heated argument, she could see Lylia stamp her feet in frustration as she scowled fiercely at her husband. At the same time, Dartanian set another large pan of water to boiling on the stove as he spoke.

"That makes no sense. If we don't start the pasta water first then there won't be any spaghetti to go with the sauce."

"The sauce takes twenty minutes, Dart." Lylia shook two boxes of thin spaghetti in her hands at him. "This takes only eight minutes to cook!"

"Oh, for the love of might! It takes a while for the water to come to a boil!" Dartanian nearly roared back.

Glaring at him as her nostrils flared, Lylia harped back, "Don't you shout at me!"

"Whoa. Are they always like this?" Veta whispered under her breath. The fight continued to escalate.

"Nah, I don't think so. It's usually only when they try to cook together. They can never agree and are always getting in each other's way." Drinian grinned, peering past her. Shaking his head he steered her toward the table. They sat together, amicably watching along with Hialey, Breydon and Megorah, unaware of the shadows waiting impatiently in the bedroom upstairs.

Chapter 27

Writhing back and forth they covered the ceiling from one corner of the living room to the next. Like boiling black oil spreading across hot pavement, the demons increased in size and number as they gathered there near the ceiling awaiting their new member. Their numbers had become so great, that the space between them and the couch had shrunk. More shadows entered through the cracked patio doorway, their screeching blending in with the rest of the chorus.

The demons were indeed restless. They could see his body drenched in sweat and their patience was waning. He jerked violently as he slept fitfully. Veranke floated down towards him and nipped at him near his ear. Cackling loudly, he gleefully soared up and away, yet still hovering close by. The hotter the man got, the closer he was to death. The woman would no longer be of consequence if they could get his soul. So they continued to breathe life into the fire within the hearth, forcing the flames to crackle and burn even brighter than before.

The key to their success was to keep the woman asleep. Her ability to see and sense them was now a liability. Zalman had entered her dreams as she slept fitfully next to the man on the couch where they had dozed off earlier in the night. He had done so in order to keep her occupied until Drinian's soul had been expelled from his body. And his death was imminent. They were sure of it, anxious for it.

Flinching at the sight of the angels soaring into the living room, the demons howled angrily. They swarmed into the corners of the room and dripped down the walls.

"Get out!" Veranke hissed boldly, confronting them. The angels each took a stance next to the couple on the couch in front of the fireplace, causing the fire within to dwindle.

"Begone!" the demon Fallen cried. "You have no business here."

Having coalesced into human form, Veranke glared at Woreash. The older angel's brow rose curiously and he clucked at him suspiciously. Staring down at Veta as she slept, he watched as her face twisted in fear.

"The Lord our God challenges your right. He knows you're meddling. Besides, your presumption that the man's soul belongs to you, solely because he can see you is simply that, presumptuous," Woreash spat back angrily. He pointed toward the woman. "And Zalman had no right to invade her mind." His words echoed the Lord's authority. Plunging his hands down through Veta's head, he glared back at Veranke in defiance as the demon hissed and spat at him angrily.

Woreash shook violently and an inky black substance began oozing from the corners of Veta's closed eyes. A soft hissing noise emanated from the demon who had invaded her dreams once he had been cast out of her. Screaming in pain and rage Zalman writhed in anguish above her, too weak from being expelled to take any shape or form.

Awaking with a start, Veta's heart thumped loudly in her ears. Staring up at Zalman wildly, wide-eyed with shock and fear, a scream lodged in her throat at what she saw floating above her. Having woke from a horrifying nightmare to yet another one, she fidgeted anxiously next to Drinian, her eyes darting around the living room.

"You may not have him," Maleeka shouted angrily, drawing Veta's attention as he withdrew his sword.

Sitting up suddenly, Veta watched as the woman she'd seen at the playground charged at the demons. Now she realized her mistake for it was clearly a man only with fine feminine features. His essence glowed brightly, causing the shadows to shrink and cower momentarily.

"Oh, we can, oh, we will..." she heard the demons snarl back just as angrily, apparently unwilling to accept defeat just yet.

Turning towards Drinian in confusion, Veta was horrified to see him shaking as though in a nightmare next to her. Sweat poured from his brow. She could feel the heat emanating from his body without even touching him. His face convulsed and his body seized then stopped suddenly, going limp. Reaching out she touched him gently with her hand. Remembering what Drinian had said about how his last illness had nearly killed him she realized, at that moment, how much danger he was in.

Glancing around the room frantically, she saw the figure of another angel glowing as Maleeka had.

"There's no time for introductions. Hurry little one," Woreash said, his age-worn face appearing haggard and tired. He seemed to slump where he floated. Hanging loosely in his hand at his side was a sword.

Veta's hand flew to her mouth. She threw the afghan off her and stumbled from the couch to the floor. Looking up at Drinian, she saw the dark shadowy substances, fighting with Maleeka to get at him.

Maleeka turned towards Veta, crying out to her desperately. "Save him Veta. I cannot hold the demons off much longer!"

"Get help," Woreash urged quietly right next to her ear, causing Veta to whirl around in surprise. "God has deemed he is to be healed by way of a human hand."

Veta fled toward the entryway stairwell, in order to find Chase. Assaulted by demons, as she neared it, she let out a strangled cry. Flailing her arms out wildly, she screamed, managing to stumble up the flight of stairs. Falling to the floor near the landing, she sobbed as a shadow attacked her, attempting to seep into her body.

"No! I am one of God's children, you cannot have me," she cried with conviction.

Upon her words, the cold surrounding her shifted away from her. Desperately, she crawled up the last few stairs. Tears filled her eyes. The thought of losing Drinian overwhelmed her and her heart ached. *God please, please help me save Drinian, she prayed desperately. He needs you, Lord. We need you to heal him so he can be a father to his children. Help me to find Chase, so he can save him.*

Shaking her head wildly, she continued to crawl along the floor, desperately hollering for help. Her voice became louder and stronger as her determination to save him grew.

"Help, Chase! Somebody help me please," she cried out in desperation and terror. Once again another demon attempted to assault her, only to be flung back by the hand of the angel, Phillipe, who was creating a safe path for her.

Brandishing his sword over her head protectively, a bright white light encased them both as he helped her along.

Having awakened from the screaming, Dante rolled out of bed. Barely taking enough time to throw on pajama bottoms, he was out of his bedroom first before Alaina, in her sleepy state, could even register what was happening. Staring toward the top of the stairs, Dante saw Veta come up from the floor, reaching out to him desperately while screaming for help once again.

Doors all along the hall to his right flung open loudly. Other members of the household came rushing out of their rooms and ran down the hall towards him. Staring back at them from the top of the stairs, looking wild-eyed and somewhat dazed, Veta gasped out a name.

"Drinian," she hollered at Dante. "He's burning up. Please help me!"

Veta could see Dante's eyes grow wide with fear. Knowing full well what that could mean, he thundered down the stairwell, passing her as he ran to the living room below.

At the same time, Megorah strode purposefully down the hall toward Veta. Not fully understanding what was happening, but sensing her distress, she knelt down before her and laid her hand upon her brow. Instantly, she realized something was terribly wrong. Feeling the chill emanating from the front stairwell; the hairs on the back of Megorah's neck prickled uneasily. Staring back into Veta's horrified eyes she watched the woman gaze out into the space near the chandelier.

"How many are there?" Megorah asked her angrily. She could hear Dante holler for Chase from the living room below them. The panic she heard in his voice was troubling but she knew whatever was wrong Chase could handle it.

"Get out of our house you filthy demons," she cried out angrily. Witnessing Chase and Dartanian running past her, they disappeared down the stairwell. Feeling someone coming up behind her, she turned suddenly, flinging out her arms. Seeing Hialey, Alaina and Crisalya behind her, as Lylia cowered in her bedroom doorway at the far end of the hall, Megorah halted them from coming closer.

"Wait!" she cried. "It's not safe yet."

Trembling, Veta could feel the icy cold of the presence of the shadow, attempting to filter its way in through the bright light of the angel's protective arc. She watched in amazement as two more angels waged a ferocious war with a dozen demons within the entryway. The sight was so frightening that her heart went out to the angel's having to battle the demons.

From her vantage point at the top of the stairs, Veta could also see Dartanian shoot back out into the foyer from the living room. Within seconds, Royce and Breydon came running down the stairs towards him.

"Get dad," he shouted at Royce in a panic. "And tell him to bring ice to Drinian's room. Lots and lots of ice! Breydon, we need your help getting Drin up to his room and into the tub."

Without a word, Royce spun around and sped back up the stairs, sprinting off towards the opposite side of the house, without a backward glance. Having put the pieces together he had a full understanding of the seriousness of the situation.

Glancing up at Veta briefly, Dart's gaze rounded on Megorah as Breydon pelted into the living room.

"Drin's burning up with fever. Can you handle..."

Megorah's eyes flew open with fright. "Go. Just go!"

Dartanian disappeared back into the living room as Veta came up off the floor. Shaking noticeably, her eyes darted around the entryway. She realized suddenly, she could no longer see any of the shadows or the Guardians. Panicking, it occurred to her what that must mean. Turning towards the stairwell in order to descend the stairs, Megorah and Crisalya stopped her.

"No! Let go!" Veta struggled to get past them.

"Veta, Honey. They'll take good care of him. You can't help him right now." Crisalya said, trying to calm her down. She could see her becoming visibly hysterical.

"Let go of me. I've got to get down there," she screamed.

Megorah forcefully grabbed Veta's arms, managing to pin her to the wall with her sister's assistance.

"I can only imagine what you must have gone through just now, Veta," Megorah spoke calmly. "But you need to…"

"You don't understand." Veta sobbed, going limp against the wall. "The demons are fighting to keep the angels from saving him. I have to help stop them somehow."

Stunned by her words, the two sisters drew back from her, completely shell shocked. Taking advantage of the opening, Veta took a deep breath and bravely walked unsteadily, but quickly, back down the stairs into the living room.

The shadows within the room were thick in numbers, making it feel as though, she was walking amidst an actual war zone. Were it not for the glowing bright light surrounding the Guardians, she might not be able to see more than a few feet before her eyes. Gasping, suddenly chilled to the bone, a demon near her fell right through her, then exploded upon being lanced by an elderly angel's sword. The angels silver eyes gleamed with holy light. He deferred his head towards her briefly, acknowledging her ability to see him. Then spinning on the spot in a circle, the elderly angel sliced three more demons through the middle in quick succession.

More demons flitted about Dartanian and Breydon as they struggled with Dante and Chase to lift Drinian from the couch. Each one was being hindered by an individual demon as the angels fought to prevent them from their efforts. One particularly devious demon was assaulting Drinian by wrapping itself around him. The dark-haired angel was having difficulty impeding its efforts.

"That one is, Veranke. He's one of the strongest," Phillipe explained, floating protectively next to her while nodding toward Drinian.

"Why are they doing this?" Tears streamed down her face. Her eyes darted about her in almost a daze at what she was witnessing. "Is this what it's like for him all the time?"

"They believe his death will mark the end of the prophecy," Phillipe explained above the clang and clatter of the fight. "For Drinian its worse for all he sees is the darkness of the demons. He never sees the holy light of the Guardians as you do. On the plus side, he and you typically only see them in this form rather than their true form."

"Their ... true form? This isn't how the demons normally look?"

"Oh, heavens no. No man or woman could possibly handle seeing all the demons in their truest form. God is not cruel and he is aware of man's limitations."

"This cloudy black face-less form is frightening enough." She shivered. Her lips quivered and her teeth began to chatter. "I cannot even imagine what they must look like..."

"In their truest form?" Phillipe nodded towards Drinian. "Oh, yes. It is truly terrifying for man. Your fiancé has only seen them in that state a few times and each time he went into shock."

"Wait a minute, did you say prophecy?" Veta asked suddenly in confusion, finally registering what he'd said moments before. She was still recovering from the notion of only seeing the darkness for it instilled within her a strong yearning to protect the feverish man before her. "What prophecy? I don't understand." She could see tears in Phillipe's beautiful drawn face as he stared upon Drinian, while the men began to carry him from the living room. The sounds of clashing swords, snarling demons, and the grunts and groans of the Guardian angels as they fought, echoed within the walls of the living room, making it hard for her to hear.

"Oh, sweet, Veta. There's so much more going on here than even the Blackthorne family could possibly imagine."

"Please, Phillipe. Isn't there anything I can do?" she sobbed into her hands in despair, looking up in time to witness the dark spirits swirling around the ceiling after the men heading toward the entryway.

"Anything you can do for him? Drinian sees them and they know this. So, for as long as *they* can see him, they will torment him." Phillipe's mouth quirked into a mysterious smile. "So, you tell me. What can *you* do for *him*?" The angel asked her kindly as he gazed upon her, his eyes bearing within them God's holy light. "Tell me, Veta, do you have a voice?"

Understanding dawned on her in an instant, as she stood facing the angel. Distraught at the possibility of losing the father of her children, she raged suddenly, taking strength from Phillipe at her side.

"No!" she screamed at the top of her lungs as Royce and Rafe sped into the entryway. Carrying bags of ice, they stopped suddenly at her stricken face.

Veta stomped through the furious foray toward the stairwell, where the men had nearly dropped Drinian because of the demon called Veranke. The men all stared at her in astonishment as they paused briefly where they stood.

"I said no!" she shouted again, only louder. Veta could see the one called Veranke bend down towards Drinian. "Get away from him you monster. You can't have him! I won't let you," she finished on an ear-splitting scream.

"Veta, what the…" Startled by her reaction, Dartanian stared at her. Unable to see the demons, he had no way of knowing she wasn't talking to him, though her gaze was downcast toward Drinian.

The mass of demons in the entryway began to shriek and writhe in pain the instant she began screaming. They halted in their foray and turned their luminous red eyes toward her. Gnashing their teeth angrily, they snarled at her with fury. The angels, seeing an opening with the distraction, eliminated one demon after another. An explosion of what looked like black powder erupted into the air as one demon after another was swiftly dispatched. Lifting up from Drinian, Veranke furiously swooped towards her with his scowling visage but she stood fast before him, never wavering an inch as the black powdery substance fizzled all around the entryway, disappearing through the floor.

Chin held high, Veta glared back at the monster as her body trembled with fury. She refused to allow her fear to overwhelm her as it did before. The demons numbers were dwindling fast, and she knew she had God on her side.

"Who do you think you are, to order me about?" Veranke sneered with an angry evil grin. "You have no power over me. I can destroy you!"

"I am your worst nightmare, Veranke."

Horror and understanding flooded Rafe's face at her words.

"No, Veta. Don't talk to them," he urged.

"They will never sway me for Jesus Christ is *my* Lord and Savior," she cried out.

A bright white light crackled all around her, glowing and growing as she spoke, causing the angels near her to smile radiantly, though the Blackthorne's could not see it. "*I* am the one who is in love with Drinian and will be marrying him on Friday," she declared, situating the demon Veranke with a fierce glare. "You can't have him! He was never yours in the first place! I may not wield any power over you, Veranke, but the one thing I know, as sure as I can see, is that I do, however, wield the power of prayer."

Dropping to her knees, she clasped her hands together before her. Bowing her head in determination Veta began to pray reverently and urgently.

"In the name of the Father, his Son and the Holy Spirit, I pray that God and Jesus Christ in all their might will make Drinian invisible to all demons. Protect him from their sight Lord for you have a plan and a purpose for his life. A plan for his work through this ability you have blessed him with. Blind all demons of his presence so that they may no longer impede your will where he is concerned; whatever this prophecy may be. If this is your will, Lord; then so let it be. So let it be. Amen."

Raising her head, she lifted up from the floor and watched in wonder as a heavenly light filled the entryway. Hearing, Veranke and the remaining demons within, cry out in agony as they first covered their ears than their eyes, she peered up at the angels near her with a look of wonder on her face.

"God has heard your prayer, Veta. For now, Drinian is safe. I must warn you it will not last forever. When two become one, they shall see him again."

"I don't understand." The remaining demons fled from the house in defeat, including Veranke. "What does that mean?"

"In time you will see. For now, he needs tending to."

Flicking her hand towards the men still holding Drinian on the stairs, she willed them to continue their progression upwards towards her fiancé's.

"Go, please," she encouraged them as both Royce and Rafe strode past her in order to follow behind them.

Rafe sensed another presence nearby as he had on the landing several nights before. He almost wished he had the ability to see what she must be witnessing now. He had the strong feeling something highly significant had just transpired within his own home and he had missed it.

"Breydon, Dart! Don't let him fall," Rafe called, noting that they seemed to be managing the task much easier now than they had in the living room. They carried him up the stairs now with ease as though he weighed nothing. "Get him to the bath in his room." Glancing back down at Veta as he held four large bags of ice in his hands, Rafe faltered for a moment at the glow he saw upon her face.

"Please, help him," she whimpered. Her eyes gleamed with a radiant light the likes of which he hadn't seen since his own wife.

Megorah and Crisalya looked on in awe from the landing with Hialey and Alaina just behind them. Though they could not see what Veta could, they were able to sense something momentous was happening. The chill in the air suddenly disappeared and it was replaced immediately by an overwhelming and comforting warmth.

Dartanian and Breydon had Drinian by the shoulders, while Chase and Dante had his feet. The men exchanged curious glances, each observing the sudden ease with which they were now carrying him. Not saying a word they quietly moved Drinian's unconscious form past the women at the top of the stairs, disappearing down the hallway as they went.

Maleeka knelt down next to Veta as she slumped over suddenly at the bottom of the stairs. She appeared exhausted. Staring back at the man in front of her in fascination, she eyed him with relief and took a shaky breath.

The angel smiled at her with tears in his eyes. "I am Maleeka and this is Woreash. Please be sure to tell them this. Thank you for what you've done. Now, he has a chance at some peace for a time."

"Will he be okay?" She glanced up towards the older angel who hovered near them. She could see his eyes crinkle as he smiled weakly and shook his head.

"I suspect he will be fine now, though he has a rough road ahead of him yet." Woreash sighed while glancing toward the upstairs hallway. "But he has a chance he might not have had before, were the demons able to know his whereabouts."

Veta could feel hot tears drip down her face as she bowed her head toward them in deference. Feeling hands upon her shoulders, she looked up, startled to see Megorah and Crisalya suddenly next to her. Their faces were filled with concern, as well as something else of which she couldn't read.

"Who are you talking to, Veta?" Crisalya asked tentatively, already having a suspicion as to who it was.

Peering up at them in wide-eyed amazement, Veta understood, at that moment, the significance of what she'd just done and seen, even as the angel whispered to her the news. Glancing back at the messenger, still kneeling next to her, new tears sprang forth with joy, at the sudden knowledge she had secretly been given.

Seeing the angel next to her nod, she turned back to the Blackthorne sisters and spoke quietly to them, but loud enough for everyone in earshot to hear.

"The angels Woreash and Maleeka."

Chapter 28

When Breydon heard Veta scream the first time, he'd rolled off his bed, banging his head on the nightstand as he went. Since he had the bad habit of sleeping naked, he'd had to throw on a pair of pajama pants before rushing out the door. His bedroom was further down the hall than most, so he'd figured one of his brothers would reach her first. Not surprisingly, Dante had apparently gotten to her before anyone else. His reaction time was the fastest, and his room was near the front of the house.

Initially, Breydon felt gratitude toward Veta for waking them in time in order to save his brother. But now, he just stood in the upstairs hallway near the front entryway staring out at her, seething angrily at her declaration.

He'd thought her behavior had been odd. Her frantic screams, gesticulating arms, and public prayer had given them quite a show. The ability to be able to see the angels and demons would explain away some of what they'd just witnessed. The presence of the shadows alone would definitely account for the difficulty they had in lifting Drinian from the couch. He was the largest of the four brothers and solidly built like a brick stack house but, between himself, Dante, Dart as well as Chase, they should have been able to pull him from the couch without any problem. After all, they'd done it before fifteen years ago. Yet, he didn't want to believe it was possible that she could really see these two angels in particular. Because if what Veta said was true, that would mean what Alaina had told everyone when she'd first arrived nearly three weeks ago now, was also mostly true as well.

He hadn't wanted to believe that at the time either.

The ability to be able to tell when someone was lying or not would typically put Breydon at quite an advantage over others. It was one of the reasons why he'd become a lawyer in the first place. The problem with knowing truth versus a lie was that, when he was confronted with an undeniable truth he didn't want to believe, it was often a huge slap in the face, like now for example.

Sensing his anger, Megorah tensed next to Veta, willing him to stay calm. She could barely see him from where she stood but she could feel him seething and see his eyes spark with fire as he stepped out into the upstairs landing.

Charging down the stairs, hands balled into fists, Breydon scowled at Veta. His eyes narrowed and his teeth clenched when he challenged her statement.

"You claim you're seeing Maleeka and Woreash? Right now?" He roared, startling her so she shrunk back from his overbearing countenance. "Who do you think you are?"

It was one thing for Alaina to have spoken to them in a dream, but Veta was claiming she was both seeing and speaking with them. He had witnessed the Guardian angels battling an unseen force in the foyer and living room and had even seen and felt the bright warm light that had engulfed the entryway after she'd prayed. But Breydon could not see the two angels she spoke of who were supposedly standing next to her now.

"Breydon, calm down." Hialey knew full well her attempts to get him to cool it was likely in vain.

Striding back into the entryway, Dartanian and Dante watched in trepidation as their younger brother confronted Veta. She appeared weak when she attempted to stand, and wobbled on her legs as though exhausted, requiring help from Megorah and Crisalya just to stay up.

"That's funny, Veranke asked me the same question," she said quietly. "Only he was a little more frightening." Voice shaky, she gazed back at his furious visage in confusion, her body still trembling slightly from the experience. Her arms and legs hummed with what felt like static energy. Becoming extremely anxious by the way Breydon was looking at her, she cringed.

"Veranke," Dante repeated curiously. "I've heard that name before. Isn't that the demon that…"

"Caused Drinian to give you that scar when you were three?" Dartanian finished for his twin brother. They exchanged interested glances.

"As I understand it, he's also the shadow that caused the death of Drinian's horse." Rafe emerged from the upstairs hallway. He was drying his hands on a towel, and the sleeves of his robe were wet up to his elbows. "He and another demon called Fallen, as well as one called…."

"Zalman," Veta finished for Rafe while staring at a spot next to him.

Acknowledging her accuracy, one eyebrow rose in question as Rafe continued. "According to Drin, that one likes to break into people's dreams."

"I can attest to that," Veta whimpered. She raised one hand to her head and shook it as though trying to clear it. She appeared frazzled and extremely shaken up.

"Royce and Chase said they're going to stay with Drin for the moment," Rafe said on a side note as he eyed her inquisitively, and then took in Breydon's glowering form. Settling his gaze on Veta in the end, he could see her face was drawn and tired yet somehow still lit with a warm glow. Worried she might fall, he came forward and gently took hold of her arms, guiding her to the stairs.

"You should sit down. Now, am I to understand you saw two angels by the name Maleeka and Woreash?" He asked her kindly, as she did as he requested. He then stepped back so everyone could see her.

Veta's head bobbed up and down. "I have a better understanding now of what Drinian…."

"You still haven't answered my question," Breydon snarled, interrupting her. He glared with fierce eyes her way.

Confused by his hostility and unsure of exactly what his question had been, Veta gave him a perplexed look. She could hear Megorah trying to get him to calm down but was distracted by Maleeka.

"Breydon is angry at your claim because he cannot see me or Woreash," Maleeka said. The hurt and pain in Breydon's eyes were obvious, and he yearned to be able to comfort him. Seeing Woreash shake his head and stare him down, he stopped speaking.

"But I thought he could see angels." Veta looked at the angel standing next to Rafe. Noting the direction of her gaze, Rafe stared down and to his right, eyeing the spot curiously. Without realizing it, she had also gained the attention of everyone else in the room.

"He can ... just not the two of us. Now tell Rafe to stop staring. I always stand to his right, always will," Maleeka said.

After relaying the message in almost a distracted fashion, the patriarch stared back at Veta appearing stunned.

"I don't understand. Why can't Breydon see you?"

Breydon moved towards Veta as though to speak but was stopped by Rafe who held up his hand. Wanting to hear what she was saying in order to determine legitimacy, he shushed his children.

"We are not messenger angels or Guardians. We've already shared this with Alaina by way of a dream, but you wouldn't have any way of knowing that yet."

Startled by what Maleeka was saying, she didn't see or hear Lylia padding softly down the stairs towards them. "You're not a messenger or Guardian? Then what are you? Wait a minute, you told Alaina in a dream, but do the rest of them know?"

Lylia stopped halfway down the stairs, looking around the entryway, taking everything in. "Yes, we know. Alaina was kind enough to tell us," she said in response to what Veta had just asked. Everyone turned, peering up towards her in surprise at seeing her there.

"What do you mean?" Veta was confused. She glanced back and forth between Lylia and Maleeka.

With a long-suffering sigh, Lylia explained. "Two and a half weeks ago, Alaina showed up with Dante and claimed she'd received word from the angels Maleeka and Woreash that she was pregnant. It seems they were also kind enough to share with her about the Blackthorne's abilities as well," she finished, sounding more than a little cross. Crossing her arms under her chest, she hugged herself tight. She acted as if she were anxious to be around her. "Let me guess, they have news for you. You're not having twins, are you?" Lylia became thoughtful, as one eyebrow quirked in a questioning fashion.

Glancing down at her waist, Veta laid a hand upon it self-consciously, feeling all eyes upon her. Smiling softly, she glanced toward the upstairs hallway, a worried expression on her face.

"You're right. It seems we're gonna have a handful with triplets," she said softly, eliciting several gasps and startled looks from around the room.

Lylia chuckled softly. "You say you're seeing Maleeka and Woreash now, right? So why not ask them why they haven't told you the best part yet? You know, why it's so significant and all. This way you get to hear it straight from the horse's mouth, as they say," she giggled mischievously, looking as though she was enjoying Veta's confusion.

"Lylia," Dartanian exclaimed in disgust at her behavior. She acted as though his family's situation was some sort of game.

"What? She's a part of this family now, whether the rings on her finger yet or not," she said in a huff. Pulling at the ties on her white lacy robe, Lylia stepped forward revealing her perfectly manicured toes in her two-inch heels and pointed toward the foyer floor below her. "If you're going to tell her about your gifts before she's even wed, then at the very least have the decency to tell her everything," she said with bitterness in her voice. Her gaze roamed from one family member to the next. Turning away from their anxious expressions, she regarded Veta with disappointment. "You see the reason why this is all happening now..." She gestured toward Alaina then back at Veta. "You and Alaina being pregnant that is - is because their mother Lilyandhi called on a divine messenger while giving birth to the triplets."

"I don't understand. Why does that matter?" Veta felt like she'd missed something. Glancing toward Maleeka, she could see him turn away from her and gaze imploringly at Woreash.

"You must allow me to explain her error," Maleeka pleaded with Woreash.

"No, all in good time. They must come to the knowledge on their own." Woreash replied, hushing Maleeka as he bowed in deference.

"It matters because by doing so, Drinian's gift was ripped in half," Lylia said. "Breydon got the ability to see what he does by default because he was the next child born who could handle the gift. If Megorah had come first then she'd probably be seeing them instead." Turning towards Megorah, Lylia forced a smile. "Bet your glad you were born last. Then you'd be the one tortured..."

Megorah interrupted her, attempting to placate Lylia to no avail. "I understand you're angry, Lylia but..."

"No," Lylia said quietly, while adamantly shaking her head. "No, you really don't." Turning back to Veta she continued explaining. "What Alaina said would seem to be true as is proven through you. Seeing both angels and demons are meant to be all one gift. Which makes sense really as seeing them separately seems to cause side effects," she stated callously, meeting Breydon's glare. Rolling her eyes, Lylia shrugged as though becoming bored. Yawning loudly, she continued, "You're seeing both spiritual entities, you know things without knowing why, and I suspect now, you have the gift of a 'Voice of Conviction' am I right?" she smirked. Her eyes seemed to twinkle. Lylia had heard Veta hollering and praying from where she had been hiding around the corner at the top of the stairs. "One gift per child." Lylia shrugged again and ticked off each gift with her fingers.

"She is correct," Woreash said, his expression serious.

Perplexed, Veta inquired of the angels, "One gift per child. But Drinian has a 'Voice of Conviction' as well doesn't he? It can hurt the shadows."

"Indeed," Woreash agreed. "He was bestowed the gift of 'Voice' by God when it became clear upon the death of his horse, Rohn, that he would need a way to protect himself and others from the demons which plague him."

"We are always present," Maleeka raised a hand to halt her from speaking further. "But Drinian was one of the first who could see them and managed to survive to adult age. God deemed he should have a choice over how he utilized his ability to see them. Without the ability to see the messengers and Guardians, he had no real effective way of using his gift properly, which is why the Lord bestowed the 'Voice of Conviction' upon him fifteen years ago."

"I see." Veta's brow furrowed in thought at everything she was learning.

"So," Lylia interjected, suspecting the angel present had completed delivering its message. "You and Drinian, it would seem, get to have triplets too. I'm sure Chase can help you find out for sure sometime next week. Either way, both events or pregnancies if you will, are significant as they will aid in fulfilling…"

"A prophecy," Veta finished for her in understanding, winning her a raised brow from both Lylia and Rafe.

"Yes, so it would seem. Though no one seems to know exactly what that prophecy is. Although, there is speculation it will aid in correcting Drinian's ability." Lylia was unable to disguise the emotional catch in her throat.

"You seem to have a pretty good grasp of the situation, Lylia. You almost act as though you have the knowledge we don't." Crossing his arms over his chest, Rafe stared Lylia down. His eyes bore into hers suspiciously, while regarding her with both concern and even sympathy. Her envy of Veta and Alaina's pregnancies was obvious. Clearly, she had been hurt by hers and Dartanian's inability to have more children.

"Rafe, you'd be surprised at what I know now, as opposed to what I didn't know when I got married," she spat back angrily. Her expression was haughty and arrogant as if she truly did hold secrets of her own.

Turning abruptly, Lylia began regally ascending the stairs only to stop suddenly. Glancing back, her expression had softened and she peered over at Rafe, who watched her carefully.

"How is Drinian by the way? Will he be okay?" Her expression led Rafe to believe, she was truly concerned.

"It's too soon to tell." He watched Veta out of the corner of his eye.

"I guess it's a good thing Veta woke us when she did. She may well have saved his life. Maybe even his soul from the sounds of it." With that, Lylia walked out and back to her room.

Veta's face flooded with heat at Lylia's statement. She could feel everyone's eyes on her. Choosing to ignore them, she watched instead as Maleeka and Woreash floated up toward the stairs, gazing at Lylia as she went."

"What is it?"

"Are you worried?" Maleeka asked the elderly angel, not responding to Veta's inquiry. They hovered two feet above the stairs as though suspended in mid-air by ropes while watching Lylia disappear around the corner of the upstairs landing.

Nodding, he replied. "Yes, very. I have not been able to get through to her."

"Maybe I better go check on Lylia," Dartanian said. "She was pretty upset to hear that you had been told about the family's secret Veta. Try not to judge her for her behavior right now." Glancing back towards his dad, he couldn't help but wish that he could stay. It seemed Veta might actually be conversing with angels, and he desperately desired to hear what they had to say.

"I'm so sorry," Veta said quietly, having been distracted from the angel's conversation. She remembered full well why Lylia was so angry and could almost sympathize with her.

"It's not your fault." Dartanian shook his head regretfully. Seeing his father waiving him on, he ducked his head in frustration and paused before heading back upstairs.

"Just come get me when you need me again," he said without looking back and hurried along after Lylia.

Chapter 29

The rest of the night, the men had Drinian back and forth, from his bed to the bathtub. Between numerous ice baths and several doses of Paracetamol, they were eventually able to get his temperature to an acceptable level. Though still just barely less than one hundred Chase was satisfied that Drinian was out of danger for the moment.

Becoming almost belligerent at her insistence Veta refused to leave Drinian's side during the duration much to Rafe's annoyance and amusement. Once she had shared with the family what the angels had to say, the divine beings explained she would likely not be seeing them again then promptly disappeared. Realizing she was now expecting triplets the family stood in stunned silence outside Drinian's bedroom for a while. Eventually, they returned to their own rooms.

The day wore on into the late afternoon. By then, Drinian was still not completely lucid and had to be placed in another ice bath when his temperature spiked again. Concerned he was becoming dehydrated, the doctor surprised everyone by dragging an infusion pole from his bedroom closet. After affixing an IV bag to the pole, he prodded for a vein from Drinian's left arm. Unable to get a good stick he switched arms and with a little help from Crisalya was able to get an IV drip going, as well as pull a little blood for testing if it became necessary. Around midnight, however, it finally began to hold steady once again at a hundred degrees.

Worried for Drinian, Veta had not allowed herself to sleep while he was feverish. Around dinner time Thursday evening, Rafe insisted she come down and eat with the family for at least a brief meal. Picking at her dinner, without really eating much, she eventually decided to return to the bedroom.

After dinner, Chase found her passed out on the hallway floor in front of his son Ethan's room, while on his way to check on Drinian. Making sure she hadn't bumped her head, he picked her up and carried her to the bedroom. Laying her next to Drinian, he figured they would both be better at ease in each other's presence.

The ordeal with the demons had been harder on her than what she'd let on for she slept through Drinian's next fever spike. It finally broke early that morning. While she slept next to him, he'd been told by his father about the prayer she had said over him at which point Breydon entered the room. Sharing with his brother what he'd seen immediately following her prayer, Drinian's eyes glowed in wonder.

"The battle was fierce even before she started shouting and said that prayer, Drin. But from where I stood, it was like all movement on both sides must have stopped for the briefest moment. They looked bemused."

"They? Meaning the angels?" Drinian asked.

"Yes. The next thing I know they're smiling like God himself had entered the room and they began spinning through the air, slashing and whirling about with their gleaming swords so ferociously." Breydon paused. "Drin, I've never seen anything like it."

Stunned, Drinian stared at his father in wonder.

"She's stayed with you throughout your feverish state." Rafe was tickled by the woman's protective nurturing nature for his son. Leaning back, he rested his booted foot upon his left knee as he shrugged. Cocking his head to one side, he looked past his son towards the woman sleeping peacefully next to him. Then after a moment, both men quietly left in order to give him time to rest.

Drinian had been truly touched. When he'd realized that her 'Voice of Conviction' meant she was pregnant with triplets, he'd wanted to do something for her.

Chase had refused to allow him out of bed until the next day, so he'd asked Dartanian to ride out to his house and bring back the roses for her.

It wasn't until noon on Friday when she finally awoke again. The infusion pole and IV bag had been removed as she slept. Over half a dozen vases of flowers, as well as a couple of teddy bears and balloons, were sitting around the room when she woke instead. Though most of the arrangements were assortments of different kinds of flowers, the largest arrangement held a dozen long-stemmed Black Baccara roses. Since it had been set right next to her on her nightstand it was the first thing she saw when she opened her eyes.

Gasping audibly, she reached out and gently touched the velvety petals of one of the flowers. Pulling one from the vase she sniffed at it and then rolled onto her back, holding the rose close to her chest as she smiled.

"You like?" she heard a deep male voice say next to her. Turning, she saw Drinian propped up in bed with multiple pillows. A stand with a large pitcher of ice water had replaced the infusion pole. There was a tray setting across his lap too. He'd clearly been getting ready to eat some lunch.

"You're awake!" Veta sat up cautiously, not wanting to spill his chicken soup. Smiling brightly, she stared back at him, holding the rose in her lap. Gazing upon her face affectionately, his hauntingly pale blue eyes sparkled.

Her green eyes appeared drowsy, and she had a crease along her cheek from her pillow. Her face, though clear of makeup was slightly flushed. Her hair was tousled from turning in her sleep. At some point, she'd switched to one of his long sleeve flannel shirts and the buttons had been left undone rather provocatively close to her chest. She looked awful sexy for a woman who had just woke up, and Drinian found he was enjoying the view of her awake about as much as when she was asleep.

"They're absolutely beautiful." Her face lit up with delight.

Smiling back at her it turned suddenly into a frown. "I'm afraid I have some bad news though."

"What's wrong?"

"We can't get married." He could see the expression on her face fall instantly.

"I see." She looked away dejectedly.

Grinning, from ear to ear, his eyes twinkled mischievously. Chuckling softly, he reached out and gently ran his hand along her arm, causing her to shiver noticeably.

"I have been ordered by Chase to stay bedridden for the next twenty-four hours. So we have to move the wedding until tomorrow, upon his insistence. Can you believe the nerve?"

Her head spun around in surprise. Then her expression changed suddenly, and she gave him an impish grin.

"Who says we have to get out of bed to get married?"

For an instant, there was no sound. She'd shocked him into silence.

Without warning, he laughed out loud and pulled her towards him, nearly knocking over his tray, sloshing some of his soup from its bowl. Not wanting to get her sick again, he opted to kiss her softly on the forehead instead, as he rested his head against hers briefly.

"That's what I said but dad seemed to think the pastor would have a problem with that." Chuckling, he trailed kisses down her forehead and cheek. "Besides, for whatever the reason they seemed to think I might attempt to initiate some rather strenuous activity if we had it today."

Giggling, as he boldly ran his hand along her hip and back around to her bottom, Veta reached up and touched her hand to his face. Marveling at how handsome he was, she sighed in relief at seeing his features so alive and vibrant. She'd been so worried about him since Wednesday night she hadn't been able to concentrate on anything else since. Her traitorous cat, Little Drin, had even opted to find a new home in Katana's room – Megorah's eldest daughter – because she'd been so distracted.

"I can't imagine, what would have given them that idea." She smiled at him.

"Well, you know, I've never really been one to follow orders much." Drinian's hand continued to roam. Finding the buttons on the front of her shirt near her waist he began pulling them apart. Sliding his hand inside he ran his fingers up along the skin at her waist, causing her to inhale sharply. They stared at each other intently.

Whimpering softly at his touch, Veta was quickly becoming excited. Arching into him as he kissed her down her neck and along her collarbone, she realized there was something in her way.

"You're gonna knock over your lunch tray," she said breathlessly as he bent his head.

"You know, I really just don't care." Drinian boldly moved to open her shirt, so he could see all of her rather than just feel her.

In that same moment, he heard his bedroom door open suddenly. Footsteps could be heard padding towards his bed. His head came up suddenly, and he pulled her shirt tightly closed. Fortunately, her back had been to the door so the intruding party couldn't see how close he had come to see her shirtless. Though, the obviousness of their activity wasn't lost on Chase. He stood, hands on hips, glaring at Drinian, as the man scowled right back at him.

Peering over Veta's shoulder after seeing her wide-eyed and embarrassed expression Drinian could have killed with a look.

"Ever heard of knocking, Doc?" He growled.

"I told you no messing around. Don't make me have to separate the two of you."

"Couldn't even if you tried," he declared with a mulish stare. Seeing Chase wasn't going to back off, he sighed heavily. "But if you must know, I made a promise to her to wait, so it wouldn't have gone very far anyway," he said with a sigh. Sitting back up in bed properly, he adjusted the tray so it was no longer dangerously close to falling off the edge.

"Hmm. I don't believe *I* ever made such a promise." Veta smiled mischievously at no one in particular.

"Don't tell him that," Drinian exclaimed, trying to keep from laughing while shushing her. "Cause then, he really *will* try and separate us."

"Something tells me my attempts to do so would be in vain," Chase said dryly, though the sparkle in his eye betrayed his attempt at seriousness. "I'm glad to see you both doing better. You had us a little worried, Veta. You'd been sleeping for so long…"

"I'm sorry. I guess I just didn't realize how tired I was."

"No worries you needed the rest and you need to eat too." Chase took in her complexion and thinning frame. He was becoming concerned she hadn't been getting enough nourishment, for her or the babies. "I'll let them know you're awake so we can bring you a tray. I'm assuming you're going to want to eat with this character?"

Seeing her nod he strode back towards the bedroom door. Stopping at the bedroom doorway, Chase glanced back towards them as though having almost forgotten something.

"By the way, Megorah was hoping you could pry yourself away from him for a little while after lunch if you were awake. She pulled the dress down from the attic this morning. They'd like to have you try it on." With that, Chase turned and left the way he came.

"They want me to try on a dress. What's he talking about?" Veta asked as she stole a piece of fruit from his plate. She licked the yogurt off of the strawberry while grinning coyly back at him. Drinian groaned and shivered at the sight, staring at her longingly.

"He's talking about mom's wedding dress. It's kind of a tradition. Every woman in the family has tried on

Lilyandhi's dress to see if it would fit but even if it does you don't have to wear it unless you want to." He leaned back then, and really looked at her hard. Recalling how tall she was, and after taking into consideration her frame, he stared at her thoughtfully.

"You're looking at me funny."

Shaking his head, Drinian responded with a shrug. "It's just odd is all. Mom had told Meg before she'd passed away that one of the brides in our family would wear the dress one day." Seeing her questioning glance he explained. "Mom had the gift of foresight. So far no one has been able to wear it because it hasn't fit right. Not even Lylia. She was the closest of everyone who tried it on. Frankly, with your build and height, I just can't see you fitting in it either."

Catching Drinian's disappointed expression, she couldn't help but wonder if there was significance to the dress being worn again. She was quickly discovering there was still so much about him and his family to learn. It made her anxious to know more.

"Would you like to see me wear it?" She filched another piece of fruit.

"I would love it if you could wear it," he admitted longingly. "It would lend credence to much of what she told me before she died."

Sensing there was something important she still did not yet know she sat up straight and peered back at him with a quizzical look. Reaching out, she took his hand into hers and laid it next to the flower in her lap.

"What did she tell you?"

They sat in silence for a while as the question hung in the air. Drinian had never told anyone everything that his mother had said to him. Not even his father. So when he'd learned of Alaina's pregnancy he was the only one who, at the time, knew the significance of it. Now, with Veta also being pregnant, he couldn't help but wonder if there was even more to it than what she had said.

A nagging thought tugged at the back of his mind as though there were pieces of a puzzle which he was supposed to be connecting. Staring at her thoughtfully, he decided it was time for someone else to know what he did, especially after what had happened Wednesday night. If anyone was deserving to know, it was definitely Veta. She had more than proven she was trustworthy when she saved him from the demon Veranke. After a while Drinian inhaled deeply and squeezed her hand, having made a decision.

"I'm going to tell you everything you need to know and some you might not want to know. You've proven to me, in more ways than one, that I can trust you with this."

Before he could say anything more the door opened and in walked Megorah with a tray for her. After agreeing to try on the dress sometime after lunch, his sister left. Before long Veta was listening intently to Drinian as he told the story of his family and their history, as well as what had happened fifteen years before while eating her chicken soup and fruit salad.

Chapter 30

Taking a deep breath, Drinian finally appreciated, for the first time, how hard it must have been for his brother to explain their history to Alaina. Frowning momentarily, it occurred to him it had likely been even more challenging, as Dante wasn't initially able to tell her the whole story before she'd arrived at the Blackthorne Horse Ranch.

"To begin with, you need to know my parent's background." He pulled a photograph off his end table and brought it over for her to see. "By knowing that you'll understand better how we've come about our abilities and why they are so strong."

Gazing at the picture, Veta noted that the woman in the picture, standing next to Rafe reminded her of Megorah. "You told me a little bit already about how your mother was Indian but you never said which tribe," she said curiously while sipping her soup. Staring longer at the picture, she realized the woman's eyes were a similar pale blue to Rafe's and found the coloring odd for an Indian woman. Laying it next to her she continued to eat.

"She was full-blooded Mandan Indian. My father, however, is…"

"Did you say Mandan Indian?" She dropped her spoon in surprise, grabbing up the picture next to her once again. The eyes made more sense now, knowing the tribe she'd come from.

"Yes, why?"

"A full-blooded, Mandan Indian in Montana? How did she get here?"

Noting her awe-struck expression, Drinian almost laughed aloud.

Realizing she'd probably sounded rude, she winced.

"Sorry. I guess it makes sense though because there were some in that tribe, who had light colored hair and grey or even blue eyes like your mother... What was her name again?"

"Lilyandhi."

"Oh, right. It's a beautiful name. By 1838 though, there were only a hundred and twenty-five full-blooded Mandan's left." Seeing Drinian's raised eyebrows and humorous expression she smiled weakly.

"You seem to know a lot about my mom's background already." He leaned back, staring at her curiously.

"I may be a CPA, but I also studied art in college and took some pretty thorough history courses as well. I've always been fascinated by Native American history specifically. I don't really know why. If I'm recalling my history correctly, the Mandan Indian nation is currently enrolled in the Three Affiliated Tribes of the Fort Berthold Reservation that is located in North Dakota. That's why I was surprised to hear about your mother. Typically full-blooded Indians tend to stick to the reservations."

"History tells us many of them were killed off and, yeah, they were placed on reservations like most of the

Indian tribes," Drinian said. "What they don't tell you, is that a small band of the Mandan tribe along with Indian Chief Black Bear and his wife Timid River Rabbit, my mother's parents, managed to escape to the Rocky Mountains near the Flathead Valley area."

Raising an eyebrow at Drinian she eyed him suspiciously.

"You say your grandfather was a Chief? I don't mean to poke holes in your story, or be disrespectful Drin but…"

"I know where you're going with this. No one has ever heard of him I'm sure, and a band of full-blooded Mandan's so far into this territory is rather odd. They weren't typically nomadic as they'd build permanent settlements along riverbanks. I'm telling you what my mom was told by her father. He claimed to be Chief and full-blooded…"

"Ah, I see, and since there were so few left there wasn't really anyone to discredit him."

"Exactly, my mother attempted to investigate his accounts after his death but the few Elders left of the Mandan tribe were not very forthcoming which is, I suppose, understandable. Either out of fear or embarrassment, they did not wish to claim a man who fled with his wife, children and a few Indian braves."

"Did they shun your mom?"

"I'm not exactly sure how she was treated. She was not very talkative on that aspect. But I don't believe they completely disregarded her or they would have never allowed her to leave Dante with them when he was three."

"Wait, what?"

"That's a whole other story which we'll get to in more detail in a bit." Drinian sighed heavily, rubbing at his face almost wearily. Veta could sense it was a sore subject and opted not to push him.

"Long story short, there was an incident that involved the three of us when we were about three years old. The accident nearly killed me so they sent him to live on the reservation. It wasn't until Dante returned home twenty-two years ago when mom died, that we discovered from him that there was a tribe within the tribe no one ever talks about. Two brothers, born over two hundred years ago, who'd shown an aptitude for reading minds and foreshadowing events. They had split over differences. One believed their gifts could be harnessed and used against the white man. The other believed it should be kept a secret from the white man for fear of their tribe's decimation."

"One guess as to which half of the tribe your mom was from." Veta nodded with an appreciation of the situation as she finished her bowl of soup.

"Yeah, in the end, it was a really bad move on Chief Black Bear's part." Crossing his arms behind his head Drinian stared up at the ceiling, deep in thought.

"Why?"

"The tribes already in this area did shun them out of fear, and because of that more died due to illness than what would have had to."

"Afraid, you mean because of their abilities?" She took a guess. Seeing him nod she took a sip of her tea and waited patiently for him to continue.

"My father, on the other hand, was born in 1955 to Rathbourne Blackthorne."

Giggling suddenly, Veta covered her mouth. "Rathbourne?"

Grinning back at her, Drinian rolled his eyes. "I know. What was great grandpa Blackthorne thinking, right? They were of the European elite though, so they tended to use odd names back then. Anyway, Rathbourne was of

Scottish descent. The way Dad tells it, they were aristocratic snobs so they stuck to their kind until he met my grandmother Saphire who was a gypsy girl. It was love at first sight the way dad makes it sound. Rathbourne became thoroughly entranced by her."

"That is a fascinating mix." Veta's eyes grew wide. "That would make you half Indian, one-quarter Scottish, and one quarter, what Romani?" At his raised brow, she elaborated as to her guess. "The term gypsy is slang for those of Romani descent who tended towards wandering. For some of the Romani, it's considered an offensive term, akin to negro for blacks."

"Huh, I guess I never fully realized that. But yeah, I think I do recall dad mentioning something about Romani at one point so that sounds about right. But you see now why we are the way we are? It's more than just these abilities passed down through mom. With your knowledge of history, you may be aware that some gypsies, or Romani – sorry – were thought to be able to foreshadow the future and had a tendency toward dabbling with magic. Grandmother Saphire was one who could do this. It was quite strong in her from what I understand. Being as Grandpa Rathbourne was an avid Christian and convicted by his faith, he ruthlessly attempted to squelch these gifts of hers."

Becoming queasy at his words she asked tentatively, "Have you ever…?"

"Dabbled in magic? Oh, no. Definitely not." His response was adamant. "I must stress, we have never messed with magic for those abilities are derived from the devil, as far as we are concerned, and dad does not tolerate such things. As I said, Rathbourne was a born again Christian and raised dad with strong Christian beliefs."

"Hence, his initial protective nature of me." She now had a better understanding of the man. Breathing what probably looked like a sigh of relief at hearing this, Veta rubbed her brow. She would admit she had been concerned he had been leading up to the possibility of occult practices.

"Wait a minute." She looked at him suddenly as a thought occurred to her. "Rafe said the gifts run down both lines of your family. Does that mean that he has a discerning ability?"

Nodding as he looked back at her with the gypsy eyes she presumed were passed down through his father, he shifted uncomfortably next to her. "He actually has more than one."

"But I thought Lylia said..."

"I know. In dad's case it's a little different because our Scottish heritage also has us descending from a long line of Weir-deVere's which spans back more than seventeen hundred years that he's aware of," he said, placing his hand gently over her mouth.

Wide-eyed with shock at the news she mumbled against her hand. "My lips are sealed." Veta was aware that one of the abilities was the gift of 'Knowing', but she noted that Drinian hadn't really specified what Rafe's other gifts were.

All of the Blackthorne children knew of Rafe's extensive lineage and what he was capable of, but not all the spouses had been told. Alaina had figured it out on her own as the result of her ability to discern thoughts, and Drinian suspected the same of Royce as well for he seemed to be able to pick things up that others did not. To his knowledge, no one else knew about Rafe's gypsy background. Though all were aware of his gift of

'Knowing,' most were unaware of his other abilities for good reason.

"Grandma Saphire was gorgeous so I can see why Rathbourne fell for her." Drinian continued. "There's a picture in dad's study. She had beautiful long jet-black hair and crystal-clear blue eyes much like dad's." He pointed towards his own. "So this unique feature comes from all sides of our family background. His family did not approve of the match, as you can imagine, and though he'd come from old money he had a lot of his own. So after they married they left Scotland and immigrated to Montana, settling in the Flathead Valley Area. Soon after my grandmother Saphire had identical twin boys, Rafe and Rourke."

"Your dad has an identical twin?" She sat up straight, her head swiveling around suddenly in surprise.

"He doesn't talk about him and he won't," he said darkly. "But I mention it because it's important. None of us has ever met him. Uncle Rourke moved back to England in their twenties before dad met mom."

Sensing that Drinian's mood had changed drastically for some reason, she eyed him cautiously. It seemed the more he discussed of his uncle, the more agitated he became.

"But, why is that so significant?" Moving her tray out of the way, she sat it on the floor. Taking up the mug of tea, she held it in her hand as she listened. She was enthralled, to say the least. It felt like story-time to her.

"Here's the part where you're going to learn some things no one else in the family knows." Seeing her curious expression he set his own tray out of the way as well. Grabbing hold of her legs as he leaned forward, he pulled her closer to him. In hushed tones, he continued.

"Dad has always told us that he and Rourke had a heated dispute and that his brother left but he's never gone into detail about it. Before mom died she told me what really happened between them. She felt at least one of us needed to know and, for whatever the reason, she told me."

"Are you sure you want to tell me this?" She was a little anxious at his tone. Though she couldn't help but be curious, Veta wondered if it was a good idea for him to be telling her something even his own brothers and sisters didn't know.

"Mom entrusted me with this for a reason." Drinian paused, looking her in the eye. "I cannot say for sure why but I get the feeling it's important for you to know. I believe it may hold some significance to the prophecy she made."

Caught off guard, her eyebrows shot up upon hearing that Lilyandhi had made the prophecy the angels had referenced. Veta realized, at that moment, she was truly at a turning point. She'd known when she'd found out about his family and their gifts that she was being entrusted with something of great importance. As her mind began connecting what she knew, to what she was learning now, she was almost overwhelmed by the sheer magnitude of a whole way of life she'd never known existed before. And how rare, the kind of family in which she was marrying must be; one with an extensive lineage and so strong in faith in God that the Lord had blessed them with intense discerning abilities.

Feeling a little like Lucy when she'd found the land of Narnia in the back of the wardrobe, Veta took a deep breath and slowly set her mug down. Taking his hands in hers she decided right then and there. She not only wanted but needed to know everything in order to be able to fully understand the man she was marrying, as well as the children she was carrying.

Drinian watched the play of emotions cross her face as she sat pondering what he'd just said. The range of her expression had gone from shock to fear and then finally to acceptance in a matter of a few seconds. He could feel her small soft hands in his. He squeezed them gently when he watched her nod her head, as though to say she was ready to hear the rest.

"Dad only told mom this once but she seemed to remember it well. There was a girl, barely a woman, whom both Rafe and Rourke had become sweet on shortly before their twentieth birthday. Pretty blonde thing, really small like Hialey I guess, with brown eyes. Dad could see Rourke had taken quite a shine to her more so than most of the ladies he'd been seeing. He could tell the girl seemed to prefer him more than Rourke for some reason, but he opted instead not to hinder his brother from pursuing her, and pursue her he did for nearly six months, which was a lot longer than any other girl he'd ever dallied over."

"They were all expecting him to announce his engagement when without warning he just stopped seeing her. Rourke refused to say why. The girl, having made several attempts to see him again, appeared to be quite distraught by his sudden distant behavior. A couple of months went by when suddenly the girl was dumped off at the ranch by her father with bags in tow. Come to find out she was a few months pregnant and Rourke was the father. So this girls' dad expected him to marry her but he refused. According to mom, Rourke stated he wouldn't marry a whore who'd spread her legs so easily."

Feeling Veta tense at the comment, he held her hands firmly as he continued to tell the story.

"For obvious reasons she became distraught. She informed Rathbourne and Saphire that Rourke had promised to marry her if she would sleep with him, but that he'd dumped her mere days afterwards."

"Oh, no!" Veta gasped.

"Rourke was furious with her."

"Are you serious?" Her face was incredulous.

"Violently furious. So much so he beat her up pretty good, too. The foreman at the time tried to stop him. Rourke nearly killed him for his efforts. Grandpa Rathbourne, along with the rest of the hands, managed to finally get him off of her but by then it was too late. She'd been permanently disfigured and miscarried."

"Oh my!"

"It tore grandma Saphire up badly to see the violence her son was capable of. Especially towards a woman."

"What happened to that poor girl?" Veta paled noticeably, hoping she'd never have to meet Rathbourne.

"Here's where it gets kind of sketchy. No one's really sure. According to mom, not even dad could find her and he searched something fierce from what I understand. He'd hoped to try and make amends somehow but she disappeared from the hospital the day after Rourke left town. You see, dad was not there when this happened initially, as he was on his way back with several new horses from Colorado. He returned within days of it going down. At the time both this girl and the foreman were down at the hospital. Dad didn't believe what everyone said until he went down and saw them himself."

"According to mom, the second dad saw what Rourke had done to her he went and confronted him. Seems he blamed himself for what happened to her. Both, because he'd given Rourke his blessing to pursue her, and because he figured if he'd been there he could have stopped him from beating her."

"They got into one of the worst fights ever seen outside Mother Tethers Saloon. My dad almost killed Rourke and probably would have too, if the Sheriff at the time hadn't shot him just to get him to stop."

"The Sheriff shot your dad?" She stared at him dubiously.

"Yes, got him in the leg. Grandma Saphire was so broken up over what had happened to the girl and between her sons that she died a month later. Rathbourne blamed both dad and Rourke for his wife's death. The day they buried her he decided it was best to return Rourke to England, so Rathbourne left the Ranch to Rafe and he's never been back."

"That's just not right Drinian. Saphire was Rafe's mom. How could his dad blame him? If anything it should have been on Rourke. If he hadn't hurt that girl like that…"

"Thing is, mom says dad felt more responsibility for what happened then what he ever let on. He'd witnessed firsthand the darkness within his brother before. There had been other incidences earlier in their life. Some with the ranch hands, some with his treatment of their horses and, on occasion, when he'd hit a girl in front of Rafe at school I guess."

"Mom never elaborated on these stories but explained that dad had thought he'd put Rourke pretty well in his place after the last incident with a girl at the school. Apparently, Rourke had promised he had it under control, which was a lie of course. But dad loved his brother and was blinded by that." Pausing there in his story, Drinian debated for a moment on whether or not to continue. In the end, he decided it was all or nothing."

"And this, right here, is why I believe mom wanted me to hear this story."

Confused, Veta blinked and stared back at him, not understanding what the significance was. Seeing her confusion he explained.

"There is a ... a dark side to the Blackthorne heritage and it's found only in identical twins. One is always born pure of heart. The other is born with very dark tendencies. Like, in the story of Cain and Abel in the Bible."

Chapter 31

Veta was too stunned by this news to say anything initially. The way he made it sound, one of his brothers - either Dante or Dartanian - had been born evil and after having met them she couldn't imagine that was true.

"Anyone can have a dark side to them. It's human nature. Even the Bible tells us that. Mitch was, for the most part, a good husband. He treated me and the kids quite well. I would have never guessed he'd taken part in raping me but he did, and he kept it from me for years."

"I understand what you're trying to say but what I'm talking about is different. There are people who have dark moments when they make a bad decision and then regret it. Dartanian can tell you all about that. When he sees black surrounding a person, he knows that individual is struggling with dark thoughts, or intentions, at that moment but that can change in an instant."

"Explain."

"Just last Wednesday, Dart said he watched the local librarian walking into a church for choir practice, and the color surrounding her was black. Seeing what he was, he followed at a distance into the church in order to try and gauge what was going on. Afterwards, she stopped and talked with the pastor and as they spoke the color around her changed."

"Changed how?"

"At first, the blackness diminished to a thin line about her head. Then it disappeared altogether. For a short time, he saw nothing. Neither black nor white. Then, without warning, it became white. She had apparently been wrestling with something. During her conversation with the pastor, she'd been relieved of the burden."

"I see. So, when Dartanian looks at people he sees either black or white surrounding their body? Never grey?"

"No, he only sees it around their head, from their shoulders up basically. It's rare when he sees it surrounding a person's entire body unless they are standing alone. And it's either: black, white or nothing at all. There are some people he's not able to discern anything from for some reason, even when he is concentrating," Drinian explained. "The thing is, there are people who have an inherent nature that leads toward darker tendencies. If a person like that is not brought up right, they could become evil."

Veta's brow furrowed. Troubled by what he was saying, she found herself deep in thought. She supposed he was right, that there could be something to what he was saying.

Drinian watched his fiancée gnaw on her bottom lip, pondering what he'd told her so far. He knew it was a lot but that he needed to tell her, so she was prepared for their future to come. Reticent at having to throw more at her, he grimaced at his next words.

"Thing is, what most in this family don't know, is that Saphire would have had a third child but she was only pregnant once."

"But, I thought you said…"

"One of mom's journals shares of a vision she had; a gypsy woman birthing three babies, not two. Later on, it tells of another vision she had around the time we were about three and a half years old. It's of Rathbourne pulling a small child from the river nearby here and trying desperately to revive him as Saphire is screaming in the background. There are two small identical boys of the same age standing nearby. One is watching the events intently with almost relish, the other looking upon his brother with horror."

Stunned at what she'd just heard Veta became uneasy. Glancing around the room, pieces of the story he'd been telling her, began falling into place in her mind like a jigsaw puzzle.

"Why did your parents send Dante away?" she asked suddenly.

"Because Dante nearly got me killed. We were three and a half years old. None of us could swim but we got it in our heads that we could. We'd gone down towards the river nearby and were playing on the bridge. The demons: Veranke, Zalman and Fallen, were already messing with me a lot by then. They were in rare form that day. They convinced me I could breathe underwater so I told my brothers I could."

"Dante had developed an aptitude with his ability real fast. The angel at his side warned him what was happening, and he thought it was funny. So, Dante told Dart it was true and that he believed me, then told me I should prove it to him. So I tried."

She gasped audibly, imagining the scene playing out.

"Dart tried to stop me but Dante convinced him it wasn't necessary, that I'd be fine. See that's the thing about discerning a person's thoughts. When you know what someone is thinking it can give you an advantage over others because you can convince a person with a weaker mind to do things they might not otherwise do. So, Dart stood back and watched as I, thoroughly convinced I'm capable of doing this, dove into the river. The shadows assaulted me the moment I hit the water. Dante laughed at first, thinking it was funny but then he realized he could no longer hear my screams in my head because I was drowning, so he frantically dove into the water after me. But the shadows converged on him too.

"Three demons against two three-year-old kids. How did you guys even survive?"

"Because mom had that vision I was telling you about at the same time we were wandering down to the river. She didn't know why but she felt strongly it was an omen of sorts. She alerted dad and he came tearing after us. He got there just as Dante knocked his head on a rock in the water."

"If he hadn't, history would have repeated itself," Veta said, sounding relieved.

"Yup. Afterwards, they set us down individually and asked us what happened. Once they had our stories they managed to piece it all together. The way Dante responded to what happened though, disturbed dad a great deal. When mom told him of her vision he finally remembered what had happened to his other brother when they were that age. Rourke had caused Randulf's death too, just as Dante had nearly caused mine.

The difference, in this case, was that Dante had the gift to discern thoughts. Rourke didn't. Rathbourne chalked it up to an accident, thinking boys will be boys. But dad, well, I think he knew better. He could see the same darkness in Dante that he'd seen in his brother. He was determined to find a way to help him and protect us. So they sent him away."

"Does Dante know about his dark side?" Seeing Drinian shake his head Veta stopped; mouth agape.

"He knows there was an accident of course. He remembers it. I don't believe he realizes fully the extent of this because he was never told about what happened with Rourke and mom said the key was to not treat him as though he was being punished. We were so young Veta. At that age, you just don't know any better."

"He needed to learn to control his gift while being taught to live by God's laws. That darkness is always in him. I'd daresay it's a constant internal battle for him much like what I go through with the shadows, only worse. He has learned to temper, or control it, over the years. But if he feels threatened, or if someone he loves is threatened or harmed, that darkness comes out. It's awful hard to get him under control then."

"I get the feeling from you that he lost control once. When he returned home, sometime after your mom died maybe? Like Rourke did with this woman."

Screwing up his face in a half-hearted gesture of affirmation, Drinian leaned back against the bed, resting his head. Thinking quickly about how he wanted to respond, he leaned forward and explained.

"Yes, and no. It's different with Dante than how it was with Rourke. See, dad's brother had no compunction or remorse for the things he did, because he'd never learned to appreciate how his actions affected other people. Rathbourne was either unaware of, or in denial over his son's true nature, so he never took the time to teach these things, believing it was inherent within him, but it wasn't.

Dante, on the other hand, was taught very early on. He understands and can experience compassion. I tend to think that is partly because of his ability. If he weren't able to discern thoughts, I think he'd probably be just like Rourke was and dad made sure he was trained to hone that darkness within for other purposes so it was never used against an innocent."

"What does that mean?" she asked a bit anxiously.

"It means dad found an outlet for him that allowed him to utilize his darker tendencies for a greater purpose. Unfortunately, this is where I have to stop where Dante is concerned. There is much about the past fifteen years of his life I just don't know. Mostly because it's classified."

Mouthing the word classified, she realized she understood what he meant. Rafe admitted to her Monday night that he'd been involved with the CIA at one point. Clearly, the other purposes of which Drinian was referring to was in relation to services within that branch of government.

"All of this is important to know though I must admit, I *have* digressed a bit. In the end, losing his family how he did in that summer of 74' hit dad pretty hard I guess. That's when he started becoming a regular down at the local tavern. It was while visiting the bar on his twentieth birthday in March of 1974, that he met and became quickly infatuated with my mother, Lilyandhi, who had gotten a job there as a waitress."

"Somehow I have a hard time seeing your mother, the beautiful woman in that picture, as a waitress," she said dryly, momentarily baffled at the visual of Lilyandhi Blackthorne, with her small frame and long hair, handing out beers to a bunch of men at a bar. Stating as such, Drinian chuckled, trying to imagine her waiting on a bunch of drunken men himself.

"The way mom told the story it was love at first sight. They met and were married within a couple of months. Though, I get the feeling we don't have the whole story on that."

"Why do you think there's more to it?"

Drinian replied heavily, his gaze seemed to drift internally to memories past. "I get the feeling by things I've overheard over the last forty years that Chief Black Bear wasn't a gentle man with mom. Possibly even her brothers too. They, like so many Native Americans, couldn't hold their liquor. In either event, dad has always been very adamant that we learn to treat women with the proper respect, which is good because it's only as it should be."

Much to Megorah's annoyance, their lunch together ran late. Not wanting her to leave without having finished telling her everything, Drinian continued by explaining about the prophecy Lilyandhi had made. Listening intently, Veta learned that his mother had requested to speak with him one last time, right before she'd died. When they spoke, she explained that one day there might be a way for Drinian to finally be free from the incessant tormenting of the demons which plagued him.

At the time even Lilyandhi had not fully understood how exactly it would transpire. She believed that the answers might somehow lie within her journals. One journal, in particular, had stories which held significance to his situation. Drinian explained his mom gave that journal to him upon her death, as a way of giving him hope, that he would not forever be afflicted with the shadows all-consuming presence, his entire life.

It was a lot to take in. Being a history buff much of it was fascinating to Veta. Some of it was a bit frightening, particularly when he explained, that he believed the demons had been trying to prevent him, from finding peace. But after hearing him explain what Alaina had told everyone when she'd arrived, she set her spoon down slowly and gazed at him thoughtfully.

"Don't you find these two pregnancies kind of odd?" She glanced up at him to see if he'd caught on to what she was trying to get at.

"How do you mean?" The way he hedged in his response led Veta to believe he knew where she was going with her line of questioning.

"Neither Alaina nor I was supposed to be able to have any more children. At the same time, all of the men in your family aren't supposed to be able to have children either and yet here we are, both Alaina and I, pregnant once again. With triplets at that."

An unsettled feeling hit the pit of her stomach. Thinking back to the day she rented the cabin, she recalled the look Freedom Raines had on her face when she chose it for her. It was as though she'd known something was going to happen to her. Was it possible there were others like the Blackthorne family with such abilities? To assume otherwise would be rather presumptuous.

And would the birth of these children, really be enough to right his mother's wrong?

"How exactly will the births of these particular children fix this for you?" Veta asked, still not entirely convinced it could be all there was too it.

"Honestly, I'm not exactly sure yet. That has not been made clear to me." Drinian proceeded to explain that he wanted to read back over the journal of his mom's, in order to see if there was a correlation between their births and the string of numbers and symbols he'd seen inside it. But having lent it to Megorah, who in turn loaned it out to Alaina, it had managed to come up missing. He also

391

explained that Alaina had said she'd taken notes as well, but that she couldn't find those either.

"Does she remember when or where she lost them?"

"She told me the last time she saw the journal and notes was the day of the wedding rehearsal dinner for her and Dante. She thought she'd had them in her hand when she had an anxiety attack and fell out in the hallway near Drinian's room. But Lylia said she only saw the checkbook register in her hand and nothing else when she came upon her."

"That's odd." Veta was thinking a lot of Lylia's behavior had been weird lately. She thought they were becoming fast friends when they'd first met, but when she'd become sick Lylia had never come to visit her and all the other women in the house had. She barely talked to her when she did see her, and even then it was as though she were avoiding her.

Remembering the statement Rafe made Wednesday night about Lylia seeming to know more than what she was saying, Veta couldn't help but wonder if there might be something to that. Not wanting to be the cause of any bad feelings amongst the family, she debated on whether she should even say anything.

"What is it? You look like you've got something really bothersome running through your head." Drinian gulped down the last of the tea Crisalya had made for him. It was his second cup today, and it seemed to be helping a lot. Grateful to his sister and Chase for their care and remedies, he made a mental note to thank them for it later.

"Nothing, it's just…." Sighing heavily she opted to speak her mind rather than keep it in. They were going to be married after all, and they needed to be able to openly communicate with each other. "The way Lylia was acting the night you got sick was downright peculiar. I recall your dad making a comment at the time that she seemed like she knew more than what she was saying." She paused then, uncomfortable with the idea that was stirring in her mind.

"Spit it out, Honey." Drinian had a suspicious thought of his own percolating in his mind, as he watched her troubled expression.

"Is it possible she does know something? Do you think maybe she did actually find the journal and notes but isn't saying anything for some reason?"

"Truthfully, the thought hadn't occurred to me until now. Breydon wasn't around when she was asked, so I don't know for sure if she was telling the truth. I suppose anything is possible." The notion that his sister-in-law might have been less than honest with him about his mother's journal bothered him a great deal. Years before, when he'd first purchased the building with the apartment Veta had rented, Lylia had come around looking for a rental herself. It was because of him that she'd even met Dartanian in the first place.

"The question is, why? I mean, if it's true she has it, why would she hang onto it and not say anything? After all, it was given specifically to you by your mom. Why would she keep it from you?"

"That, my dear, is the question of the day. Because I can't imagine what significance it would have for her."

Chapter 32

Wedding Day
Saturday, June 6, 2015

The wedding went off without a hitch. Though Lilyandhi's wedding dress had not fit, as everyone had hoped, Veta managed to find one at the last minute at the Bridal Boutique in town. She'd been annoyed at Megorah and Crisalya's pigheadedness about not altering their mother's wedding dress in any way. When she'd seen it hanging on the mannequin in the upstairs library on Friday afternoon she'd fallen in love with it instantly. Wanting to be able to wear it for Drinian, she'd asked for permission to take it to be altered. The Blackthorne sisters had refused her suggestion, regretfully stating that if it didn't fit then it wasn't meant to be.

Instead of spending Friday afternoon with her fiancé as she'd hoped, she had been stuck in the Bridal Boutique trying on dresses. Fortunately, she'd been able to find one she liked that fit and she'd looked absolutely stunning in it. Elegantly made of a sheer satiny fabric it was sleeveless and dipped low both in the back and front. It had left little to the imagination as it fit her like a glove around the waist and hips. Trailing long to the floor it had a short train in the back and a slit cut high up the front revealing her shapely legs. Choosing to skip the veil this time around, she'd worn her hair classically pinned up, with a simple diamond studded tiara that complemented the shimmering satiny fabric of the dress.

Megorah and Crisalya had been able to locate some Irises at Veta's request. But last minute she'd opted instead to carry one of the Black Baccara roses from her vase. Wrapping the lacy handkerchief Lylia loaned her around its stem, she then tied a sky blue and an emerald green silk ribbon around it. Both Drinian and his family had been truly touched at the symbolism behind her gesture when they saw her walking down the steps next to Rafe. Having nearly brought Drinian to tears upon seeing her with the rose and ribbons, he'd had trouble getting through their vows.

The real surprise of the evening occurred when Drinian presented Veta with a three-tiered cheesecake with cherries for their wedding cake. Crying tears of joy, she had happily smeared an infinity symbol across his face, eliciting an unexpected food fight that left Lylia cowering under the kitchen table near the patio for an hour. Though the children had thoroughly enjoyed their parent's angst, Lylia clearly had not. Angrily stomping from the room with cherries dripping from her dress, she'd refused to assist with clearing up the mess even though it was hers and Dartanian's night for cleanup.

As though the heavens had sent it as a gift, the sky opened up with rain showers, as they were enjoying the remainder of cheesecake with coffee. Taking each other's hand they'd quietly stepped out onto the patio and strode out onto the lawn while Chase shouted at them angrily from the patio doors.

"I ain't hauling either of you into any more ice baths!"

Giggling together like a couple of kids, Veta kicked off her shoes and hiked up her skirts. Taking off at a dead run for Drinian's cabin she sped along. He ran behind her, enjoying the view of her bare legs as she ran barefoot in the grass along the path. Reaching the cabin they tumbled to the floor in the entryway off the back patio, ignoring the open doors, pouring rain and flashing lightning in the sky.

"Aren't you going to carry me over the threshold?" she asked, breathing heavily from the exertion of their run through the forest.

"Carry you? You beat me over the threshold, silly." Drinian grinned. Fumbling with her skirts, he discovered to his delight that the only lingerie she was wearing was her thigh high stockings and garter belt. She giggled next to him as he stared down at her, his eyes wide with shock. "Oh, Lord, help me. Had I known that...."

"We would have never made it through the ceremony," she finished for him, laughing as she spoke.

Lifting her from the floor, he carried her up the steps to his room and tossed her onto the bed. They spent all Sunday in their room coming out only long enough for food and drink. By early Monday morning, they'd been called to the Ranch house at Rafe's request, hoping they'd come and get, as he put it, their smarmy cat.

Apparently, Little Drin had taken it upon himself, to relieve Rafe of all of his writing utensils from his desk, and since he was tired of tripping over him every time he attempted to walk through a door, he wanted the cat gone.

After showering, Veta dressed in a green cotton summer dress and sandals. She was standing in the living room when her husband came down to meet her.

"What took you so long?" She smirked, her eyes twinkling with mischief.

"Somebody jumped me on the way to the shower then stole it before I could take one." Giving her a devilish grin he reached out suddenly, pulling her towards him and wrapped her in his arms. Taking in her scent he sighed next to her. "I don't know what I did to deserve you but I'm awful glad you're mine now."

"Isaiah 26:3-4," she said, garnering a perplexed look from her new husband. "It says; 'You, Lord, give perfect peace to those who keep their purpose firm and put their trust in you. Trust in the Lord forever, He will always protect us.' The demons tried to kill you as a child and they've tortured you for forty years. Through it all, you have maintained your faith in God. How many men and women can say that?"

Brow furrowing in thought, Drinian stood quietly holding her, content with her in his arms.

"God's angels protected you Wednesday night, the same way they did for you as a child and fifteen years ago when you lost Rohn."

"Hhhmmm. I believe you may actually be right," he said as he kissed her brow. "You know … I'm in love with you."

She smiled brightly. "I know. As am I with you."

"When do you think that happened?"

At first, she giggled but then became serious. "Before either of us were even born, I'd wager."

Leaning into him, she could feel his solid chest against her back and reveled in the contentment she felt with him next to her as he was. After a while, they headed out the patio doors and down to the pond. Walking hand in hand, she waived to the ducks. They strode on by and marveled at the warmth and beauty of the June summer day as the sunshine reflected upon the water.

The shadows had kept their distance, for the most part, but Veta was beginning to get used to their occasional irritating intrusions. It seemed her prayer had truly been answered, for the demons could no longer see Drinian, though he could still see them. This proved to be somewhat entertaining when the terrible three attempted to frighten her in the shower just that morning. Not realizing he had entered the bathroom to shave, he managed to elicit ear-splitting screeching from them. They fled the bathroom in pain and agony after he shouted them out. The shadows could no longer use their intimidating oppressive ways against him as they had so often before. He had enjoyed a peaceful night sleep next to his new wife rather than hours of restlessness and was feeling exceptionally well as a result.

On their walk to the ranch house Drinian gave his new bride fair warning she might be in for some ribbing from his family since it was their first time there as a married couple.

Looking forward to seeing them all again, especially Hialey, Veta found herself surprisingly content for the first time in over a year.

Striding across the lawn toward the kitchen patio Drinian observed her pause and glance over at the playground, her expression a mix of thoughtfulness and confusion.

"What is it, Honey?"

"The first time I saw Maleeka was near the playground," she said quietly, having made the connection on their wedding day.

He faltered at her words, suddenly realizing what she was saying. His gaze flitted thoughtfully toward the playground even as he continued to walk.

"You're referring to the woman in white. You were trying to tell me about her the day I got sick." His head bobbed in recollection. "That's right. I'd disregarded it, thinking the woman was just one of the cleaning ladies."

"Maleeka has such fine features. I thought he was a woman at the time. I'm surprised that I could see him then and wonder why God allowed it when he's one I shouldn't see. The more I think about it … he seemed awfully alarmed by it at the time." She stepped onto the patio allowing herself to be guided, albeit unnecessarily by her husband's large gentle hand.

"The angel might well have been just as surprised as you were to discover you were seeing him."

"I almost wonder if it was God's way of alerting him to your illness. You know? That something was wrong maybe?"

"Could be. Have you seen either of them since that night?" He halted unexpectedly, having just stepped into the kitchen. Concern was laced in both his expression and voice.

Shaking her head, Veta sighed sadly. "I haven't seen anything but shadows lately. I guess I thought…"

"You thought you'd be seeing the angels all over the place, didn't you?" Breydon answered for her. "Like you do the shadows."

She glanced at her brother-in-law sheepishly. "Yes, I guess I did."

"Angels are not like demons. They are not typically intrusive, nor do they intentionally impose upon a person's life, unless necessary. Most angels only make their presence known when God deems their message, or sometimes even their protection is required," Breydon explained good-naturedly.

"I suppose that makes sense."

"No worries, I've no doubt you'll see more in time." Breydon stepped toward the counter and took two mugs from Royce. Carrying the coffee mugs over to them, he handed them off. Seeing the one given to her had a tea bag in it she eyes him curiously, her brow lifting in question. Noting her expression of disappointment at receiving tea, rather than coffee, he chuckled.

"Crisalya saw you guys coming. She said you required tea this morning; something about needing a boost of energy?" He winked at her and Crisalya grinned widely, taking a seat at the table.

Blushing, Veta rolled her eyes and looked up at her husband.

"Don't say I didn't warn you." Drinian chuckled, his mouth quirking up on one side in a grin of his own. He took a long drink of hot coffee and sighed. Their conversation of a moment before had clearly not been forgotten. Veta could tell it was time to move on to a topic not quite so heavy but was saved the need to do so by her new father-in-law.

"Good. You're here." Rafe growled, stalking into the kitchen from the stairwell. "When are you going to get that flee bitten varmint out of here?" Clearly grouchy, he appeared to be limping as he rounded on them from the other side of the kitchen, drawing everyone's attention. Wearing charcoal dress slacks, a starched white-collar shirt and tie, he looked like he was ready for a lawyer's office, rather than a ranch. Dropping his suit jacket over a nearby chair, along with his overnight bag, he scowled.

"Don't mind dad. He's just irritable because your cat seems to be able to elude his bedroom security system *and* because he keeps tripping him." Dartanian smirked. He set down with a plate full of eggs, bacon, and hash brown potatoes. Seeing Veta eying his breakfast hungrily, he got up, pulled her towards the table, and set her down in front of his plate. Stepping around her, he headed back towards the stove to fill another plate for himself.

"What? Little Drin? He would never do that." Veta eagerly dug into her plate of eggs. Seeing Dante come into the kitchen from the stairwell she waived to him in greeting since her mouth was full. Watching him nod towards her in acknowledgement, she noticed he was wearing a t-shirt and jeans with chaps, as Royce turned to him with a thermos of coffee and a breakfast burrito in his hand. Before Dante could speak, Royce handed the items off to him. The man smiled gratefully back at him.

"Didn't you hear? Dad renamed him," Megorah said, gaining Veta's attention. She and Crisalya sniggered. Exchanging humorous glances across the table from her with Hialey, they looked like they were all struggling to keep from laughing.

Halting at the patio door before exiting, Dante turned suddenly towards Rafe. "Uh, yeah. About that dad, you may want to lay off…" Dante started but was interrupted by the sound of a cat meowing loudly, drawing everyone's attention. Their heads swiveled in order to see where it had come from.

Seconds later a black cat with one white paw came streaking through the kitchen from the pantry, carrying a pen in his mouth. Rafe had just turned towards Dante after filling his plate with food and missed seeing the cat come up behind him. Stepping backwards out of Royce's way, he tripped over the cat as it sped past him towards the living room.

Swearing irately and loudly at the cat, Rafe lumbered backwards, and his plate flew out of his hand. Catching himself barely in time, he would have fallen to the floor had he not managed to snare his hand upon a nearby chair.

Mere seconds later Alaina bounded into the kitchen from the living room holding the cat. Little Drin was still carrying one of Rafe's pens in its mouth. Face flaming with anger she glowered at Rafe as she strode purposefully toward him.

"Aha! I have *you* to thank for teaching that to my sons," Alaina cried, sticking the cat's head into Rafe's face.

Yanking the pen from the cat's mouth, Rafe's steely crystal-blue eyes met the cat's innocent stare.

"That's all I've heard all morning long, both my boys singing you little 'bleep' at the top of their lungs." Dropping the cat on the floor in front of him, Alaina placed her hands on her hips. She stared her father-in-law down indignantly. "Now hear this – no more," she hollered loudly at Rafe while pointing at him with her index finger. Glancing over at Dante, her eyes widened in both astonishment and irritation.

"You knew! You knew and didn't say anything," Alaina declared hotly at her husband. The man cringed openly, realizing the angel at her side had been kind enough to bust him.

Having disappeared into the pantry as she yelled, Rafe could be heard rummaging through boxes and canned goods. He was in there for several minutes and could be heard swearing repeatedly before Megorah finally decided it was time to investigate. Striding toward the pantry door, she was deterred from going further when her dad came charging out of the pantry, both hands full of pens.

"Oh, I'm sure it's just your imagination, *Dad*." Rafe mimicked his daughter's voice. "Little Drin couldn't possibly be taking off with *all* the pens in the house." His face florid, he thrust his arms out towards Megorah as he glared. She backed away anxiously, though her eyes were filled with mirth. "Just my imagination, huh?" he vented in disgust, returning to his own voice.

Megorah covered her mouth and bent over, bursting out laughing. A chorus of laughter erupted from everyone else in the room at the same time.

Walking in with a newspaper in hand, Chase looked around the kitchen at everyone as they laughed. Slapping the paper on the table in front of him in disgust, he stared at his wife in annoyance.

"What happened this time?" he said irritably, peering around him.

"And once again Chase misses everything." Royce chuckled under his breath, though loud enough for everyone to hear, eliciting a few more chuckles from everyone.

Clapping Chase on the shoulder, Breydon smiled good-naturedly. "Don't worry Doc. One of these days you'll have one up on us."

"Wow," Veta said out of the blue. "I see what you mean, Cris. The sheer entertainment value alone would bring me back home."

Chase rolled his eyes heavenward and gave Veta an irritable look while Dante slipped out the patio doors, continuing to chuckle as he went.

Watching Chase stride toward the fridge as she ate, Veta could see he'd apparently just been out for a run since he was wearing jogging shoes and shorts. Opening the fridge he reached for bottled water, twisted off the cap and took a long drink as a cell phone went off, the sound interrupting the remaining laughter. Everyone grabbed for their phones until Rafe could be heard grumbling from the kitchen floor that it was his as he answered it.

"Hello?"

"Am I speaking with Agent Pearson?" Rafe heard a familiar male voice say on the other end.

"Yes," he grunted in annoyance while dropping the remainder of his food from the floor back onto his plate. Bent over in a kneeling position, he sat up on his heels and glanced at the watch on his wrist.

"I hear a noise in the background. Are you in a restaurant?"

"I'm attempting to eat breakfast," Rafe said crisply in answer. "Why are you calling? I cannot get there any sooner."

"On the contrary, I've been ordered to tell you to enjoy your retirement."

Bemused by the statement, Rafe responded directly, "Why?" He waved his hand frantically in the air, in an attempt to gain quiet around him. "I thought you needed … my expertise in this particular case?" he said cautiously, not wanting to raise any awareness, as to the true nature of the trip he was taking this morning.

"Your assistance is no longer required." The inflection in the tone of voice on the other end was of a serious nature, evoking within Rafe a chilling sensation. "The Director asked me to thank you for your many years of service and to tell you to enjoy your early retirement."

Senses on high alert, Rafe came up off the floor. His face went white.

"I see," he said shortly, forcing a neutral tone.

Mcgorah's head popped up from her breakfast, staring at her father in concern. Though his expression was placid, she sensed an inordinate amount of anxiety and fear emanating from him, which was highly unusual.

"You're sure you no longer need…"

"Mr. Pearson, you are relieved of duty. I trust you can find something else to occupy your time. Good day, Sir." Severing the connection, the phone went silent.

Accustomed to such abrupt endings to his phone conversations, Rafe would normally dismiss it without a second thought. This time, however, he stared at his phone, the sudden firming of his jaw the only sign that anything might be wrong. Attempting to neutralize his emotions, he schooled his features into a blank expression. He sensed he'd gained an audience anyway.

"Everything okay, dad?" Breydon asked.

Hialey's head spun around at the question, her curiosity piqued.

"It would seem my meeting has been cancelled." Rafe shrugged half-heartedly. The corners of his mouth lifted, the smile not quite meeting his eyes. Tapping at the screen of his cell phone he sent off a quick, silent inquiry to his contact at the Central Intelligence Agency where he'd just been relieved of duty.

Disturbed by his father's evasive response Breydon tensed, sensing there was more to it than what he was saying. He watched his father send, what appeared to be, an urgent text. Becoming distracted by three sudden faint flashes of light barely visible from the hallway near the entryway, he peered surreptitiously up through the divider between the living room and foyer.

"Well, that's good then," Crisalya said, oblivious to her brother's curious behavior. She licked frosting off of her fingers from her glazed cherry blossom donut. "I hate it when you have to take those business trips. I always worry something will happen to you while you're traveling."

"I don't think you'll have to worry anymore about such trips, Cris." The tension coiling within Rafe's gut threatened to spring forth, which would belay what he was otherwise saying. "Today's would have been my last anyways," he said grimly, gaining Royce's attention. His finger rapidly continued to fly across the phone's screen. In his own world, he mouthed three words without thinking as he tapped them into the phones messaging box.

"Steven Adam Jameson."

Royce had been staring at Rafe, a hawk-like expression on his face. Contemplating the potential meaning of the name he guessed his father-in-law was typing, he tapped his own knuckles on the counter, his brow furrowed. Gnawing on his bottom lip in agitation, he watched as Rafe moved to lift his overnight bag from the floor, thought better of it, then left it there as he hastily headed back upstairs. Noting he was still texting on his phone as he went, Royce grimaced then ducked his head. He moved towards the cupboard.

Reaching back behind the regular canisters of coffee, Royce pulled out a package marked, 'Death Wish', knowing somehow that his father-in-law, and quite possibly even Dante, was going to need it today. Quickly emptying the contents of one of the pots into the sink, he filled it with enough water to make twenty-four ounces of the most aromatic and potently caffeinated blend of coffee he was aware of. Then, grabbing two twelve-ounce insulated coffee mugs with lids from another cabinet, he set them next to the pot and proceeded to prepare the rest of the items he suspected they would require.

Chapter 33

Scooting back from his chair as he watched his dad head back upstairs without eating, Breydon grabbed up his briefcase from the floor. Wiping his mouth with his napkin he reached over, pulled his wife towards him and gave her a quick kiss.

"See you at dinner time. Love you," he said absentmindedly as he stood. Feeling Hialey yanking him back down, he chuckled. She gave him a long drawn out kiss. Noticing their parents kissing, their boys, Cody and Seth stuck their fingers in their mouths and began to gag. Their reaction made the children around them giggle and laugh.

"*That's* how you're supposed to kiss your wife before you leave for work," Hialey exclaimed after she was through with him, causing even Lylia to grin and chuckle as she got up to head down toward the playroom.

Casting a sheepish glance in Lylia's direction as she went, then peering over at his brother, Breydon stood once again, throwing his suit jacket over his shoulder. "Hey, Drin, walk me out to my car."

"You actually expect me to leave the presence of my new, beautiful wife for your company instead?" Drinian gave his younger brother a look that said he was nuts. Catching Breydon's eye, he sensed something was up and exhaled in exasperation. "Oh, all right. I'll be right back, Honey."

Nodding that she understood, Veta continued to inhale her breakfast. She scratched at Little Drin's head, enjoying the entertainment around her.

Following his brother out of the kitchen, they headed in silence toward the entryway and out onto the porch. Taking the stairs down from the porch, they walked in step with each other. They quickly found themselves on the walkway, heading towards the drive and the garage.

"Watch your back," Breydon said quietly, without warning or preamble. "And Veta's too."

Startled, Drinian looked back at his brother in alarm. "What's going on?"

"Just this morning in the entryway, as I'm finishing breakfast, I saw him again."

"You saw who?"

"An angel on the fence."

Drinian stopped walking and turned to stare at his brother. "Wait a minute. Do you mean…"

"Yup. I'm not familiar with this one as I hadn't seen him much before. He came around asking questions about how to find his way into the 'Shadow Clan' a few days ago. I think, initially, the angel confused me with you," Breydon said, reverting to a term his brother used to use as a child for the demons.

"Are you serious?"

"Yes. I've only seen this happen a couple of times before; divine messengers on the fence, unhappy with their current existence. In his case, I sensed there was something more to it."

"You could tell he was lying?" Drinian had never realized his brother's gift to discern truth could extend to angels as well.

"I only mention it because this morning in the entryway I saw him arguing with two others."

"Why didn't you say…"

"Drin, stop, I'm trying to tell you something significant here." Breydon held up his hand in order to get his attention. "He crossed just now."

"What do you mean?"

"I mean, the angel phased out right in front of me, as dad was heading upstairs. Veta may not have even noticed him, because it happened that quickly. The first time I'd ever seen it happen was when I was a kid, and I didn't understand what was going on. The second was when I was in college. At the time there was an older angel present. He explained to me that the angel in question had chosen to switch sides and, therefore, was no longer in God's favor."

"Are you serious?"

"Serious as a heart attack, bro. They can either be tossed out by the Lord, or the angels can accomplish it on their own by going willingly. Even they have a choice." Breydon punched the garage door opener. Watching the door open, he paused a moment, then turned toward his brother. "I don't know exactly what this means. I gather the angel was attempting the switch in some warped way to try and help hinder the demon's plans somehow."

"How do you figure that?"

"Because, the two messengers he was arguing with kept saying, that what he was trying to do wouldn't work." Eyeing each other with troubled expressions,

Breydon banged on the hood of his car. "Look, something is going on out there right now. These heavenly messengers, they're restless. I've been seeing more lately than what I do usually, which is why I made that comment to Veta."

"You have any idea what's going on?"

"Man, if I knew I'd tell you. All I do know is that Meg's been getting some pretty unsettled vibes lately." Opening the trunk of his car Breydon threw his briefcase in and shut it. Clearing his throat he went on. "And it all started about a month before Dante showed up with Alaina."

Starting the car with his clicker, Breydon turned towards Drinian. Seeing his furrowed brow, he clapped him on the shoulder.

"Not trying to rain on your honeymoon parade here..."

Drinian halted him before he could say anymore. "Would you say it started thirty days before they showed up here?" He asked anxiously.

"That's what I said isn't it?"

"No, Breydon, this is important. What day did they arrive home?"

"I don't know. It was a Sunday, like May 17th or some such. I'd have to look at a calendar for sure. Why?" Breydon watched his brother begin to pace back and forth in front of him while spouting numbers off as if he were going mental.

Drinian's hands balled into fists in frustration. Growling suddenly, he swore.

"What's with *you*?"

"There's a pattern emerging here, Brey. I think it's got something to do with mom's prophecy." Continuing his pacing he glanced over at his brother while wiping a hand across his brow. "The problem is I don't have the journal anymore for reference."

"Still can't find it?" Breydon could appreciate his brother's dilemma.

"No." Drinian shook his head. "But I have a sneaky suspicion I might know what happened to it."

"You think maybe the shadows had something to do with its disappearance?" Breydon leaned up against his vehicle.

"No, well, maybe inadvertently." Drinian stopped pacing. Hands on hips, he turned away and stared back towards the house. "Are you going to be back here later on tonight?"

"Yes. Hialey and I decided to stick around probably for a few more weeks before heading back home. She seems to be having too much fun with the entertainment factor." Breydon grinned humorously. "She seems to think being around our family is better than watching television. Something about some old television drama called Dallas."

Chuckling, Drinian smiled back at him. "There might be something to that." Then he laughed, thinking of the incident with the cat and his dad just this morning. "Are Dart and Lylia still staying here for the rest of the summer too?"

"They have been, but I'm betting they'll be going back home soon."

"Shoot. I want to get you in the same room with, Lylia. I have a question or two for her I need to be answered."

"Good luck with that. I haven't seen much of her. Aside from this morning, she seems to be avoiding me." Seeing his brother's curious expression Breydon shrugged, folding his arms across his chest. "But then Lylia's been avoiding most of us lately, and I'm pretty sure she and

Dart might be on the outs right now, which is partly why I would imagine."

"Why do you say that?"

"Because Dart's been pretty grouchy since you got sick."

"What's that got to do with…"

Laughing out loud, Breydon reached forward and slapped his brother on the shoulder. "It's got nothing to do with you. Why else do we Blackthorne men become increasingly irritable?" he asked, giving his brother a meaningful look.

"Right," Drinian rolled his eyes in understanding. "She cut him off didn't she?"

"He hasn't said anything but by the way he's been stomping around here and the way she's been avoiding us, I'd say that's likely what's going on. Dartanian wants to stay at the house for the summer; she wants to go back… You do the math." Breydon finished on an exhale. "Honestly, sometimes I wonder how the two ever got together. There are times I can't help but think he picked the wrong woman because she's nothing like I would have imagined for him."

Shrugging off his brother's comment, Drinian couldn't help but find himself nodding in agreement. On more than one occasion he'd thought the same thing.

"Dart is going to become evil if she has. Shoot, he's the worst out of all of us."

"I figure we lived through your dry-spell so we can live through his." Breydon chuckled, winning himself a dark scowl.

"Wait a minute." Breydon pulled away from his car abruptly, finally putting the pieces together. "You think Lylia took it? I thought she told Alaina and Meg she hadn't seen it."

"She did."

"And you think she's lying."

"Not accusing anything, merely positing a theory right now." He glanced towards the house uneasily.

Whistling softly, Breydon eyed his brother apprehensively. The possibility that their sister-in-law might be withholding his mother's journal from the family was a disturbing notion. The fact that it was missing alone was upsetting enough, but to find out someone within the family might actually be refusing to return it made his blood boil. It could, however, explain a lot of her behavior lately if it were true.

"Tread carefully, Drin. Cause this theory could go south on us real fast, whether true or not."

"You're not telling me anything I don't already know."

Chapter 34

Heading back from his fishing trip, Damien Biardon's stomach rumbled loudly in aggravation. It was later than he'd promised his wife, Ciara, he'd be heading home but he knew she wouldn't be too upset. She was very amicable that way. Catching her text before he had gotten in the vehicle he groaned in irritation.

Pizza again.

Every Sunday night it had to be pizza. This time she was making the homemade kind from a box that she liked so much. According to her, she'd grown up on it. Personally, he thought it tasted horrible and greasy but he couldn't get her to stop making the stuff. Apparently, it was also cheap. Since cheap was what they could afford it was one of the reasons why she'd make it so frequently.

Not bothering to respond back right away he'd been debating about what he wanted to do. Damien had been craving Chinese food for several weeks now. There was a restaurant on his way home that had a buffet. It would be the perfect opportunity to get his fix in. He had twenty left on his card which would be just enough for the meal and a couple of pack of cheap Menthol's. He could swing in and eat there at the restaurant then text her on his way out that he was heading home and wouldn't need to eat since he'd eaten with his buddies from the fishing trip. It was a small white lie as far as he was concerned. He figured it was better than hurting Ciara's feelings.

Knowing full well he should just go home and eat with his three children and his wife, as he promised that morning before he left, Damien pulled off at the sign for the buffet.

"No don't," the angel in the vehicle next to him spoke urgently. He watched the man pull up next to an old dilapidated Chevy truck. "Damien, you've been doing so well lately. Go home to your wife and children. Keep your promise and eat with them instead. It is Sunday after all."

Shaking his head, as his hand stilled upon the keys in the ignition, Damien sighed heavily. A war waged within him as he sat staring out the windshield at the open sign of the restaurant. Even with the windows of his car up, he could already smell the mouth-watering aroma of the fried wontons and egg rolls.

Pursing his lips, he grimaced. "Nope, can't take it anymore," he said aloud. "I got to have my Chinese. I cannot eat that disgusting homemade pizza tonight." Grabbing his keys he shoved them in his pocket and headed inside the restaurant.

Head bowing in disappointment, the angel sighed heavily. He watched him disappear through the restaurant doors. "I tried Lord. You know, I tried." Raising his head to the ceiling of the car, he then disappeared himself.

Allowing the waitress to show him to his table, Damien ordered his drink then headed straight for the buffet. Not normally on his guard much anymore and anxious to eat, he missed seeing the man in the corner of the room on the opposite side quickly lower his baseball cap over his face.

The man with the prison tattoos on his arms watched the man who'd just entered the restaurant closely, his pale green eyes darting around the room anxiously. He slowed his eating pace immensely. Ben O'Leary smiled, formulating a plan in his head, as he assured himself that it was definitely the same man. He couldn't believe his luck. Ten years prior he had aided in facilitating the identity transformation of the very man who had just walked into the restaurant and was now eating at a table alone. The guy had paid him really good for his services too, but Ben figured he'd be good for several thousand more just to keep quiet.

Biding his time until the man appeared to have finished eating, Ben watched as the guy stood, left money on the table, and then headed for the restroom near the back. Not bothering to leave money behind for payment, Ben got up and headed straight for the front of the restaurant. Exiting the door without looking back, he slipped around the edge of the entrance and waited. Moments later the door opened once again and out strode the man he'd been waiting for.

"Steven Jameson," he said loudly, practically sniggering when the man tensed noticeably but kept walking. Strolling quickly after him Ben hollered again. "Yeah, I know it's you, Steven Adam Jameson. It would be in your best interest to stop and talk to me."

Pivoting on his heel, Damien swiveled around and met the man's gaze. He couldn't fathom how he had missed seeing the guy before. Normally so in tune with his surroundings, he'd made the mistake of dropping his guard. Cringing inwardly upon recognizing the man, as the same one who had given him his new identity in the first place, he sequestered his emotions and kept his cool.

"I don't know you, nor do I know a Steven Jameson. So buzz off!" Damien said brusquely, noting with agitation the dark outline around the man's entire body. He tensed and moved to turn.

"Man, I'm the frog who gave you the name you're currently using Mr. Damien James Biardon." Seeing the man's mouth twitch, Ben cackled. Flinging out his tatted arm, he pointed towards him. "That's right! I know it's you, man. You want to keep your happy new existence and your freedom then you're gonna pay me ten thousand to keep quiet."

"Pay you?" Damien flared angrily, his finely-honed control slipping. His eyes grew dark and deadly upon Ben O'Leary.

Knowing all too well what the dark cast around the man meant, Damien could tell Ben had no good intentions whether he was to pay him or not. Even if he had that sort of money, which he didn't, Ben would still turn him in regardless.

Squaring his shoulders, while drawing himself up to his full six-foot height, Damien's jaw clenched. He gritted his teeth. "I ain't paying you anything."

Ben tried to shove a business card in his front pocket.

In one swift movement, Damien grabbed the man's outstretched wrist with his left hand and twisted it. In the same moment and motion, his right hand came together in a loose fist. He threw a swift uppercut to the man's jaw, knocking him backwards and down.

Stunned, Ben huddled on the ground with his hands cupped protectively over the bottom portion of his face. He groaned in agony. Barely registering the squealing sound he'd emitted upon being slugged, he attempted to quickly shake off the punch, marveling at how adept Steven still was at putting a man down. Glancing in his direction, he noted the man backing away and then turning towards his car. Paying close attention to the vehicles make and model, Ben called after him.

"You're gonna regret this! You'll see. There's a reward out for you man!"

Flinging open his car door, Damien got hastily back into his vehicle and slammed the door. Glaring back out at the man, he started the car and sped off, knowing full well Ben was likely getting his plate number even as he spun the tires on his vehicle to get away. He would have cracked the man's neck right there, but the location was too public. Too many people had seen him

Swearing aloud, Damien banged at the wheel of his car. What had he been thinking? Kicking himself for stopping in the first place, he flexed his right hand as the food in his stomach became a knotted mass of instant indigestion. If he'd just headed home, he would have never run into the frog and wouldn't be in the precarious position he was in now. He knew he had a mess to clean up. If he didn't deal with it properly, he'd have to disappear once again for good.

Snarling furiously, Damien realized suddenly that he wouldn't be able to do that quite so easily this time. Yanking the card from the front pocket of his t-shirt where it was falling out, he flipped it over and peered down at the number with a calculating stare. There were three children involved now. One in particular who was in grave danger of being forced into the same kind of life he'd been trapped in for over ten years.

Growling deep in his throat, his face twisted darkly, his eyes filling with contempt. He was such a sweet little boy; he couldn't and wouldn't let them get their hands on him. Not his son. Damien knew he had to find a feasible way to protect them, or he was going to wind up getting his children and wife killed.

Or worse.

And there was most definitely a worse option than death.

Hearing his cell phone going off, Damien reached for it as it lay in the seat next to him. Peering at it anxiously, he noticed the text was from Ciara again.

"Damien? Something's wrong. What is it? Where are you, Honey? I'm worried about you," he read aloud. Closing his eyes briefly as he drove on home, he groaned internally. How was it she always knew when something was wrong?

Seven miles away, Ciara Biardon placed her cell phone back on the counter with a shaking hand. Breathing heavily, she couldn't quite dispel the feeling that something was wrong but couldn't figure out what.

The buzzing sound of the timer erupting pulled her from her revere, forcing her to concentrate instead upon pulling the pizza pans from the oven. Setting the pans on the stove to cool, she reached for the kitchen shears in order to cut the pizza as she called her children to the table.

"Pizza is ready!" Glancing into the living room, she watched all three of them run from the boy's bedroom. Noticing the light had been left on Ciara rolled her eyes in exasperation as the youngest son by mere minutes raced into the room, hollering for pizza.

"Good grief! How many times do I have to tell you to turn off the lights, Dartanian?"

Epilogue

Are your eyes bugging out like mine are right now?

That's right, I, Vortigern Black have returned. I told you I would.

As the reader, you're probably thinking something like, 'More gifted fictional characters? Good grief! There's too many already … and I hate cliffhangers!'

Maybe your eyes aren't warbling in your head but mine was because I happen to know that the people within the stories the author and I are telling you about are real, which means my head was spinning after I read this the first time.

The kid's name is Dartanian, eh?

And who is this Damien guy and Ciara chic? They appear to be gifted like the Blackthorne's and RavenCroft's are. Is it possible they're related somehow?

Whooooee!

There is definitely a lot going on in this series. It's almost impossible to keep up. I don't even know where to begin other than to say I bet I know where this is going.

Sort of.

I mean, every RavenCroft and Blackthorne triplet so far has met a woman and found themselves shortly thereafter expecting a bunch of babies. It seems only fitting to presume that Dartanian would be next. Right?

Tell you what, let's just run this down now, shall we?

In book one, it was Kahner and Sable and they're now expecting triplets.

In book two, it was Dante and Alaina, and her ultrasound shows three babies.

In book three, Kalabernus met Ariana and soon she had three buns in the oven as well.

And now, in book four, Drinian and Veta have met and are also, shocker of not really a shocker, expecting triplets too.

Noticing a trend are we?

What is it with the whole three baby thing? Kahner wasn't kidding when he mentioned in book one that multiple births tend to run in the family. That was quickly proven to be fact toward the end of that story when Sable was leafing through the Blackthorne family tree. Triplets truly do abound. Sheesh!

Do you suppose that's what this whole prophecy of Lilyandhi's is about? The fact that the Blackthorne family tree is about to see a plethora of activity? If one takes another look at a portion of that prophecy listed at the beginning of this story it could make you think that maybe. Now how did that go again? Oh, right...

A seed shall lie within her womb
Three times blessed we can presume.

It's right there within the prophecy all right. Or is it? Besides, if you're like I was at this point in the story then you're scratching your head in confusion. Cause every story seems to start with a portion of a worded prophecy. But in Kayos Begins, the one Alaina discovers in the journal of Drinian's is a bunch of numbers and symbols, not words. Do you remember that? Here, let me help you out...

2000_4-19//15//2015_(30)^(4-19=3)(5-18=2)(6-16=1?!)

Do you remember those numbers and symbols? Looks like a jumbled mess until you consider how Alaina figured out some of it were dates.

But now ... wait a minute.

If the numbers and symbols are Lilyandhi's prophecy then where the heck is the poetic prophecy at the beginning of these books coming from?

Yup, this is why I was scratching my head.

Doesn't that imply that there's more than one prophecy? If that's the case, then who foreshadowed the one being divided out throughout each book? Is it also one of Lilyandhi's or did someone else make it?

Ah, who knows.

Either way, we got a lot of babies coming so far. Literally, a dozen babies on the way. Can you imagine what their diaper bills are going to be like? Wowsers! I think Dante had the right idea when he mentioned buying stock in Pampers or some such in volume two after he found out Alaina was pregnant. Though I get the feeling like it needs to be a family investment.

Clearly, there was a pattern here until suddenly at the end of this book we have a random chapter about a guy named Damien who, let's face it, sounds like a bit of a jerk. For sure he's a liar because, once again, we have someone who isn't who he claims to be and he has a wife named Ciara plus three kids. No big red flags there until you learn they've got a son together by the name Dartanian.

Now, what do you suppose that means?

Granted, it's not like our good Sheriff Blackthorne has any kind of solitary rights to the name Dartanian or anything, but it does lead one to wonder if something is about to happen with the third Blackthorne triplet.

After the baby trend I started noticing, when I was reading through all this the first time around, I would venture to guess that Dartanian was about to hit the baby lottery too, which as you know would definitely please Lylia to no end. But this last chapter has me completely thrown off.

Huh, makes a body wonder. I guess we won't know until the next Blackthorne story.

I was awfully glad to see Drinian finally find a match in this here tale though. That said, even I felt the scenario in which it occurred left a little to be desired. I was also struck by the similarity between the two stories of Drinian and Veta's with that of Kalabernus and Ariana from volume three. Granted, Ariana was being tormented by a stalker rather than literal ghosts from her past like Veta but both women were being about as equally tortured as the men they ended up getting involved with. Oof, especially Veta.

I'm not trying to lessen the severity of being stalked for over nine years like Ariana was but to lose three kids and a husband. Then to find out the man you'd married was one of the men who had assaulted you in the first place, and that he was her twin boys real father because of it.

(Vortigern shivers.)

That just seems wrong to me on so many levels.

What kind of poor excuse for a human being does that to someone? I can only imagine how that must have messed with her head. It left me wondering how Veta could still possibly believe in a loving God when that had happened to her.

Anyway, one could argue that a woman would have to have endured a life of difficulty in order to be able to understand and appreciate what the two men had lived through. Almost seems like someone or something had been preparing them for the experience of carrying children gifted with such a cursed fate of seeing shadowy demonic beings.

What I also found interesting about this tale was how Drinian left us with a bit more information about Rafe and his own two brothers when he started telling Veta about him and his family. It left me wondering whether there was any significance in the tale he told about the woman that Rafe and Rourke fought over forty years ago.

Plus, the ending there in the kitchen with Rafe learning he was no longer needed for a consult with the CIA also seemed a bit leading as well. There'd been mention of him having worked for the government before in Kayos Effect but nothing more had really been said until now. One can only hope Ms. Christine will finally shed some light on what's going on with that situation in the next Blackthorne story. Before we get into all of that though, we're gonna have to return to the RavenCroft's for as it would happen there is also more to that story as well.

I'll catch you in the next one.

A Note from the Author

Thank you for taking the time to read my story. I truly hope you enjoyed it. And if you wouldn't mind... Please be sure to leave a review of Total Kayos at amazon.com. I'd love to hear from you! I'd also like to welcome you to experience...

Deadly Karisma
An Unfortunate Lineage
Volume V

OR, if you're disinclined toward reading Secular fiction at this time, (and there is nothing wrong with that, of course) you may skip on to...

Kayos Knows
An Unfortunate Lineage
Volume VI

OR, if you're ready to skip to the finale then feel free to skip over everything and go straight to it.

Karisma Kayos: Out of Time
An Unfortunate Lineage Finale
Volume VII

Either way, I hope you're enjoying the series so far!

Delaine Christine

CHARACTER LIST OF SUSPECTS

Rathbourne Blackthorne - The former owner of The Blackthorne Horse Ranch. He is the father of Rafe, Rourke and Randulf (deceased) Blackthorne. He returned to Scotland with his son Rourke after his wife, Saphire, passed away in 1974. He still lives there with his unmarried son today.

Saphire Blackthorne - Is the deceased mother of the triplets Rafe, Rourke and Randulf (deceased) Blackthorne. She was a gypsy woman with unique and mesmerizing emerald eyes and unmatched beauty. She was married to Rathbourne Blackthorne.

Rafe Blackthorne {A.K.A, David Pearson} - Is the patriarch of the Blackthorne household and owner of The Blackthorne Horse Ranch in Kalispell, Montana. He is secretly employed within the Central Intelligence Agency under an assumed name. He was married to Lilyandhi Blackthorne (deceased.)

Lilyandhi Blackthorne - The deceased matriarch of the Blackthorne clan. She is the mother of Rafe Blackthorne's six children. Originally of Mandan Indian descent, she was the last of her particular tribe. She has maintained many of the journals left behind by her descendants and authored a few of her own.

Dante Blackthorne {A.K.A, Agent Franclin (Franc) Kastle} - Is the identical twin to Dartanian Blackthorne. He recently married Alaina Jordan (Astraia O'Kahner) and adopted her three children: Sayleena (6), Saruman (4) and Storman (4) Blackthorne (Jordan-Thatcher). They are currently expecting triplets.

Alaina Blackthorne {A.K.A, Alaina Jordan, Astraia Thatcher (O'Kahner)} - Widowed on April 19, 2015, she recently re-married to Dante Blackthorne. She is also the mother of his adopted children Sayleena (6), Saruman (4) and Storman (4) Blackthorne. She is currently expecting triplets fathered by Dante Blackthorne.

Drinian Blackthorne - The second born in the set of triplets within the Blackthorne clan. He is six feet, six inches tall and the largest, as well as the most handsome of his brothers. A carpenter at heart, he owns and manages several rental properties.

Veta Rohann (Gaylord) - Widow to Professor Mitchell Gaylord she had three children: Casey (13), Aaron (13) and Sarah (8) but they are deceased. Even amidst such a tragic loss, her faith has never wavered. Taking a leap of faith she travels from Maryland to Montana believing God is leading her along a new path.

Dartanian Blackthorne - The third son born in the set of triplets within the Blackthorne clan. He is an identical twin to Dante Blackthorne. The Sheriff of Breckenridge County, he is married to Lylia Blackthorne and father to her daughter Kayla (3).

Lylia Blackthorne - The wife of Dartanian Blackthorne, she has a daughter named Kayla (3) who is not Dartanian's biological daughter. She has a teaching degree and home schools most of the children at The Blackthorne Horse Ranch. Lylia's origins are unclear for it seems she was switched at birth.

Breydon Blackthorne - The fourth in the order of birth. He is the fraternal twin of Megorah Blackthorne (Ryans) and the prosecuting attorney for Breckenridge County. He is married to Hialey and is the adopted father of her two boys, Cody (6) and Seth (4) Blackthorne.

Hialey Blackthorne - The wife of Breydon Blackthorne. She owns an upscale lingerie shop called Hialey's Place. She has two children from a previous marriage, Cody (age 6) and Seth (age 4). Her refreshingly open and honest personality often gets her in trouble.

Megorah Ryans - The fifth child born in the Blackthorne family, she is the fraternal twin of Breydon Blackthorne. Megorah is married to Dr. Chase Ryans. They have three children together: Katana (12), Ethan (10) and Katie (8). She owns and manages The Ryans Real Estate and Rental Agency in Whitefish, Montana.

Dr. Chase Ryans - Owns a local family practice in Whitefish, Montana just north of The Blackthorne Ranch, but assists at the local hospital in the ER. He is married to Megorah (Blackthorne) Ryans and they have three children: Katana (12), Ethan (10) and Katie (8.)

Crisalya Howard - The baby of the Blackthorne family. She is an ER nurse, working in the local hospital along-side Dr. Chase Ryans. She also assists her husband, Royce Howard at the popular local coffee house, The Coffee Haven. They have one son together, Aiden (2-1/2).

Royce Howard - The owner of a local coffee house and popular hang-out called The Coffee Haven. He is married to Crisalya (Blackthorne) Howard, the youngest of the Blackthorne clan. They have one son, Aiden (2-½).

Marshall Howard - He is an older half-brother of Royce Howard and also the owner of the Howard's Motel in Whitefish, Montana

Cody Howard - He is an older brother of Royce Howard and the co-owner of a construction and repair shop in Kalispell, Montana.

Freedom Raines - She is the receptionist at The Ryans Real Estate and Rental Agency and is forever making mistakes or mixing things up. She speaks with a rather unusual and odd accent making her hard to understand at times. Is it possible she has a gift of her own?

Deputy James Pike - He is a fairly new deputy with the Sheriff's Department. Infatuated by Crisalya Howard (Blackthorne) he has a bad tendency towards keeping tabs on her and all but one within the Blackthorne clan are unaware of his stalking. Is it possible there might be history there?

Phillipe (angel) - One of God's many messengers and protectors of innocence, he is present during many of Veta's tragedies. He is described as exceptionally tall with shoulder length blonde hair and pale blue eyes.

Woreash (angel) - One of God's many Holy Warriors he is determined to see God's will through. As with all angels, he is very tall at around seven feet in height. He is described rather oddly as elderly in appearance with white or pale grey hair and silver eyes.

Maleeka (angel) - One of God's many Holy Warriors he has a short temper. He is short on patience and has a comical personality while in battle. He seems to follow Woreash's lead. Also exceptionally tall he is described as having feminine features with long dark or black hair to the waist and bright blue eyes.

Zalman (fallen angel/demon) - This particular demon is thought to have been present at the birth of some of Lilyandhi Blackthorne's ancestors before his fall from grace. Could it be he holds a grudge against her ancestors and by extension the Blackthorne family?

Veranke, Zalman and Fallon (The Troublesome Three) - They are three particularly loathsome and bothersome demons, who plague Drinian incessantly.

Photo by Rosemary MacDaniel

Delaine Christine

Who is this woman really?
Does anyone even know?
And what part of this here story
Is about her, do you suppose?

It's so hard to say at this point
There's so much of her now within

For more about the series
and the author

vortigernblack.com

smashwords.com/profile/view
/DelaineChristine

Or to Contact the Author:
delainechristine15@gmail.com